Secrets of the Morning

Books by V. C. Andrews

Flowers in the Attic
Petals on the Wind
If There Be Thorns
My Sweet Audrina
Seeds of Yesterday
Heaven
Dark Angel
Garden of Shadows
Fallen Hearts
Gates of Paradise
Web of Dreams
Dawn
Secrets of the Morning

Published by POCKET BOOKS

V.C. ANDREWS™

POCKET BOOKS
New York London Toronto Sydney Tokyo Singapore

This book is a work of fiction. Names, characters, places and incidents are either the product of the author's imagination or are used fictitiously. Any resemblance to actual events or locales or persons, living or dead, is entirely coincidental.

An *Original* Publication of POCKET BOOKS

POCKET BOOKS, a division of Simon & Schuster Inc.
1230 Avenue of the Americas, New York, NY 10020

V.C. Andrews is a trademark of Virginia C. Andrews Trust

POCKET and colophon are registered trademarks of
Simon & Schuster Inc.

Cover art by Richard Newton

Printed in the U.S.A.

Dear Virginia Andrews Readers,

Those of us who knew and loved Virginia Andrews know that the most important things in her life were her novels. Her proudest moment came when she held in her hand the first printed copy of *Flowers in the Attic.* Virginia was a unique and gifted storyteller who wrote feverishly each and every day. She was constantly developing ideas for new stories that would eventually become novels. Second only to the pride she took in her writing was the joy she took in reading the letters from readers who were so touched by her books.

Since her death many of you have written to us wondering whether there would continue to be new V. C. Andrews novels. Just before she died we promised ourselves that we would find a way of creating additional stories based on her vision.

Beginning with the final books in the Casteel series, we have been working closely with a carefully selected writer to expand upon her genius by creating new novels, like *Dawn* and *Secrets of the Morning,* inspired by her wonderful storytelling talent.

Secrets of the Morning is the second book in a new series. We believe it would have given V. C. Andrews great joy to know that it will be entertaining so many of you. Other novels, including some based on stories Virginia was able to complete before her death, will be published in the coming years and we hope they continue to mean as much to you as ever.

Sincerely,

THE ANDREWS FAMILY

PROLOGUE

As we descended through the billowing clouds, New York suddenly appeared below me. New York! The world's most exciting city, a city I had only read about and heard about and seen pictures of in magazines. I gazed through the window and held my breath. The tall skyscrapers seemed to go on forever and ever, past anything I could have imagined.

When the stewardess began telling us to fasten our seat belts and pull up the backs of our seats, and the no smoking sign was flashed, my heart began to thump so hard I thought the nice old lady beside me would hear it. She smiled at me as if she did.

I sat back and closed my eyes.

It had all happened so fast—my discovering the truth about my abduction and confronting Grandmother Cutler with the lies, a confrontation that forced her to promise she would get Daddy Longchamp, the man I had mistakenly believed to be my father, paroled quickly. In exchange, I had to agree to go to the Bernhardt School for Performing Arts in New York, something Grandmother Cutler arranged so she wouldn't have to put up with a grandchild who she claimed wasn't really a Cutler. My mother confessed to having had an affair with a traveling singer, my real father, and then conveniently, she fell into one of her nervous states and retreated from any responsibility. Grandmother Cutler could do anything she wanted with me, just as she could do with anyone else at Cutler's Cove, including her son, my mother's husband Randolph.

What a horror life at the hotel had been after I had been returned to what was considered my real family. How would I ever forget Philip's forcing himself on me and Clara Sue's spite that eventually resulted in poor Jimmy's being carted off by the police after he had run away from a horrible foster home? Now I was caught between two worlds—the ugly world back at the hotel where there was no one I could turn to or depend upon, and the frightening prospect of New York City where there was no one I knew.

Even though I was going to do what I had always dreamt of doing: train to be a singer, I was terrified of setting foot in a city so big. No wonder my breath was caught in my throat and my heart threatened to drum through my chest.

"Is someone coming to meet you at the airport, dear?" asked the old lady sitting next to me. She introduced herself as Miriam Levy.

"A taxi cab driver," I muttered and fumbled for the instructions I had been given and had placed in my purse. I must have looked at them twenty times during the flight, but still had to gaze at them again to confirm what was to happen. "He's going to be down by the luggage carousel and he's going to hold up a card with my name on it."

"Oh yes, many people have that done. You'll see," she said, patting me on the hand. I had told her that I was to live in an apartment house with other Bernhardt students. She said the location was in a very nice neighborhood on the East Side. When I asked her what she meant by the "East Side," she explained how the streets and avenues were divided into east and west and so I would have to know whether 15 Thirty-third Street, for example, was East or West Thirty-third. It seemed frighteningly complicated. I envisioned myself getting terribly lost and wandering forever through the long, wide avenues with thousands of people rushing by and not caring.

"You mustn't be afraid of New York," she said as she adjusted her hat. "It's big, but people are friendly once you get to know them. Especially in my neighborhood in Queens. I'm sure a nice girl like you will make friends quickly. And just think of all the wonderful things there are for you to see and do."

"I know," I said, putting my brochure about New York City back in my carry-on bag.

"What a lucky girl to be flying to New York to attend a famous school," she said. "I wasn't that much younger than you when my mother brought me over from Europe." She laughed. "We thought the streets were really paved with gold. Of course, it was a fairy tale."

She patted my hand again.

"Maybe for you, the streets will be paved in gold, for you fairy tales will come true. I hope so," she added, her eyes twinkling warmly.

"Thank you," I said, even though I no longer believed in fairy tales, especially fairy tales coming true for me.

I held my breath again as the plane's wheels were lowered and we approached the runway. There was a slight bump and we were rolling along. We had touched ground.

I was really here.

I was in New York.

1

A NEW ADVENTURE, A NEW FRIEND

We filed out of the plane slowly. When we entered the airport, Mrs. Levy spotted her son and daughter-in-law and waved at them. They came forward and hugged and kissed her. I stood back watching them for a moment, wishing that I had some family anxiously awaiting my arrival, too. How wonderful it must feel to arrive after a big trip and have people who love you waiting there to throw their arms around you and tell you how much they've missed you, I thought. Would I ever have that?

Once Mrs. Levy found her family, she forgot about me. I started after the crowd of passengers since we were all headed for the same place—the luggage carousels. But I was like a little girl at a circus for the first time. I couldn't stop looking at everything and everyone. On the walls there were large, colorful posters advertising New York shows. The kind of musicals I had only dreamt about seeing were loudly announced all around me. These stars and these shows, could they be only minutes away? Was I foolish to dream that someday I would be featured on one of these beautiful posters?

I continued down the corridor gazing up at the huge sign advertising a perfume by Elizabeth Arden. The women in all the advertisements looked like movie stars with their glamorous clothing and jewels and beautiful, radiant faces. As I spun around, I heard a voice over the public address system announcing arrivals and departures.

A family went by me speaking in a foreign language, the father complaining about something and the mother pulling her little wards by the hand as quickly as she could. Two sailors strolled past me and whistled and then laughed at my surprise. Farther down the corridor, I saw three teenage girls in a corner smoking cigarettes, none of them much older than I was, and all wearing sunglasses even though they were inside. They glared at me angrily when I stared, so I looked away quickly.

Never had I seen so many people in the same place at once. And so many rich people! The men in soft dark suits and polished black and brown leather shoes, the women in elegant silk dresses and coats, their diamonds glittering on their ears and necks as they clicked down the corridors in their high heels.

After a while I began to be afraid I'd gone in the wrong direction. I stopped and stared hard around me and realized that none of the other people from my plane were nearby. What if I got lost and the taxi driver who had come to fetch me left? Who would I call? Where would I go?

I thought I saw Mrs. Levy hurrying down the corridor. My heart jumped for joy and then plunged when I realized it was just another elderly lady wearing similar clothing. I wandered to my left until I spotted a tall policeman standing by a newspaper booth.

"Excuse me," I said. He peered down at me, over his open newspaper, his forehead creasing in tiny folds under his wavy brown hair.

"And what can I do for you, young lady?"

"I think I'm a little lost. I just got off the airplane and I'm supposed to go to the luggage carousel, but I started looking at posters and . . ."

A light sprang into his blue eyes.

"You're all by yourself?" he asked, folding his paper.

"Yes, sir."

"How old are you?" he asked, squinting with scrutiny.

"I'm almost sixteen and a half."

"Well, you're old enough to get about by yourself if you pay attention to directions. You're not very lost. Don't worry." He put his hand on my shoulder and turned me around and explained how to get to the luggage carousels.

After he finished, he waved his right forefinger at me.

"Now don't go looking at all the signs, you hear?"

"I won't," I said and hurried off, his light laughter trailing behind me.

By the time I got to the place where the baggage was the passengers were all squeezing and crowding around to get their bags. I found a small opening between a young soldier and an elderly man in a suit. Once the soldier saw me, he pushed to the right so I would have more room. He had dark brown eyes and a friendly smile. His shoulders looked so broad and firm under the snug uniform jacket. I saw the ribbons over his right breast pocket and couldn't help but stare.

"This one's for marksmanship," he pointed proudly.

I blushed. One thing Mrs. Levy had advised me on the plane was not to stare at people in New York and here I was doing it again and again.

"Where are you from?" the young soldier asked. Above his other breast pocket was his last name, WILSON.

"Virginia," I said. "Cutler's Cove."

He nodded.

"I'm from Brooklyn. That's Broooooklyn New York," he added, laughing. "The fifty-first state, and boy did I miss it."

"Brooklyn's a state?" I wondered aloud. He laughed.

"What's your name?" he asked.

"Dawn."

"Dawn, I'm Private First Class, Johnny Wilson. My friends call me Butch because of my haircut," he said, wiping his right palm over his closely cut hair. "I wore it like this even before I joined the army." I smiled at him and then noticed one of my blue bags go by.

"Oh, my luggage!" I cried, reaching out in vain.

"Hold on," Private Wilson said. He slipped around some people to my left and scooped out my bag.

"Thank you," I said when he brought it back. "I have one more. I'd better keep my eyes on the luggage."

He reached over and lifted his duffle bag out from between two black trunks. Then I saw my second bag. Once again, he stabbed into the pile and got it for me.

"Thank you," I said.

"Where are you heading, Dawn? Any place in Brooklyn?" he asked hopefully.

"Oh no, I'm going to New York City," I said. He laughed again.

"Brooklyn's in New York City. Don't you know your address?"

"No. I'm being picked up," I explained. "By a taxi driver."

"Oh, I see. Here, let me carry one of your bags to the gate for you," he offered and before I could say anything, he lifted it and started away. At the gate there was another crowd of people with many holding up signs with names written on them, just as Mrs. Levy had predicted. I searched and searched, but I didn't see my name. A lump came to choke my throat. What if no one was here for me because they got my flight mixed up? Everyone else seemed to know where he or she was going. Was I the only one arriving in New York for the first time?

"There it is," Private Wilson said, pointing. I looked in the direction and saw a tall, dark-haired man who looked unshaven and tired and very bored standing with the card: DAWN CUTLER.

"With a name like Dawn, that could only be for you," Private Wilson remarked. He led me forward. "Here she is," he announced.

"Good," the taxi driver said. "I got my cab out front but there's an airport cop on my back. Let's get movin'," he said, hardly looking at me. He took both my suitcases and lunged forward.

"Thank you," I said to the soldier. He smiled.

"Have a good tour of duty, Dawn," he cried as I followed the lanky cab driver out of the airport. When I looked back, Private Wilson was gone, almost as if he had descended like some sort of protective angel to help me in a moment of need and then disappeared. For a few moments, I had felt secure, safe, even in this huge place with crowds and crowds of strangers. It was almost as if I had been with Jimmy again, with someone strong to look after me.

As soon as the taxi driver and I burst out of the airport, I had to shade my eyes to see where I was going. The sun was that bright. But I was glad it was a warm, summer day. It made me feel hopeful, welcome. The taxi driver showed me to the cab, put my suitcases in the trunk, and opened the rear door.

"Hop in," he said. A policeman was approaching rapidly, his face glum.

"Yeah, yeah, I'm goin'," the taxi driver cried and moved around the car quickly to get behind the wheel.

"They don't let you make a livin' here," he explained as he pulled away from the curb. "They're on your back, day and night." He drove so fast I had to hold onto the handle above the window, and then he came to a quick stop behind a line of cars. A moment later, he shot out of the line, found a space, and wove our cab in and out with an expertise that made me gasp. We nearly collided a number of times, but soon we were on open highway.

"First time in New York?" he asked without turning around to look at me.

"Yes."

"Well I have heartburn every day, but I wouldn't live anywhere else. Know what I mean?"

I didn't know if he was waiting for a reply or not.

"Just live and let live and you'll be all right," he advised. "I'll tell you what I tell my own daughter—when you walk in the streets, keep your eyes straight ahead and don't listen to nobody. Know what I mean?" he asked again.

"Yes, sir."

"Aaa, you'll be all right. You look like a smart cookie and you're going to a nice neighborhood. When someone mugs you there, they're polite about it," he said. "They say, 'Excuse me, but do you have ten dollars?' "

He gazed into the rearview mirror and saw my look of shock.

"Just kiddin'," he added, laughing.

He turned on his radio and I gazed out at the approaching skyscrapers, the traffic, and the hustle and bustle. I wanted to save and savor all of this ride, my entrance into New York, and ponder the memories later. It did seem overwhelming. What did Grandmother Cutler really hope would happen to me when she arranged for me to come here? I wondered. Did she think I would panic and beg her to let me return? Or did she hope I would run off and she would never have to lay her watchful, suspicious eyes on me again?

I felt something tighten in my heart. I wasn't going to turn and run away, I told myself. I would be determined and strong and show her I was just as strong as she was, even stronger.

We went over a bridge and into the heart of the city. I couldn't stop looking up. The buildings were so tall and so many people were on the streets, going in and out of them. Car horns blared, other cab drivers shouted at each other and at other drivers. People rushed across streets as if they thought drivers were deliberately aiming for them.

And the stores! All the stores in the world were here, famous ones I had read about and heard about like Saks Fifth Avenue and Macy's.

"You're going to give yourself a neck ache, you keep doin' that," the cab driver said. I felt myself redden. I hadn't realized he was watching me. "Know when you're a New Yorker?" he asked, gazing at me through the rearview mirror. I shook my head. "When you don't look both ways crossing a one-way street." He laughed at what I imagined was a joke, but I didn't understand it. I guess I had a long way to go before I would be a New Yorker.

Soon we were going up very nice streets where the people seemed to be dressed better and the sidewalks were a lot cleaner. The fronts of the buildings looked newer and better cared for, too. Finally, we stopped in front of a brownstone house with a cement stairway and a black iron railing. The double doors were tall and looked like they were made of fine dark oak wood.

We pulled to a stop and the cab driver got out and put both of my bags on the sidewalk. I stepped out of the car and gazed about slowly. This was to be my new home for a long time now, I thought. Overhead I saw two airplanes climbing into the deep blue sky speckled with small, fluffy clouds. Across from us was a small park and beyond that, just visible between some trees was water, that I guessed was the East River. I couldn't stop looking at everything and, for a moment, forgot the taxi driver was still standing beside me.

"The fare's taken care of," he declared, "but not the tip."

"Tip?"

"Sure, honey. You always tip a New York cabby. Don't forget that. You can forget anything else."

"Oh." Embarrassed, I opened my purse and fumbled through the change. How much was I supposed to give him?

"A buck will be enough," he said.

I plucked one out and handed it to him.

"Thanks. Good luck," he said. "I gotta get back to the grind," he added and hurried around the cab just as quickly as he had at the airport. In moments, he drove off, his horn groaning as he cut in front of another car and spun around a corner.

I turned and looked up the small cement stairway. Suddenly it looked so high and forbidding. I took hold of the handles of my luggage and began my slow ascent. When I reached the landing, I put the bags down and pushed the buzzer. I wondered if it worked or anyone heard it inside because nothing happened. After a long moment, I pushed the buzzer again. Seconds later, the doors were pulled open dramatically by a tall, stately looking woman. I thought she was at least in her late fifties. She stood straight with her shoulders back like the women in the textbook pictures demonstrating perfect posture, the ones who parade about with a book balanced on their heads, and her brown hair had streaks of gray throughout it.

She wore an ankle-length, navy blue skirt, and pink ballerina slippers. Her ivory blouse had billowing sleeves and a wide collar with the two top buttons undone so her necklace filled with large, colorful stones was clearly visible. She wore a heavy-looking earring with smaller versions of the same imitation or precious stones on her left earlobe, but none on her right. I wondered if she knew one was missing.

Her face was heavily made up, her cheeks streaked with rouge as if she had put it on in the dark. She wore dark eye liner and had such long eyelashes, I knew they just had to be false. Her lipstick was a bright crimson.

She stared at me, drinking me in from head to toe. Then she nodded to herself as if to confirm a thought.

"I suppose you're Dawn," she said.

"Yes, ma'am," I replied.

"I am Agnes, Agnes Morris," she declared.

I nodded. That was the name on my instruction sheet, but she looked like she expected a bigger reaction from me.

"Well, pick up your luggage and come on in," she said. "We have no servants for that sort of thing here. This isn't a hotel."

"Yes, ma'am," I repeated. She stood back to let me pass, and as I did so, I got a whiff of her strong, almost overpowering cologne. It smelled like a combination of jasmine and roses, as if she had sprayed one scent on, forgot, and then sprayed another.

I paused in the entryway. It had a cherry wood floor and a long, rather worn looking oval rug. The Oriental pattern was almost faded. As soon as we stepped in and I had closed the second set of doors behind me, a grandfather clock on my right chimed.

"Mr. Fairbanks is introducing himself," she said, turning to the tall clock encased in a rich mahogany wood. It had Roman numerals for numbers and thick, black hands with ends that looked more like tiny fingers pointing to the hour.

"Mr. Fairbanks?" I asked, confused.

"The grandfather clock," she said as if I should have known. "I have given most of my possessions names, the names of famous actors with whom I once worked. It makes the house more . . . more . . ." She looked about as if the words were somewhere in the air to be plucked. "More personal. Why?" she asked quickly, "do you disapprove?" Her eyes grew small and she pulled her lips so tight the corners became white.

"Oh, no," I replied.

"I hate people who disapprove of something just because they didn't think of it first." She ran the palm of her hand up the side of the grandfather clock cabinet and smiled as if it were indeed a person standing there. "Oh Romeo, Romeo," she whispered. I shifted my feet. The suitcases were heavy and I was standing with them in my hands. It was as if she had forgotten I was there.

"Ma'am?" I said. She snapped her head around and glared at me as if to say "Who was I to interrupt?"

"Continue," she said, waving toward the hallway.

Directly ahead of us was a stairway with a thick, hand-carved brown balustrade. The gray carpet on the steps looked as worn as the entryway carpet. The walls were covered with old pictures of actors and actresses, singers and dancers, framed clippings of theater reviews and pictures of performers with accompanying articles. The house itself had a pleasant musty scent to it. It looked clean and neat and a great deal nicer than most of the places Daddy and Momma Longchamp had taken Jimmy and me and Fern to live in. But that seemed ages and ages ago now, as though it all happened in another life.

Agnes stopped at the entrance to a room on our right.

"This is our sitting room," she said, "where we entertain our guests. Go in and sit down," she directed. "We'll have our first talk immediately so there are no misunderstandings." She paused and pursed her lips. "I suppose you're hungry."

"Yes," I said. "I came right from the airport and I didn't have anything on the plane."

"It's past the lunch hour and I don't like Mrs. Liddy having to work around the students' whims, eating and not eating when they feel like it. She's nobody's slave," she added.

"I'm sorry. I really don't mean to put anyone out." I didn't know what to say. She had been the one to suggest eating and now she was making me feel terrible for confessing I was hungry.

"Go on in," she commanded.

"Thank you," I said and turned to enter. She seized my shoulder and stopped me.

"No, no. Always hold your head high, like this, when you enter a room," she said, demonstrating. "That way everyone will notice you and sense your stage presence. You might as well learn the correct things right away," she said and sauntered off down the corridor.

As soon as she was gone, I turned back to the room. The sunlight through the pale ivory sheers was misted and frail and gave the sitting room a dreamlike quality. The chintz sofa and matching side chair with its high back and cushioned arms were both worn and comfortable looking. On the coffee table were copies of theater magazines and an old rocking chair sat across from the sofa.

In the corner to my right, next to a beautiful desk, was a table of dark oak with an old-fashioned record player just like the one in the RCA logo, and a pile of old records beside it. The top record was the aria from the opera *Madam Butterfly.* Over the fireplace mantel was a painting of a stage play. It looked like the balcony scene from *Romeo and Juliet.*

On the other side of the room was a piano. I looked at the sheet music opened on it and saw it was a Mozart concerto, something I had played in Richmond. I felt like sitting down and playing it now. The tips of my fingers tingled in expectation. It was as if I had never been away from it.

Behind the piano were shelves filled with copies of plays and old novels and a glass case full of things from plays: old programs, pictures of actors and actresses, props, including a colorful mask like the kind worn at fancy costume balls, some glass figurines and a pair of castanets with a note under it that read, "Given to me by Rudolph Valentino."

My gaze fell on a silver framed photograph of what had to be a very young Agnes Morris. I took it into my hands to look at it more closely. Without the heavy makeup, she looked fresh and pretty.

"You shouldn't touch things without permission." I jumped at the sound of Agnes's voice and pivoted to see she was standing in the doorway, her hands pressed to her chest.

"I'm sorry, I was just . . ."

"Although I want the students to feel at home here, they must respect my possessions."

"I'm sorry," I said again. I put the picture back quickly.

"I have a number of valuable artifacts, things that you can't replace no matter how much money you have because they are associated with memories, and memories are more precious than diamonds or gold." She came farther into the room and gazed at the picture.

"It's a very nice picture," I said. Her face softened some.

"Whenever I look at that picture now, I think I'm looking at a complete stranger. That was taken the first time I appeared on a stage."

"Really? You look so young," I said.

"I wasn't much older than you." She tilted her head and swung her eyes so she gazed toward the brass light fixture on the ceiling. "I had met and worked with the great Stanislavsky. I played Ophelia in *Hamlet* and got rave reviews."

She peered at me to see if I was impressed, but I had never heard of Stanislavsky.

"Sit down," she said sharply. "Mrs. Liddy will be in shortly with your tea and sandwiches, although you mustn't expect to be waited on hand and foot after this."

I sat on the sofa and she sat in the rocker across from it.

"I know a little about you," she said, nodding, her eyes small and her lips tucked tightly together. Suddenly, she reached under the waist of her skirt to produce a letter. What an odd place to keep it, I thought. She held up the envelope as if to show me she possessed some valuable secret thing. The instant I saw the Cutler Cove Hotel stationery, my heart began to flutter.

She took the letter out of the envelope. From the way it was folded and creased, it looked like she had been reading it every hour on the hour since it had arrived. "This is a letter from your grandmother. A letter to introduce you," she added.

"Oh?"

"Yes." She raised her eyebrows and leaned forward to peer right into my face. "She has told me about some of your problems."

"My problems?" Had Grandmother Cutler put my dreadful story in writing? Why? Did she hope to make me seem freakish and curious even before I had begun here? If she had, it was only to make sure I failed to follow my dream.

"Yes," Agnes said, nodding and sitting back in the rocker. She fanned herself with the letter. "Your problems at school. How they had to transfer you from school to school because of the difficulties you had getting along with other students your age."

"She told you that?"

"Yes, and I'm glad she did," Agnes replied quickly.

"But, I didn't have any trouble at school. I've always been a good student and . . ."

"There's no point in denying anything. It's all here in black and white," she said, tapping the letter. "Your grandmother is a very important and distinguished woman. It must have broken her heart to have had to write these things." She sat back. "You've been quite a burden to your family, especially to your grandmother."

"That's not so," I protested.

"Please." When she raised her hand, I saw that her fingers were turned and twisted with arthritis and her hand looked more like the hand of a witch. "Nothing matters now but your next performance."

"Performance?"

"How you behave here while you are under my wing," she explained.

"What else did my grandmother write?"

"That's confidential," she said as she folded the letter. She stuffed it back into the envelope and returned it to where she kept it under her skirt.

"But it's information about me!" I protested.

"That's not the point. Don't be argumentative," she said before I could respond any further. "Now then," she concluded, "since you do have this unfortunate past history, I'm afraid I'm going to have to consider you under probation."

"Under probation? But I've just arrived and I haven't done anything wrong."

"Nevertheless, it's a precaution I must take. You must not violate a single rule," she warned me, shaking her long forefinger. "No one stays out later than ten P.M. on weekdays and no later than midnight on weekends, and only when I know where he or she is going.

"Excessive noise is not permitted ever. And no one is ever to be messy or in any way damage or vandalize my home. You understand that while you are here, you are a guest in my house, don't you?"

"Yes, ma'am," I said softly. "But since the letter from my grandmother was about me, can't you tell me what else she said?"

Before she could reply, a plump, round-faced woman with blue-gray hair and friendly eyes, who stood no more than five feet tall, arrived carrying a tray with a sandwich and a cup of tea. She had roller-pin arms and small hands with pudgy fingers and she wore a light blue dress with a yellow flowered apron over it. I felt warmth and friendliness in her smile immediately.

"So this is our new Sarah Bernhardt, is it?" she asked.

"Yes, Mrs. Liddy. Our new prima donna," Agnes said and twisted her mouth up into her cheek. "Dawn, this is Mrs. Liddy. She's the one who really runs the house. You are to listen to her the same as you would listen to me. I will not tolerate anyone being nasty to Mrs. Liddy," she emphasized.

"Oh, I don't think this one will be anything but nice, Mrs. Morris.

Hello, m'dear." She put the tray on the coffee table and stood back with her hands on her hips. "And welcome."

"Thank you."

"Pretty one," Mrs. Liddy said to Agnes.

"Yes, but the pretty ones are often the ones who get into the most difficulty," Agnes snapped.

With both of them staring at me, I felt as if I were encased in glass just like the theater artifacts.

"Well, m'dear," Mrs. Liddy said, "I'm in the kitchen most of the morning. If there's anything you need, you can come see me there. We like everyone to have his or her bed turned down by ten at the latest on weekends and once a week we do a thorough sweep of the house. Everyone helps."

"Yes," Agnes said, cutting her eyes toward me. "We all work here. The girls tie their hair up, slap on the oldest blouse and skirt, and roll up their sleeves, just like the boys. Windows are washed, bathrooms scrubbed down. I compare it to breaking down a set," she added. "I imagine you know what that means, don't you?"

I shook my head.

Agnes's eyes widened as though she couldn't believe what she was hearing.

"When a play has finished its run, the actors and the crew tear down the scenery so the next play can begin."

At that point Mrs. Liddy smiled at me and left.

"Have you ever had piano lessons?" Agnes asked.

"A little," I said.

"Good. You will play for us during our artistic gatherings. I try to bring everyone together once a month for recitals. Some of the students recite lines from plays; some sing, some play instruments.

"But, that will be later on when the school year begins. I don't have many students here during the summer session. Actually, there are only two at present. But in the fall, we'll pick up three more. The Beldock twins are returning, and one, Donald Rossi, is brand new, just like you.

"Trisha Kramer has agreed to share her room with you. If you can't get along with Trisha, I will have to move you into the attic or ask you to leave. She's a delightful young lady and a promising young dancer. It would be dreadful if anything happened to make her unhappy here. Do I make myself clear on that score?" she asked.

"Yes, ma'am." I could only wonder what lies Agnes had passed on to my prospective roommate.

"And I especially don't want you disturbing the other student who is here," she warned. "His name is Arthur Garwood." She sighed and shook her head. "He's a sensitive young man studying the oboe. His parents are quite famous: Bernard and Louella Garwood. They play in the New York Philharmonic Orchestra.

"Well, I see you enjoyed your little snack. I will show you the rest of the house and take you to your room."

"Thank you." I stood up. "Should I take this tray back into the kitchen?"

"Absolutely. According to your grandmother, you are quite used to being waited on, but I'm afraid . . ."

"That's not true!" I exclaimed. "I've never been waited on."

Her eyes grew small and watchful and for a long moment she stared at me.

"Follow me to the kitchen. We'll come back for your suitcases after I've shown you the rest of the house."

I followed Agnes out and down the hallway. The kitchen and the dining room were at the far end. The kitchen was small with a kitchenette table and chairs in the center and a window that looked out on another building, which meant there would be no sunlight here in the morning. Even so, Mrs. Liddy had everything looking so spick and span: the light yellow linoleum shining, the appliances glittering clean, that the room sparkled.

The dining room was long and narrow with a big chandelier of teardrop glass. The table could easily seat a dozen or so people. Right now it had a crystal centerpiece with a vase of flowers beside it and four place mats set at the far end, which I quickly imagined was there for myself, the other two students and Agnes Morris.

"Trisha set the table this morning," Agnes explained. "Each of the students takes his or her turn for a week setting the table and clearing the dishes. And no one complains," she added pointedly.

There were no windows in the dining room, but the right wall was covered with a long floor-to-ceiling mirror, which made the room look even longer and wider. The opposite wall was peppered with pictures of dancers and singers, musicians and actors. From the way some of the pictures had faded into sepia, I knew they were quite old. The floor was carpeted in dark brown and the carpet looked far newer than the rug in the entryway.

Agnes led me through the dining room to a short corridor. She explained that her room was here and Mrs. Liddy's room was at the far end. She paused at her door and her eyes seemed to soften a bit.

"If you ever need to talk, just knock softly on my door anytime," she said. I was surprised, but happy she had finally said something nice to me.

"It's one of the reasons why my house is so popular with the out of town students. I, having been in the theater, can appreciate the problems performing arts students face. I understand and I can empathize." Sometimes, when she spoke to me, she made her gestures so big, it was as if we were both on a stage before an audience and our conversation was dialogue written for a play.

"Knock like this," she said and tapped gently on her own door. "Then wait. I'll say, enter. You turn the handle slowly and open the door gradually, an inch or so at a time," she said in a loud whisper and demonstrated. "I hate it when doors are thrust open."

I stared at her, fascinated by her every move, the soft way she spoke. I had never had anyone take such care showing me how to enter a room. Then my eyes swung from her to the doorway and I saw the curtain. It was in two sections, draped from the ceiling to the floor about five feet or so inside the door. Anyone who came into the room would have to separate the curtains and walk through, just like he or she would separate a curtain to enter a stage. Before I could ask about it, she closed the door softly and turned to me.

"Do you understand everything I've told you?" she asked.

"Yes, ma'am."

"Good. Let me show you your room."

We returned to the sitting room to pick up my luggage and then proceeded up the stairway to the second floor, which contained four bedrooms. There were two bathrooms on this floor, one on each side.

"Now," Agnes said, pausing in front of the bathroom on the left, "although everyone could use either one in an emergency, I like to keep this one reserved for males and the other one for females. We mustn't abuse our bathrooms," she emphasized. "We must always keep the others in mind and not be selfish and take up too much time doting on ourselves.

"As long as I've had students here," she said softly, "I haven't had any problems having both boys and girls. That's because we all use discretion," she said. "We don't spend inordinate time alone with a member of the opposite sex and never close the door when we are alone. Am I quite understood in this?" she asked.

"I'm afraid you have been misinformed about me," I said and felt the tears burning under my eyelids.

"Please, my dear Dawn. Let's not bring a single note of unpleasantness into this opening scene. Let it all go like clockwork—all of us in tune with each other, all of us taking cues from each other. I just know we'll have curtain call after curtain call after curtain call. Don't you?" she said, smiling at me.

I didn't know what to say. Curtain calls for what? Using the bathrooms fairly? Not getting into trouble with boys? What cues did she mean? All I could do was nod.

She opened the door and stepped into the bedroom.

"It might not be as large and elaborate as what you've been accustomed to, but I am rather proud of my accommodations," she said.

I didn't reply. I could see it would do no good to defend myself right now. Her impression of me had already been poisoned by Grandmother Cutler.

The room was sweet. There were two white post beds with headboards and a night stand between them. The night stand had a lamp with a bell-shaped shade on it. The floor wasn't carpeted, but there was a rather large pink throw rug between the two beds. The bedding matched the pink in the rug. Each of the two small windows on the right above the two student desks were covered with white cotton curtains that had lace edging. There were shades on the windows, both drawn up at present to permit whatever sunlight squeezed in between this building and the one beside it. There were two dressers, and a large closet with a sliding door.

Agnes told me the bed on the right and the accompanying dresser were mine. Trisha had a picture of an attractive couple who I guessed were her parents on her dresser and a picture of a handsome boy who could be her brother or her boyfriend beside it. On her desk were textbooks and notebooks neatly piled beside each other.

"Well, I'll leave you to get yourself settled in," Agnes said. "Trisha should be coming home from school in an hour or so. Remember, you are a guest in my home," she said and started out. At the door she spun around and added, "Act One," and left.

I put my suitcases down and gazed around the room again. This was to be my new home for a long time. It was cozy and warm, but I was sharing it with another girl and that was something that both frightened and excited me, especially after the warnings Agnes had given me. What if we didn't get along? What if we were so different that we ended up hardly speaking to each other? What would happen to my dream of becoming a singer?

I began to unpack, hanging up my clothes and putting my underthings and my socks into the dresser drawers. I had just placed my suitcases at the rear of the closet when the door was suddenly opened and Trisha Kramer burst into our room. She was an inch or so taller than I was and wore her dark brown hair drawn back from her face and pinned up in a chignon that I thought very sophisticated. Over black leotards she wore a floating chiffon black dress, and on her feet were silver dancing shoes.

Trisha had the brightest green eyes I had ever seen with eyebrows trimmed just the way fashion models wear theirs. Although she had a perfect little nose, her mouth was a little too thin and too long. But her soft, wonderful peaches and cream complexion and sleek figure went far to compensate for any imperfections.

"Hi," she exclaimed. "I'm Trisha. Sorry I wasn't here to greet you, but I had dance class," she added and did a pirouette. My smile widened into a laugh. "That, I want you to know, took me nearly a month to perfect."

"It was good," I said, quickly nodding. She bowed.

"Thank you, thank you. Don't do another thing," she said before I could utter a word or move. "Just sit down and tell me everything about yourself. I've been starved . . . starved!" she emphasized with big eyes, "for female companionship. The only other person living here now is Bones and you've already met Agnes," she said, swinging her eyes toward the door and back.

"Bones?"

"Arthur Garwood. But let's not talk about him just yet. Come," she said, taking my hand and pulling me to sit on my bed. "Talk, talk, talk. Where did you go to school before? How many boyfriends have you had? Do you have one now? Do your parents really own a famous resort in Virginia?"

I just sat there smiling.

"Maybe tomorrow we'll go to see a movie. Would you like that?" she asked, grimacing in anticipation of a yes.

"I've never been to a movie," I confessed.

"What?" She sat back and stared at me, her smile frozen. Then she leaned forward.

"Don't they have electricity in Virginia?" she asked. For a moment we stared at each other, and then I started to cry.

Perhaps it was all of it finally coming to a climax: discovering the parents I had known and loved for more than fourteen years were not really my parents, being dragged off to live with a family that didn't really want me back, discovering that the boy I thought might be my first boyfriend was really my brother and the boy I thought was my brother was the boy I really liked the way a girl should like a boy; having to have a vicious, jealous sister, Clara Sue, and a mother who doted only on herself. And now, being shipped off as part of a bargain with a grandmother who despised my very existence for reasons I still didn't quite understand—all of it came raining down upon me.

As I looked at Trisha with her vibrant eyes and bubbly personality, her excitement over things like rock and roll and boys and movies, I suddenly realized how different I was. I had never really had the chance to be a young girl and a teenager. I had been forced because of Momma Longchamp's illnesses to be the mother. How I had longed to be like Trisha Kramer and others like her. Could I be? Was it too late?

I couldn't stop the tears from flowing.

"What is it?" Trisha asked. "Did I say something?"

"Oh, Trisha, I'm sorry," I said. "No, you're perfect. Agnes had me thinking you'd be horrible."

"Oh Agnes," she said, waving the air, "you can't pay attention to anything she says. Did she show you her room?"

"Yes," I said, nodding and wiping away my tears, "with the curtain."

"Isn't it a gas? She thinks she lives on the stage. Wait until you see the rest of it. Did you get your class program card yet?"

"Yes." I dug it out of my purse and showed it to her.

"Great! We have English together and vocal music. I'll take you over to the school now and give you a grand tour. But first, let's change into sweatshirts and jeans and sneakers, and go get ice cream sodas and talk and talk and talk until both our throats get dry."

"My mother bought me only fancy things for school. I don't have a sweatshirt," I moaned.

"Oh yes you do," she said, jumping up and going to the closet. She pulled out one of her own, a bright, blue cotton one, and tossed it at me.

I hurried to change as Trisha and I talked a mile a minute, giggling almost after everything we said. When we finally started out, Trisha stopped me at the door.

"Please, my dear," she said, assuming Agnes Morris's demeanor. "Whenever you enter or leave a room, always hold your head high and your shoulders back. Otherwise, you won't be noticed."

Our laughter trailed after us as we bounced down the stairs.

I wasn't in New York more than a few hours.

And already I had a friend!

2
EXPLORING THE BERNHARDT SCHOOL

Even though Trisha took me to a luncheonette only two blocks away from our student house, I couldn't help being afraid of getting lost. The streets were so long and I found I had to walk very quickly to keep up with her. My eyes darted all about as I took in the traffic, the people, the stores and other apartment houses, but Trisha kept her gaze down and talked as she hurried up the sidewalk to a corner and then turned to lead me down another street and up another. It was as if she sensed traffic and people or had eyes in the top of her head and didn't have to worry about bumping into someone or being hit by a car.

"Quickly," she cried when I hesitated behind her, "before the light changes on us." She grabbed my hand and tugged me off the sidewalk. Drivers honked their horns at us because the light did change when we were only three quarters of the way. I was terrified, but Trisha thought it was funny.

The cashier at the luncheonette, the bald-headed, stout elderly man behind the counter and even some of the waitresses knew Trisha and waved and said hello when we entered. She slid into the first empty booth and I followed, happy to be safe and have a place to rest.

"I've never been to Virginia," Trisha began. "My family's from upstate New York. How come you don't have a thick, southern accent?" she asked quickly, just realizing it.

"I didn't grow up in Virginia," I said. "My family traveled around a great deal and we didn't always live in the south."

The waitress came to our table.

"Want a black and white?" Trisha asked me. I didn't know what it was, but I was afraid to show just how stupid I was.

"Fine," I said.

"All the kids from the school come here," she said. "They have a juke box. Want to hear some music?"

"Sure," I said. She jumped up and went to the juke box.

"Isn't that great?" she said, returning. "Now hold it a sec," she said without pausing for a breath. "What do you mean, your family traveled around a lot? Agnes told me your family owns a famous hotel and has for a long time. From the way Agnes described it, it's practically a historic site."

"It is."

She shook her head. "I don't understand."

"It's complicated," I said, hoping to leave it at that. I was sure that once I told her my story, she would regret having me as her roommate.

"Oh, I'm sorry if I sound like I'm prying. Mr. Van Dan, our English teacher, says I should be writing the gossip column for a newspaper."

"It's a little hard for me to talk about it all right now," I said, but I could see that only interested her more.

"I'll wait. We've got plenty of time to poke into each other's business," she added. I had to laugh.

"Is that a picture of your brother or your boyfriend next to your parents' picture?" I asked. "Since we're being snoops, that is."

"My boyfriend back home," she said, nodding. Then she held her arms out and cried, "I'm an only child. And I'm very spoiled," she added. "Look what my father sent me last week." She extended her wrist to show me the beautiful gold watch with two diamonds in it, one for twelve and one for six.

"It's very beautiful." My compliment was sincere, but I couldn't help the tears that began to fill the furrows at the bottom of my eyes. Would I ever know who my real father was, much less meet him and have him love me the way a father should love a daughter? According to Grandmother Cutler, he couldn't have cared much less about my birth and was happy to get away without any responsibility. But deep down I harbored the hope that Grandmother Cutler was lying about this, just the way she had lied about other things concerning me. In my secret, putaway heart, I dreamt that because I was in New York, the capital of entertainment, I would somehow find my real father. And when I found him, he would be overjoyed to see me.

"He's always sending me presents," Trisha continued. "I suppose I'm a Daddy's girl. What's your father like? Do you have any brothers or sisters? I can ask that right now, can't I?"

"Yes. I have a brother and a sister. My brother Philip is older, and my sister Clara Sue is a year younger." I thought about Jimmy and Fern and how hard it still was not to call them my brother and sister. "My father is

. . . a very busy man," I added dryly, thinking about Randolph and the way he had always managed to be doing something whenever I needed him.

"Say no more," Trisha said and leaned over the table. "So what do you do?"

"Do?"

"Your talent, silly. I'm going to be a dancer. But you already know that. So?"

"I sing, but . . ."

"Oh great, another singer," she said, sighing. Then she flashed a smile and her face brightened, her eyes like Christmas tree lights. "No, I'm just kidding. I can't wait to hear you sing."

"I'm not really that good."

"You made it into Bernhardt, didn't you? You passed their gruesome audition. Didn't you just hate the way they looked you over? But someone important thinks you've got talent," she said. "Otherwise you wouldn't be here."

What was I to say? If I told her Grandmother Cutler pulled strings to get me in, Trisha might resent me for it. I would have to explain how it was all part of an arrangement and then I would have to tell her everything.

"Anyway, before long, Agnes will have you singing at one of her gatherings."

"Was she really an actress?"

"Oh yes, and she still is. I don't mean on the stage or screen, but in real life. And she has all these old actor friends who come over for tea on Sundays. It's fun to listen to them reminisce. Did you meet Mrs. Liddy?"

"Yes. She's very nice."

"She and Agnes have been together for ages and ages. Sometimes, she's the only one Agnes will listen to, but don't worry, you'll love it here. You'll see. Just don't let Bones get you down."

"Why would he do that?"

"He's always so glum. I swear if he smiled, he'd crack his face," she said as the waitress brought our ice cream sodas.

"Why do you call him Bones?"

"When you see him, you'll know. Yummy," Trisha said and started sipping on her straw. Her personality was like a warm summer day. I had never seen such a happy, exuberant girl. "Better get to your soda," she said. "We have a lot to do and I have to get back to help with dinner. It's my week."

"Oh. Right."

Trisha insisted on paying. When she put down a tip for the waitress, I told her what had happened with the taxi driver.

"He had the nerve to ask?" She shook her head. "What am I saying? Of course, he had the nerve; he's a New York cabby. Come on," she said, taking my hand. Oh no, I thought, not another race down the sidewalk.

We hurried out of the luncheonette and turned left.

"How do you know which way to go? It all looks so confusing," I said. I had already forgotten from which direction we had come. The streets looked so similar.

"It's easier than you think. It won't take you long to find your way around. The school's only a block up and a block over," she added as we walked on.

"My boyfriend's name is Victor, but no one calls him anything but Vic," she said. "He writes a couple of times a week and calls once a week. And he's visited me twice already this summer."

"That's very nice. You're lucky to have someone who cares so much about you."

"But I've got to tell you a secret," she said, stopping and pulling me closer as if all the strangers passing by us on the sidewalk would be interested in our conversation.

"What is it?"

"There's a boy I like at the school—Graham Hill. He's s-o-o-o handsome. He's a senior, studying acting." Suddenly, the corners of her mouth drooped sadly. "But he doesn't even know I exist," she said. She looked down at the sidewalk and then snapped her head up. "Let's hurry," she said, charging off again and tugging me behind her. "They'll still be in rehearsal and we can get a look at him."

Hurry? I thought. What were we doing before?

When we came around the corner, I saw the Bernhardt School across the street. There was a very tall, iron bar fence around the grounds with vines threaded through most of it. The entrance opened on a driveway that snaked up and over a small knoll before reaching the gray stone building that reminded me of a castle because it was tall and round, but what looked like a more recent addition with a flat room ran off to the right. In that section the windows were larger. Off to the left, I saw two tennis courts, both presently in use. On one court two couples were playing doubles. Even with the sounds of the traffic, the horns honking, we could hear their occasional laughter.

The sky above had become a darker blue with a puffy, cotton ball cloud here and there. The breeze that lifted the strands of my hair and made them dance over my forehead was warm and salty. Beyond the school I could see the water that had been visible from the front steps of our apartment building.

"Come on," Trisha commanded as soon as the light turned green.

The grounds of the school surprised me. I hadn't thought I would find green grass, or flower beds, or the water fountains with benches and slate rock pathways in the middle of New York City. And there were great maple and oak trees with long thick branches casting cool shadows in which some students now sat or reclined, some reading, some talking softly, dozens of white and gray pigeons strutting bravely about them. It looked more like a beautiful park than school grounds.

"It's very pretty here," I said.

"It was once owned by a multimillionaire who loved Sarah Bernhardt, the famous actress, and decided to create this school in her name after she died. The school has been in existence since 1923, but everything's up-to-date. Ten years ago they added the new buildings. There's a plaque right there," Trisha said pointing to the fence. When we crossed the street, I stopped to read it.

TO THE MEMORY OF SARAH BERNHARDT
WHOSE BRIGHT LIGHT LIT UP THE STAGE
AS IT HAD NEVER BEEN LIT BEFORE

"Isn't that the most romantic thing you've ever read?" Trisha said, sighing. "I hope someday someone very rich falls in love with me and has my name engraved in marble."

"Someone will," I said and she smiled.

"Thank you. It's very nice of you to say that. I'm so glad you're here." She threaded her arm through mine to walk me through the entrance.

I looked up at the circular entrance to the school. This close, it looked even more intimidating than I had imagined. In those hallowed halls, really gifted people practiced and developed their talents. Many of its graduates were famous. These teachers saw the best and finest. Surely someone like me would stand out like an unripe tomato in a basket of ripe ones. I had only just learned how to play the piano and I had never had formal voice lessons. And after all, Grandmother Cutler had gotten me in without an audition. No one had said I had enough talent to enroll. My head bowed with the panic I felt.

"What's the matter?" Trisha asked. "Are you tired?"

"No. I . . . maybe we should wait until tomorrow," I said, pausing in the driveway.

"You're not afraid of this place, are you?" she asked quickly. By the way she asked, I suspected she had had similar feelings on first arriving. "Come on," she added, urging me forward. "Everyone is very friendly here and everyone understands what it means to be a performer. Stop worrying."

Once again, she was pulling me along. I was beginning to feel like a puppy on a leash. We hurried up the driveway to the front entrance. A tall, slim man in a light blue sports jacket and matching slacks was just coming out. He had silvery gray hair and a silvery gray mustache which contrasted sharply with his cerulean eyes and rust complexion.

"Trisha?" he said as if he couldn't believe it was she.

"Hello, Mr. Van Dan. This is Dawn Cutler, a new student who just arrived. I'm showing her around."

"Oh, yes," he said, gazing at me from head to foot. "You're going to be in my class."

"Yes, sir," I said.

"Well, I look forward to seeing you tomorrow." He turned toward Trisha, his eyes twinkling. "Subtract fifty percent from whatever Trisha tells you, Dawn. She has a propensity for hyperbole," he added and continued on.

"What did he say?" I asked, grimacing.

"I tend to exaggerate," she said and giggled. "He's very nice and very funny in class. See," she said, "I told you people are friendly here."

When we entered the school, we were greeted by an enormous mural in the lobby. It ran up the wall almost from the floor to the ceiling. It was a portrait of Sarah Bernhardt with her left hand up as if she were reaching for something and her eyes tilted toward the heavens.

"This way," Trisha said and we went off to the right over the light brown marble floors. Late afternoon sunlight was filtered through the high, stained-glass windows, painting a rainbow of colors over the walls. Trisha led me down a long corridor. We stopped in a smaller lobby in front of two sets of double doors. On a large bulletin board was a poster advertising an upcoming production of Chekhov's *The Sea Gull.*

"This is the amphitheater," Trisha explained and opened one set of doors softly. She gestured for me to get closer, and I peered in over her shoulder.

It was a large auditorium with seats in a semicircle facing a stage. At the moment there were a half dozen people on the stage rehearsing a scene. Trisha pressed her right forefinger up against her lips and indicated I should follow her down the aisle. About midway to the stage, she stopped and directed me to sit beside her. For a few moments we listened as the young director explained where he wanted one of the actors to stand during the scene. Trisha leaned over to whisper in my ear.

"That boy all the way on the right is Graham. Isn't he dreamy?"

He was a tall, blond-haired boy with chiseled facial features. His hair lay lazily over his forehead and he leaned back against a wall as if he were totally uninterested in whatever was going on.

"Yes," I said.

After a moment she urged me to get up and we retreated up the aisle.

"Come on," she said as soon as she closed the doors behind us. "I'll show you the classrooms and the music suites and the dance rehearsal room."

Although our tour was done with lightning speed, I felt more secure about attending the classes the next day. Now I knew where most everything was. When Trisha saw what time it was, she hurried us out through a side exit and took me on a shortcut over the grounds to what was the delivery entrance for the school. We burst out on the sidewalk and rushed to the corner. All we had to do was go down another block and we were at the apartment building.

The moment we entered, Agnes Morris popped out of the sitting room as if she had been hovering at the door.

"Where have you been?" she demanded, her hands on her hips.

"Dawn and I went to George's Luncheonette to have ice cream sodas and then I took her to the school to show her around," Trisha said. "Why?"

"Why didn't you see if Arthur wanted to go along? He might have liked to go for an ice cream soda, too. You're usually more thoughtful, Trisha," she said, eyeing me. "Don't let anyone influence you badly." She pulled herself up haughtily. "Hereafter, sign out when you leave so I will know you are gone. Is that clear?" she asked, directing her glare at me again.

"Sign out?" Trisha said incredulously.

"Yes. I'm leaving a pad on the small table in the entryway here. Name and time from now on," she said. "I took Arthur to your room to introduce him to Dawn and there was no one there," she added, making it sound like the most horrible thing ever.

"I'm sure he didn't mind," Trisha replied and swung her eyes toward me.

"Nonsense. Of course he would mind. It was like walking out on a stage and having no audience. Come along, Dawn," she said. "I'll introduce you now. I don't like Arthur being slighted."

Trisha and I followed Agnes up the stairway. We stopped at a closed door and Agnes knocked softly. There was no reply, nor did anyone come to the door. Puzzled, I turned back to Trisha, who only shrugged. Agnes knocked again.

"Arthur? Arthur, dear?"

A few moments later, a very tall and exceedingly thin boy opened the door. He had a prominent Adam's apple. I could hear Daddy Longchamp saying, "Now there's a bean pole."

Arthur had large, sad, black eyes the same color as his ebony black hair, which was long and straggly. It looked like he had never taken a brush to it. He had a long, lean nose and a mouth with pencil-thin lips. His face was narrow with his chin almost coming to a point. Against his jet-black hair and eyes, his skin looked very pale. He made me think of wild mushrooms growing in damp, dark places in the forest.

Arthur wore a black cotton shirt that ballooned out around him as though it was filled with air. It was tucked into charcoal-gray slacks.

"Good afternoon, Arthur," Agnes said. "Here is the young lady I promised you would meet: our new student." She stepped back so I could step forward. "Dawn Cutler, meet Arthur Garwood."

"Hello," I said, extending my hand.

"Hello." He looked down at my hand as if he first had to inspect it for germs and then took it and let it go so quickly, I wasn't sure we had actually touched. He glanced at me quickly, but I thought I saw the glint of interest in them even though he dropped his gaze to look down at the floor.

"Arthur, as I told you, is a very talented musician," Agnes said.

"I'm not talented," he snapped, looking up sharply. His dark eyes flared.

"Of course you're talented," Agnes said. "You're all gifted young people or you wouldn't be here. Well," she said clasping her hands together and pressing them to her bosom, "I hope you all become very good friends and years and years from now, when all your names are up in lights, you will remember how I first introduced you."

"I'll never forget it," Trisha said. I looked back and saw her smiling.

"Let's all get ready for dinner," Agnes said, not hearing Trisha's sarcasm.

Arthur Garwood took that as a cue to close his door. His action caught me by surprise and I had to step back quickly or get my foot caught. Trisha saw the look of shock on my face and seized me under the arm to pull me to our room. As soon as our door was closed, she burst into laughter, laughing so hard she made me laugh, too.

"See what I mean about Bones?" she said, holding her stomach. "I'm not talented," she said, making her voice deep to imitate him.

"Why is he so unhappy?" I asked. "I don't think I've ever seen such deep, melancholy eyes."

"He doesn't want to be here. His parents made him come. Maybe, when you want to put yourself into a depression, you'll get him to read you some of his poetry. Anyway, thank goodness you're here," she added, "so I don't have to face that all alone." She began to undress to take a shower.

"You can use the other bathroom to shower," she said. "You don't have to wait for me."

"But I thought Agnes said that was supposed to be for the boys?"

"It is, but Arthur never showers and dresses for dinner. He wears the same clothes day in and day out, and there's no one else here yet."

I chose a pretty pink princess-shaped dress to wear to my first dinner at the student house, laid it out on the bed, and then scooped up my bathrobe and went to take a shower. I had just gotten undressed and stepped into the stall when I heard the doorknob turning and saw the lock snap open. It was obviously faulty. It happened so fast, I had no time to do anything. Arthur Garwood stepped in with a towel over his shoulder, his eyes down. I screamed, covering my bosom the best I could with my left arm and hand while my right hand dropped to shield the nudity beneath my waist. Arthur looked up. The moment he saw me, his mouth dropped open and his pale complexion turned so red, he looked feverish. Then I reached out and pulled the shower curtain around my naked body.

"I . . . oh . . . sorry, I . . ." He stepped back and closed the door quickly.

My heart was thumping like a tin drum and it wasn't just because the door lock had given way and caused an embarrassing moment. My mind reeled back to the memory of my brother Philip and what had happened between us at the Cutler Hotel. I felt myself grow nauseous and dizzy, from the memories, and I had to pause and sit on the edge of the bathtub and take deep breaths. Even so, I couldn't stop thinking of Philip's hands touching my body, his lips pressing down on my breast as he babbled and pleaded and forced himself on me that day at the hotel. I'd never been able to reveal what had happened that day because Jimmy was hiding in the hotel and I didn't want to endanger him. How horrible it had all been. The vivid images were like tiny knives poking at my heart. I embraced myself and rocked back and forth for a few moments until my nausea subsided. Then, after a few more deep breaths, I got up and showered, turning the water almost as hot as it would go, so hot that it burned and hurt as it splashed down on me. Perhaps I hoped I could burn and scrub away the shame of my thoughts and memories. But I know now I'll never be free of them.

When my skin was so raw and red I couldn't stand it any longer I got out and dried myself quickly, slipped into my robe and hurried back to my room. Trisha was already dressed and was just finishing her hair. I shut the door behind me and lay back against it, closing my eyes.

"What's wrong?" she asked. "You look upset."

I quickly told her that Arthur Garwood had walked in on me.

"It brought back bad memories," I muttered when I'd finished and sat on the bed.

"Really?" Trisha started to sit beside me. Then she looked at her watch. "Oh, I've got to go down and help Mrs. Liddy. We'll talk later tonight. We'll go to bed early and put out the lights and talk until we both fall into a drop dead sleep, okay?"

I nodded. I couldn't help it. Part of me wanted to keep all my twisted secrets locked in my heart, but another part of me longed more than anything for someone to confide in. If only I had a normal mother like other girls did—a mother you could laugh with and bring your problems to, who would hold you and stroke your hair when you were hurting. My mother was a frail, fragile flower to whom nothing sad could ever be spoken.

All the people I really loved were gone from my life, and all the people who were in my life now were people I could never love: suspicious, cruel grandmother Cutler; Randolph, my detached, distant always too busy father; my pale, frantic mother; Clara Sue, my vicious sister, and Philip, who wanted to love me in only the ways a brother should never love a sister. I needed a friend like Trisha desperately, perhaps too desperately. I hoped and prayed she wouldn't be like so many others and eventually betray me. But sometimes, we have no choice but to trust someone, I thought.

After Trisha left, I got dressed, brushed out my hair and went down to my first dinner at the student house.

If Arthur Garwood had been too shy to look at me before, he was terrified of our even crossing glances now. His cheeks still looked rosy with embarrassment and he only looked up from his plate when he absolutely had to.

The dinner was wonderful: pot roast and potatoes with a delicious gravy. Mrs. Liddy did something wonderful with the vegetables, too. I had never tasted spinach and carrots quite like this. For dessert we had sponge cake soaked in wine and covered with macaroons, almonds and whipped cream. Mrs. Liddy told me it was called a trifle.

After Trisha had helped serve the food, she sat down beside me, but we didn't have much chance to talk. Agnes Morris dominated the conversation at the table with her stories about different actors and actresses she had worked with and known, plays she had performed in, and where she had gotten her training. She appeared to have an opinion or a story about everything, even the spinach when I squeezed in a compliment about it.

"Oh, that reminds me of a funny story," Agnes said. I looked at Arthur. He had been stealing glances at me all night, but whenever I caught him doing so, his blush returned and he looked back down at his plate. "About a horrible young actress, I knew, whose name will remain anonymous because she has become quite the rage in Hollywood these days. She was about as conceited a person as you could find," she said, looking at me pointedly. "Why, she couldn't pass even a store window without stopping to gaze at herself.

"Anyway, this young lady pursued a young man, a rather handsome, debonair young man, until she persuaded him to take her to dinner and then a ride through Central Park, which she hoped would be very romantic. It wasn't and in fact, when he brought her home at the end of the evening, he simply shook her hand and said good night. Not even a quick, good night kiss," Agnes emphasized.

"Well, my conceited friend was quite upset, as you might imagine. She hurried up to her room to cry into her pillow, but when she stopped to look at herself in the mirror in the hallway, as she always did, what do you think she saw? A piece of spinach stuck right between her two front teeth!" Agnes clapped her hands together and laughed. Trisha looked at me and raised her eyes. I turned toward Arthur who nearly smiled. His lips trembled and he shook his head.

I offered to help Trisha clear the table, but Agnes repeated how we each had to take our own turn. She practically ordered me to follow her into the sitting room so she could show me her scrapbook.

"Of course, Arthur can come along, too, if he likes," she said and Arthur uttered his first words of the evening.

"Thank you, but I have to finish my math homework so I can *practice,*" he said, twisting his mouth on the word, "practice," as if it were a profanity. Arthur stole a last glance at me, and shot off. He couldn't be more shy if he were a turtle, I thought.

It turned out that Agnes didn't have only one scrapbook; she had five and all full to the last page. She had saved every single word ever written about her, even reports and notes written by her grade school teachers. Sentences were underlined, especially ones like "Agnes shows a dramatic tendency."

"Here's a picture of me at the age of two dancing on the veranda."

The picture was so old and faded, it was impossible to make out her little face, but I smiled and said it was remarkable. Agnes had things to say about each and every scrap in the scrapbooks. We had only gone through a book and a half when Trisha returned from her kitchen chores to rescue me.

"It's time for me to do my English homework," Trisha announced from the doorway. "I thought I would show Dawn what we have done so far so it will be easier for her to catch up."

"Oh, of course," Agnes said.

"Thank you," I said, getting up. I shot a look of gratitude toward Trisha and backed away from the sofa.

When Trisha and I reached the stairs, we rushed up, both of us swallowing our giggles until we closed our bedroom door.

"I know what that's like," Trisha said. "She tortured me with it the first few nights I arrived. Of course, I was trapped," she added. "I had no one to save me like I saved you.

"I wonder what's caused this new insanity about signing in and out?" Trisha said. "Agnes was never like that with us before."

"It's all my fault," I said.

"Your fault? You mean because you weren't here to be introduced to Arthur. No, I think . . ."

"It's because my grandmother wrote a letter about me to Agnes and told her some horrible things. Agnes told me I'm already on probation."

"Probation? Agnes said that? How odd. She rarely enforces any of the rules or cares. Most of the time, she can't recall them herself. But why did your own grandmother do such a thing?" Trisha asked.

Before I could reply, there was a knock on the door and then Agnes poked her head in.

"There's a phone call for Dawn," she said.

"A phone call?" I looked at Trisha.

"I forgot to tell you that we don't permit phone calls after seven o'clock at night, unless it's a dire emergency or it has something to do with the school. Since this call is long distance, I made an exception and said I would get you," Agnes said. "You can take it in the sitting room."

"Is it my mother?" I asked getting out my bathrobe slowly.

"No. It's someone called Jimmy," she said.

"Jimmy!" I hurried past her and bounced down the steps to the sitting room to scoop up the receiver.

"Jimmy!"

"Hi, Dawn. How are you? I hope I didn't get you in trouble by calling this late. The lady who answered sounded upset."

"No, it's all right. How are you?"

"I'm great. I've got some big news to tell you and since I've got to leave tomorrow, I thought I'd better try to phone."

"Leave tomorrow? Where are you going?"

"I've enlisted in the army, Dawn. I'm going to boot camp tomorrow," he said firmly.

"The army! But what about school?"

"The recruiting officer explained how I can get my high school diploma while I'm in the army, and I'll learn a skill I can use when I get out."

"But Jimmy . . . the army . . ." I paused, my heart racing as I recalled that helpful soldier at the airport, the one who had reminded me of Jimmy. Had that been an omen, a prophecy?

"It's all right, Dawn. It will be good for me. I want to be on my own and not passed from one foster home to another." Jimmy's voice rang with determination.

"But Jimmy, when will I see you?" I cried.

"Right after boot camp, I'll get a leave and come to New York to see you. I promise. There's no one else for me to see anyway, no one else I care about but you, Dawn," he said softly. The image of his sweet face flashed before me, his dark eyes shimmering, crying out for the love we both had thought was forbidden between us. Now that we knew it wasn't, we were like infants learning how to walk, tottering and stumbling along, searching for the right words, the right way to act toward each other. After years and years of living as a brother and sister, it was so difficult to cast off those identities and put on new ones.

"I miss you, Jimmy," I said. "More than ever now that I'm in New York. It's so big and scary."

"Don't worry, Dawn. I'll be there before you know it and I know you're going to do well."

"I've already made a friend, my roommate, Trisha Kramer. She's very nice. You're going to like her."

"See? I knew it."

"But Jimmy, you should try to find Daddy, especially now that you're going into the army. He needs you, Jimmy. I hate to think of him coming out of that horrible prison and being all alone. He doesn't have Momma; he doesn't have Fern; and he doesn't have you."

There was a silence between us.

"Jimmy?"

"I've written him a letter," Jimmy confessed.

"Oh Jimmy, I'm so glad."

"I did it mostly because you wanted me to," he said, putting a manly gruffness into his voice.

"That makes me happy, Jimmy, to know you did something nice because of me," I said softly.

"Uh, huh," he said quickly. "What about your new family? Are they going to come to visit you?"

"They say they are. Jimmy . . ."

"Yes, Dawn?"

"You're still my real family," I said. He was silent on the other end for a long moment.

"I've got to hang up, Dawn. I've got to pack and do some things yet."

"Be careful, Jimmy. And write me. Please!" I begged.

"Of course, I'll write you. Just don't become a big star too fast and forget me," he teased.

"I'll never do that, Jimmy. I promise."

"Bye, Dawn."

"Bye."

"Dawn!" he cried.

"Yes, Jimmy?"

"I love you," he said quickly.

I knew how hard it was for him to say it, to put into words feelings we had believed sinful.

"I love you, too, Jimmy," I said and then I heard the phone click dead. I was about to cradle my receiver when I thought I heard another click. Had Agnes Morris been listening? Maybe Grandmother Cutler had employed her as a spy.

It wasn't until I cradled my receiver and stood up that I realized tears were streaming down my cheeks. They dropped off my chin. I scrubbed my cheeks with my palms and walked slowly out of the sitting room and up the stairs.

Trisha was in bed, reading a magazine when I entered. She dropped the magazine quickly and looked at me with eyes full of questions.

"Who's Jimmy?" she asked.

"The boy I believed was my brother for years and years and years," I said. Her lips gaped open.

"You thought was your brother?" she asked. I nodded.

"A boy who you thought was your brother? A grandmother who writes nasty letters about you? What kind of a family do you come from anyway?"

I could see it was time to tell her some of my story. If I was going to have a friend, a true friend, I couldn't keep too many deep, dark secrets from her. I had to trust her, take my chances and trust her with my tale. I could only hope and pray she wouldn't betray me and spread my story all over the school, a story that would make me seem like something freakish to the others, especially people who didn't know me.

"Will you promise not to tell anyone what I tell you?" I asked her.

"Of course," she said, her eyes wide with excitement. "Cross my heart and hope to die," she said, drawing an X over her breasts. I nodded and sat down on my bed. She went to her knees and sat back on her legs, tossing her hair over her shoulder and folding her hands on her lap. She looked like she was holding her breath.

My thoughts took wing to Jimmy and I recalled the way we would lie awake for hours and hours talking, lying beside each other in our pull-out sofa and whispering deep into the night. I lay back and looked up at the ceiling.

"Shortly after I was born, I was kidnapped," I began and told her my story.

For the longest time, Trisha didn't ask a question, didn't say a word. After a while she lay back in bed and folded her arms across her chest and listened. I think she was afraid to interrupt because she thought I might stop talking. After I told her all about Momma and Daddy Longchamp, Fern and Jimmy, and described how life was for us, I quickly skipped to my return to Cutler's Cove. I was too ashamed to tell her about my short romance with Philip when I was attending Emerson Peabody in Richmond and what had happened between us at the hotel afterward.

"Clara Sue sounds horrible," Trisha finally said. "What a mean thing to do to Jimmy."

"If I never see her again, it will be too soon," I replied. Trisha was quiet for a long moment and then she sat up and turned to me.

"When you came out of the bathroom after Arthur had walked in on you, you said it had brought back bad memories. What bad memories? Something else at the hotel?" she asked perceptively.

"I was almost raped when I took a shower," I said, deciding to make something up. "By a hotel handyman."

"Oh, that's awful. What did you do?"

"I fought him off and he ran away. The police are still looking for him." I turned away so Trisha couldn't see the lie in my eyes. All of a sudden, chills went up and down my spine and I was almost dizzy with fear over how she would react to my story. What had I done? New York was my one and only chance for a new life where no one knew about the strangeness of my past. Why had I confided these things that should be buried ten feet underground and never seen again? With my heart going as fast as a speeding train, I looked at Trisha, terrified that I might see loathing in her eyes.

"You're so lucky!" she suddenly exclaimed.

"What?" Had I heard right? "Lucky?"

"You've had such an exciting life and nothing ever happens to me," she moaned. "I went to just one plain old public school in a small town, had only one real boyfriend, and hardly ever went anywhere. Oh, we've been to Palm Beach in Florida dozens of times, but that's no fun for me. I'm always trapped in some stuffy hotel and forced to dress and behave perfectly because so many rich and important people are always staring at each other and especially each other's children. If I have a hair out of place, my mother gets hysterical. We get our manners out of Emily Post. I can't even put an elbow on the table!"

She jumped over to my bed and sprawled out beside me on her stomach.

"But when I become a famous dancer, I'm going to be outrageous," she declared firmly. "I'm going to dress wildly, have dozens and dozens of glamorous boyfriends, all with shady reputations, smoke cigarettes in long pearl cigarette holders and be seen in elegant places. Wherever I go there will be reporters snapping pictures. And I won't get married until I'm . . . I'm almost thirty! And it will be someone so rich, his name will open doors and make people scurry about like wild rabbits. Doesn't that sound exciting?" she asked me.

"Yes," I said not to hurt her feelings, but deep inside I was torn apart by my desires. I wanted to become a great singer, and I wanted to taste fame and experience the world—there was so much out there that I'd never seen or done. But, if I opened my secret heart and looked inside I knew I'd see my strongest hope. I wanted to have a family and love and cherish my children so they would never feel the way I did now. I couldn't wish that on anyone.

Trisha turned over on her back. "Does Agnes know all this stuff that happened to you?"

"She doesn't know anything but whatever lies Grandmother Cutler wrote her in that letter. I don't even know what the letter said—I'd love to get my hands on it."

"We will," Trisha vowed.

"How?"

"When we know Agnes is out for a while and Mrs. Liddy is busy, we'll sneak into her room and search for it."

"Oh, I don't know if I could ever do that," I said. Just the thought of it made my heart thump.

"Leave it up to me," Trisha said. "O-o-o-o," she squealed, "this is the most excitement I've had in ages."

"I'd rather not have any of it," I muttered, but she didn't hear me or care to.

She made me go back and describe in more detail what it was like to move from one town to another, one school to another. We talked until we both confessed to being tired and finally put the lights out.

I fell asleep quickly, exhausted from my trip and all that I had done since I had arrived; but sometime in the middle of the night, I awoke to the sound of rainfall: my first summer storm in New York City. The staccato beats on the roof overhead were military drums to take me into memories I had hoped to ignore, memories of my first night at Cutler's Cove when I found myself in a strange new world with my strange new family. How I had missed Momma and Daddy Longchamp, Fern and Jimmy.

I got out of bed. Trisha was fast asleep, her breathing deep and regular. I moved carefully so as not to wake her, and I went out to go to the bathroom. On my way back to the room, I heard an odd sound. I listened and realized it was the sound of someone sobbing and it was coming from Arthur Garwood's room. I drew closer to his door and listened.

"Arthur?" I called. "Are you all right?" I waited. The crying stopped, but he didn't reply. I listened a bit longer and then returned to my room to wonder about this dark, brooding boy who shut himself up in his own body.

3
THE LETTER

Summer that used to move like a caterpillar flew by and before I knew it, I was opening my eyes to greet a late August morning. My stay in New York and attendance at the Bernhardt School of Performing Arts had taken me on a roller coaster of emotions. The panic I had felt the first day of class didn't diminish immediately, even though Trisha had been right: everyone was friendly and encouraging, especially our teachers who were less formal than my public school teachers. In all my classes except math and science, we sat in a half circle facing the teacher who usually spoke to us in a conversational tone. My speech instructor even told his students to call him by his first name!

And most of the students were different too. The chatter in the cafeteria or in the lounges was always about theater or movies or recitals. We didn't have a basketball or football team. Everything was centered around the arts. Usually, I sat and listened when the others talked about their favorite performers and productions. I was ashamed to admit that I had yet to go to a real play, especially to a play on Broadway. Of course, I told Trisha, who immediately arranged for us to go see a matinee.

Nearly every day at school, some new announcement was posted on the general bulletin boards advertising auditions and opportunities, mainly for the seniors. I couldn't imagine myself asking someone to pay me for performing, not for a long time. Trisha felt the same way about herself, but we always stopped to read the bulletins, pretending we were planning on attending the auditions.

I received many compliments and a great deal of support from my vocal teacher and fellow music students, but if anyone kept me from losing my head, it was my piano teacher, Madame Steichen. She had been a concert pianist in Austria and was famous. It was considered a great honor to be in her class, although for me it was quite frightening at first. I could see from the way my fellow students acted when they entered her classes that she would be quite different from our other teachers. She ran a general class in music and gave individualized lessons.

Madame Steichen always dressed formally for class, dressed as if she were performing for an audience herself. She usually entered just before the beginning of the class and never tolerated anyone coming late. We were all seated and waiting and we could hear her shoes clicking down the corridor as she approached. When she entered, no one made a sound. Rarely did she smile.

She was tall and thin, with long, graceful fingers that seemed to have minds of their own when she brought them to the piano keys. Never had I seen such intensity in anyone's eyes as I saw in her dark gray eyes when she demonstrated. I was very impressed and very excited about being one of her students.

She always wore her hair pinned firmly back in a bun. She wore no makeup, not even a touch of lipstick to brighten her pale red lips. Sitting beside her on the piano stool, I saw the little brown age spots on her wrists and on her temples. Her skin was so thin, the tiny veins that ran over her eyelids were quite visible.

Yet her frail body was deceptive. She was firm and strong in class and never hesitated to sting her pupils with caustic criticism whenever she thought it necessary. At least twice, she nearly had me in tears.

"Why did you tell me you had piano lessons?" she demanded the first time I sat down to play the piano for her. "Did someone tell you I was tone deaf?"

"No, Madame, but I did have lessons. I—"

"Please," she said, cutting me off with a sweep of her hand. "Consider yourself just beginning. Forget everything and anything you were told. Do you understand me?" she demanded, her small, intense eyes pinning me to my desk.

"Yes, Madame," I said quickly.

"Good. Now, let us go back to the fundamentals," she said. For the rest of the day she treated me as if I had just been told, "This is a piano."

Toward the end of the summer though, she paused at the conclusion of a lesson and stared at me for a long moment. My heart began to beat in anticipation of her telling me I should give up the piano. Instead, she brought her shoulders back, nodded, and looked down her nose at me to say something I considered spectacular.

"You appear to have a natural instinct for music. In time I believe you can become of concert pianist class."

Then she pivoted on her soft shoes and left me sitting there with my jaw dropped open. Of course, I rushed out to tell Trisha and we celebrated with a double fudge chocolate sundae at George's Luncheonette. We both felt so good about it that we even tried to get Arthur Garwood to come when we saw him walking over the school grounds. He stared at us as if we had asked him to jump off the George Washington Bridge. For a moment when he gazed only at me, I thought he was going to come, but then he shook his head, thanked us, and walked off quickly. All summer long he had kept to himself, but I sensed he wanted to talk to overcome his shyness and talk to me, especially if I were alone.

Except for Trisha and a few other friends I had made in classes, I had no one else to share my happiness with. I could write Jimmy a letter, but I couldn't call him. I had begun to feel truly like an orphan. Cruel Fate had stolen away my family and left me with a family that didn't want me. It was as if I had no family at all, no past, no present, no future. Other girls my age could rattle on and on about their childhood, their brothers and sisters, grandparents and parents. They could talk about trips their families took together, their wonderful holiday dinners, funny things their little brothers and sisters said and did, but I had to sit with my mouth sewn shut.

My real mother Laura Sue never came to New York to visit me as she had promised the day I left Cutler's Cove. However one night on the last Monday in August, she called to see how I was doing and to recite her excuses for neglecting me all summer long.

"I haven't been well," she said, "since the day you left. First, I came down with this horrible summer cold. It nearly became pneumonia and then I developed an allergy that simply puzzled the doctors.

"Oh yes, I had more than one doctor. Randolph brought in allergy specialists, one after the other, but I couldn't stop my eyes from watering and every once in a while, I broke into these spells of sneezing.

"You can imagine how it has been. I have hardly been down in the hotel."

"I'm sorry to hear it, Mother," I said. "Maybe if you came for a visit to New York, you would leave your allergy behind," I suggested.

"Oh no, the allergy has left me as mysteriously as it came. I'm fine now, except I'm quite run-down and the doctors advise me to continue my bed rest awhile longer. I'm sorry; I so wanted to take you shopping in New York.

"Are you having a good time? Enjoying the school?" she asked.

"Yes," I said, wondering whether she really cared. I knew that if I said no or tried to describe problems she would immediately have a fainting spell and jump off the phone so fast my head would spin.

"Good. Maybe in a month or so, I will be able to travel. In the meantime, I'll see to it that Randolph sends you some money so you can do some shopping with one of your friends, okay?

"I'd send Randolph, but the hotel's been busier than ever and Grandmother Cutler is depending on him."

"I'm sure," I said dryly, "she doesn't depend on anyone but herself."

"You must not talk like that, Dawn," my mother chastised. "It won't do any of us any good. We must make the best of the situation. Please, don't bring up any controversy, not now, now that I've gotten up enough strength to talk to you."

"Why does it take so much strength for you to talk to me, Mother? Is it because of the clouds of lies that hover above us?"

"I have to go now, Dawn. I'm getting tired," she said quickly.

"When will you tell me my father's name, Mother? When?" I demanded.

"Oh dear. I can't talk like this over the phone. I'll speak to you again, soon," she said and hung up before I could say another unpleasant thing. Right after she did, I once again heard a second click. It sent a chilling ripple through my body. Agnes Morris did listen in on my phone calls, I thought. It enraged me and when I went upstairs, I told Trisha.

"She's spying on me," I said. "I'm sure of it. And all because she believes the lies my grandmother wrote."

"We've got to get a look at the letter," Trisha concluded. "Let's try tomorrow night when she goes to the theater with her friends. I'm sure she won't lock her bedroom door."

"Oh, Trisha, I don't know. What if we're caught?"

"We won't be. You want to see the letter, don't you?" she asked. "Well?" she pursued.

"Yes," I said. I looked into her eyes. "I want to see that letter very much."

The next night we sat in the sitting room and pretended to be interested in Agnes Morris's scrapbooks. It almost kept her from going out with her friends because she lingered so long to explain this picture and that and tell anecdotes about her performances and fellow actors. When Mr. Fairbanks, the clock, bonged out the hour, she realized she had to hurry to dress to meet her friends.

After she left we went looking for Mrs. Liddy and found that she had gone into her room to listen to the radio. Trisha looked at me and nodded. She went to Agnes's door and discovered it was unlocked, just as she had expected. When she turned the knob, I thought a dozen butterflies had been frightened inside my chest. It felt like their wings were flapping against my heart. I hesitated.

"What if she comes back while we're in there?" I asked.

"She won't. She's gone to a show. Come on," Trisha whispered. I looked back at Mrs. Liddy's closed door. The music from the radio could still be heard, but she could still come out and see or hear us. That would be terrible, I thought. Then I thought about Grandmother Cutler and how she would glare at me with her gray-stone eyes shooting devilish electric sparks.

"All right," I said and followed Trisha into Agnes's room. I hadn't seen past the curtain before. Trisha parted it and we entered.

It did feel like I was walking onto a stage and entering a set. We found the bedroom dimly lit by a small Tiffany lamp on the desk to the left. Agnes had an antique white cast-iron bed with white pine night stands on either side. There were oversized pillows and a white down comforter with pink trim. The wall on the right held an enormous mirror. A long vanity table was covered with jars and tubes of makeup, cold cream and powders. In the left corner were bottles of perfume, so many it looked like a shelf in the cosmetic section of a department store. As we drew closer, I could see that a ring of small bulbs lined the mirror. It even smelled like back stage.

There were two matching dressers on the left and a closet between them, the door now closed but a sign over it read, EXIT. I turned to Trisha with a smile of confusion on my face.

"She's taken things from stages and put them in this room. That's an actual makeup table from an old theater. And those drapes," she said, nodding toward the windows, "were made from actual stage curtains.

"Every morning she leaves this room, she pretends she's starring in a new play," Trisha added. I looked at the pictures on the walls. They were all pictures of Agnes wearing different costumes from the different productions she had been in. I recognized some of them from the scrapbooks.

Suddenly, it all struck me as being very sad. Agnes lived in the past because she had no present and no future. Every day she wove her memories together on a loom of fantasy to avoid facing reality, facing the fact that she was no longer young and beautiful and in demand. She lived vicariously through her talented residents. I began to wonder how much of what she had told us was part of an illusion.

"If the letter is anywhere," Trisha said, "it's probably on that desk."

We went to it and began to search through the papers piled in a rather disorganized manner—bills were mixed in with personal letters, theater periodicals and advertisements. We didn't find Grandmother Cutler's letter there. Trisha opened the drawers and rifled through them, but again, we came up empty-handed.

I touched Trisha's shoulder and indicated she should be quiet when I thought I heard footsteps in the corridor outside the door. We listened, but heard nothing.

"We better go," I said.

"Wait." Trisha gazed around the room. "This letter, it's probably part of some sort of scene in her crazy head. A secret correspondence . . ." Trisha mused aloud and studied the room like an amateur sleuth. "I remember this play we put on last year, a mystery . . . Agnes was there, of course . . ."

She walked slowly toward the bed.

"Trisha, let's forget it," I pleaded. Surely, if Mrs. Liddy came out, she would hear us searching in the room. Trisha held her hand up to indicate I should be quiet while she thought. Then she lifted the comforter a bit, knelt down and stuck her hand between the mattress and the box spring. She ran her hand along the side of the bed, came up with nothing and went around to the other side to do the same thing. "Trisha."

"Wait."

She knelt down out of sight. I stepped back to listen at the door. A moment later, Trisha stood up smiling with the letter in her hand. We met at the desk and Trisha took the letter out of the envelope and spread it before us in the light of the small Tiffany lamp. I read it softly, aloud.

Dear Agnes,

As you know I have enrolled my granddaughter Dawn in the Bernhardt School and asked Mr. Updike to have her housed in your residence. I am relying on our friendship. I hate to place such a formidable burden on your shoulders, but frankly, you are my last hope.

This grandchild has been a terrible problem for us all. My daughter-in-law is absolutely beside herself and has nearly had a number of serious nervous breakdowns as a consequence. I can't tell you how much my son Randolph has aged because of this . . . this . . . I'm afraid I have to say it . . . bad seed in our family.

The irony is she has musical talent. Since she has done nothing but gotten into trouble in one public school after another because of her juvenile delinquency, which includes sexual promiscuity, I thought sending her to the school of performing arts might help. Perhaps if she is made to concentrate on her talents, she will be less of a delinquent.

The fault lies with all of us. We have spoiled her. Randolph has rained gifts upon her ever since she was an infant. She's never done a true day's work at the hotel. No matter what we ask her to do, she always complains.

Furthermore, I'm afraid she has become a rather sneaky person, not above lying right to your face. She even went so far as to steal from one of my elderly guests.

Even though I have warned her against it, she might stay in contact with some public school friends who have been bad influences on her. Watch out for that and please be sure she lives up to your rules and does whatever she is supposed to do. I will, of course, be speaking to you shortly in more detail about all this.

You don't know how much I and my family appreciate your willingness to take on what I would have to honestly admit is a major problem child.

At this point we are afraid of the bad influence she will have on Philip and Clara, who are both doing so well.

Rest assured, I will not forget you.

Sincerely yours,
Lillian Cutler

Trisha looked up at me and then put her arm around my shoulder.

"The entire letter is one big lie," I said. "One big, horrible, cruel lie. A bad seed, sexually promiscuous, spoiled, a liar and a thief! And she hates my mother, hates her," I said through my tears. "I can't believe she wrote that I would be a bad influence on Clara. You know some of the things she did to me and to Jimmy."

"You expected something like this," Trisha said softly, her hand on my shoulder.

"I know, but to actually see it all in writing. She's the most atrocious, loathsome woman I have ever met. I wish there was some way I could get back at her," I said, clenching my teeth.

"Just be a success," Trisha said calmly. "Be everything she says you're not."

I nodded. "You're right. I will try harder and harder and every time I get an A or receive a compliment, I'll think of how she has to accept it."

"We better put this back," Trisha said, returning the dreadful letter of lies to its envelope. She shoved it between the mattress and the box springs again and then we slipped out of Agnes's bedroom and quietly made our way out of the corridor, but when we turned toward the stairway, I paused and looked back. I just had the feeling there were eyes on us in the darkness. A shadow moved.

Trisha didn't know I had stopped. She kept moving up the stairway, but I took a step back and saw Arthur Garwood, his back pressed against the wall. Because he was so thin and he was wearing his usual black shirt and black slacks, it was nearly impossible to see him. Although he must have known I had spotted him, he didn't step forward. Instead, he continued to press himself to the wall and cling to the darkness. I started to call out to

Trisha, but didn't. Instead, I just turned back and followed her up the stairway to our room. As soon as I closed the door behind me, I told her.

"He just kept standing there in the dark?" she asked.

I nodded and embraced myself because the incident had left me cold.

"He doesn't want us to know he was spying on us. Don't worry, he won't say anything to Agnes," she assured me.

"How did he know we were going to sneak into her room?" I wondered.

"He might have just been following us or . . ." Her eyes went to the door. "Maybe he's been listening in on our conversations," she concluded. "If I ever catch him doing that, I'll give him something to be sad about. Forget about him," she said quickly. "He's just weird."

I nodded, but it was easier said than done. Arthur's slim silhouette lingered on the inside of my eyelids. For a moment I wondered if maybe it hadn't just been a shadow, my overworked imagination. I went to the door and opened it a crack to peer out just to see if I would catch him returning to his room. I saw nothing.

"Forget about him," Trisha advised again. "He's not worth the worry."

I closed the door and Trisha turned on the radio so we could listen to music while we did our homework. Afterward, I had a terrible time falling asleep because of the letter. My mind reeled with the images and memories of my every conversation and confrontation with Grandmother Cutler, from the first time we met when she told me I would have to change my name from Dawn to Eugenia to our showdown when I let her know I had discovered the truth about my abduction and her involvement in it. She wasn't a woman who took defeat gracefully. In ways I feared I was yet to discover, she would work her revenge.

At the end of the summer session, the Bernhardt School closed down. Some seniors remained to practice and prepare for auditions, but most teachers and students took advantage of the short break between the summer and the fall semesters to go on holiday. I had already decided that I wouldn't return to the hotel. I really didn't want to return, and no one at the hotel, my mother included, even asked if I were returning, much less insisted I do. Agnes seemed to expect it.

Trisha went home of course. I couldn't blame her. She was anxious to see her parents and her boyfriend, as well as some of her old friends. She kept inviting me to go home with her, but I thought I would only be in her way.

"Maybe you'll change your mind afterward," she said and wrote out directions for me to take a bus upstate.

"I'll call you in a few days," she warned, "and nag you to come. I hate leaving you here alone," she added, looking as if she would burst into tears.

I was to be alone. Even Arthur Garwood left. His parents stopped by to pick him up the day before Trisha left, and we happened to be downstairs at the time, so we got to meet them. When Agnes introduced me and Trisha to Arthur's mother and father, I thought he might very well have been adopted. He didn't look anything like either of them. Arthur's father was short and almost completely bald. He had a pudgy face with a small, tight mouth and beady hazel eyes.

Arthur's mother was an inch or so shorter than his father and built like a pear. She had strawberry blond hair, light blue eyes and fair skin.

The only thing I sensed they shared with Arthur was their dour personalities. They hardly spoke and seemed only concerned about keeping to their schedule. They were embarking on what they called a work-holiday. They were going to participate in a chamber music recital in Boston, after which they would do some sightseeing and go to Cape Cod. Arthur was reluctant to go along, but they were insistent. He didn't say good-bye to anyone, but just before he walked out the front door, he turned and looked at me with those large, melancholy eyes and for the first time, I felt more sorry for him than anything else.

I didn't realize just how lonely I would be without Trisha until everyone was gone and I was upstairs, alone in my room. I did some reading and then decided I would go out and buy a notebook to keep as my journal. Our English teacher had suggested we do something like this, for other reasons. He wanted us to write down impressions and descriptions we could then draw upon later when an assignment required them. I wanted the journal as a way of helping myself to understand my kaleidoscope of emotions.

I kept busy during the day helping Mrs. Liddy, who said she always used the end of the summer break to do a thorough cleaning of the house.

"Usually, there's no one here," she said, but she didn't say it with any resentment. She smiled immediately.

Cleaning the rooms from top to bottom one at a time reminded me of my work as a chambermaid at the hotel. I wondered about some of my friends from the hotel, like Mrs. Boston, the chief housekeeper for the family, and Sissy, who by taking me to Mrs. Dalton, had unknowingly helped me to discover the secret of my abduction.

I dove into the work, getting on my hands and knees to scrub the floors and dusting and polishing the furniture until everything, no matter how old it was, glimmered like new. I washed the windows and cleaned them down to the smallest speck of dust so that it was nearly impossible to tell whether they were opened or closed. Every once in a while, Mrs. Liddy stopped by from a room she was doing and stood in the doorway, her hands on her hips, shaking her head. Later that afternoon she brought Agnes up to see my work.

"Isn't this wonderful, Agnes?" Mrs. Liddy said, clapping her hands together. "We've never had a pupil work as hard as this, have we? My own mother back at our rooming house in London didn't get our rooms as sparkling clean."

"Yes," Agnes said, gazing down. "I'll have to write a letter and tell your grandmother about this."

"Yes," I said. "Why don't you? Although that's not why I'm doing it. You might ask how someone who is so spoiled and selfish knows about cleaning rooms," I added, a small, tight smile around my mouth. Mrs. Liddy's eyes twinkled amusingly.

"Perhaps you're changing," Agnes said and walked away, leaving me feeling infuriated.

I passed my time visiting the museums and window shopping on Fifth Avenue. One afternoon, I went into the Plaza to just sit in the lobby and watch the fancy-dressed people coming and going. I tried to imagine Jimmy and me staying here for one glorious week. I would buy some beautiful dresses and we would go to the expensive restaurant and maybe even dance in the ballroom. I thought of my tall, strong Jimmy, his dark eyes staring down at me, a slight smile teasing his full lips, his hands warm and protective as he held me in his arms. Small shivers, delicious and terrifying, went through me at these thoughts.

Of course, Jimmy wouldn't want to dress up and he wouldn't want to put on airs and be someone he was not; but maybe, when he returned from being in the army, he would be different, older and perhaps even more ambitious. Why shouldn't he want the same things? I thought.

After I had returned from a day at the Museum of Natural History, I lingered in the sitting room, tapping out a melody on the piano. I never heard Agnes come up behind me, but suddenly, I felt someone else in the room and turned to see her standing there staring at me in the strangest way. For a moment I thought she was angry I had played the piano without asking her first.

"My father was a talented pianist," she said, "but he didn't think it was honest work for a man so he did nothing with it."

"Oh. Perhaps that's where you get your talent from, Agnes."

"Yes, perhaps," she said. I had never seen her look so melancholy. She was even dressed in black and wore little makeup and no jewelry, which was very unusual.

"Do you have brothers and sisters? I didn't see any pictures of any in your scrapbooks," I said.

"No, I was an only child. My mother went through such a time giving birth to me, she swore she would have no other." Agnes sighed.

"Didn't you ever want to be married?" I asked. The way she stared back at me I expected she would bawl me out for prying into her private life. Suddenly though, she smiled.

"Oh, I had plenty of opportunity, but I was always afraid of marriage," she confessed.

"Afraid? Why?"

"I was afraid marriage would clip my wings and put me in a gilded cage like a beautiful canary. I would still sing, but my voice would be filled with longing and dreams. It is very difficult to be a good wife and mother and live a life on the stage," she lectured. "Show people are a different breed. You will understand in time what I mean when I say our first love is the stage and no matter what promises we make to our loved ones, we will never betray our first love and never really sacrifice when it comes to our careers.

"Something happens to us when those lights go on and we hear the applause. We make love to an audience, you see. Actually," she said, looking about the sitting room as if we were on a stage, "I have been married all this time, married to the theater."

"Don't you think I can be a singer and still have a husband and a family?" I asked, desperation stealing through me at the thought that I would be forced to choose between my dreams.

"It's difficult. It will depend entirely on your husband, how understanding and loving he is and whether or not he is the terribly jealous type."

"Why jealous?"

"Because he will have to see you sing of love to other men and kiss them and recite vows of love so convincingly that audiences will believe you love these men."

I had never thought of these things before. It brought a heaviness to my heart that made it feel like a lump of lead in my chest. I tried to imagine Jimmy sitting in the audience watching me do the things Agnes described, Jimmy who seemed so tough to the outside world, but who I knew to be easily wounded.

"But," she bragged, "I did crush some young male hearts. Do you know what is in this vase I keep under lock and key?" she asked, approaching one of the cabinets. I had simply assumed it was a valuable antique.

"No. What?"

"The ashes of Sanford Littleton, a young man who was so in love with me he committed suicide and left instructions for the remains of his cremated body to be given to me," she said and followed it with a shrill laugh.

"Oh don't look so glum. You don't have to plan your whole life this moment," she chastised. I wasn't glum; I was shocked. She turned to leave and then pivoted on her heels to look back at me. "A letter came for you today," she said.

"A letter?"

"Yes. Mrs. Liddy brought it up to your room when she went up with some linen."

"Thank you," I said and ran upstairs to find the letter on my bed. I had been expecting a letter from Jimmy telling me about his plans for a visit to New York, but I saw from the envelope that it had been forwarded here from the Cutler Cove Hotel. When I turned it over, I saw it had been opened and resealed with tape. But the name and return address made my heart leap. It was a letter from Daddy Longchamp, the man I had grown up thinking was my father, and who still seemed much more like a father to me than Randolph Cutler ever had.

I threw myself on the bed and opened the envelope quickly. I saw from the date on the top of the letter that it had been mailed nearly three weeks ago.

Three weeks! How horrible, I thought. How long had it been kept at the hotel? And I just knew Grandmother Cutler had read it. What right did she have to do such a thing?

I tried to put aside my rage for the moment but I might as well have tried to hold my breath for three hours. I was still shaking with anger as I read.

Dear Dawn,

I am pleased to tell you that I have been released from prison. I'm still not sure how or why it happened so fast, but one day the warden called me in to tell me my parole hearing had been moved up. But jail ain't been the worst part of all this. The worst part's been my knowing how much I hurt you and Jimmy and Fern. I never meant it to be this way and I'm sorry. I surely wouldn't blame you for hating me forever, and I do hope that you're having a good life now that you're living with your real folks who I know are rich. At least you'll never have to scrimp and save the way we usta. No more grits and peas for dinner.

I've got me a good job. The prison authorities located it for me. I'm a maintenance man in a big laundry. I also got a nice little apartment not too far from where I work. It's going to take me a while to earn enough money to buy me a car, but I can't travel far for a while anyways on account of the parole rules.

The nicest thing that's happened is Jimmy calling and writing me. We're becoming good friends again and I'm mighty proud of him. He says he keeps in contact with you, too. It hurts me that Fern is off living with strangers, but I've been told she's living with good people who are well-to-do folks and can give her what she needs and then some.

Of course, I'm hoping that someday soon I can get her back. I asked my parole officer about that, but he says that's something he don't know nothing about just yet. All he said was if the family goes ahead and adopts her, I'd have big problems. I'm just afraid it's going to take an army of lawyers to straighten it out, but since I'm to blame, I can't complain much.

Anyways, I wanted to write to you to tell you I'm sorry for the hurt and pain I caused you. You was always a good girl and I was always proud to be your daddy even though I really wasn't.

The truth is I miss Sally Jean and you and Jimmy and Fern so much it hurts like a punch in the chest. Some nights I don't sleep at all remembering. We had tough times, but we had each other then.

Well, that's all. Maybe someday me and you will meet again. But I don't blame you if you don't want anything more to do with me.

God bless you.

Daddy

P.S.: I wrote it because I still think it.

I clutched the letter to my bosom and sobbed, rocking back and forth on the bed. I cried so hard it hurt my stomach. Tears streamed down my face and soaked my blanket. Finally, I took deep breaths and choked back my tears. Then I stuck Daddy Longchamp's letter between some pages of my journal and went to my desk to write back to him.

I told him I didn't hate him and I knew everything. And I couldn't wait for the day we would meet again. I wrote pages and pages, telling him about my life at the hotel, how awful my real family was and how being from a family that had a lot of money didn't make life happier for me. Then I told him about New York and my school. The letter was so fat, I had a hard time putting it into an envelope. I sealed it and rushed out to get it mailed. Because of the delay, his letter having gone to the hotel and being kept there so long, he probably thought I didn't want anything to do with him. I wanted to tell him that wasn't so as fast as I could.

Trisha called a few times that first week to try to get me to take the bus to visit her and her family. I told her about my strange conversation with Agnes and what she had told me was in the vase in the glass case.

"Oh don't believe that story," Trisha said. "It's something she took from a play."

"I hope you're right. I feel funny every time I go in there now."

I promised I would seriously consider visiting her, but I had a wonderful surprise occur early one morning when Agnes knocked on my door to tell me I had a phone call from Madame Steichen.

"I've returned to the school early," she declared and paused as if that explained everything.

"Yes, Madame?" I said.

"I have an hour between nine and ten free every morning beginning today."

"Yes, Madame," I said. "I'll be there. Thank you."

"Very good," she replied and hung up.

I felt like I was walking on air and when I attended these special lessons, I sensed a change in Madame Steichen's attitude toward me. Her voice was softer, her commands given with a more loving tone. Also, I noticed that when my other teachers, and even teachers I had not yet had, learned about my special lessons with Madame Steichen, they treated me differently as well. It was as if I had achieved some celebrity status.

Trisha was the first to return from the summer break. We stuffed three hours worth of conversation into the first hour we spent together. I told her about the things I had been doing in New York and described my lessons with Madame Steichen. She was very excited and impressed. Then I showed her my letter from Daddy Longchamp. She read it and cried and was outraged when I explained how long it had been kept at the hotel and how it had been read.

Afterward, we went to George's for what had become our famous ice cream sodas and to listen to the juke box.

We returned to the house slowly. It was a very hot and humid late summer day, so we were grateful for the long, thick shadows cast by the sun's falling behind tall buildings, as well as the slight breeze coming off the East River. Even in summer though, the traffic and the pedestrians didn't slow down. I had come to see that New York had a rhythm of its own and anyone who wanted to live and work there either took on that rhythm or was run down by it.

A second big surprise was awaiting my arrival at the house. Agnes stepped out of the sitting room, smiling.

"It's about time you've come back," she said. "You have a gentleman visitor, Dawn."

"Visitor?" I shrugged at Trisha. Jimmy wouldn't come without calling first, I thought. We walked quickly to the sitting room doorway, but the moment I looked in, I felt as if my feet were nailed to the floor. I didn't want to go a step farther. Sitting there and smiling up at me was Philip.

"Hi, Dawn," he said, leaning back on the sofa with his arm across the top. He looked more handsome than ever with his thick, flaxen hair brushed up in a wave and his cerulean blue eyes twinkling mischievously. "I was able to get away for a day to come see you before I have to return to school."

"Isn't that nice?" Agnes said, smiling. I didn't say a word. "Why don't you introduce Trisha to your brother?" she asked when I didn't move.

"I didn't ask him to come," I said sharply.

"What?" Agnes looked at Philip as if he had to translate my words.

"I thought you might be glad to see someone from the family," Philip said, his arrogant smile fading quickly.

"You were wrong," I said. I felt blood rush to my face and my stomach turned sick somersaults with anger and fear. I couldn't look at Philip without remembering his lips and hands all over my body. "I don't care to see you. Just leave me alone," I said. "Leave me alone!"

I turned and ran toward the stairway.

"Dawn!" Agnes cried. "You get right back here."

I took the stairway two steps at a time and rushed up and into my room, slamming the door quickly behind me. Then I threw myself on my bed and folded my arms across my chest as I glared up at the ceiling.

I wouldn't pretend all was hunky-dory, I thought. I wouldn't forget what he had done to me.

A few moments later Trisha came in. She closed the door softly behind her and stared at me, her mouth agape.

"How could you do that to your own brother? He's so cute and he seems very nice. I mean, I thought it was only Clara Sue and Grandmother Cutler who . . ."

"Oh Trisha," I said. I bit down on my lower lip.

"What?" She came to my bed quickly and sat down.

"I lied to you that day when you asked me why I was disturbed about Arthur walking in on me in the bathroom."

"Lied?"

"I told you it was a handyman who had attacked me."

"But then . . . who did it?"

"Philip," I said. "My brother." I buried my face in my pillow. "I'm so ashamed," I moaned. "And he has the nerve to come here and act as if nothing happened between us."

"How horrible," Trisha said, stroking my hair. "Poor Dawn. You have so much to try to forget."

I turned around to look up at her. I could tell she no longer saw my life as some kind of fantasy. No longer would she regret how boring her own life seemed next to mine. Facing reality had made me grow up more quickly than I would have liked, but I had no choice.

4

A VISIT WITH JIMMY

When it was clear to Philip that I wouldn't come back down and visit with him, he left. He had brought me a box of candy that he told Agnes to give to me with the message that he would call me some time in the near future.

"Your brother was heartbroken," she said. "And such a nice young man, too." She sighed and then looked at me harshly and shook her head. "That's not the way for a well-bred young lady to behave," she chastised. "Your grandmother was hoping your manners would improve here."

I bit my lip to keep myself from uttering any reply. I wanted to shout back at her, to cry out and tell her she didn't know what she was talking about; she had no idea what sort of terrible things had happened to me and if there was anyone who had to have her manners improved, it wasn't me; it was Grandmother Cutler who lorded it over everyone as if her hotel was her plantation and we were all her slaves. But, I said nothing. Instead I went to help Mrs. Liddy since it was my turn. I gave her Philip's gift of candy, which she was more than pleased to accept.

By late afternoon Agnes was back to her old self, flitting about the apartment house, all excited about a luncheon she was going to attend on the weekend in honor of the contribution to the theater made by the Barrymores. She was full of stories about Ethel and John and claimed she had been in two productions with Lionel Barrymore. By evening the excitement centered on the impending arrival of the other student residents.

The next day the Beldock twins were the first to arrive. Agnes called Trisha and me down to meet them and their parents. I knew the twins were fourteen, but when Trisha said they were small, I had no idea how small. They were like cupie dolls, both standing less than five feet tall. But they were adorable with their button noses and small, round mouths. They had chestnut-brown eyes and hair the color of summer hay, which they had cut in an identical style at their shoulders and tied with pink ribbons.

They wore identical pink and white dresses with saddle shoes. I was sure that for one to look at the other was the same as looking in the mirror. Even the dimples in their cheeks were in the exact same places.

I loved the way they anticipated each other's moves and often finished each other's sentences. Trisha had already told me that Samantha was called Sam and Beneatha was nicknamed Bethie by all their friends. They were both clarinet players and so good at it that they were already first seats in the orchestra.

But I found myself even more fascinated by their parents, a young, vibrant couple. The father was handsome with that all-American wholesome, devastatingly good-looking face and charming manner. He was at least six feet tall with a suntan that highlighted his silvery blue eyes. It was their mother from whom they had obviously inherited their small facial features and graceful hands. She had warm blue eyes and a tooth paste advertisement bright smile. I loved her mellow voice and the loving way she held and kissed the twins.

How I envied them their happy childhood. They looked like the perfect little family, always secure, always comfortable. When I lived with Momma and Daddy Longchamp, we had love in our home, but the strain of making enough to feed, clothe and shelter us kept Daddy Longchamp grouchy and sad most of the time, and all I could remember about Momma was her being sick or tired and defeated. And, of course, the family I had now was far from perfect.

What made some children lucky enough to be born to happy homes? Were we like seeds in the wind, some falling on fertile, rich earth, some scattered onto bone-dry land full of shadows and darkness, fighting their way toward every inch of sunlight? I wondered if someone first meeting me, someone like Mr. or Mrs. Beldock, could take one look at me and see how miserable I was inside, how poor my soil had been and still was.

Trisha and I helped the twins move into their room. They were full of stories about their summer.

"Oh Trisha," Sam said, "we're so happy . . ."

"To be back," Bethie concluded. "That's all we've been talking about."

"Our return to Bernhardt," Sam added, nodding. "And it's so much fun to meet someone new," she said, turning to me. I had to smile at the way they organized their things, one reminding the other what drawers each had last year and where each piece of clothing had been hung.

Trisha and I invited them into our room and spent the rest of the afternoon talking about music and movies and hairstyles.

Agnes was truly worried about her last student resident, Donald Rossi, because he didn't show up all day. Then at dinner, the door buzzer was heard and she got up from the table to greet him. He had been delivered by his father's chauffeur because his father, a famous comedian, was performing at some nightclub in Boston. The chauffeur carried Donald's bags as far in as the entryway and then left. Agnes brought him in to meet us immediately.

Donald was a short, very plump fifteen-year-old with curly blond hair and freckles even on his nose. He had an oval-shaped face with remarkably rubbery lips that twisted through all sorts of contortions whenever he spoke, usually attempting to do some imitation of a famous movie star like James Cagney or Edward G. Robinson. I had never met anyone as forward and nervy the first time he was introduced to new people.

"I'm starving," he said and plopped himself down next to Arthur who acted as if someone with the plague had just been placed at the table. He cringed and pulled his chair as far to the left as he could.

"Wouldn't you like to bring your things to your room first, Donald?" Agnes asked him.

"Oh, they'll wait," he said. "But my stomach won't," he added and laughed. Then he looked at Arthur. "Looks like you let your suitcases come first all the time," he said and laughed at his own joke. Arthur shot a glance at me and then his face reddened. "That reminds me of a joke my father just told me," Donald said, stabbing a dinner roll with his fork quickly as if he thought it might run off the dish. "These two guys were starving to death in the desert when they come upon this dead camel. The first guy says, 'I'm dying for a camel sandwich but I can't get over the smell.' 'Smell?' the second guy says, 'I can't get over the hump.' " Once again, he roared at his own joke.

The twins gaped at him, both their mouths open the same way. Arthur sighed and shook his head.

"Oh dear, Donald," Agnes said, "I don't think the dinner table is the proper stage for that kind of humor, do you?"

Donald looked up from his plate of food. All through the telling of the joke, he had been dipping his serving spoon into one thing after another and dropping gobs of potatoes and vegetables on his dish. Now he was hacking off a chicken leg.

"Oh, you want food jokes, huh? All right," he said, pushing on. "There was this rotten apple at the bottom of the barrel, and this housewife comes along and starts digging down because she thinks she's going to get the best apples on the bottom, only she comes up with a handful of gook, see . . ."

"Excuse me, Donald," Agnes interrupted, "but dead camels and rotten fruits are not the sort of things we like to hear about when we're eating."

"Oh." He stuffed the roll into his mouth in one gulp and chewed thoughtfully for a moment. "You know the one about this midget who dies and goes to heaven?" he began.

There didn't seem to be any way to stop him short of shooting him. I looked at Agnes. She took a deep breath and shook her head. Like it or not, our little student residency family had been formed. The twins had their room, Arthur had his, Donald, thank goodness, was the farthest down the corridor, and of course, Trisha and I had ours.

Before the week was out, Arthur and Donald had a bad argument when Donald continued to tease him about his weight. Agnes interceded and a fragile truce was declared, but it got so we didn't look forward to dinner as much as we had before because it was only a matter of time at most meals before snarling and snapping started between Arthur and Donald. It came again the week Donald had kitchen duty. Somehow he had gotten into the kitchen without Mrs. Liddy knowing it and skinned all the meat off a piece of chicken. He served Arthur the bones with a teaspoon of potatoes and one pea. It was funny and Trisha and the twins started to laugh, but Arthur became enraged and left the table.

Agnes asked Donald to go up and apologize to him.

"There has always been peace in this house," she lectured. "We've always been a good cast and a good cast can't perform well if there is dissension."

"Hey, I'll do anything for show business," he said, flicking an imaginary cigar and leaning over like Groucho Marx. He was incorrigible, but he did go up to apologize. He returned soon after saying he didn't mind talking to a door if the door would at least squeak.

Later, when I met Arthur in the hallway alone, I advised him not to pay so much attention to Donald.

"He's an exhibitionist," I said, "trying to be like his father. Just ignore him and he'll stop teasing you."

"I thought you considered him funny," Arthur snapped.

"Sometimes, but most of the time, he's just obnoxious. I don't like to see anyone teased and made the butt of someone else's jokes."

Arthur's face softened.

"You're right," he said. "He's not worth it."

I smiled and started away.

"Dawn," Arthur called. "I . . . um . . . wondered if I couldn't show you some of my poetry one of these days. I think you might like it."

"Why of course you can, Arthur. I'd be very happy to read it. Thank you for asking," I said. I never saw his face light up so quickly and his normally dark eyes turn so bright.

"Okay," he said.

I didn't tell Trisha because I knew she would advise me against becoming involved with him in any sort of way, but I did feel sorry for him. I thought he was easily the loneliest and saddest boy I had ever known.

Not long after the new school year had begun, I received a letter from Daddy Longchamp. He said he had been heartened and grateful for my letter. He claimed he missed me a great deal and he had wanted to say so in his first letter, but he didn't think he had a right to anymore. The rest of his letter was filled with details about his apartment and job. He sounded more hopeful because he was making some new friends, one in particular being a widow in the same apartment building.

I decided I would try to write to him at least twice a month.

One afternoon, a few days after Arthur had asked me to read his poetry, I heard a knock on my bedroom door. Trisha was still at dance practice. I was sitting on the floor, my back against the bed, doing my English homework.

"Excuse me," he said when I said, come in. He stood back, not daring to take a step in.

"Hello, Arthur. What can I do for you?" I asked. He had the strangest way of peering at me, making his eyes small and leaning so that his shoulders turned in, making him look like a bird.

"I was wondering, if you weren't too busy that is, if you would want to look at my poems."

He was carrying a notebook under his arm.

"Sure," I said. "I'd love to. Come on in."

He hesitated a moment, looked back and then entered.

"Sit down," I said, patting the spot beside me.

"On the floor?"

"Sure, why not? It's very comfortable down here. Trisha and I always sit on the floor when we do our homework."

It took Arthur a few moments to fold those long legs of his comfortably, but he did it and then handed me his notebook. It was a thick one.

"You have a lot of poems," I said, impressed.

"I've been writing them a long time," he said dryly.

"Who else has seen them?" I asked, opening the cover.

"Not too many people," he said, "that I wanted to see them. Of course, there are always people who will poke their noses into someone else's business," he added and I guessed he was referring to Trisha who had told me she had once snuck a look at his poetry when he left the notebook on a table in the sitting room.

I turned the page and read. Trisha had been right. All of his poems were about dismal subjects: animals dying or being deserted, stars that burned out and became black spots invisible in the night sky and someone dying from some horrible disease. I thought they must be good, even so, because they made me feel sad and afraid and reminded me of my own bad times.

"These poems are very good, Arthur," I told him. He turned his head and allowed his eyes to meet mine. They looked like dark pools in the forest, deep and so still they seemed frozen. Looking into Arthur's eyes was like looking through a keyhole of an otherwise locked door. I saw the sadness and the loneliness inside and I felt the emptiness. "I know they're good because they make me sad and make me remember when I felt like this in the past.

"But if you can write so well, why don't you write poems that will make people feel happy?"

"I write what I feel," he said, "and what I see."

I nodded, understanding. When I read the poem about the beautiful dove that broke its wings and had to stay on a leafless branch until its heart gave out, I thought about Momma Longchamp growing weaker and weaker after Fern's birth until she was like a beautiful bird whose wings had been clipped. I recalled the day her heart gave out, and in remembering I felt anew my need for a mother or daddy to hold me close and stroke my hair when I was sick or scared.

Tears began to stream down my cheeks.

"You're crying," Arthur said. "No one has ever read my poems and cried."

"I'm sorry, Arthur," I said. "It's not because your poems are bad." I handed the notebook back to him. "It's just hard for me to read these things and not think about my own painful times."

He looked astonished for a moment. Then he nodded slowly, his thin lips pressed together with understanding and his protruding Adam's apple bobbing as he swallowed.

"You don't like your family, do you?" he asked and before I could reply he added, "I know about the letter of lies your grandmother wrote to Agnes."

"You followed us that night and saw us sneak into her room to read it, didn't you?" I accused him sharply.

"Yes. I know you saw me that night." He looked down at his long-fingered hands folded in his lap and then looked up. "I listened through the door and heard how angry you and Trisha were after reading it. Why does your grandmother dislike you so?"

"It's a long story, Arthur."

"Are you angry about my following and spying on you?" he asked, holding his breath.

"No. But I don't like to be spied on. It makes me feel dirty all over and gives me the creeps."

He nodded, and we were both silent and tense for a long moment.

"I don't like being with my parents," he confessed. "I hate going home and I can't stand going on holiday with them."

"That's terrible, Arthur, a terrible thing to say about your mother and father. Why do you say it?"

"They're always disappointed in me. They want me to be a professional musician. They're determined that that's what I will be. I practice and practice, but I know I'm mediocre. My teachers know it too. The only reason they tolerate me is because of who my parents are."

"Why don't you just tell them how you feel about it?" I asked.

"I have, dozens of times, but they refuse to listen. All they say is keep practicing; it takes practice. But it takes more than practice," he emphasized, his eyes widening. "It takes some talent too. It has to be in you to be something. My parents can't see that they want to make me into something I'm not."

"You're right, Arthur. They're just going to have to understand. Someday, they will, I'm sure."

He shook his head woefully. "I doubt it. I don't even care anymore." He took a deep breath, his narrow shoulders rising and falling. Then he looked at me with those beady eyes again.

"I'm going to write a poem, just for you, Dawn," he said quickly. In fact, it will be about you," he said, "because you're different," he added and then blushed when he realized how emphatically he said it. "I . . . I mean . . . you're very nice." He stood up so quickly that he almost stumbled and fell over.

"That's very kind of you, Arthur," I said. "I look forward to reading it."

He stared at me a moment and then smiled for the first time. A moment later, he was gone.

I shook my head in amazement and wiped the last lingering tear from my cheeks.

The next day I had a wonderful surprise waiting for me when I returned from school. Jimmy had written to tell me he was getting his leave the following week and he would use the time to visit Daddy Longchamp and then swing around to see me. He would be in New York on the weekend and be at our apartment house by twelve o'clock to take me to lunch. I couldn't contain my excitement. Every night I planned the things I would wear. I wondered aloud about changing my hair style. Trisha said I was driving her insane.

"You would think a movie star was coming," she said. "I never got so excited about my boyfriend's visits," she said a little enviously.

"It's been so long since I've seen Jimmy and so much has happened to both of us. Oh Trisha, what if he's met so many pretty girls that he thinks I'm still a child next to them," I moaned.

She laughed and shook her head.

"If he likes you as much as you say he does, nothing can change the feelings you have for each other," Trisha declared.

"I hope you're right."

The next day we went to Saks Fifth Avenue. I was in luck because there were two beautiful models in the cosmetics department lecturing customers on the proper way to apply makeup. I chose a different shade of lipstick and bought some perfume. The model showed me how to put on eye liner and blush and even gave me some advice about my hair. I used some of the money my mother had sent me to buy a new sweater and skirt outfit I had seen in a fashion magazine.

I was on pins and needles from the moment my eyes snapped open the day Jimmy was to arrive. I had been practicing with the makeup just the way the model had shown me, and after I was finished I brushed my hair long and hard till it shone like a fairy princess's. I put on my new sweater and skirt and then I nervously looked in the full-length mirror. I couldn't believe my eyes. Excitement had made my cheeks flush pink and my eyes sparkle, and the soft blue wool molded itself gracefully around my breasts and waist before falling to my knees, like a dancer's skirt. I couldn't help thinking, conceited though it was, that I looked beautiful.

I was too nervous to eat breakfast. Although summer had lingered into late September and it was still warm, the sky was overcast and dreary. I was afraid it would rain—I'd had so many fantasies and daydreams about Jimmy and I walking through the city, his strong hand holding mine. Trisha went to the library to get some research books for a term paper we had to do. By the time she returned, it was after noon and Jimmy still hadn't arrived.

"He's late," I cried. "Maybe something happened and he can't come."

"He would have called you, wouldn't he? Stop worrying. It's not so easy traveling through New York, you know. You're chewing your nails down to your finger bones," she declared. I pulled my fingers from my lips.

"Here," she ordered, giving me one of the books. "Take out your notebook and go down to the sitting room and read and wait."

"Oh, I just couldn't, Trisha," I moaned.

"It will help you pass the time until he comes. Just do it," she commanded. "I'll sit and wait with you."

We went downstairs. As the hours ticked by I began to get discouraged. I took out my mirror and checked and rechecked every few minutes, primping and patting my hair. Arthur Garwood returned from Saturday instrumental practice and looked in, his pencil-thin lips twisting into a smile, but when he saw Trisha was there with me, he snapped himself back as if he were connected to an enormous rubber band and continued up to his room. Finally, after we'd waited nearly four hours we heard the door buzzer sound. Trisha and I looked up at each other. Agnes was out shopping with friends and Mrs. Liddy was in the kitchen.

"Should I let him in?" Trisha asked.

"No, no, I'll do it," I said and took a deep breath. "How do I look?"

"Not any different from the way you looked five minutes ago when you asked," she said, laughing.

I stood up and went to the entrance. I closed my eyes and for a moment pictured Jimmy back at the hotel in the hideaway when we had told each other our most secret feelings and thoughts about each other. Those moments and those words seemed more like part of a childhood dream, a fantasy. Had time and distance changed the way we felt? My heart began to pound in anticipation. I opened the outer doors to greet him.

Jimmy looked so much taller in his uniform. His face had lost its innocent softness and become firm and full in a mature way. His dark hair was short, of course, but that didn't take away from his good looks. It seemed to emphasize his hazel-brown eyes, Momma Longchamp's eyes. He stood tall with his shoulders back, confidence radiating from him. As he looked down at me, I saw his eyes soften and warmth flooded through me.

"Hi," he said. "I'm sorry I'm so late, but a bus broke down and I got a little lost. You look so pretty."

"Thank you," I said. I didn't move. It was as if we had both jumped ahead years and years and were afraid to treat each other the way we had when we were growing up side by side as brother and sister.

"Aren't you going to invite him in?" Trisha asked, standing directly behind me.

"What? Oh. I'm sorry, Jimmy. This is Trisha, my roommate. Trisha, this is Jimmy."

Jimmy stepped forward and took Trisha's hand.

"Pleased to meet you," he said. He nodded toward me. "Dawn has told me a lot about you."

"And she's told me a lot about you, too," Trisha countered. They both looked at me as if I had given away state secrets about each. "Shall we go into the sitting room?" Trisha asked, that silly smile frozen on her lips.

"What? Oh, yes," I said and led Jimmy in.

"Very nice place," he said, sitting down on the small sofa and gazing around at the pictures and mementos.

"Would you like something to drink?" Trisha asked. "Dawn seems to have forgotten her manners," she teased. "Agnes would be very upset."

"No thank you," Jimmy said. There was a long moment of silence and then we all started talking at once.

"How is Daddy Longchamp?" I asked.

"How's school?" Jimmy asked.

"What's it like being in the army?" Trisha asked.

We all laughed. Then Jimmy sat back, a lot more relaxed. He seemed so different to me, so calm and so much stronger. I had always felt so much younger than him, so much like his little sister. Now his quiet maturity made me feel even more distant.

"I like the army," he said. "Like they tell you at boot camp, I've found a new home."

I raised my eyebrows on the word "home," and he turned to wink at me.

"But it's okay. I like the guys I'm with and I'm learning about engines and mechanics in a way that will be handy when I get out." He turned back to me. "I'm sorry about being late. I was supposed to take you to lunch, now it will have to be dinner. If that's all right, that is," he added.

"Oh . . . of course," I said.

"You'll have to tell me a good restaurant. I don't know much about New York," he explained to Trisha.

"Oh, go to Antonio's on York and Twenty-eighth," Trisha suggested.

"That's too expensive," I said. We had never gone to eat there, but we had stopped to look in at it and it looked very fancy.

"Don't worry about it," Jimmy snapped, that fiery light I remembered in his dark eyes flashing for a moment to announce his pride. "Anyway," he said, his eyes filling with a mischievous twinkle, "you're too dressed up for anything cheap."

I blushed so fast and hard, I felt the heat rise in my neck. When I looked at Trisha, I saw that silly, satisfied smile on her lips.

"Well, then, let's go," I said. "I'm starving."

"She should be; she's been too nervous to eat all day," Trisha revealed.

"Trisha!"

Jimmy laughed. We got up and walked out.

"Have a good time," Trisha said.

"Thank you," Jimmy said.

"He's very handsome," she whispered in my ear.

When we stepped out of the apartment house, I discovered he had a taxi cab waiting.

"Why didn't you say something, Jimmy?" I cried, knowing what that would cost. "The meter's been running all this time."

"Don't worry about it," he said. "After what I've been through, I deserve to splurge and there's no one I care to splurge with more than you, Dawn. You really do look great," he added as he led me to the cab.

Suddenly, a brilliant sun peeked through the dreary clouds and across the street, trees in vivid colors lit up. It warmed my heart, but made me feel like I had entered a dream, stepped into one of my fantasies.

Here were Jimmy and I, practically two orphans who had been brought up a step past utter poverty, getting ready to go to a fancy New York restaurant. How strange and confusing time and events had been. It was hard to determine what was real and what was a dream. Maybe for the moment, I thought, it was better not to try.

The restaurant was as fancy as it looked. When we entered, we were asked if we had reservations. Of course we hadn't, but the maître d' studied his book and then nodded his head. I think he was impressed with Jimmy's uniform.

"I can take care of you," he declared and showed us to a corner table. It seemed to me that everyone at the restaurant was looking at us as we walked through it to sit down. I was so nervous I nearly sent my silverware flying to the floor when I took the napkin out from under it to put it on my lap. We were asked if we wanted cocktails.

Cocktails! I thought. How old did the waiter think I was?

"No, we'll just go right to dinner," Jimmy replied and smiled. "We're starving."

"Very good, sir," he said and left us with the menus. When I saw the prices, my heart stopped.

"Oh Jimmy, some of these dinners cost as much as our week's food bill was."

"I told you not to worry about it," he said. "I haven't spent a penny of my army pay until now," he admitted. And then he told me with pride thick in his voice how he had given Daddy Longchamp some money.

"Tell me how he really is, Jimmy," I said after we had ordered. Jimmy's eyes darkened and the corners of his mouth tightened the way they would whenever he fought back anger or sadness. He gazed down at the table and fingered his silverware.

"He looked a lot smaller and a lot older to me. I guess prison does that to you. His hair was grayer, his face thinner, but when he set eyes on me, he brightened considerably. We had a long talk about that had happened and he explained why he and Momma did what they did, how they thought they were doing the right thing since your real Momma and Daddy didn't want you and since he and Momma had tried and failed to have another baby."

Jimmy looked up quickly, his eyes watering.

"Of course, he still admits it was wrong and he's very sorry for the pain and suffering he caused all of us, but I couldn't help but feel more sorry for him than I felt for myself. It's broken him and with Momma gone, he really has nothing."

I wasn't as strong as Jimmy; I couldn't keep my tears from pouring over and out of my lids. He smiled at me and leaned over the table to wipe the tears from my cheeks.

"But he's happier now, Dawn, and he sends you his love. He's made some new friends; he likes his new job."

"I know. He wrote to tell me that."

"But I bet he didn't tell you he has a lady friend," Jimmy said with a wry smile.

"Lady friend?"

"She's cooking for him and I had the suspicion she was doing a lot more, but they didn't want me to know about it just yet," he said, his smile spreading.

Of course I was happy that Daddy Longchamp had found some companionship and wasn't going to be lonely any more. I knew what it meant to be lonely and how it made your heart heavy and even bright sunny days look gloomy and dark. But I couldn't help thinking about Momma and that made hearing about Daddy Longchamp and another woman painful to me. My expression must have shown my confusion because Jimmy reached across the table and took my hand in his.

"But he told me no one could ever replace Momma in his heart," Jimmy said quickly.

I nodded, trying to understand.

"Daddy described how hard he's been working to locate Fern," Jimmy said, "but he can't get any details. It seems everyone's sworn to secrecy about it. He was told that was the way they protect the family that took her in and the way they protect her from being bothered later on."

"But he's her real father!" I protested.

"And a man with a prison record," Jimmy reminded me, "who doesn't have any money or a real job or a wife to help raise a child. Of course, he still hopes that someday . . ."

"Someday we'll find her, Jimmy. And we'll bring the family together again," I said with clear and sharp determination.

Jimmy smiled and nodded. "Sure we will, Dawn."

It wasn't until after our food came that we broke loose with talk about ourselves. Jimmy described his training, his friends and some of the things he had seen and done. I told him about school, about Madame Steichen, more about Trisha and described the other students in our apartment house, especially poor Arthur Garwood. After a while it seemed I was doing all the talking and Jimmy was listening, eyes wide.

"This is certainly a lot different for you than any of the other places we've been," he concluded. "But I'm glad you're with people who see how talented you are."

Then he broke the bad news: how he was really in New York because he was going to be shipped out to Europe tomorrow afternoon.

"Europe! Oh Jimmy, when will I see you again?"

"It won't be as long as you think, Dawn, and I'll write often. Don't look so worried," he said, smiling, "there's no war on. All soldiers go on a tour of duty someplace. This way I get to see some of the world and Uncle Sam pays my way.

"We don't have much time together, Dawn," he added with a serious look in his eyes, "let's not spend one moment of it unhappy, okay?"

How wise he sounded. Time and tragedy had changed him. I realized that Jimmy had really been on his own most of the time since that morning the police had come to our apartment in Richmond and declared that our father was a kidnapper. Jimmy had no choice but to grow up.

I swallowed back my tears and forced a smile.

"Let's go for a walk," I said, "so I can show you my school."

Jimmy took out his wallet and paid the enormous dinner bill without blinking an eye and we left. He was surprised at how well I knew my way around the city. I explained how Trisha and I often took the buses and the subways now to go to the museums and see shows.

"You're growing up fast, Dawn," Jimmy said but looked sad about it. "And becoming so sophisticated I probably won't recognize you when I come back and you probably won't want much to do with me."

"Oh Jimmy, don't ever say that!" I cried, stopping on the sidewalk. "I'll never think I'm better than you. That's a horrible thing to say."

"All right, all right," he said, laughing. "I'm sorry."

"You mustn't even think such a thing about me. I would just as soon quit this school."

"Don't you dare, Dawn. You're going to become a star. I just know you will," he said firmly. Then he reached out and took my hand so that we walked holding hands all the rest of the way.

After I showed him the school and the small park nearby, he told me about his hotel.

"It's nothing fancy, but I got a nice view of the city because I'm twenty-eight floors up."

"Why don't you take me to see it," I said. "I've never been in a New York City hotel."

"You really want to see it?" he asked. He looked unsure of himself, undecided, and for a minute I thought he was going to say something. Then his face changed.

A second later, he had hailed a cab and we were on our way to his hotel.

Although I knew it wasn't as fancy as the Plaza or the Waldorf, it was nice. His room was small, but he was right about the view. It was breathtaking to look out over the buildings and streets and see the ocean in the distance. Jimmy stood beside me and held my hand and we gazed quietly. Then I lowered my head to his shoulder and closed my eyes, trying to swallow around the lump in my throat. I couldn't keep the tears in.

"I'm sorry, Jimmy," I said, "but I can't stop remembering things. I can't stop thinking about little Fern, about holding her and feeding her and watching her crawl and laugh; and I can't stop thinking about Momma when she was healthy and pretty."

"I know," he said, petting my hair and then kissing the top of my head.

"And I can't stop thinking about you and me back at the hotel in Cutler's Cove," I said.

"I don't stop thinking about it either," he confessed. I pulled my head back from his shoulder and looked at him. His dark eyes gazed down into mine. "Dawn," he whispered, "if you feel like crying, go ahead. I'll understand. Cry enough for me too."

He looked so sad when he said that. I couldn't cry. I reached up instead and touched his cheek. Slowly, as if we were crossing all the time and distance that had come between us, our lips moved toward each other's and we kissed softly. I turned toward him and our kiss grew more passionate. When he pulled back, I saw tears shining in the corners of his eyes.

"I still can't help the confusion that torments me inside," he said. "I think about you, dream about you, want you, and then I see you in my mind's eye growing up as my sister and it feels so wrong to think of you any other way."

"I know," I said. "But I'm not your sister."

"I don't know what to do," he confessed. "It's like there's a wall between us, a wall forbidding us to touch."

"Leap over that wall then," I said, surprised at how aggressive I was.

I took his hand into mine and drew it up and over my breast. I pressed his palm there and held it. He kissed me again and then we moved quietly to the bed. First, we just sat there, stroking each other tenderly. Then he moved closer so his head was on my forehead. His warm breath was on my face. I moved so my head tilted backward and my neck arched. I didn't feel quite real when his warm lips kissed the hollow of my throat and stayed there. My breath caught. For a long, long moment, I waited for him to move away. I felt the tingling turning into wave after wave of warmth

He closed his eyes and I closed mine and we fell asleep in each other's arms.

When my eyes snapped open, I was confused for a moment. Jimmy was still asleep. I turned softly so as not to wake him and put on the small lamp on the night stand to look at the clock. Thunderstruck, I felt my head swim. Could that be right?

"Oh Jimmy," I cried, sitting up.

"Huh?" His eyes fluttered open.

I threw off the blanket and rushed to get my clothes on.

"It's two o'clock in the morning. Agnes will be furious. We're supposed to be in by twelve at the latest on weekends and ten on weekdays."

"Oh, wow. I don't know what happened," he said, sitting up and putting on his pants.

We rushed out and down to the hotel lobby. It was so late there was no one behind the desk. It took us quite a while to finally find a cab and it was nearly three in the morning when we arrived at Agnes's house.

"Should I come in with you and explain?" Jimmy asked.

"Explain what? How we fell asleep together in bed in your hotel room?"

"I'm sorry," Jimmy said again. "The last thing I wanted to do is get you in trouble at your school."

"I'll think of something. Call me tomorrow morning. Oh, it is the morning," I said. "Don't you dare leave for Europe without seeing me one more time, Jimmy. Promise," I demanded.

"I promise," he said. "I'll come over around eleven."

I kissed him and hopped out of the taxi cab. Naturally, the front door was locked so I had to press the buzzer. Jimmy sat staring up from the cab. I waved him on and he instructed the cab driver to take him back to the hotel. A few minutes later Agnes opened the doors. She was in her robe with her hair down. Without her pounds of makeup, she looked ghostly pale and years older.

"Do you know what time it is?" she demanded before letting me enter.

"I'm sorry, Agnes. We just lost track of time and by the time we looked . . ."

"I didn't call the police, but I had to call your grandmother," she said. "I don't have to tell you how upset she was. I didn't know this boy you were seeing was a juvenile delinquent who had been arrested at the hotel."

"That's not true," I cried. "She's lying about Jimmy, just as she lied about everything else in the letter she wrote you."

"Well, if anyone's doing any lying, I think it's you, my dear," she said, pulling herself up into a stern posture. She was into a role, I thought. There wasn't much sense in arguing. "You have deceived me and after I have trusted you, too. How do you think this reflects on me and my moving down my body from the place where his lips touched me, down to the very tips of my toes.

I moaned and fell back against the pillow. He leaned over me, his arms at my sides and smiled.

"You're so pretty. I can't help loving you. There will never be anyone for me but you, and even if it takes me years and years to get past that wall, I'll do it," he pledged.

"Oh Jimmy, get over that wall now," I begged, not even believing my own words. It was as if there was someone else within me saying these things. He grew serious, his eyes darker, smaller.

Then he sat back and stripped off his army jacket and unbuttoned his shirt. I watched him, unmoving. When he began to lower his pants, I lifted my sweater over my head and unzipped my skirt. He pulled back the cover on the bed and I slipped under it, just wearing my bra and panties. We embraced and kissed. His fingers found the clip on my bra and undid it. After he removed it with my help, he pressed his face to my breasts and kissed me.

"How beautiful you are," he said with a low sigh. "I remember when you were younger. You were so shy about your body, always wanting to wear loose sweaters so I couldn't see. And if we should accidentally touch . . ."

His memories sent me reeling back to our years as brother and sister. The wall he described between us came between us again as I recalled those times when we did touch each other intimately by accident and then felt dirty and ashamed because of it. It was so hard to drive away those images and feelings.

When he pressed his manliness against me now, I shuddered both because of the excitement and because of the guilt. But why should I feel this guilt? I demanded of myself. Jimmy is not my brother; he's not!

Jimmy sensed the tightening in my body and his kisses came to a halt. He pulled himself back and looked at me.

"We're going too fast, Dawn," he said. "This is going to hurt our love for each other, not cement it. I want you, more than I want anything else, but I don't want to do anything to drive you away from me.

"Let's just lie here together, and hold each other," he said with a wisdom far greater than mine.

He put his arm around my shoulders and brought me closer to him so my head rested on his chest. For a long time, we just lay there silently, holding each other. Our pounding hearts slowed and a wonderful peace came over us. Through the window we watched the sun go down over the city. Soon the thousands and thousands of lights that made the New York skyline so exciting glittered.

standing with the school. Your grandmother was going to lodge a complaint with the administration, but I promised her this would never happen again and that you would never see this boy again.

"Also," she said, folding her arms under her breasts and stiffening into a statue, "you are restricted to this dorm for six months. You are to be in by six o'clock, even on weekends, and can go out only if you have something to do at the school and only after I confirm it. Is that clear?"

That's unfair, I thought, but swallowed back my resentment and nodded. I didn't care about going out anymore anyway. Jimmy was off to Europe tomorrow.

"Very well then," Agnes said, stepping back to let me pass. "March yourself right up to your room and be very quiet about it so you don't disturb the others.

"I'm very disappointed in you, Dawn," she called as I went by her. I hurried up the stairs. The moment I slipped into our room, Trisha sat up.

"Where were you?" she asked. "Agnes is furious."

"I know." I sat on her bed and started to cry. "I'm restricted for six months. Grandmother Cutler has seen to that."

"But where were you?"

I told her how we had gone to Jimmy's hotel room and fallen asleep in each other's arms.

"Wow," she said.

"Nothing happened, Trisha. It wasn't like that," I said, but I saw the skepticism in her eyes. "You've got to help me tomorrow," I said, remembering Jimmy would come by in the morning. "I've got to see him before he goes off to Europe."

We planned how she would wait outside and then come to get me when he arrived. Jimmy and I would visit with each other in the park. It would be there where we would say our good-byes. And then I would return to the apartment house and bury myself in my school work and my music, trying to forget the time and the distance that kept us apart.

I went to sleep dreaming about the day he would return and we would go off together to live our own lives, free of Grandmother Cutler and hateful people. I would earn a wonderful living for us through my singing and music.

Was I still a child to have such hope?

5
FAMILY AFFAIRS

After we said our painful good-byes and Jimmy left for Europe, I tried to lose myself in my work. It wasn't long before I hated time and absolutely despised the calendar that seemed to gloat and remind me continually of just how long it took for weeks and months to pass. I didn't think I would mind my punishment as much as I did, but it was especially painful to be restricted to the apartment house when Trisha and some of our other friends were free to go to movies and dances, restaurants and department stores.

One Saturday night shortly after Jimmy left and Arthur Garwood had heard about what had happened and how I was punished, he came knocking on my bedroom door. I thought it was Agnes, perhaps coming to tell me I was permitted to use the sitting room and didn't have to lock myself up in my bedroom. I was prepared to sulk and not utter a single word to her. I didn't even say, "Come in." After a moment though, I heard Arthur call my name so I went to the door. He stood there with a box under his arm.

"What is it, Arthur?" I asked. He looked like he would stand there forever.

"I thought you might want to play checkers."

"Checkers?"

He tapped the box.

"Oh."

"You don't have to," he added quickly, his face already registering disappointment, his eyes glum, his mouth drooped. He started to turn away.

"Oh, no. I'd like to," I said, not sure whether I was doing it for him or for me. He brightened immediately and we set the checkerboard up on my desk.

I was positive he was letting me win most of the time because I saw moves he should have easily made, but avoided because it would mean the game would end much faster.

"I'm working hard on your poem," he told me. "Even though I want it to be something special, it won't be much longer now."

"I'm looking forward to it, Arthur. Have you spoken with your parents about your playing the oboe?"

"A dozen times since you and I talked about it," he replied, "and always with the same result. Wait and see. Just practice. They don't want to hear anything but what they want to hear," he said. "You know I'm supposed to play a large solo part during Performance Weekend this year."

Once a year in the spring, the seniors at Bernhardt put on an exhibition of their talents during what was known as Performance Weekend. Their parents and families arrived and there were two nights of variety. Real New York critics were invited as well as producers and directors and many often attended.

"I'm sure you'll do better than you expect, Arthur," I said.

"I'll be dreadful and you know it," he said firmly. "I'm dreadful now and I've been at it forever; there's no reason to expect any changes. I told my parents and begged them to ask that I be excused from the weekend, but they were outraged that I would even suggest such a thing."

"What do your teachers say?"

"I told you," he reminded me, "they're intimidated by my parents. They aren't going to prevent me from performing. I'll be a laughingstock. Anyone who has any sense of music will see immediately just how inferior I am." He sighed and bowed his head into his cradling hands. Then he glanced upward, tears shining in his eyes. "Everyone will laugh at me."

He stared at me with those wet, beady eyes a moment.

"Dawn," he said softly, "you know music; it's in your blood and you've heard me play. I know. I've seen you walk past the music suite while I was practicing and you've heard me here. I don't know anyone who is as honest and as thoughtful as you are," he added with such sincerity it made me blush. "Please don't lie to me. What do you really and truly think of my oboe playing?"

I took a deep breath. It was usually easier to lie to people than to tell the truth about them, even though they knew you were lying. My sister Clara Sue was like that. She knew she was overweight and selfish and when I told her the truth about herself, she hated me even more for it. Many people lived in illusion and fantasy and didn't want anyone to disturb their world of comfortable lies.

I thought about Madame Steichen and how she was so dedicated and devoted to her music that she would never pretend anyone was good if he or she wasn't. Her honesty was what made her stand above so many others even though that honesty often made her seem very cruel.

And here was Arthur Garwood, who wanted to hear the truth about himself, who was depending on me to tell it to him. If anything, he needed an ally in his battle to face reality.

"You're right, Arthur," I admitted. "You don't play exceptionally well. I could never see you as a professional musician, no matter how much influence your parents have.

"But it's all right to do things to please them for a while," I added quickly. "Surely in time they will realize it too, if they are as good as everyone says they are and . . ."

"No!" he snapped, pounding the checkerboard so hard with the palm of his hand he made all the checkers dance out of their squares. "They are blind when it comes to me. If I fail, they fail, and they can't stand failure."

"But you can do other worthwhile things. Maybe you will be a great writer. Maybe you . . ."

"They won't listen!" His eyes filled with tears. He shook his head and looked down. When he took a deep breath, his narrow shoulders rose and then fell so sharply I thought he would fold up like a suit of clothes that slipped off a hanger. Neither of us said anything for a moment. I was afraid of how he might explode with frustration and anger. One moment he was docile and so soft spoken, he was barely audible; and the next moment he was screaming, his small eyes stretching open, his face red, his thin, wiry body contorted.

"I'm adopted," he confessed as though it were a crime. He spoke through his clenched teeth, telling me something I had suspected from the first day I had set eyes on his parents and saw how different they looked from him. "But they don't want anyone to know it. It's a secret we've kept all my life."

He lifted his head to gaze at me and choked off his sobs and swallowed them.

"You're the only person I have ever told," he said.

"But if you're adopted," I said as softly and calmly as I could, "they shouldn't expect you to have inherited their musical talents, right?"

"That's just it," he replied quickly. "If I don't demonstrate musical talent, they think people will conclude I was adopted and the secret will be out."

"Why did it have to be a secret?" I asked.

His body trembled and his dark eyes were bleak, warning me I was about to be shocked. Forewarned as I was, I still wasn't prepared for what I heard.

"They don't live together like a husband and wife are supposed to," he said. My look of confusion forced him to go on. "They don't sleep in the same bed. My mother has never done what has to be done to make a baby. Don't ask me how I know," he begged and I had the suspicion that spying on people and peeping unobserved at them was something Arthur had been doing all his life.

"Let's not talk about my problems," he said quickly, raising his head to face me again. "I shouldn't be so selfish and talk about myself with you incarcerated in this house for six months. It's a very unfair punishment and cruel, too. I'm very surprised at Agnes," he added, his thin lips whitening in the corners with anger.

"It's not her; my grandmother made her do it," I said. "It's all right. I'll survive." I sighed.

"I won't go out either," he said with determination. "I'll stay home every weekend night and be available to you if you want company. I'll do anything you want to do—play checkers, play cards, or just talk. All you have to do is ask."

Earnestness like that put tears in my eyes.

"Oh Arthur, I can't ask you to punish yourself like that. Don't you dare."

"I don't go anywhere important anyway," he said. "And I don't have any real friends. Besides, I can't think of anyone else I'd rather be with." He looked away quickly, embarrassed by his confession.

It embarrassed me as well and for a moment I was speechless. I thought it was best and easiest simply to pretend I hadn't heard or understood.

"The board's a mess," I said. "Let's start all over again."

"Oh. Certainly," he said, rearranging the checkers, and we played on until I told him I was tired. I thanked him for keeping me company.

After he left I thought about the things he told me. Why would a man and a woman live together as husband and wife if one of them didn't want to touch the other or be touched? Wasn't sex a way of bringing yourself as close to another person, a person you loved, as could be? And why would a woman be so frightened of it? Was it just her fear of becoming pregnant? How confusing and complicated the world was once you leave that realm in which you dwelt as a child, I thought. You lived in a bubble until one day the bubble burst and you were forced to look around and see that pain and suffering were not part of some make believe that would disappear with the blink of an eye. Certainly Arthur Garwood's wouldn't.

In a strange way my punishment had trapped me and made things difficult between me and Arthur Garwood. I didn't want him to think I could become his girlfriend, yet I didn't want to hurt him by turning him down all the time when he came by to keep me company. Fortunately, Trisha stayed with me many nights and some of the nights when she didn't the twins were around. Whenever there was anyone else present, especially Donald Rossi, Arthur didn't come by. He spoke to me only when I was alone and wouldn't do any more than look at me and nod whenever he passed me in the school corridors or in the streets if I was walking with someone else.

Then, Arthur made things even more complex when he came by one Saturday night to present me with his poem. He had it in an envelope.

"I'll let you read it by yourself," he said, backing away, "and you can come by any time you like to tell me what you honestly think about it. Remember," he said in the doorway, "be honest." Then he left.

I looked down at the envelope in my hands. He had even sealed it shut. I went to my bed and lay my head back on the pillow and opened it slowly. He had taken great pains to write it in an old English-style script. He might not be a talented musician, I thought, but he certainly had artistic talent. He had entitled the poem "Dawn."

Darkness grips the world in an iron fist.
Even the brightest stars can't loosen the hold
The black fingers of night have on the world and on me.
I am alone, imprisoned within the shadows I cast.
No one can hear my cries or my tears and no one cares.
I am like a bird without wings.
Despondent, I sit and wait without hope.
And then, you come.
You rise over the horizon, your smile so bright and so warm,
the darkness has no chance.
It melts like ice in your warmth.
Your rays touch my face and I throw off my shadows and
grow back my wings.
Then, like a bird reborn, I fly away and soar in the clouds.

I looked up quickly from the poem, but Arthur was not in the doorway. He had kept to his promise and retreated to his room, where I knew he waited anxiously. For a moment I was unable to move. These words were beautiful, but so revealing. I was frightened by the depth of feeling he obviously had for me. What had I done to cause him to feel so strongly about me? Was it merely because I had paid some attention to him and not ridiculed him? I didn't ask him to love me or to tell me his deepest secrets.

Even though I had done nothing I could see that would encourage him, his deep expression of love made me feel as if I had betrayed Jimmy. I knew he wouldn't like to hear how much another boy liked me. What do I do now? I wondered.

I could just hear Trisha say, "Tell him it was nice and walk away." But Arthur was too sensitive and perceptive for that. I had to be what he knew I was, what he hoped I would be. I had to be honest.

I rose from the bed and walked slowly to his room. The door was shut as always. I knocked softly.

"Come in," he said. He was sitting by his desk, the lamp on, the glow on his face making his face appear more like a mask.

"Arthur," I said, "this is a wonderful poem, a lovely poem. I don't deserve it."

"Oh yes you do," he said quickly.

"Arthur, I must tell you something I should have told you earlier. I am already in love with someone. I've loved him all my life and he loves me. We've made promises to each other that we would wait for each other. I haven't told many people this," I added quickly, "but I trust you with it just as you trust me with your secret."

He simply stared at me, that face of his still looking more like a mask, unmoving, not even his lips trembling.

"I'd still like you to keep the poem," he finally said.

"Oh, I want to, Arthur. And I will always treasure it. Especially some day when you're a famous poet," I added.

He shook his head sadly. "The only thing I will be," he said knowingly, "is a famous failure."

"Oh, please don't say that, Arthur."

He turned and looked down at his papers.

"Thank you," he said, "for being so honest."

I could see he didn't want to talk anymore so I thanked him again for the poem and left. I think it hurt me almost as much as it hurt him. I was never so glad to see Trisha and bask in her energy and laughter as I was when she returned from the movies that night and brought me the latest school gossip. I didn't tell her about Arthur's poem. I had already hidden it away in my dresser drawer with some of my other precious mementos, things I never wanted to lose, but things I found full of pain as well as love, like Momma Longchamp's picture, for they reminded me of what was lost and what would never be.

As more time passed Agnes's anger at me diminished. We never discussed the incident of my coming home at three in the morning anymore. I knew I had a good ally in Mrs. Liddy who sang my praises, especially when it was my turn to help with the kitchen work. I often spent time with her in the kitchen watching her work. She told me her life story, how she was made into an orphan at age eight when both her parents died from Spanish flu. Her family was separated because no one wanted to take on more than one child at a time, and there were two sisters and a brother she hadn't seen for more than twenty years.

I told her my story and how much I was afraid that a similar thing would happen to Jimmy, Fern and me. As it was we had no clues as to where Fern lived.

"Despite all that's happened," I said, "I would gladly trade my real family for the family I grew up with."

Mrs. Liddy didn't seem shocked, especially after I told her some of the things that had happened to me at the hotel and how Grandmother Cutler had treated me and was still treating me.

After my revelations, Mrs. Liddy and I became even closer. She spent time showing me some of her recipes and even let me help her prepare dinner for everyone one night. Her friendship helped me pass the time.

Finally, Agnes came to me one night shortly before the Christmas holiday to tell me she was very happy with how I had behaved these past months and had decided she could put me back on probation and end my punishment. I was surprised and thought it was all Mrs. Liddy's doing until I received a phone call a few days later from my mother.

"Randolph and I and Clara Sue are coming to New York on the weekend. We are on the way to spend the holidays on a luxury liner," she said. "We would like to come by and take you out to dinner."

"What about Philip?" I asked quickly.

"Philip's not going because he is visiting with some school friends. We knew you would be busy with your lessons over the holidays," she quickly said, "so we didn't ask you to join us, but we do so much want to see you."

"Are you really well enough to take such a trip?" I asked, barely hiding my sarcasm.

"Not really," she said, "but the doctors think it would do me a world of good and it isn't often I can get Randolph to leave the hotel. We'll see you soon," she added quickly. "Wear one of your nicest dresses because we'll go to a very fancy, expensive restaurant."

After I hung up, I wished I'd said I wouldn't go. I certainly wasn't looking forward to seeing Clara Sue. But despite my anger, I couldn't stop myself from being curious about everyone and how they looked. Laura Sue was still my real mother and regret it as much as I did, I couldn't deny the fact that Clara Sue was at least my half-sister.

They came by early that day. Agnes sent Clara Sue up to fetch me while she entertained my mother and Randolph in the sitting room with her theatrical stories and mementos. Without knocking, which didn't surprise me in the least, Clara Sue threw open Trisha's and my bedroom door and stood there gloating, her hands on her hips, her full bosom, which looked even fuller in her light blue dress with its tight-fitting bodice, rising and falling as she breathed quickly from running up the stairs. The crinoline under her skirt made it full and gave the impression Clara Sue was even bigger than she was. She'd had her hair cut and styled with a wave falling over her left eye seductively, which made her look much older. Other than that, she hadn't changed much; she was still a good twenty pounds overweight as was evident in her plump cheeks and arms.

Trisha looked up from the book she was reading while she relaxed in bed and watched me prepare for my dinner outing with my real family.

"This has to be Clara Sue," Trisha said in what I had come to appreciate as her deadpan style.

"Your room is so small for two people," Clara Sue commented as she twisted her mouth into a look of disgust. "How do you keep out of each other's way?"

"Traffic signals," Trisha said.

"Huh?"

"I don't really care what you think of our room, Clara Sue," I said, turning on her. "Besides, any normal person would have said hello first and waited to be introduced."

"They sent me up to tell you to hurry down," she whined. Then she pivoted and disappeared.

"Sweet thing," Trisha said. "I do sympathize, but try to have a good time."

"That's probably impossible," I said, gazed at myself once more in the mirror and left. As I passed Arthur's door, I saw it was open just a crack and he was peeping out. I didn't stop. Downstairs in the sitting room, my mother was laughing at something Agnes had said. They all turned when I appeared in the doorway.

Randolph was sitting beside my mother. He had his long legs crossed with his graceful hands folded over them and sat back comfortably, his soft mouth in a gentle smile and his blue eyes never looking more warm and bright. His light brown hair looked like it had grayed more at the temples and gray strains were even woven through the flaxen ones. But, he had his perennial dark tan and looked as elegant in his dark blue suit and tie as ever.

I was surprised at how well my mother looked. Her blonde hair lay on her bare, smooth, soft shoulders. She wore her gold necklace with the egg-shaped diamonds and the matching egg-shaped diamond earrings. The glitter in the precious stones matched the glitter in her deep blue eyes. Somehow, she looked even younger to me. It was as if time had no effect on her; she was immune to aging. She had a childlike quality, and her skin was as baby soft and creamy as ever with a healthy tint in her cheeks.

"Oh, how pretty you look, Dawn," she said, her voice dripping with Southern charm and gentility. "Doesn't she look absolutely beautiful, Randolph?"

"Absolutely," he said, nodding and smiling widely, his teeth gleaming white in that brown face.

Clara Sue stood behind them, her arms folded under her heavy breasts, her eyes green with envy.

"We're having such a delightful chat with Agnes, I hate to leave," my mother said.

"Oh, that's so kind of you," Agnes said, "but you mustn't let me delay your reunion."

"We do have reservations," Randolph said, ever the one to worry about schedules.

"Of course," my mother said. She held her hand out and Randolph shot into a standing position and helped her get up. She was wearing a beautiful black silk dress with a sweetheart neckline. Her bosom was lifted so that the rosy tint of her cleavage was visible. It was hard to believe that this woman, my mother, spent so much of her time locked away in her room in bed, an invalid.

She approached me and gave me a quick peck on the cheek. Then everyone said good-bye to Agnes, even Clara Sue, and we left to go to dinner. They had a limousine parked outside.

"You must tell us all about the school," my mother said after we were all settled in the limousine. "It must be so exciting for you to be around so many talented people."

I found it easy to talk about school and realized as I was describing it and my classes and teachers that I was excited about being here. Most of the time I was talking Clara Sue moaned and acted disinterested. She complained about everything at the restaurant and had her meal sent back to be cooked over. No matter what she did, neither my mother nor Randolph chastised her. No one could be more spoiled, I thought.

Randolph described their impending vacation, the ports of call they would visit and how much he and my mother had looked forward to this vacation.

"Randolph hasn't had a real vacation for over a year," my mother said.

I asked no questions about Grandmother Cutler and whenever any references were made to her, I simply ignored them. Until I asked how Sissy was. I would never forget the beautiful songs she sang when she worked. She was a very sweet girl, who felt bad about the way the others had

treated me when I first arrived and one of the chambermaids had been fired to make a place for me, someone who really didn't need the work.

"Grandmother fired Sissy," Clara Sue practically bellowed.

"Fired her? But why?" I asked, turning to Randolph. He shook his head.

"She was doing poor work," Clara Sue said with relish.

"That couldn't be true," I insisted, looking at my mother now. From the way she shifted her eyes from mine, I knew the reason lay elsewhere.

"She fired her because she told me where Mrs. Dalton lived, didn't she?" I demanded.

"Mrs. Dalton lived?" Randolph said. He looked at my mother.

"That's not true, Dawn," my mother said softly. "Please don't talk about it anymore. It's not pleasant to hear about unpleasant things now and I can't be made nervous just before a trip like this."

"But I'm right, aren't I?" I looked at Clara Sue who sat back smugly, which confirmed my suspicions. "How horrible," I said. "Sissy needed the work. It's not fair. Grandmother Cutler is so cruel, so horribly cruel."

"Now, Dawn," Randolph said, "you don't want to get yourself upset and everyone else upset, do you? We're having such a nice time."

A nice time? I thought. Who's having a nice time? On one side of me I had Clara Sue groaning and moaning and doing all that she could to make our dinner a disaster and across from me I had my mother who wanted to pretend all was wonderful and rosy, even though she knew I had been sent away after I had discovered the ugly truth.

I turned on him.

"Why did you let her fire Sissy?" I cried. "You know Sissy's a good worker and a loyal worker. Don't you feel sorry for anyone? Can't you do anything at the hotel?"

"Dawn!" My mother's eyes flared. "Oh dear," she said. "My heart is pounding something fierce, Randolph. I think I might just faint away at the table."

"Easy, my darling," he said, leaning over with concern. He took her hand into his and patted it quickly.

Why can't he see how phony she is? I wondered. Or didn't he care?

"I think we had better go," my mother said between gasps. "I need to get back to the hotel and lie down, otherwise I won't be able to go tomorrow."

"Of course," Randolph said. He signaled the waiter and demanded the check immediately.

"See what you've done," Clara Sue accused, the self-satisfaction written all over her face. "You're always causing some sort of trouble."

"Clara Sue!" Randolph chastised.

"Well she is. Look at all the terrible things she did at the hotel last summer. I told you I didn't want to take her out to dinner," she said, sitting back hard and folding her arms under her bosom, her face in a quick sulk.

"Clara Sue, please," our mother begged. Clara Sue's face folded into a small smile. She was very satisfied with herself and what had occurred.

"I feel very sorry for you," I said to her. "You have nobody but yourself and you know you can't stand yourself."

Her mouth dropped open, but before she could reply, Randolph had paid the check and helped my mother to her feet. We all started out. The ride back in the limousine was dreary. It was like riding in a hearse. No one spoke to anyone and the whole time, my mother sat there with her head on Randolph's shoulder, her eyes shut tight. Clara Sue glared out one window and I glared out the other.

When we pulled up in front of the apartment house, only Randolph stepped out with me.

"I'm sorry our dinner wasn't more pleasant," he said. "Perhaps when we return from our trip, we will be able to stop by and try again. If Laura Sue is up to it, that is," he added.

I looked back at the limousine. My mother was still lying back on the seat with her eyes closed and Clara Sue was gazing out innocently.

"I doubt she will be," I said, turned to go up the stairway and then spun around on him. "But you should demand to know why your mother fired Sissy," I cried and ran the rest of the way up the stairs and into the house without turning back.

After the holidays and the termination of my punishment, the school year moved more quickly for me. Each week I looked forward to receiving one of Jimmy's letters from overseas, and fortunately, the letters came like clockwork. He filled them with detailed descriptions of Berlin and European people and their customs. He always ended his letters with his vows of love and promised to return as quickly as he could. I filled pages and pages of notebook paper, describing every little thing I did, down to what flavor ice cream soda I had at George's Luncheonette and mailed it to him.

Daddy Longchamp hadn't written me for a long time. Then in April, I received a short letter from him which left me feeling cold and unhappy.

Dear Dawn,

I'm sorry I haven't written to you much, but I've been busy with my new work among other things. One of the other things that's kept me busy is getting to know Edwina Freemont who's had a rough life herself with her husband dying and all.

Anyway, we got to know each other real well and been keeping each other from suffering too much loneliness. One day we just looked at each other and both thought why not up and get married? Also, I've been talking to a lawyer who says if there would ever be a chance of me getting back Fern, it would improve a whole lot if I was married and there was a mother in the house. So there it is.

I hope things been going well for you. I wrote Jimmy and told him too.

Love,
Daddy

After I read the letter, all I could think about was Momma. I kept telling myself I should be understanding and think about Daddy Longchamp being all alone, especially with Jimmy off to Europe. But every time I told myself that, I saw Momma's face. Finally, all I could do was bury my own face in the pillow and bawl. I cried until my tears dried up and I could cry no more. I buried the letter with my other mementos and didn't tell anyone about it, not even Trisha.

A few weeks later, Jimmy wrote to tell me about Daddy Longchamp's marriage. He said he had expected it so he was more prepared for it than he imagined I was. He had met Edwina Freemont and said she was a very nice woman, but he admitted it still hurt him inside to know that his daddy had a new wife. He swore he would never get used to Momma being gone.

And neither would I, I wrote back, no matter how much time passed or how many new families I had.

For a while afterward, I felt there was a constant dark cloud hovering over me. The only things that made me happy were my vocal and piano lessons, receiving letters from Jimmy, and listening to Trisha go on and on about other girls. When I didn't have any lessons after school, I often stopped by to watch her at dance practice. I thought she was very good.

Trisha's seventeenth birthday was in early April. Her parents came to take her out to dinner and a Broadway show and invited me to join them. Her mother was a very pretty woman with big, green eyes and her father was a handsome, tall man who did dote on Trisha and lavished gift after gift on her, including a promise that as soon as she graduated from Bernhardt, he would buy her a little sports car.

Her parents asked me questions about my family. They had heard of the Cutler Cove Hotel and had even thought about staying there for a week one summer. Trisha threw me a glance or two when I replied to the questions, not revealing how unhappy I had been at the hotel. We went to see *Pajama Game* and after the show we went for coffee and cheesecake at

Lindy's. It was a completely glamorous evening in every way and although I knew I was lucky to have been invited along, in my deepest secret heart I was jealous of Trisha. My mother had barely acknowledged mine with a short phone call and a check stuck in a card in the mail, instructing me to buy myself what I wanted.

As April drew to a close, the excitement about Performance Weekend grew. Trisha and I often remained after school to watch the seniors rehearse.

Arthur Garwood became even more withdrawn as Performance Weekend drew closer and closer. It got so he wouldn't even come out to talk with me. I stopped by and knocked on his door a few times to try to reassure him that all would go well, but each time he didn't acknowledge my knock. Once, he even turned off his lights.

I was worried about him and told Agnes, but she said it was just performance jitters.

"We all get it," she explained. "Even the greatest performers still have butterflies in their stomachs just before they go on, even though they have performed and performed hundreds of times. In fact, they say if you are not nervous, you won't do well. Overconfidence is a liability in the theater," she declared.

"It's more than just performance jitters with Arthur," I said, but Agnes wouldn't listen.

Then, the morning before Performance Weekend, we all came down to breakfast and noticed immediately that Arthur was unusually late. Agnes became concerned and went up to his room to see if he was sick. She returned quickly and announced in a panic that Arthur was not there; that he hadn't slept in his bed.

"Does anyone know anything?" she asked frantically.

"Maybe he lost more weight and disappeared," Donald Rossi quipped.

"That's not funny," I snapped.

"No, it isn't," Agnes said. "It's so unlike Arthur. He keeps to himself and he is quiet, but he is not irresponsible. Oh, dear, and with his solo coming up tomorrow night," she cried and ran off to phone his parents.

Neither I nor Trisha saw Arthur anywhere in the school all day. Toward the end of the day, I deliberately walked by one of his classes to look in to see if he was there. He wasn't. When Trisha and I returned to the apartment house after school, we found Arthur's parents with Agnes in the sitting room.

"Oh girls, thank goodness you're here," Agnes declared. She was wringing her hands. "There hasn't been a hint as to what happened to Arthur. We were hoping he might have said something to one of you," Agnes said, looking particularly at me. Trisha shook her head.

"Dawn?"

I looked at Mr. and Mrs. Garwood. They didn't look worried as much as they looked angry and that got me angry.

"He was very nervous about his performance," I said. "He was afraid he would make a fool of himself and embarrass everyone. He's probably off hiding somewhere."

"Oh, that's ridiculous," Mr. Garwood said. "He would never do such a thing."

"Yes he would," I insisted and so vehemently, everyone turned sharply to me. "He was desperate," I said, "desperate because you wouldn't listen to his pleas."

"Dawn!" Agnes cried and looked quickly at the Garwoods. "She doesn't mean to sound insolent," Agnes started to explain.

Anger blazed through me. "Don't tell them what I mean, Agnes. Arthur has told me often how he has pleaded with you to understand. He knows he doesn't have the musical talent that both of you have, the abilities that you expect and demand in him."

"That's absolutely untrue," Mrs. Garwood snapped. "Arthur is quite talented. He . . . ."

"You're more right than you know! He's enormously talented but not the way you think."

"How dare you say such a thing?" Mr. Garwood's eyes grew small and took me in slowly from head to toe in a way that frightened me but I hoped and hoped I wouldn't back down. "Who does this child think she is?" he asked.

"I'm not a child," I snapped. "Arthur is very unhappy and he is desperate. You should listen to him. He doesn't want to disappoint you, but that's why he doesn't want to continue with the oboe."

"That's enough!" Mr. Garwood cried, rising to his feet. "If you know where Arthur is, you had better tell us, young lady."

"I don't know," I said, "and if I did, you would be the last person I would tell," I cried and ran from the room.

"Dawn!" Agnes screamed.

"I'll talk to her," Trisha said and followed me up the stairs. I slammed our bedroom door behind me and stalked around the room, fuming.

"I just knew something like this might happen," I said. "I just knew it. I warned Agnes, but she wouldn't listen, and you saw what his parents are like. They're horrible, horrible!"

"Wow. You really told them off," Trisha said.

"I couldn't help it. Arthur is in trouble; he's crying out for help and all they can think about is themselves and their own reputations. I'm sick of parents who don't really love their children. Sick of it!" I cried and flopped on my bed. Trisha sat down beside me.

"You don't know where he is though, do you?" she asked. I shook my head.

After the Garwoods left, Agnes came to our room.

"I'm so embarrassed," she began. "Nothing like this has ever happened before. The Garwoods are heartbroken."

"They're not heartbroken," I insisted. "They're worried about what their friends and relatives will say, friends and relatives they have invited to Performance Weekend. They don't really care about Arthur."

"You were absolutely rude and insolent down there, Dawn. I won't have such behavior in my house. If you don't tell me this instant where Arthur Garwood is, I will call your grandmother and inform her I have to have you expelled from this residency."

"I don't know where he is," I moaned. "He has no real friends to go to. He's just hiding out somewhere until Performance Weekend is over. Then he'll return. You'll see."

"Did you encourage him to run off?" Agnes demanded. "His parents suspect you did."

"I didn't have to encourage him. It's their own fault he did. They wouldn't listen to his pleas. Honest, Agnes," I cried through my tears, "I'm telling you the truth."

She stared at me and then shook her head.

"What are we to do?" she asked, her gaze growing distant.

Trisha and I looked at each other. Whenever anything unpleasant occurred, Agnes fell into one of her old roles. I could tell that she was drifting into some memory now, posturing and taking on the demeanor of some character in some obscure drama.

"Young people are so troubled these days. Their lives are so complicated. Don't you long for the simpler times, the quieter times? Don't you wish you could go to sleep and wake up a little girl again? I do. Oh, how I do," she said and turned to leave slowly, gracefully from our bedroom.

"She's losing it," Trisha remarked, shaking her head. "She can't handle turmoil."

"Who can?" I asked. "Who wants to?" I added.

Performance Weekend came and went and Arthur Garwood did not return. The Garwoods had the police come to the apartment house to question everyone, especially me. I told them everything I had told the Garwoods. They listened, nodded their heads and left. Agnes went off wringing her hands and Donald Rossi tried to invent new jokes about the situation.

Then, nearly a week later, I received a letter without any return address on the envelope. Something about the handwriting on the front, however, made my heart beat faster. I ripped open the envelope and read.

Dear Dawn,

There's no one else I care to say good-bye to. I'm sorry I didn't say good-bye in person. I have been putting away my money for a long time to do this. The only reason I remained as long in Bernhardt as I did was because I enjoyed being around you. But you have your own life and I know that I won't be part of it.

I've decided to go off and try to become a writer. Maybe, if I succeed, my parents will forgive me. I hope you were being honest when you told me you would always cherish the poem I wrote about you. Maybe someday we will meet again. Thank you for caring.

Love,
Arthur

Trisha thought I should give the letter to Agnes.

"But then they might hunt him down and drag him back and he will hate me for it," I said.

"There's no return address on it," Trisha pointed out. "All they know is it was mailed in New York City. This way," Trisha continued, "Agnes will know it's not your fault and Arthur's parents won't be able to blame anything on you."

"Poor Arthur," I said. Trisha shrugged.

"Maybe he's going to be happier now. He might even gain some weight," she added. I smiled, folded the letter back into the envelope and did what she had advised: brought it to Agnes, who sighed and sighed over it and thanked me.

We heard no more about it. Like so many unpleasant things that happened at Agnes Morris's resident hall, the events were never again mentioned, or if they were, they were indistinguishable from real events and fictional ones occurring in dramas. But I didn't have time to worry too much about it.

Madame Steichen began to include me in her monthly Saturday recitals showcasing her students. I sang with the chorus in two school musicals. The competition for solo parts was fierce and the seniors usually won them, even though other students often told me that I should have been chosen.

Toward the end of the school year, Madame Steichen informed me that she had selected me to be her featured student during next year's Performance Weekend. We would dedicate our summer classes to it. Everyone congratulated me on the honor and I was very proud. Even so, I promised Trisha I would find time to visit with her and her parents.

On the last day of the regular school year, Trisha met me outside the music suite, her face so red with excitement she looked like she would explode.

"Guess who's coming here next fall to teach vocal music," she cried, hugging her books to her bosom and spinning. "I just heard. Just guess!"

"Who?" I asked, shaking my head and smiling at her exuberance.

"Michael Sutton, the opera star!"

Michael Sutton was the rage of the opera scene in Europe; he had been a star in America the year before his European tour and had been and still was featured in magazine after magazine. He was young and handsome and as talented as anyone could be.

"He's going to hold auditions the week before school starts to choose his students," Trisha declared. "And even though I can't hold a note, I'm coming back early to try out. Of course, you'll have a wonderful chance, you lucky thing. You're a senior now!"

My heart began to pound in anticipation. I shook my head. Events in my short life had taught me never to count on anything, especially not a rainbow after the rain.

Still, why not hope, I thought. After all, Michael Sutton!

6
GETTING TO KNOW MICHAEL

Trisha and I were very excited the day of the audition for Michael Sutton's vocal class. We rose a half hour earlier than usual and tried on a dozen different skirt and blouse combinations before we both settled on our baby-pink blouses and pleated ivory skirts. We had bought them together during one of what Trisha called "Our weekend shopping safaris in the city." We would spend hours and hours going from one department store to another trying on different clothes, some dresses so expensive or outrageous we knew we could never buy them. But it was fun pretending even though salesladies with disapproving eyes glared down over their pinched noses at us.

Wearing identical outfits to the audition was Trisha's idea.

"Because we look like twins, we'll catch his attention," she said.

We washed and conditioned our hair and then brushed it until it seemed to glow, finishing with pink silk ribbons. Then we put on just a touch of lipstick. Neither of us needed any more color in our faces; we had both been tanned by the summer sun. We decided to wear white sneakers and Bobby socks, too. Giggling more out of nervousness than anything else now, we bounced down the stairs to breakfast and listened attentively as Agnes strutted up and down the dining room giving us advice for auditioning while we ate.

"Look confident; be businesslike, and whatever you do, don't be first," she warned.

We didn't need the warning. By the time we arrived, the music suite was so crowded that the candidates were told to line up and were given cards with numbers on them to use instead of their names. The line that had been formed stretched from the piano all the way on the other side of the long room to just outside the door. Richard Taylor, a senior and one of Madame Steichen's prize pupils, greeted us. Richard was talented but somewhat arrogant about it. He had been assigned to Michael Sutton as his teaching assistant and he was swollen with self-importance.

Richard was a tall boy, as lanky as Washington Irving's Ichabod Crane with long legs and arms and very long fingers. It was a sight to see him play the piano because his hands were so large, they looked like independent little creatures dancing over the keys. He had a narrow face with a nose that reminded me of a weather vane and a long mouth with corners that tucked in so tightly, they resembled dimples. His lips were naturally bright; it always seemed like he was wearing lipstick. He had a very fair complexion with tiny streams of freckles running through his cheeks and across his forehead. His light brown eyes were deeply set. He kept his rust-colored hair long, with strands going down his neck and under his collar.

"Just take a card and get in line," he commanded in his thin, nasal voice as the students arrived. "After the first cut, we will be taking names. Until then, numbers will suffice." He scowled at some of the candidates as if to say, "Why waste your time and ours?"

Most of the girls paid no attention to him; they strained their necks and twisted every which way to get a glimpse of Michael Sutton, who was standing near the piano with his back to us and gazing down at some sheet music.

"How many students will be in Mr. Sutton's class?" Trisha asked as she took a number card for herself and for me.

"Six," Richard replied.

"Six! Only six," she moaned.

"Will it be three girls and three boys?" one of the girls behind me asked.

"It won't be determined by sex; it will be determined by talent," Richard said and shook his head. "Where do you think you are, summer camp?"

Those students who heard his reply laughed. The girl who asked the question shrunk down behind the students in front of her. Satisfied with himself, Richard Taylor strutted toward the front of the line and then tapped Michael Sutton on the shoulder. He turned and looked our way.

I had seen pictures of him in magazines and newspapers, of course, but nothing compared to seeing him in person. He stood a little over six feet tall with broad shoulders and a trim waist. His dark, silky hair was brushed neatly on the sides with the front flowing back in a soft, gentle wave. He looked casually elegant in his white shirt and gray slacks. As he gazed over the line of hopeful candidates, his smile widened and warmed, those dark sapphire eyes sparkling with an impish glint. He had the most glamorously white smile I'd ever seen—it was like watching someone step out of a movie.

We had heard that Michael Sutton had just flown in from the French

Riviera, which accounted for his even, rich tan. I heard the sighs of girls ripple down the line in an undulating wave of "oo's and ah's."

I thought he was easily the handsomest man I had ever seen in person. Just gazing at him made me tremble and quickened my heartbeat. I was sure I would make a total fool of myself when it came time to sing for him. Maybe, I would be incapable of uttering a sound and would just open and close my mouth. The thought of it made me redden and I felt my cheeks grow very hot. Agnes had been right. I was certainly glad I wasn't at the head of the line. I pitied the girl who was.

"Hi, everybody," he said. "We're just about ready to begin." He had a soft and melodious voice with just a hint of an English accent. "First, let me thank you all for coming. Seeing so many of you here doesn't hurt my ego one bit, I can tell you that," he said and there was light laughter.

"I wish I could take all of you," he said, his face turning serious, "but obviously, that's not possible. I might choose one or two of you simply for the sake of variety, so nothing that happens here is meant to be a definitive comment on your talents and abilities. If you don't work with me this semester, I'm sure you will work with other capable teachers, maybe even more capable teachers than I."

He slapped his hands together and I saw the thin, elegant gold watch on his left wrist.

"All right, ladies and gentlemen," he continued, "I'll give you a start on this, one at a time," he said, indicating his tuning harmonica, "and I would like you to run up and down the scales for me."

He asked the first student to step forward. It grew very quiet, so still I could hear the deep breathing around me. He gave her the note and she did her scales. When she was halfway through, he said thank you and asked the next candidate to step forward. The line moved very quickly and before I knew it, I was going to be next.

I noticed Michael Sutton's eyes swing from the boy ahead of me to me. Terrified, I made my eyes flee from his long, searching look, afraid he would see how nervous I was. When I looked back at him, he was smiling. He listened to the boy for a moment and thanked him. Then he spun around to face me completely, his full, sensual lips open. For a long moment, he simply stared at me, drinking me in from head to foot. Numbness tingled in my fingers, perhaps because I had my fingers locked in so tightly together.

"All right," he said and brought his tuning harmonica to his lips to give me a note.

I started to sing and felt my throat tighten. I stopped immediately.

"That's all right," he said softly. "Try again."

This time I did my scales as best I could. When I was finished he merely nodded and I felt my heart sink. I hadn't realized just how much I'd hoped to be in his class until this moment.

"Thank you, number thirty-nine," he said and I stepped aside.

When everyone in the line had performed, Michael conferred with Richard Taylor. Then Richard stepped forward and held a sheet up before him.

"These people please remain. The rest of you, thank you," he said curtly, and then read out the numbers. Halfway through the list I heard my number called out. I couldn't believe my ears. So many students had sounded better than I had, and so many weren't as nervous and looked like they would make better students and singers. Trisha squeezed my arm.

"You lucky thing," she said enviously.

"There's still the second cut," I reminded her.

"You're going to make it. Good luck," she said and left with the other disappointed, rejected candidates.

The next step in the audition was to give Richard the sheet music for the piece we wanted to sing so he could accompany us while Michael Sutton listened, sitting in the rear of the auditorium with his pen and notebook in hand. I had decided I would sing "Somewhere Over the Rainbow," the song I had sung successfully at the music concert when I had attended Emerson Peabody in Richmond.

This time around, we had to announce our names and our song titles.

"Dawn Cutler," I declared. " 'Somewhere Over the Rainbow.' "

Once I began my song, the same thing happened to me that always happens when I sing. I forgot where I was and who was listening. I was alone, possessed by my music. All my vision and concentration went into the perfection of those notes. I traveled on a magic carpet of melody that carried me up and away from worry and pain. I forgot the past and the present. I was like an eagle soaring in the wind, obsessed and infatuated with her own ability to fly. Not the clouds, nor the stars, nothing seemed too far away.

I didn't open my eyes again until I had finished. For a moment there was a deep silence and then there was applause. The other candidates were clapping enthusiastically, forgetting for the moment that we were all competing for only six positions. I looked back at Michael Sutton. He was smiling and nodding.

"Next," he called.

Again, after everyone was finished, Michael conferred with Richard Taylor. This time, however, Michael Sutton stepped forward himself to make the announcement.

"I can't tell you all what a wonderful experience this audition has been for me," he said. "I am impressed with just how much talent there is here. And, very pressed to make a decision. But, alas, it has to be done," he added and turned to his note pad. "The following students will please remain so we can discuss your schedules," he said and then he read off the names.

My name was the last to be called out, but when I heard it, I felt my heart burst with joy. I had been chosen, selected out of all these other talented students to work with someone famous. What are you going to say and think when you hear about this, Grandmother Cutler? I wondered. Never in your wildest thoughts that horrible day when we confronted each other in your office did you even imagine that I would achieve so much. I was one of Madame Steichen's prize piano pupils, already practicing the piece I would play at Performance weekend this year, and now, I was one of six special students selected to work with Michael Sutton!

Your revenge has become a double edge sword with the sharper end pressing toward you, Grandmother Cutler.

"Please give Richard the schedules of your other classes, your required classes," Michael Sutton said, forcing me out of my hateful thoughts, "so we can plan out your private lessons. We will meet only once a week as a group. The rest of the time, I will work alone with each of you," he finished, his gaze resting on me for such a long moment that I got nervous and had to look away.

After I gave Richard my schedule, I started out. Two of the other music teachers had come in to speak with Michael, but he looked away from them and nodded and smiled at me as I started toward the doorway. I smiled back, my heart racing. Then, I tripped over one of my sneaker laces that had come loose and fell forward, catching myself just before falling on my face.

"Are you all right?" Michael called and started toward me.

"Yes," I said quickly and ran out, feeling like a complete fool. The blood had rushed into my face and I was so flushed and embarrassed, I couldn't wait to get away.

Trisha was waiting for me in the lobby.

"You made it, didn't you? I knew you would. You're going to have to tell me every little detail about every moment of your private lessons," she ordered. "I want to know everything he says to you."

"Oh Trisha, he probably thinks I'm just a little idiot. I nearly fell on my face just now while I was gaping at him stupidly on my way out!" I cried.

"Really? How exciting. See, something's happened already," she said. How she could amaze me with the way she could twist and turn things around. All I could do was laugh and go along with her.

Later that day, I had to return to the school for my summer hour lesson with Madame Steichen. I told her about my being chosen to be in Michael

Sutton's class, but she didn't seem too happy about it. We had gotten on friendly enough terms so that I felt I could ask her why she had smirked when I told her.

"He is not classical," she said. "He is not a true artist; he is a performer."

"I don't understand the difference, Madame Steichen," I said.

"You will, my dear Dawn. Someday, you will," she predicted and insisted we not waste a moment more of her precious time discussing nonsense.

After my lesson with Madame Steichen, I gathered up my sheet music and started out slowly, thinking that since I had plenty of time to get back to the apartment house before dinner, there was no point in rushing. Anyway, I felt like enjoying the remainder of the warm, late August afternoon. A cool breeze off the East River caressed my face. Above me, milk-white, tiny clouds looked like little puffs of whip cream dripped over a frosting of deep blue sky. I sat on one of the wooden benches and closed my eyes to breathe in the scent of roses and marigolds and pansies. The perfumed air and warm sunlight took me back to happy, carefree thoughts. I saw myself as a little girl, skipping rope and singing one of the rope skipping songs I had learned from girls a few years older.

"My mother, your mother, lives across the way, two fourteen, East Broadway. Every night they have a fight and this is what they say . . ."

I couldn't help but laugh at the memories now.

"Must be a very funny thought," I heard someone say and opened my eyes to see Michael Sutton standing in front of me and looking down at me with a slight smile over his lips. He carried a slim, leather briefcase in his right hand.

"Oh, I . . ."

"You don't have to explain," he said, laughing. "I don't mean to intrude."

"Oh, it's not an intrusion," I sputtered. "I was just startled."

He nodded and held his briefcase with two hands before him.

"So how was your piano lesson today?" he asked. I was surprised that he remembered my schedule so well.

"I think it went all right, although Madame Steichen is very frugal when it comes to compliments. She believes a true artist doesn't need to have others tell her when she is doing well; she knows it herself, instinctively."

"Poppycock," Michael Sutton said, leaning toward me. "Everyone needs to be stroked, to be told he or she is doing well. We all have egos that have to be petted like little kittens. When you do well, I will let you know; and when you don't, I will let you know that, too."

He straightened up again and looked back down the pathway. I held my breath. We were talking as if we had known each other for a long time. He seemed so relaxed and not at all aloof and full of conceit as I had assumed celebrities would be.

"I'm on my way to have a cup of cappuccino at a small café just around the corner. Would you care to join me?" he asked. For a moment I just stared up at him. It was as if I had to have the words translated. He smiled and tilted his head slightly. What was cappuccino? I wondered. Was it wine?

"Cappuccino?" I said.

"You could have a regular cup of coffee, instead, if you like," he said.

"Oh. Yes," I said quickly. "Thank you."

He waited a moment.

"You will have to get up if you are going to join me," he pointed out.

"Oh. Yes," I laughed and jumped up. We started toward the gate.

"So, you live in one of the school-approved residences nearby," he said as we walked.

"Yes," I said, suddenly feeling quite tongue-tied.

"And do you like living in New York?" he asked. As we turned a corner he took hold of my arm. I would have expected such a gesture would make me nervous and embarrassed but instead I found myself relaxing and feeling surprisingly safe.

"It's fun," I said, in answer to his question. "But it takes getting used to."

"My favorite city is London. You must see it one day. In London one walks in the shadow of places built centuries ago, and yet the modern world is all around you, too."

"That does sound exciting," I said.

"Haven't you traveled much?" he asked.

"Not outside the United States, no," I replied.

"Really? I thought all the students here were very sophisticated travelers," he said and I thought now he will think less of me. "But then again," he said, stopping and turning to me, "what I noticed most about you in the audition was your innocence, it seemed so sweet." We stopped walking and when I turned to him to see why he was staring at my face so intently, my heart began to flutter wildly. I found myself looking into his eyes and unable to pull my gaze away. "You have the look of someone about to be discovered, and about to discover," he said, so softly I could scarcely hear him. He raised his hand and for a moment that seemed to last an hour I thought he was going to touch my face. Then he lowered his hand to his side. "And yet," he continued, "there's something else behind those blue eyes, some wisdom that suggests you have had perhaps very painful experiences. I'm intrigued." His eyes still held mine and he seemed to drink me in. Then the moment passed and he suddenly turned away.

"Here we are," he said, leading me into the café and to a corner table. When the waitress asked if we wanted our cappuccinos with cinnamon or chocolate, I had to confess I had never had one before and didn't know which to choose.

"You look like you would like the chocolate," Michael said and gave her the order. "Tell me more about yourself. I like to get to know my students personally. I've read your file, of course, and I know you're from Virginia and your family owns a famous resort. I've never been there. What's it like?" he asked and I described the hotel and the ocean and the small seaside village of Cutler's Cove. He listened attentively, his eyes rarely leaving my face as I spoke. Occasionally, he nodded and asked about something else. I didn't speak in great detail about my family, except to say they were usually very busy with the work at the hotel.

"I haven't seen my parents for a long, long time," he said sadly. "I've been on tour, as you know. The life of a performer, a well-known performer," he added, "is very complicated. Things the rest of humanity take for granted are very rare for us. For example, I can't remember when I last had a holiday dinner with my family. I always seem to be on the road when these things come up."

He looked over his steaming cup of cappuccino and fixed his eyes on mine, which were now filled with sympathy and surprise. I never imagined that someone as famous and successful as Michael Sutton would have such unhappy thoughts. In every picture taken of him, he always looked like he was on top of the world, smiling down at the envious and the adoring.

"Yes," he said suddenly, nodding, "there is something very different about you, from your name to those blue eyes that continually change shades to match what you're thinking."

I started to blush, but he reached out and put his hand over mine.

"Don't change," he said so fiercely he surprised me with his vehemence. "Be yourself and don't let others make you over into what they expect or want you to be. When you sang for me today, you became your own person, your own special person living in your music. It pumps your blood around. I know; I have the same feelings when I sing, and the moment I saw you, saw someone who reminded me of myself, I knew I had discovered my star pupil."

Was I really sitting here listening to Michael Sutton tell me I had the potential to be a singing star? I wondered. Or was this only a dream? In a moment I will wake up and it will just be morning and Trisha and I will start debating what to wear to the audition.

I closed my eyes and then opened them, but Michael Sutton didn't disappear. He was still there, sitting across from me, gazing at me with enough admiration to make my heart pound. His eyes were laughing, full of sparkling lights as he templed his fingers beneath his chin and smiled.

"You look like you're about to cry," he said.

I swallowed back my tears of happiness.

"It's just nice to hear you compare me to you," I said. He nodded and leaned back, gazing toward the doorway of the café a moment.

"Well," he finally said, "I think when you have been blessed with a talent and have been able to be successful all over the world, you have an obligation to help others who have been blessed with talent.

"That," he said, turning back to me with a fire in his eyes now that made my heart quicken, "is why I have agreed to spend my time teaching at the Bernhardt School. I knew I would find not only talented young people here, but also young people who needed guidance and the advice of someone who has traveled the hard, high road.

"And that's why I think it's important for me to be personal, informal with my students, my special students," he emphasized. "If I can't give them the benefits of my experience, what good is it?

"Anyway," he continued, putting his hand over mine again, "I feel as if I know you well. If you are like me, you are a passionate person. You feel everything more deeply than other, ordinary people do, whether it's happiness or sadness, pleasure or pain, and then you are able to translate that experience into song through your beautiful voice. Am I right?"

"Yes," I said. "I think so."

"Of course I'm right. Do you have a boyfriend?" he asked, sitting back again.

"I do, but he's away in Europe. He's in the army."

"I see." He nodded. "Remember this, Dawn," he said leaning toward me, "passion makes us desperate."

I stared into his eyes, mesmerized. It was as if my heart had stopped. I didn't dare to breathe for fear I would shatter the fragile moment. His smile came slowly, softly and then he sat back again.

"Tonight," he declared, "there is a recital at the Museum of Modern Art, and afterward, there is a wine and cheese reception. Of course, I am one of the honored guests and now I would like you to be one as well."

"Me?"

"Yes. Be at the museum at eight o'clock. I'm sure you know how to dress. Don't look so surprised," he said, smiling. "In Europe it is *très chic* for a teacher to invite one of his prize students to a recital. Anyway, I want you to hear these people sing. There are things to learn. Each moment of our day must be a positive and worthwhile moment. From this moment on," he said, "don't let any opportunity slip through your fingers."

He looked at his watch and then reached for his wallet.

"I have to be going. Errands to do before I can be free to enjoy. I'm glad we had this informal chat and got to know each other a little better and I look forward to seeing you tonight. You will be there?"

"Oh, yes," I said quickly. My mind raced along as I considered my wardrobe and what would be proper attire. Wait until Trisha found out, I thought.

Michael stood up and we left the café. On the sidewalk outside, we parted. I watched him hail a cab. He waved just before he got in and then he was gone.

I stood there, my thoughts whirling around in my head making me so dizzy I had to lean against a street light pole and catch my breath. Was I dreaming? Finally, I started across the street, feeling as if I were walking on air. I had to look down to be sure my feet were touching the ground. I didn't even realize where I was until I found myself standing in front of the apartment house. Then I rushed up the stairs and through the door. I raced up the stairway, and burst in on Trisha who looked up from her magazine.

"You will never believe," I said with a gasp, "where I am going tonight and who asked me to go."

Then I proceeded to tell her everything in a single breath.

My stomach churned so with anticipation, I couldn't eat a thing for dinner. The food just lay there on the plate staring up at me. I picked away at what I could when Mrs. Liddy looked in because I didn't want her to think I didn't like what she had made. I had washed my hair and set it in large rollers. Agnes and Mrs. Liddy knew I was going to the recital and that Michael Sutton had invited me.

Before dinner Trisha and I had gone through my wardrobe trying to decide what was appropriate to wear to an evening recital. Most everything was too informal, we thought. Finally, we settled on my sleeveless black taffeta with the V neckline. It had a wide, black bow tie belt at the waist and a full skirt that reached between my knees and ankles.

After dinner when I went up to dress, Trisha stuck her hand into her top dresser drawer to produce her padded bra. She dangled it before me.

"Oh, no," I said, eyeing it with temptation. "I couldn't wear that."

"Of course you could. You want to look older and enhance what you already have developed, don't you? You're going to be among grown women; you can't look like a child," she emphasized. "The bodice of your dress requires it," she concluded. "Just do it," she snapped when I still hesitated.

I took it from her slowly and put it on. When I slipped into the dress and she zipped up the back for me, my image in the mirror took me by surprise. It wasn't only the padded bra. There had been subtle, but significant changes in my looks since my mother and I had gone shopping in Virginia a little over a year ago. I had been sensitive to the changes in Jimmy, but somehow not to the changes in myself.

Just as with him, my face had lost its childhood plumpness in the cheeks. I saw a more mature glint in my eyes and found that whenever I looked at anything intently now, I tended to raise my right eyebrow like a question mark. My neck looked softer, the curve into my shoulders more graceful and smooth, and my cleavage deeper with the shadow at the bottom, suggesting and promising. Even Trisha was surprised.

"You look so much older!" she exclaimed. "Here," she cried, rushing to her jewelry box and producing a gold necklace that sparkled brightly with tiny diamonds. "Wear this."

"Oh, I couldn't, Trisha. What if I lost it? I know it was a special gift to you from your father."

"All his gifts to me are special," she shrugged. "Don't worry, you won't lose it and you need something around your neck with that deep neckline. Or should I say, 'plunging neckline'?" she teased.

"I look like a fool, just like someone trying to appear ages older, don't I?"

"Absolutely not," she insisted. "I'm just kidding. Don't you dare change into something else, Dawn. Now march yourself right down those stairs and call for a cab this instant before you lose your nerve. Go on," she insisted.

Agnes was waiting for me at the bottom of the stairway. For a moment I thought she was going to insist I turn around and change into something that would make me look far less enticing and more my age. But suddenly, her dark brown eyes brightened and she brought her hands to the base of her throat.

"For a moment," she said, her voice nearly breathless, "I thought I had fallen through time and was looking at myself coming down that stairway in a melodrama I starred in when I was only four or five years older than you." She sighed and shook her head.

"I have to call for a taxi," I explained and started toward the sitting room. Lost in one of her memories, Agnes could go on for hours.

"Yes, but wait right here afterward," she ordered and rushed off. She returned with a mother-of-pearl white shawl and draped it over my shoulders. "Now," she said, standing back, "you look fully dressed and elegant and like one of my girls."

My heart was racing so quickly when I walked out and down the stairs to get into my cab that I thought I just might fall in a faint and have to be carried off to a hospital. I felt myself trembling after I got into the taxi. For a moment I couldn't remember where I was going.

"Which museum?" the cab driver asked again.

"The Museum . . . of Modern Art," I gasped.

"Right," he replied and shot off.

When we arrived I sat there a moment and gaped at the crowd of richly dressed sophisticated men and women stepping out of taxi cabs and limousines and then making their way toward the front entrance of the museum. Here and there I saw some young people, but they were all with their parents. I paid the cab driver and emerged from the taxi so slowly I was sure he thought I was attending a function I despised. After he drove off, I stood there hoping to spot Michael Sutton, but he was nowhere in sight. Finally, I walked to the front entrance and followed some people through the doors.

Small groups were gathered in the lobby. So many people appeared to know each other. I saw no one who looked as alone as I was. I waded through the sea of laughter and conversation, making my way slowly toward the recital. Signs directed me. When I reached the doorway of the room, I found an elderly lady sitting at a desk with a list of names before her. She looked up at me expectantly and smiled. Were we supposed to have tickets?

"Good evening," she said and waited for me to give her my name.

"Good evening. I'm Dawn Cutler," I said.

"Cutler?" She looked down at her list of invited guests. "Cutler," she repeated. "I'm sorry, I don't . . ."

I felt the blood rush into my face as other people around me stared and waited impatiently to go ahead.

"You were sent an invitation?" the elderly lady asked me, still smiling in a friendly manner.

"I'm . . . I was invited by Michael Sutton," I stammered quickly.

"Oh. A guest of Mr. Sutton's. Yes, yes. Go right on inside and take whatever seat you like," she said.

I moved into the recital room quickly and gazed around, searching desperately now for Michael. I knew no one else here and didn't know where to go. I tried not to look confused and frightened, but it seemed to me that everyone in the room was looking at me: people who were seated turned to look back, others entering paused to gaze at me, none smiling. I was sure I stood out like an ugly weed in a bed of roses.

Finally, out of desperation, I hurried down the right aisle and took the first available seat. I looked back at the doorway, hoping to see Michael Sutton enter. The moment he did, I thought I would go to him. Finally, just before the recital was to begin, he did come, dressed in a tuxedo and black tie. But I didn't move. On his arm was a beautiful woman with flaming red hair, her ears dripping diamonds. An excited usher greeted them immediately and led them down the other side of the recital hall to reserved seats right up front.

I was stunned. He didn't even look for me; surely he hadn't even asked if I had arrived, for he would know I had and sought me out, I thought. Did he expect I would be waiting for him in the lobby? He hadn't said so. Was I supposed to go to him now? When I strained my neck to look over the people in front of me, I saw there were no empty seats beside him.

Before I could do anything, the recital began and I had no time to think. It consisted of stars from the Metropolitan Opera House singing famous arias. The voices and the music were so overwhelming that while the recital was conducted, I forgot everything else: forgot about being embarrassed or alone, forgot about sitting among strangers who seemed very disinterested in me, even forgot about Michael Sutton, who appeared to have overlooked the fact that he had invited me.

After the applause had ended and the crowd had begun to make its way out of the recital hall, I lingered so that Michael would see me. So many people were gathered around him as he made his way up the aisle; I didn't know how I would get to him, short of elbowing my way through the pack of admirers. He didn't see me and I was too embarrassed to shout out. Instead, I bowed my head and followed the audience to the wine and cheese reception.

Waiters and waitresses moved around a big room carrying trays of wine in tall, thin glasses and trays of hors d'oeuvres. I took a glass of wine and waited to catch sight of Michael. Finally, I saw him in the middle of a crowd of people all the way across the room. I made my way as gracefully as I could, even though I felt like running to him. When I got there, I stood back, waiting for him to notice me. It seemed to take ages because his eyes were fixed on the beautiful redheaded woman, who was with him. She kept her arm threaded through his and threw her head back to laugh and nudged him with her shoulder every time he said something.

Finally, he turned my way. His eyes brightened with recognition.

"Dawn," he cried. He held his hand out and I took it to move through the crowd. "Wasn't it wonderful?" he asked, his face flushed from the wine and the conversation, as well as the heat from the people who closed in around him.

"Yes. I wasn't sure whether I was supposed to meet you in the lobby so . . ."

"This, ladies and gentlemen," he declared, turning to the people who stood closest to us, "is one of my new pupils."

"Oh, that's right, Michael," the redheaded woman said, laughing, "I forgot you are to be a teacher, too, this year." She whispered something in his ear and he laughed loudly. Then he turned back to me.

"Did you get something to eat, a glass of wine?"

"Yes," I said, holding up my glass.

"Good. Well enjoy yourself. We'll talk about this when we have our first private lesson," he said and patted me on the hand. I waited with baited breath for him to say more, but he returned his attention to the people around him.

I stood there dumbly, wondering what else I was to say or do. After a moment his friends and the redheaded woman led him off toward another gathering of people and I was left standing alone.

Michael hadn't even really introduced me to anyone; he hadn't told anyone my name. I looked around. Could everyone see my embarrassment? Everywhere I turned, eyes were on me. How foolish I must appear standing by myself with a glass of wine in my hand waiting for someone to say something to me, I thought. I saw a man lean over and whisper to the woman beside him, who laughed loudly at whatever he'd said. They were surely laughing at me. My heart felt right up against my throat and I broke out in a cold sweat.

I wanted to run out of the room, but I knew that would only draw more attention to me. Slowly, with my head bowed, I made my way toward the door. When I finally found myself in the lobby, I lifted my head and felt the tears stinging behind my eyes. Afraid someone would see me in tears, I charged out the entrance of the museum and hurried to the street. Once there, I took deep gasps. I was a tight wire inside, stretched so taut I thought I might break and cry hysterically.

Without realizing what I was doing or where I was going, I turned left and began to walk. I don't know how far I walked or what directions I took, for I turned wherever there was a green light. Finally, I stopped and looked around and realized I was lost. But what frightened and shocked me even more was the realization that I had left the museum carrying my wine glass. What if someone had seen me leave and thought I had stolen it? If I was described to the woman who had been seated at the desk at the door to the recital hall, she would know who I was and tell Michael Sutton.

I could hear her saying it: "Your prize pupil stole a wine glass and went rushing out."

I turned about desperately, looking for a place to throw it. Suddenly, I heard someone say, "Hi, honey. Slumming tonight?"

I spun around to face a man with an unshaven face with eyes that looked more like empty sockets. When he smiled, he revealed a mouth missing many teeth. I could smell his whiskey breath. He looked like he had slept in his faded brown rain coat and creased pants. His sneakers were torn at the sides.

When he laughed, I pivoted as quickly as I could and ran as fast as I could in my high-heeled shoes. Agnes's white shawl flew off my shoulders, but I didn't stop to retrieve it because I heard the horrid man shout. Just as I reached a corner, one of my heels gave way. I threw off my shoes and kept running, not looking back. I ran as hard and as fast as possible until I came to a busy intersection. There, I took hold of a light pole and caught my breath. Passersby glanced at me, but no one stopped to ask me what was wrong or if he or she could help.

I was finally able to flag down a taxi cab.

"Must've been some party," the driver said after I got in. I realized my hair was a mess, the strands flying everywhere. Tears had streamed down my cheeks. My dress was rumpled and I was barefoot. Yet, I still clung stupidly to the wine glass I had taken from the reception. I gave the cab driver my address and sat back, my eyes closed all the way.

When we arrived, I quickly paid the fare and rushed up the stairs and into the house. The moment I entered, I heard voices from the sitting room and remembered Agnes was having some of her theatrical friends over. I tried slipping by the door, but Agnes had heard me come in. She stepped out of the sitting room.

"Dawn," she called. "Come and tell us about the reception." As I drew closer to her, she realized something was wrong. "What happened?"

"Oh Agnes," I cried. "I got lost and lost your shawl. I'm sorry."

"Oh dear. You never got to the reception? But how could that be? Surely the taxi took you directly there."

"No, afterward," I explained. She stared at me and then looked at the glass in my hand.

"I don't understand," she said, shaking her head. "Why do you have that glass?"

"I . . . I don't know!" I cried and rushed past her and up the stairs.

Naturally, Trisha was up and waiting to hear about my exciting evening, but as soon as she took one look at me, her smile turned to a look of shock.

"What happened to you?"

"Oh Trisha, I'm so embarrassed. It wasn't a date with Michael. He hardly spoke to me. I ran out of the reception and forgot to give back this glass. Then I got lost and a horrible man came after me so I ran and ran, losing a shawl Agnes had given me as well as breaking off a heel," I cried and fell on my stomach on my bed.

"I don't understand what you're saying," Trisha said. I spun around and screamed through my tears.

"I'm saying it's no good to try to be someone you're not. I shouldn't have dressed up like this. I shouldn't have even gone. Grandmother Cutler's right. I'm a nobody who was dropped back on the doorstep of rich, fancy people; but everyone can see I'm not one of them and I don't belong."

"That's stupid. Of course she's not right about you. Anyone can get lost in New York at night. Stop crying," Trisha demanded. "So you forgot to give back a glass. Big deal. At least you forgot. Other people probably swipe them on purpose, even rich, sophisticated people. Anyway, did Michael Sutton see you run out?"

"I don't know," I said, grinding back my tears.

"So?"

"I felt so foolish," I repeated. "No one spoke a word to me, not even the people I sat next to. They're all so stuck up. I felt like I was in a room filled with Grandmother Cutlers."

"They'll be sorry," Trisha said, sitting beside me and stroking my messy hair. "Someday, they will all come to hear you in a recital and you can remind them of this night."

I looked at her and shook my head.

"Anyway," Trisha said, taking the glass and putting it up on my dresser, "we have a real souvenir, a memento marking your first night with Michael Sutton, whether he knows it or not."

She widened her eyes and we both laughed.

Thank goodness I had Trisha, I thought, the sister I had never known. I would trade Clara Sue for her in a moment. Grandmother Cutler was wrong: blood wasn't always thicker than water.

7
PRIVATE LESSONS

Now that I was a senior, my enthusiasm for beginning my second year at the Bernhardt School was greater than my enthusiasm for beginning my first. When I strutted through the campus and saw the faces of the new students green with anxiety, I couldn't help but feel a sense of superiority. Also, I enjoyed some celebrity as Madame Steichen's star pianist and as one of the six students chosen to attend Michael Sutton's classes.

I knew that Agnes had done her duty and reported these events to Grandmother Cutler because my mother, during one of her so-called stronger moments, phoned to congratulate me.

"Randolph has told me everything," she said. "I'm very proud of you, Dawn. It's so reassuring to know you really do have musical talent."

"Perhaps my father would like to be reassured too, Mother. Why don't you tell me who he really was so I can inform him of my whereabouts and achievements," I replied sharply.

"Why must you always bring up unpleasant things, Dawn? Will there never be an end to it?" she moaned with emphatic desperation. I could see her going into a faint on the other side of the line. I was sure she was calling me from her bed with her back braced against two large fluffy pillows and the blankets drawn up around her like a snail's protective shell.

"Knowing who one's father is is not supposed to be an unpleasant thing, Mother," I said with even more viciousness.

"In this case it is," she replied quickly. Her depth of deep feeling took me by surprise. How could anyone be that bad? I wondered.

"Mother," I begged, "please tell me about him. It isn't fair. Why is it an unpleasant thing?"

"Sometimes," she said, dropping her voice and speaking slowly, speaking like someone in a daze, "good looks and charm are only thin, surface deceptions hiding a stream of evil and cruelty. Intelligence, talent, whatever people think are blessings, don't always mean the person is a good person, Dawn. I'm sorry I can't give you anything more than that."

What strange and enigmatic advice, I thought. It dropped me into a whirlpool of questions and made the riddle of my birth and aftermath even more mysterious.

"Tell me this, Mother: does he still perform? Is he still an entertainer?"

"I don't know," she said quickly. At least he was still alive, I thought. She didn't say he was dead. "One of the reasons I called," she continued, her voice changing radically, rising and becoming melodious and happy, "was to see if there are things you need in your wardrobe now that you will be doing more and more performing."

"I don't know," I said. "I suppose there are."

"I have instructed Randolph to set up some accounts for you at some of the better department stores. He'll be sending you instructions today. Get whatever you need," she said.

"Does Grandmother Cutler approve?"

"I have some money of my own over which she has no control," Mother explained, some pride and satisfaction in her voice. "Anyway, congratulations on your accomplishments, and if you think of it, write me occasionally to let me know how you are doing."

Why the sudden interest in my life? I wondered. Was her conscience gnawing at her? I made no promises. Before I could say anything anyway, she began to describe her headaches and a new medication the doctor had prescribed. Then she announced she was exhausted and our conversation ended.

But the things she had said about my real father's evil nature lingered in the closets of my mind like some foul odor you could never wash away. What did that mean? If I inherited my father's musical talents, did I also inherit his depravity? How I longed to be face to face with him and judge him for myself. I would demand to know why he left without ever trying to learn anything about me. Was it because of Grandmother Cutler's power, her threats and what she could do to destroy anyone's career and life? Or was it really simply a matter of my father not caring about anything or anyone but himself, being the selfish playboy he had been described as? There were so many undercurrents flowing here that I didn't understand. Deceptions, deceptions. How was I ever going to learn to swim in an ocean of deceit?

And so while other students at Bernhardt had only pleasant thoughts to accompany them on their first days of classes, I had to move about in a fog, my only bright spots coming when I was singing or playing piano.

When fall finally descended on New York, it fell quickly, pressing the mercury in thermometers down dramatically at night and quickly turning the green leaves a crisp yellow and brown. Now whenever Trisha and I or I by myself waited at a corner for the traffic light to change, dead leaves scuttled the lawns, chased over the street and came to nestle near my feet like brown dried-up ducklings. But the sharp, clear air was invigorating. It felt good to have my cheeks tingle.

In fact, I felt good all over, and instead of blossoming in the spring with the flowers, I bloomed in autumn. Perhaps it was because my confidence had been nourished by my musical achievements. Whatever the reason, when I gazed at myself in the mirror on September mornings, I saw a wiser look on my face.

After I had gotten over my disaster at the recital at the museum, I had taken a second, harder look at the girl who gazed back from the mirror. She was almost seventeen; her life had changed radically and those changes had carved away some of that innocence. She had a sharper look in her eyes, more pronounced cheekbones and a tighter jaw. Her lips were firm, the curves in her neck and shoulders more graceful. Her breasts were full and shapely and her waist small. Perhaps she wasn't yet a woman, but she was knocking on the door.

Of course, I told Michael Sutton nothing about what had happened to me after I had run from the wine and cheese reception at the museum, and, apparently he knew nothing about it. During our first class, which was his general session with all the students, he asked me again how I had enjoyed the music and I told him it had been truly wonderful. I thanked him for inviting me. After that he turned to his lesson for the day.

The way the private lessons were staggered, I didn't have mine until a week later. When I appeared, I found Richard Taylor at the piano. Michael Sutton had not yet arrived. From the way Richard spoke and acted, I understood that promptness was not one of Michael Sutton's virtues.

"Yesterday," Richard said dryly, "he didn't show up until half of the period was over. It's not like working with Madame Steichen. That's for sure," he quipped and went back to tapping aimlessly on the piano keys. I sat on a wooden folding chair and took out my math homework. Nearly fifteen minutes later, Michael walked through the door casually and didn't even apologize for his lateness. He said he hated keeping to schedules; it was the one drawback to teaching.

"Creative people have to be motivated, have to be in the mood," he explained as he unwrapped his light blue scarf from around his neck and unbuttoned his soft wool coat. "School administrators don't understand that." He draped his things over a chair and beckoned me to the piano.

"We'll begin with the scales," he said, "and your breathing. Breathing," he emphasized, "is the key. Forget melody, forget the notes, forget your voice. Think only about your diaphragm," he preached.

Almost as soon as I began, he stopped me and turned to Richard Taylor, who was already smirking.

"See what I mean, Richard? None of the students here have been taught properly. No sense in wasting any more of your time today. We won't be needing the piano."

Richard folded the music books and left without saying a word, not even a quick good-bye to me. As soon as he was out the door, Michael turned back to me and smiled.

"He's a talented young man," he said, nodding toward the doorway, "but a bit too serious." He leaned closer to me to whisper. "He makes me nervous." He went to the doorway to close the door.

"But," he said, returning, "I meant what I said about your breathing. It's causing you to put too much strain on your throat. I bet your throat aches after you've been singing for a while, huh?"

I nodded.

"Of course. Let's try it again. We'll do it the way a European teacher of mine taught me."

He took me by total surprise when he stepped up behind me and encircled me with his arms. He held my elbows in his hands and drew me back against him.

"Relax," he whispered in my ear. I felt his breath on my neck, his chest pressed to my shoulders. The sweet aroma of his after shave lotion floated around my face and filled my nostrils. Then he pressed the palm of his right hand just under my breasts to my diaphragm.

"Now take a deep breath," he said, "and push my palm away by breathing out."

I felt his right forefinger graze the underside of my left breast, and for a moment I could do nothing. He had taken my breath away, not prepared me to do breathing exercises. Surely, I thought, he felt my body trembling and he felt the drumming of my heart. His breathing quickened, too.

"Go on," he coaxed. "Take a deep breath."

I did it and when my shoulders lifted, his hand slid closer to my bosom so that he was practically supporting it with the surface of his thumb and wrist.

"Good. Breathe out, press my hand away. Think about it as you do it. Concentrate, concentrate," he said and I did so. He made me repeat it. I did it nearly a dozen more times and suddenly, I grew dizzy, so dizzy my legs felt wobbly. I moaned and lost my balance, falling against him even more. He tightened his grip on me and held me fast.

"Are you all right?" he asked quickly. I tried to speak, but I could only nod. Then I heard him laugh. "You hyperventilated. It's nothing. You over-oxygenated your blood. Just sit down for a moment," he said, guiding me back to the wooden folding chair. Then he squatted beside me and took my hands into his. "Okay?" He squeezed my hands gently and rested his forearms on my knees.

I nodded, trying to find a voice that didn't quiver, but my face felt so flushed and my heart was still pounding that I was afraid to utter a sound, positive my voice would crack. When I looked at him so close to me, I saw a depth in his dark eyes that made me spin in a different way. It made me feel light, airy, eager to fall into his arms and have him hold me. My body began to grow warm in the most intimate places. I had to turn away because I was sure he could see these things happening in me and I was blushing just as much from embarrassment as I was from the heat that fanned out from my heart and rushed through my breasts.

"Just rest a moment," he said, "and we'll go back to the scales."

He patted my knee and stood up. He went to the piano and looked at some papers for a few moments.

"Okay," I finally said.

I know I didn't sing as well as I could when we went through the scales afterward. He made me do it repeatedly until he said I had combined the proper breathing with the notes.

"Fine. That's good," he declared, taking my shoulders in his hands and holding me out before him as he drank me in with that titillating fixed look of his. "You are already wonderful with your natural talent," he continued, "but when you do it correctly, you will reach the full height of your potential and you will become a true diva. They will flock to you and thrill just to be in your shadow.

"Do you know what happens to me when I'm with someone like you?" he continued, making me tremble more with each and every wonderful word. "I feel younger, stronger, able to go on and do even greater things. It makes me want to stretch out my own talents, extend myself further than I had ever dreamed."

He laughed and released me. Then he went to the piano and tapped on a key to give himself a note. As soon as he had, he vocalized the scales, holding his arms out toward me as if he were singing the most romantic love song. Then he did begin to sing a love song, a song he had made famous. He beckoned me to join in and indicated I should use the sheet music on the piano, but I shook my head. I knew the music well.

When I started to sing along with him, his eyes widened with pleasure and surprise. He stepped closer to me to take my hands into his and we sang to each other just the way we would sing were we on the stage in front of an audience. My voice intertwined with his, he taking me up higher and higher. His fingers tightened on mine and he drew his face closer to my face as the song came to an end.

On the stage it ended with the man and woman kissing. And so did it end this way now, even though I never thought he would actually do it. First, I felt his hot breath on my face, and then as he continued to draw me closer to him and himself closer to me, I knew it was going to happen. I closed my eyes and his lips touched mine, softly at first, almost as if we were both made of air, and then, he pressed his mouth firmly onto mine. The contact sent an electrifying flash of heat through me. I felt myself go limp. He held onto me and then slowly lifted his lips from mine. My eyes fluttered open and I gazed up into his, which seemed to call to me with such passion and desire, I could only stare and wait to see what he would do next, for I recalled what he had told me in the café: "Passion makes us desperate."

I was both frightened and thrilled by my thumping heart. I was afraid I would fall into a faint again.

"I had to do that," he said softly. "You sang so well. For a moment I thought I was really on the stage and when I'm on the stage, I do what is called for, what must be done to make the music real to the audience. That's the mark of a professional. I'm sure you understand."

I didn't, but I nodded.

He smiled at me, gazing at me intently again with those dark piercing eyes.

"We've had a very productive lesson," he said. "How do you feel?"

I was feeling so many different things at the moment, I didn't know how to respond. I was still overwhelmed by his kiss and still trembling from his touch and intense gaze.

"Fine," I finally said. He laughed and kissed my forehead.

"You're a very beautiful young woman, do you know that?" he asked. "It's rare to find someone with such a beautiful voice who also has such a beautiful face. I'm not embarrassing you, am I?"

I shook my head slowly, my eyes still locked in his stare.

"I wouldn't talk like this with any of my other students, but I sense that you are special. Your talent makes you different, makes it possible for you to be older faster because you are more perceptive, more sensitive. Like me, you grow with every passing moment and with every experience.

"Educators don't know anything about this," he said disdainfully, his face filled with disgust. "They do things by the book, even in a school like this; but we'll be different because we are different. You don't mind, do you?" he asked. I wasn't sure exactly what he meant, but I said no anyway, my "no" coming out so softly, I wasn't sure myself whether or not I had actually spoken.

"Good!" he exclaimed. "Good," he repeated softly and then he spun around quickly and went to the chair where he had placed his things. He began wrapping his scarf about his neck, smiling at me as he did so.

"I've got to run off," he said. "I have a dozen errands to do. I'm having a few people over tonight. Nothing special, just some hors d'oeuvres and champagne." He stared at me a moment and then he picked up his jacket and put it on as he approached me again.

"Can you be discreet?" he asked me.

"Discreet?"

"Keep a secret," he said, smiling, "especially if it's special?"

"Oh, yes, yes I can," I said. "I'm not close to anyone except my roommate and I don't tell her everything." I thought he was going to ask me not to tell anyone he had kissed me.

"Good." His stare lasted so long this time, as he debated whether or not to go any further with what he wanted to say. "I'd like to invite you to my apartment this evening," he finally said. "There should be some very interesting people there for you to meet, only . . ."

He turned to be sure the door of the music room was still closed. "Only the administration here wouldn't quite understand my inviting a student. Obviously, these limited-minded people would frown on such things, but rubbing elbows with theater people is good for the juices; it's stimulating. However," he warned, "if you should even mention it . . ."

"Oh, I wouldn't say a word!" I exclaimed. He pressed his forefinger to my lips and gazed back again. "The walls have ears," he said. I nodded, holding my breath. He smiled softly.

"I'm at the Parker House on East Seventy-second Street, apartment 4B," he said. "Come at eight, but remember . . . not a word to anyone, not even your roommate. Promise?"

"Yes," I said.

"Fine. See you later," he said starting away.

"Oh. What should I wear?"

"Nothing special. Come just as you are, if you like," he replied and was gone.

For a long moment, I simply stood there looking after him. Did I really hear what I thought I had heard? I spun around and looked at the piano. Did what happen here really happen? I pressed my hand to my heart as if that would slow the pounding. Then I picked up my things and started out, walking slowly, like someone still passing through a dream and afraid only of something happening to waken her.

Trisha noticed something different about me immediately when we met in our room after school. She was full of her usual energy, spinning one school incident after another, weaving in characters and events so quickly, she summarized her entire day in fifteen minutes. I listened, my face frozen in a small smile, my eyes on her, but my mind in a completely different place, my ears hearing a different voice, Michael's voice.

"Have you heard a thing I said?" Trisha suddenly asked.

"What? Oh. Yes, yes," I said quickly, unable to prevent a rush of blood into my face. It was as if my thoughts were visible. Trisha tilted her head to one side and studied me a moment. Then her eyes widened and she practically jumped off the bed.

"I know that look!" she exclaimed. "You met someone, didn't you? Someone you like very much and you're head over heels in love. Come on, tell me," she whined when I didn't respond.

"I . . ."

"Oh, Dawn," she moaned with impatience, "you can trust me. I've told you millions of things I wouldn't tell anyone else and you've told me very intimate things about yourself and your life and I've never said a word to anyone, have I? Well?"

"No, you haven't," I agreed. I was so tempted to tell her what had happened at the vocal lesson. The need to tell someone was building and building inside me like a balloon, filling with air. I was afraid that if I didn't say something, I might explode with excitement.

And yet, I recalled my promise to Michael. He had asked me if I could keep a secret; in other words, could I be mature? How could I betray him the first chance I had? What if Trisha said something to someone without realizing it, and it got back to Michael?

I bit down on my lower lip to keep the words from spilling out.

"Well?" Trisha said, curling her legs under her and sitting back on them. "Tell me!" she squealed.

"Yes," I confessed, "I did meet someone."

"Oh, I knew it. You had the look in your face from the first moment I set eyes on you. So? Who is he? He's a senior, right? It's not Erik Richards, is it? I saw him looking at you the other day and whispering to his friends. He has such dreamy eyes! It is Erik, isn't it?" she concluded quickly.

"No," I said. "It's someone else." I bit down on my lower lip again to think a moment. I could tell her without telling her, I realized.

"Then who is it? Tell me!"

"He's not a student at Bernhardt."

"He's not?" She deflated quickly from disappointment, but then rose again with an even greater curiosity.

"No. He's older, a lot older," I added. Her eyes widened even more and her mouth dropped open. "I met him at George's Luncheonette," I said, spilling it out as soon as I concocted it. "We talked and talked and then he began to meet me at the school . . . to walk me home. He walked me home today."

"How old is he?" Trisha asked and held her breath.

"He's easily in his early thirties," I said.

"Thirties!"

I nodded.

"What's his name?"

For a moment I was stumped. My mind spun like a top passing every boy's name I had ever known.

"Allan," I said. "Allan Higgins. But you must swear and promise not to say a word to anyone."

"I won't. Of course, I won't," she said, drawing her fingers across her mouth as if she were closing a zipper. "What does he look like?"

"He's tall, six feet two or three, and he has eyes the color of almonds and dark brown hair. He has a very sensitive face, the kind of face you can look into and trust. He's very, very polite and considerate. We've had some wonderful talks while he walked with me."

"But a man in his thirties!" Trisha shook her head. "What would he want with you?" Her eyes brightened with another outrageous thought. "He's not married, is he?"

"He was, but his wife died after they had been married only three short years. He said he hasn't even looked at another woman until now, and the only reason he looked at me was because I reminded him of her."

"What does he do?" Trisha asked in a breathy voice.

"He's a business executive. I know he's doing well because he has an apartment on Park Avenue. He's invited me there," I said. "Tonight," I added.

"Tonight! What are you going to do?" she asked.

"I want to go, but I don't want Agnes to know where I'm going, of course. I'll tell her I have a special piano lesson and I have to go to the library to do research for a term paper. Will you help me and back me up if she asks any questions?"

"But to go to his apartment, a man you just met and a man in his thirties!"

"I can trust him; I know I can. He's so sweet. We're just going to listen to music and talk."

She shook her head, astonished.

"Was he ever at the luncheonette when you and I were there together?"

"Yes, he was, but he didn't have the nerve to speak to me, which shows you how timid and polite he is."

"I don't remember anyone like that," she said sadly. "Will you introduce me to him?"

"When he's ready. Right now he's understandably reluctant to meet anyone."

I waited to see how she would accept my story.

"All right," she said, "I'll back you up at dinner if Agnes asks you any questions, but be careful," she warned.

"Thank you. I knew I could trust you."

"Over thirty," she muttered to herself. I hid my smile and turned to my homework so I would have nothing to keep me from going to Michael Sutton's.

Even though Michael had told me to come as I was dressed, I changed into a nicer sweater, my pink one with the mother-of-pearl buttons. It had been one of the first things my mother had bought me in preparation for my attending Bernhardt, and when I put it on now, I noticed it was tighter around my bosom. I slipped into a dark blue, pleated wool skirt and chose a pair of dark blue loafers. I wore my hair loose and down and borrowed Trisha's tiny pearl earrings.

"Why are you so dressed tonight?" Agnes asked suspiciously. I told her I had to return to the school for a special piano lesson and there might be some people there to listen. I mentioned that I had to do some work on a term paper, too. Trisha played along by complaining about the assignments, flashing conspiratorial glances at me from time to time. I almost got caught in my lie on the way out when Agnes noticed I didn't have any books in my hands.

"I'm just reading and gathering information at the library tonight," I told her quickly. "I'm working with another girl." She accepted my explanation and I left.

Michael lived in a fancy apartment house. The lobby had a gold marble floor, red leather sofas and chairs, glass tables in brass frames and a long box filled with bright flowers and plants. A doorman showed me to the elevator, and my finger trembled with excitement as I pressed on Michael's door buzzer. A moment later he appeared dressed in a beautiful charcoal-gray suit made of the softest cashmere wool I had ever seen or felt.

"Hi," he said. "Very prompt. My other guests should take lessons," he added and stepped back.

His apartment was luxurious, from the marble entryway to the sunken living room in which he had a circular silk sofa, a large glass-top table in a black metal frame, and an enormous fireplace. The floor was covered with a deep, soft, marshmallow-white rug. The floor-to-ceiling windows were hung with off-white satin drapes. Right now, they were pulled back to provide an unobstructed view of the night skyline.

I stepped into the living room and instantly recognized the music playing on the stereo to be Tchaikovsky's "Sleeping Beauty."

"What a beautiful apartment," I said.

"Thank you. A little home away from home," he said, closing the door behind me. "You didn't tell anyone you were coming here, did you?" he asked, squinting with concern.

"Oh, no."

"Good." He smiled and indicated I should have a seat on the couch.

"I shouldn't offer you any cocktails," he said, following behind me, "but I guess I can give you a little white wine. Would you like that?"

"Oh, yes," I said.

"Just make yourself comfortable."

I went to the center of the sofa and sat down. I was so nervous I didn't know what to do with my hands. First, I folded them on my lap. Then I thought that looked silly, made me look like a school girl at her desk, so I put my right arm over the back of the sofa and dropped my left over my lap. I crossed and uncrossed my legs.

"You look very nice," Michael said, bringing me my glass of wine.

"Thank you." I took the glass with both hands, afraid that my trembling would cause me to spill some on the sofa.

"Actually," he said, sitting beside me, "I'm glad you arrived before the others. It gives me a chance to get to know you even better without any distractions." He took a sip from whatever he had in his glass and put the glass on the coaster on the table. Then he leaned so close to me, we were practically touching.

"Let's see," he continued, that impish glint returning to his sapphire-blue eyes. "I know you attended a private school in Richmond and you sang a solo there at the spring musical and you were a spectacular success."

"I was just one of many people performing that night," I said.

"Uh, huh. And then your family realized you were talented and sent you to Bernhardt. Do you miss being away from home?"

"No," I said, perhaps too quickly. He raised his eyebrows. Then he nodded to himself.

"That's right. You were away from home when you went to that private school, but you're not with your brother and sister anymore. Doesn't that bother you?"

"We don't get along that well," I said, unable to hide a smirk.

"I understand. I don't get along that well with my two brothers. We rarely see each other and they never come to any of my performances. You're lucky to have a family that's at least supportive," he said. "It's paid off; they've raised a very nice young lady, as well as a talented one."

"Thank you," I said, but it was nearly inaudible and I couldn't keep the tears from breaking free of my lids.

"Something wrong?"

I bowed my head as the tears streaked down my cheeks and dropped off my chin. I hated all this deception, all these lies. Michael was so sincere and so devoted to his singing and had been so wonderful to me, making me feel so special, and here I was telling him one false thing after another.

He reached out and lifted my chin.

"Dawn?"

When I gazed into his dark eyes, I saw the confusion.

"Oh Michael, I don't really have any family," I said. "My mother lives in her bedroom most of the time, doting on herself and being waited on hand and foot. My sister hates me, is very envious of me, and my brother . . . my brother . . ."

"Yes?"

I started to cry harder, sob like a baby. My shoulders shook. He put his arm around me quickly.

"Now, now, it can't be all that bad. Whatever it is, it's behind you. You're away from it and you're here at Bernhardt and working with me," he said. He kissed my forehead and brushed away some strands of my hair that had fallen over my eyes. Then he reached into his smoking jacket pocket and produced a handkerchief with which to wipe away my tears. As he did so, I gazed into his eyes. I felt like an instrument of yearning, filled with a ravenous desire for romantic fulfillment and I know he saw it in my face, for his expression changed into a more thoughtful one.

"There's something bewitching about you, Dawn. I knew it the first time I set eyes on you at the audition. One second I look at you and you are a naive, young girl, and then I blink and your face changes and you become a provocative, seductive woman, a woman who seems to know exactly what she's doing."

He was mistaken, I thought. I never intended to be seductive. I hadn't started to cry for that reason. I shook my head and mouthed a "No," but he placed his right hand gently on my cheek.

"Oh yes, you do," he said. "Maybe you're not aware of it yourself, aware of your feminine power, the power you have and will have over men."

"Some women, women like you," he continued, "can turn a man into a boy in seconds . . . just like that," he added, snapping his fingers, "and make them beg, plead for a favorable look, a touch, a kiss. I've been all over the world, you know, and I have seen these women, have made a fool of myself from time to time over them. So I know from where I speak."

His eyes shone beautifully with unused tears. How deeply he felt the things he said, I thought. He was right when he told me that great actors, great singers, all great performers feel things more deeply.

"I don't mean to make it sound bad. You can't be bad. You can only be wonderful. If any man suffers because of you, it's his own fault," he added, sounding almost furious about it. Then his face softened again. He smiled and touched my cheek, gently.

"You will put this power to great use on the stage, believe me," he said. "The audience will feel it."

I started to smile, but he remained very serious.

"You haven't had many boyfriends, have you?" he asked.

"No."

"I'm glad," he said so definitely that I looked at him with surprise. "I like working with someone who is pure and innocent. When you sing with me, it will be like making love, making love for the first time each time we sing together."

I held my breath. He paused, but I didn't know what to say or what he expected of me. Sing with him? Where? When? Silence thicker than a fog came between us. He didn't take his eyes off mine. Then the tips of his fingers glided down my cheek and over my lips.

"I was very impressed with you today," he whispered, "especially after I kissed you at the end of the song. You really did understand. Do you know the difference between a stage kiss and a real kiss?"

I shook my head.

"A stage kiss looks passionate, but the two people hold back the passion. I've had to kiss women I could barely tolerate looking at.

"But I didn't have that problem with you today," he added quickly. "There was already something between us, some invisible cord tying us to each other, pulling us to each other. In fact, I'm having trouble keeping my lips away from yours right now. Does that frighten you?"

"No," I said, even though it did. It made me tremble like a little girl to hear him say such things, things I had dreamt he would say to me.

He took my wine glass from me and put it on the table. Then he turned back to me, moving his face toward mine slowly, and ever so slowly, brought his lips to my lips. I closed my eyes the moment we touched. This time my lips parted beneath his prolonged kiss. I gasped because his tongue touched mine, but I didn't pull away. When he lifted his lips from my mouth, I started to open my eyes, but he kissed them shut, kissing my eyelids softly and then kissing my cheek and moving down to my neck.

"Oh Dawn," he whispered, "you are a lovely creature, a most exquisite young woman. I have seen beautiful women all over the world and you are one of the most beautiful."

Me? I thought. One of the most beautiful women in the world? He must be saying these things and doing these things just to make me feel better.

"You and I will be spectacular together. I will make you into one of the greatest singing stars. I can't wait until you and I sing together, for we will put this passion we feel toward each other into our music and our music will be extraordinary. Do you want that?"

What could I say? I had fantasized about my picture on billboards, my name in lights. And here was Michael Sutton telling me the whole world would know about me. We would be on Broadway together. We would be in movies. Grandmother Cutler would die a thousand deaths. She would hear and see my name everywhere.

"Yes," I said, thrilled that at long last I would prove Grandmother Cutler wrong. "Oh yes, yes."

"Good." He pressed himself closer to me. "You must not be afraid of deep feelings and feeling deep passion. You will need to find these feelings when you sing. They are hidden inside you, waiting to be discovered. I'll help you find them," he said, and I felt his hands slide down my arms to my waist. His fingers slipped under my sweater and his palms were against my naked skin as his hands climbed quickly to my breasts. He pressed them and leaned against me more so that I had to slide back along the sofa. A moment later, he was looking down at me.

"I want to be the first to bring you to ecstasy," he whispered, "the first to take you to heights you've only read about or dreamt about. I knew that today, understood it at the end of our lesson. It's only fitting we share the greatest moments together, that I be the one to introduce you to real passion, for I will be the one who will bring you to your ultimate singing capabilities. You can't sing about the ultimate moment of love if you haven't experienced it.

"You understand what I'm saying, don't you, don't you?" he demanded, a frantic note in his voice. I was both terrified and electrified, excited and frightened, but I could do nothing more than nod and close my eyes as his fingers continued to caress my breasts.

"Dawn," he whispered, "the first light of day." He backed off the sofa and knelt down beside it to slip his hands under me. Then he lifted me into his arms. He kissed the tip of my nose and started to carry me toward his bedroom.

"But . . ." I turned toward the doorway. "Your other guests . . ."

He smiled and shook his head.

"They were very rude being so late. We won't answer the door, should they come," he said and continued to carry me across the living room. He leaned against his bedroom door and it swung open.

A small lamp on the night stand by his bed cast a soft glow over the room. The blanket had been drawn down on the bed. Michael lowered me gently to the sheets. He took off his jacket and the crisp white shirt beneath it quickly and leaned over me, flooding my face with kisses. I started to open my eyes when he pulled back, but he put the tips of his fingers on them and whispered, "Don't open your eyes until I tell you to."

I heard the sounds of the rest of his clothing being taken off and then I felt him beside me. I started to open my eyes again, but he brought his lips to them so I would keep them closed. Then he lifted my sweater up and over my head and he continued to undress me while I lay there quietly, gazing into the darkness behind my eyelids, my heart pounding.

"Now open your eyes," he said softly.

With his eyes he began his lovemaking, and in his eyes I drowned, afraid to look at anything else. He lay beside me at first, not touching, not kissing, not moving. His chest was barely inches from my naked breasts. My body tingled everywhere in expectation of his touch. The anticipation was like torture.

"You are stunning, almost too beautiful to disturb, like a magnificent flower that should only be admired and never plucked. But I don't have that kind of restraint and then again, you should not be denied the splendid ecstasy that comes when two talented and beautiful people make love."

With that he brought his lips firmly to mine. Skin to skin we pressed, just holding close at first and thrilling in the exaltation of sharing what the other had to give. With each touch of his lips, of his hands I was shot through with electrifying sensations, until at last I was wild to have him enter me, no longer tender, but fervent with his own fierce, demanding need to reach the same heights I was seeking.

He cupped my breasts in his hands and kissed the tops of each, each kiss feeling like a drop of warm rain. His hands endlessly roamed and sought all my most intimate places. Then he turned and twisted until he had fixed himself over me. He lifted my legs and closed them like a scissors around his waist. I uttered soft cries as he pressed on, calling to me over and over as if seeking me to do more, but I wasn't sure what more I should do. He was still the teacher and I was still the student.

Finally, hot juices spurted forth to warm up my insides pleasantly and then it was all over. Spent, he fell forward, his body fully over mine, his breathing as heavy and as fast as mine. For a few moments, he did nothing else nor said anything. Then he kissed me quickly on the forehead and rose.

"Wasn't it wonderful?" he said. "Wasn't it like hitting the greatest notes, feeling yourself soar to the greatest heights? Well?" he said with some irritation when I didn't respond immediately. But I was thinking about it, trying to relive the moments and see if I could recall the feeling being as magnificent as he had said.

The problem was I had been so concerned about being a good lover and doing everything right, I thought I might have missed some of the ecstasy he assured me had been there.

"Yes," I said quickly.

He smiled with satisfaction.

"I told you passion makes us desperate, but being desperate brings us to the height of our very being, the ultimate of our essence, places us in exquisite danger. You will sing great songs," he declared and laughed.

"I'm hungry," he said. "Making love always increases my appetite." He started to dress quickly. I sat up and began to put on my clothing. "Would you like something to eat?"

"No," I said. "Thank you. I'll just use the bathroom a moment."

"Of course. Come out when you're finished and watch me eat something. You can finish your wine. Then," he said, nodding more like a teacher now than a lover, "I'll call a cab for you and you will get back so you don't miss your curfew."

He left me alone. As I finished my dressing, I gazed around his bedroom, and as if I had been in a daze the whole time, I suddenly realized where I was and what I had done.

What had I done!

I had made love without the slightest restraint or hesitation. I had permitted Michael to carry me off and seduce me, but I believed, I prayed, that his words were honest and sincere. He did see me as someone beautiful, someone to cherish, someone to love because I was like him. We were blessed with a talent that made us different, made us feel things more intently. It was good; it was meant to be that two people such as he and I would find ecstasy together.

And yet, I couldn't help feeling guilty. Was Grandmother Cutler right about me? Was I the spawn of some evil, sinful act between my mother and an itinerant singer who didn't care about the consequences of his actions? Was I as spoiled and as vain as my mother who wanted to be treated like a princess and be young and beautiful forever and ever?

Just like my mother, I had my singer lover, I thought.

But Michael was different; he had to be. He wasn't some wandering crooner looking for a good time and not caring about his career and his art. Michael loved me because he saw something exceptional in me. We would be beautiful together; we would sing duets on the stage, duets that people would remember forever and ever because we sang to each other sincerely, with a passion that made our voices even greater.

No, I declared to myself, I would not feel bad; I would not feel guilty. I would feel fulfilled and I would be fulfilled. Michael had turned me into a woman, his woman, and I would wear my new identity with pride; although for a while at least, I would have to keep it all secret.

8
VOWS OF LOVE

I joined Michael in his kitchen and watched him make himself a sandwich and coffee. He insisted I have a cup of coffee and sit with him as he ate. He described how pleased he was with his work at the Bernhardt School and how excited and happy he was to be back in New York.

"Although," he said, "I thoroughly enjoyed traveling through Europe and singing in the great theaters with their wonderful histories, singing before the richest, most cultured audiences. I have played in Rome, Paris and London. I have even performed in Budapest, Hungary," he bragged.

I sat there hypnotized by his voice and the stories he told me about his travels and performances.

Suddenly, he leaned back in his chair and stared at me in a more scrutinizing manner, his head tilted to the right, his eyes fixed on mine.

"Earlier," he said, "when you were complaining about your family, you never mentioned your father. What is he like? Is he still alive?"

I thought for a long moment. Michael had taken me into his life, touched me in the most intimate ways a man could touch a woman, trusted me, wanted me. I didn't want to permit anything false between us. His eyes were full of concern and sincere interest. I believed him when he had said that music had already wed us to each other, bound us in ways other people could not understand.

"I don't know what my father is like," I began and told him my story. He listened without moving a muscle. Our roles had been reversed: now he was mesmerized by me and my tale of kidnapping and discovery, being returned to a family I despised and learning the truth of my abduction. "I know everything," I concluded, "except my father's name."

Michael nodded slowly, his dark eyes thoughtful as he digested what I had told him.

"Your grandmother sounds like a strong-willed and powerful old woman. She would tell you nothing about your real father?"

"No, and my mother is so terrified of her, she won't reveal anything either."

He nodded, lowering his eyes sadly. Then he looked up, brightening with an idea.

"Perhaps I can help you find your real father," he said.

"Oh Michael, can you? How? If you could do that, it would be the most wonderful gift you could ever give me," I cried.

"I have some good friends, agent friends, who must know agents who placed these singers and performers in resort hotels during the period you described. I'll get them to investigate and come up with some names for us. At least, we can narrow it down and proceed from there," he concluded.

"He might be a performer working in New York. You might even know him!"

"Very possibly," Michael agreed. "Let me work on it. In the meantime, young lady," he said, sitting back, "we had better get you on your way. Besides obeying your curfew at the residence, I'd like you to be fresh and energetic when I work with you. For obvious reasons, however, I won't be able to treat you any differently from the way I treat my other students. And you must continue to keep everything we do and say to each other under lock and key."

"I will," I said. "Here in my heart," I added, my hand over my breast.

"You are so lovely . . ." he trailed off.

I couldn't help blushing at the compliment. He got up to kiss me on the cheek and then phoned down to the doorman to hail a taxi cab for me. At his apartment doorway, he kissed me softly on the lips and pressed his cheek to mine.

"Good night, my little diva," he whispered.

I felt like I floated to the elevator. When I descended to the lobby, the doorman had my taxi waiting. He escorted me out and opened the cab door for me, tipped his hat and said good night. I gave the driver my address and sat back, lost in the memory of all that had happened.

Michael had singled me out and made love to me first through my music and then the way a man and a woman were meant to make love. I wondered if Michael's other guests had arrived and knocked on the door. I felt that we'd never have heard their annoyed knockings and ringings, so intent had we been on our own world, on our own happiness.

I didn't think about Trisha until I started to open our bedroom door. I should have known she would be waiting anxiously for my return and would want me to tell her every detail of my secret evening with the older man I had invented. She was lying in bed, doing her homework, but she slapped all her books closed the instant I entered the room.

"I couldn't wait until you got back," she said. "Tell me everything." She sat up and folded her hands on her lap. Just as before, I decided to mix fantasy and fact. As I got ready for bed, I began.

"He has a beautiful apartment in a very fancy building with a doorman in the lobby." I described Michael's apartment in detail, feeling confident Trisha would never go there. "He has pictures of his dead wife in every room," I added. "One great big one over the fireplace, and it's true: we do look a lot alike. She was even my size in dresses and shoes, and he's kept all her clothing. He wanted to give me some things, but I refused to take anything. I did try a few things on and everything was a perfect fit."

"That's eerie," Trisha said, eyes wide.

"Yes, but maybe it was Fate that brought us together. Some things are just meant to be."

"You mean you're going to see him again and again?"

"Oh yes, but always secretly," I emphasized. "I told him we shouldn't even meet at the school anymore. If Agnes should somehow find out, she would be sure to phone Grandmother Cutler, and she might use it as an excuse to ship me off someplace else. You can't imagine how spiteful she can be."

"What did you do at his apartment?"

"We drank a little wine, listened to music and talked."

"What did you talk about so long?" Trisha asked, looking skeptical.

"First, he talked about himself and his wonderful marriage, how much he had loved his wife and how much she had loved him. It was very sad. I cried. And then I told him my story and he cried for me. He had lost his parents at a young age and knew what it was to feel like an orphan.

"But do you know what he's going to do? He's going to see if he can help me find my real father. He has friends in important places, just like Grandmother Cutler, and he's going to make some inquiries and have some people do some research. He said he might even hire a private detective to track him down."

"He did? But that could be very expensive," Trisha said.

"He said that money doesn't matter to him when it comes to me. He wanted to give me some of his wife's jewelry and expensive perfume, but I told him I would have trouble explaining where I got them. He's very understanding and doesn't want to do anything that might cause trouble for me."

Trisha's eyes grew smaller, more perceptive.

"You must have done more than just talk with a man in his thirties," she insisted. I looked away quickly and began hanging up my things. "You did, didn't you?"

"We kissed," I admitted, "and I wanted to do more, but Alvin said we must not rush headlong into things."

"Alvin? I thought you said his name was Allan."

"It is. Did I say Alvin?" She nodded. "I can't imagine why. Oh," I said. "He has a younger brother named Alvin. I'm just so tired and confused and full of happiness." Trisha looked skeptical a moment, but then accepted my explanation.

"When will you see him again?"

"Soon," I said, "but for obvious reasons, we have to be very discreet about it. He won't call me unless it's very, very important."

"You're having a secret romance," she said unhappily. She sat back against her pillow and folded her arms under her bosom, her face in a pout. I sat at the foot of her bed.

"What's wrong, Trisha?"

"Nothing," she said. Then she looked up at me. "You're having all this romance and adventure, and I can't get anyone good-looking to say more than two words to me." Then, just as quickly as she had gone into a pout, she snapped out of it and smiled. "I think I'll start flirting with Erik Richards, since you're not interested in him," she said. "He did sit near me at lunch yesterday, and he didn't ask me a single question about you."

"Erik Richards? Of course," I said excitedly. "I think you and he would be perfect together."

"Maybe he'll ask me to the Halloween dance," she concluded. She turned to me. "What if someone from the school asks you?"

"Oh, I couldn't go. I couldn't be with anyone else now. I'd only be thinking of . . . Allan," I said, "and it wouldn't be fair to the boy who had asked me."

"But you'll miss all the good school fun. Are you sure you want to have a boyfriend so much older than you are?" she asked.

"As I told you," I sang and stood up, "it's something Fate brought about."

I ran to the bathroom to wash and brush my teeth. I hated lying to Trisha. She had been such a good friend to me, right from the beginning. Looking in the mirror I saw the face of a liar. I'd felt so happy earlier with Michael, but could love turn me into a loathsome thing? How ironic and sad if I finally found love and happiness and safety and in doing so did things every bit as evil and dishonest as the things Grandmother Cutler did. I eased my conscience by telling myself that someday, perhaps someday soon, Michael would let me tell her the truth. I looked again into the mirror studying the girl's face caught in there. My face was flushed from everything that had transpired tonight. My eyes glittered in a way I'd never seen before—I saw power within them. The truth was, I'd never again be able to go to some dance with some silly school boy, not for the reasons I'd told Trisha, but because I now knew the joy of love with a masterful older man.

Michael was true to his word when he said he wouldn't treat me any differently from the way he treated his other students at Bernhardt. In fact, I thought he was even colder and more formal with me since our evening together in his apartment. He stopped calling me Dawn in front of other students and called me Miss Cutler, instead. Whenever we passed by in the corridors, he smiled quickly, but just as quickly shifted his gaze back to whomever he was with as if he were afraid whoever accompanied him would immediately feel the electricity that crackled between us.

For the next few weeks, he had Richard Taylor present at every one of our private sessions and when he worked with me, he acted as though he were ages and ages older than I was. He didn't put his hands on me, nor did he speak about anything other than our music, and he always excused me before he excused Richard so we couldn't be alone together even for a moment afterward.

I worked and waited for him to ask to see me again. I hardly ever left the house at all, for fear I might miss a phone call. I knew if I weren't there, he wouldn't leave his name. Trisha became very suspicious as to why I hadn't gone on any other dates with my secret boyfriend.

"You haven't mentioned Allan for days and days," she said, "nor have you gone out secretly at night to meet him. Did he run off with another woman?"

"Oh, no. He had to go away on business," I told her, "but he will see me the moment he returns."

Finally, one afternoon after my private vocal lesson, Michael asked me to remain. We waited for Richard Taylor to leave and then Michael closed the door.

"Oh, Dawn," he said, coming to me quickly and taking my hands into his, "I'm so sorry I've been so terribly distant these past few weeks. I know you must think I'm horrible and I'm deliberately ignoring you."

"It bothered me," I admitted. "I was afraid you thought I had given away our secret. I kept hoping you would speak to me soon. I didn't want to do anything to endanger you at the school."

"I know," he said. "You've been wonderful about it. Very patient." He kissed me quickly on the cheek and stepped back. "A few days after you came to my apartment, the head of the school called me in to speak to me about my methods. It seems other teachers were whispering about me behind my back. I know it's just professional jealousy. They've all gotten wind of my criticism of their techniques, and some of them can't stand the attention I receive while they are hardly recognized.

"Anyway, the head asked me if I would be somewhat more formal in my student-teacher relationships. I thought perhaps someone had seen us together when I took you for coffee that day, or maybe Richard had even sensed something and told people. Naturally, I was afraid for you, too, so I thought we should cool it. I'm sorry if I've hurt you," he added.

"Oh Michael," I cried, "you can't hurt me. I understand."

"I thought you would," he said, smiling and taking my hands into his again. "Anyway, I can't stand being this way with you and not seeing you when I want to, when I need to. Can you come to my apartment again tonight, the same way, without anyone knowing?"

"Yes," I said quickly, thrilled that he had finally asked me to return.

"Wonderful." He let go of my hands and hurried to gather his things. "I've got to move along to my next appointment. Come at the same time. Don't disappoint me," he pleaded and left.

I was so excited about Michael and our rendezvous, I didn't hear a word spoken in any of my other classes and hated the clock for ticking so slowly. The only one who noticed anything different about me, however, was Madame Steichen. She interrupted our lesson and my playing by slapping her wooden pointer so hard over the top of the piano, it splintered into three different pieces and flew off in three different directions. I practically jumped off the piano stool.

"What do you call this . . . this stupid tapping on the keys?" she sneered, her face twisted and witchlike.

"Practicing," I said softly.

"No," she flared, her eyes red with rage, "this is not practice; this is wasting time. I told you, you can't play like an artist if you don't connect your very being with every note. Your fingers cannot be separated from your very soul. Concentration, concentration, concentration. What are you thinking about while you play?"

"Nothing," I said.

"That's what your playing is . . . nothing, just sounds. Will you concentrate or are you here to waste my time?" she demanded with ice in her words.

"I'll concentrate," I said, my eyes burning with tears.

"Begin again," she said. "And rid your mind of whatever it is that is distracting you."

She peered down at me, her eyes small, almost like two microscope lenses scrutinizing my face.

"I don't like what I see in your eyes," she said. "Something is corrupting you from within and it is affecting your music. Beware of whatever it is," she advised and then stepped back, folded her bony arms under her small bosom and glared in anticipation.

I shakily began again, this time putting all my concentration into my playing, forcing my thoughts away from Michael. Madame Steichen wasn't happy, but she wasn't dissatisfied enough to interrupt. At the end of the lesson, she stood before me, her shoulders lifted, her neck so straight and tight, it looked like the neck of a statue, and her head very still.

"You must make up your mind," she said slowly, her words sharp and cutting, "whether you want to be a performer or an artist." Her eyes took on a glassy stare. I had to bow my head and look down.

"An artist," she continued, "lives for her work. That's the difference between an artist and a performer, who is usually a person infatuated with himself and not with the beauty of what he creates. Fame," she lectured, "is often more of a burden than a blessing. This country is very foolish when it comes to its entertainers, celebrities," she said, spitting the words. "They worship them and then suffer when they discover their gods of stage and screen have feet of clay.

"Keep your feet on the ground and your head out of the clouds," she preached. "Do you understand?"

I nodded, my head still bowed. She spoke as if she knew about Michael and me. But how could she? Unless . . . Richard Taylor, I thought, my heart racing with fear.

"Dismissed," she snapped and pivoted quickly to march out of the music suite. I was left listening to the clicking of her heels as she walked down the corridor, each click feeling like a slap across my face.

I hurried out of the school and, without lifting my eyes, charged across the campus to the sidewalk. I rushed across streets, not seeing anyone.

It was a gloomy, overcast late fall day. The sky was a sea of bruised, angry-looking clouds threatening to drop a cold, hard rain over the city. The wind found every opening in my jacket and filled me with a chill that made me walk even faster. When I arrived at the apartment house, I charged up the stairs and through the doorway. I wanted to run up to my room and bury my face in my pillow.

But a package on the small table in the entryway caught my eye. It was where Agnes left all our mail. This package was very big and covered with stamps. I recognized the handwriting immediately: it was a package from Germany, from Jimmy. I scooped it into my arms and hurried down the corridor to the stairway.

Trisha wasn't back from a late dance practice, so I was alone. I sat on my bed and slowly unwrapped the package. Then I lifted the cover off the box and gazed down at a beautifully embroidered satin pillow with silk tassels. It was bright pink with hearts and forget-me-nots. The letters were in black and spelled out I LOVE YOU in German as well as in English. For a moment I just held it on my lap, unable to move, unable to think.

I hadn't thought very much about Jimmy these past few weeks. When his letters arrived, they sat for days on my dresser unopened. And then when I finally opened them and read them, I read them quickly, almost as though I was afraid of his words, afraid to read how much he loved me, afraid to hear his voice in my mind and see his face before me.

He had already noticed something different about my last letter. It was much shorter than any of the others and I hadn't written over and over just how much I missed him. He wondered if I were sick and he hoped his gift from Germany would cheer me up. In the letter with the pillow, he wrote, "Just knowing you're lying back with your head on this pillow makes me feel good. For me it's like you were lying back with your head on my lap."

I threw the letter down and covered my face with my hands. I didn't want to betray Jimmy, and yet, I couldn't help loving Michael. I knew how it was going to break Jimmy's heart to learn about Michael and me when it finally came out. I couldn't stand the idea that he would hate me for it.

Twice I sat down and tried to write a letter to Jimmy explaining what had happened and how it was nothing I could have planned on happening. It was just part of my musical life, I wrote, but that didn't sound any better than anything else I had written. In the end, I tore up both letters and decided I would wait to write him.

I put the satin pillow back in its box and hid it away in my closet. If I kept it on my bed, I would see and feel it every day, and every day I would hate myself for the moment when Jimmy would find out about Michael and me.

"I have a present for you," Michael said as soon as he opened his apartment door to greet me. "It's on my bed. Go put it on," he added, stepping back. He was holding a glass of wine and had soft music playing and the lights low. "I'll pour a glass of wine for you."

"What is it?" I asked, a little alarmed. He looked like he had already drunk quite a bit of wine himself.

"Just go and see," he said.

I moved quickly through the apartment to his bedroom. There was a long, white box on the bed. I opened it and looked down at a sheer, pink silk nightgown, so filmy and transparent I might as well be naked. Did he want me to put this on now? I wondered.

"Do you like it?" he asked from the doorway.

"It's very nice," I said.

"Very nice?" He stepped up behind me and took my shoulders in his hands before kissing me softly on the back of the neck. "It's very expensive, too. Put it on. Nothing else," he added. "I've dreamt all day about you in it," he said and kissed me behind the ear before turning to return to the living room.

His kisses had made me tingle all over, and just the thought of wearing nothing but this nightgown made me tremble and my heart pitter-patter.

Slowly, I got undressed and then slipped the nightgown over my head. It felt no heavier than a breeze. I gazed at myself in the mirror and saw how my nudity was quite visible. Wrapping my arms around myself, I walked slowly to the bedroom doorway and peered out. Michael had put on one of his own recordings. He was sitting back on the sofa, a tight, amused smile on his face. When he saw me, his smile widened and he sat forward.

"Come in. Don't be so shy," he said. "You look absolutely breathtaking." He poured another glass of wine and held it out for me to take. I walked toward him, my arms still wrapped around my bosom.

"I'm embarrassed," I said, hesitating.

"Don't be," he replied, his face becoming very serious and intent. "Not with me, not ever with me." He put down the glass of wine, stood up and kissed my forehead. Then he pried my arms apart gently and looked down at me, his eyes full of desire. We kissed, a long kiss, but a soft one. Wonder filled me. He did love me. It was in his voice, in the way he held me.

"You're trembling. Are you cold?" he asked.

"No, not cold."

"You poor thing, so innocent still. I told you," he said firmly, "we are special people, linked forever and ever by our talent and music. You believe me, don't you?" he asked. I nodded.

"I know what we will do," he said, smiling again, his eyes twinkling impishly, "we will make it official."

"Official?"

"Of course. We will bind ourselves formally by taking formal oaths. Just like a wedding ceremony," he added and took my hand in his to turn me about so he and I faced the mirror. In the subdued lighting, we looked like phantoms. It was as if we were in another room and our shadows had met secretly for their own clandestine lovemaking.

Michael had us step closer to the mirror. He looked so slim and sensual. One of his love ballads was playing on the stereo, almost as if he had planned it perfectly.

"Now, Michael Sutton," he said, facing the mirror, "do you take this beautiful, young singer, this siren of song, this new goddess of the stage and screen, to have and to hold, to protect and to cherish, to be your lifelong romantic lead until the curtain is drawn down and the applause finally ends?

"I do," he replied to his own question.

"And you, Dawn Cutler," he said, turning toward me and making his voice deep and serious, "do you take this handsome young man, this shooting star of the musical stage and screen, to have and to hold, to protect and to cherish, to be your romantic lifelong romantic lead until the curtain is drawn and the applause finally ends?"

I stared up at him, my lips trembling. Oh, how I wished this were truly a real ceremony and we were taking these vows in a big, fancy church, before a clergyman with hundreds of special guests present, people from the theater and the newspapers. Of course, all the Cutlers would be there, especially Grandmother Cutler, chafing at the bit, but forced to smile every time someone congratulated her. Clara Sue would be burning up inside from envy and my mother would have to deal with someone other than herself being the center of attention.

"Well?" Michael asked again.

"Yes," I said. "I do."

He turned back to the mirror.

"Then by the power invested in me by the gods and goddesses of the theater, I hereby declare you Michael and you Dawn to be male and female leads for the rest of your natural lives. You may kiss the bride with real passion and not with a stage kiss," he said, turned and scooped me into his arms for a long, hard kiss, his tongue searching for mine. He followed it with a shower of kisses over my forehead and cheeks. Then he lifted me into his arms, laughing.

"Time for the honeymoon," he whispered and carried me back to his bedroom.

This time our lovemaking was different. It lasted three times as long as the first time, and I cried out often, each time finding myself at a greater height of ecstasy, just as he had promised. Then, when I thought we were finished, he started to turn me and pull me over him. Unsure of what was happening, I became stiff.

"Relax," he said. "There's another way," he whispered and guided me until I was riding him.

When our lovemaking ended, we lay still, listening to each other's quickened breath, our hearts still pounding.

"Now that's a honeymoon," Michael finally said and kissed me on the cheek. The tiny glow of the small lamp made his eyes shine. He touched the tip of my nose. "Are you happy?" he asked.

I didn't know how long the rapture between Michael and me would last. I longed for passion undying, for ecstasy everlasting. Yet my suspicious self guessed that nothing as glorious as what Michael and I had could go on indefinitely. He would soon tire of me, a child whose experiences and sophistication couldn't compare with his or the other women he knew.

"I am happy," I said, "but every time I've been happy in my life, something has come along to destroy it."

"That won't happen this time. We were meant to live fantasy lives, lives that go on happily ever after, just like in the movies or in the great novels. You must not be afraid to enjoy life and enjoy it with me."

"I don't want to be afraid," I said. "I want everything you said to come true."

"Then it will," he declared and waved his hand in the air. "I wave my magic wand over us. Nothing can stop us or hurt us or come between us."

"Oh Michael, do you mean that? Really mean that?"

"Of course," he said. "Didn't we take the oath before the magic mirror?" He kissed me again and then turned over on his back and put his hands behind his head. I rose to go into the bathroom.

When I looked at myself in the bathroom mirror, I saw my face was still quite flushed.

Still naked, Michael came up beside me and put his hands on my shoulders. He looked into the mirror as he kissed my neck, holding his lips there a very long time. Then he ran his lips over my shoulders and brought his hands back to my breasts, watching himself as if he and I were in a movie.

Later, Trisha took one look at me after I slipped into our bedroom and knew I had done more than listen to music and talk with my older man.

"That's a hickey on your neck," she said. The powder I had splashed over it was all but gone. "What happened tonight?" she asked. "And don't tell me you just sat sipping wine and talking."

"Oh Trisha, I made love and it was wonderful, more wonderful than I imagined it would be."

"I knew it," she said. "I knew that a man in his thirties wouldn't be satisfied only holding hands and talking."

"Oh, but Trisha," I said, "I'm really in love, more in love than I thought possible. And we've made promises, even taken oaths together."

"Oaths? What sort of oaths?"

"To have and to hold and to cherish each other, just like marriage vows," I told her, but she scrunched up her face and shook her head.

"My mother told me men will say anything to get you to do what they want."

"No," I said. "That's not the way it is with us. We're special together. He needs me, even more than I need him. He's been all over the world and has seen many different beautiful women, yet he wants me. Me!

"Oh please, please, Trisha," I begged, "be happy for me."

"I'm happy for you, but I can't help worrying about you also," she said.

Trisha's words were like cold raindrops trying to pierce the roof on my house of love. They bounced off and were then dried away by the bright light that came when I recalled Michael's loving smile. Trisha and I lay awake in bed for a long time talking. Rather, I did the talking and she did the listening.

I spun a tale of wonder and joy. I told her Allan was already making plans for the day I graduated. We would take a long honeymoon, on a luxury liner, and then return to New York to live in a fancy apartment while I auditioned for parts in musicals. A few times I became so involved in my story, I nearly said "Michael," instead of "Allan." I had to keep catching myself, stopping my tongue that wanted more than anything to be truthful.

"It sounds very nice," Trisha said when I finished. "Just be careful," she warned.

I fell asleep that night dreaming about Michael's and my mock wedding ceremony and praying with all my heart that what we had pretended would someday become reality.

I went to Michael's apartment at least once a week after that. After our lovemaking we would sip wine and listen to music and talk about our careers. Michael had many offers for roles to play waiting in the wings and promised that he would soon be arranging for me to have auditions so that I could join him on the stage.

"Of course," he said, "I wouldn't put you in a tryout until I believed you were ready. We will have to work harder and harder on your lessons and get you to the point where no one will want to turn you away."

He hadn't forgotten about his other promise to help me find my real father. He said that his agent friends were still looking into a history of performers who traveled the beach cities and would have played a hotel like Cutler's Cove. He claimed it wouldn't be long now before we would have a list of names and could go about crossing off those who were obviously not my father.

"What will we do with the names that remain?" I asked.

"Perhaps you will get your mother to tell you a little more and then we will be able to narrow it down to one or two. Let's wait to see how many there are first," he replied.

Of course, I was impatient and excited about someday confronting my real father. I had made up my mind he couldn't be worse than my mother. He was a victim, just like me.

The weeks passed more quickly for me now, and before I knew it, we were about to begin our Thanksgiving holiday. Everyone was leaving to spend it with their families. Michael asked me to remain behind after our private lesson that week and as soon as Richard Taylor left, he turned to me.

"What are you going to do with your holiday? Are you going back to the hotel?" he asked.

"I don't want to," I said, "and no one really wants me to. My mother hasn't phoned for weeks."

"Good," he said. "I'm not going anywhere either and I have an idea if you can find a way to manage it so no one knows."

"What idea?" I asked excitedly.

"I want you to come to my apartment and stay with me for the entire long weekend. We'll have our own holiday. Would you like that?"

"Oh yes, Michael," I said. "I would love it. I'll cook our Thanksgiving dinner. I'm a good cook, you know."

He laughed at my exuberance.

"I don't doubt you are. But no one must know, of course, and we won't be able to go about the city together. People recognize me and if you are seen with me . . ."

"I'll find a way, Michael. I will," I promised and spent the rest of the day thinking about it. I considered telling Agnes I was returning to Cutler's Cove, but then I was afraid she would speak to Grandmother Cutler and they would discover I had been lying. I was desperate for an idea when Trisha gave me one by asking me if I would like to come home with her for the holidays.

"Oh, Trisha," I said, "I would, I really would, but at a different time. Allan has asked me to spend the holiday with him, only I didn't know how I could manage it until now. That is, if you will go along with it."

"What do you mean?" she asked.

"I'll tell Agnes I'm going home with you for Thanksgiving," I said.

From the way Trisha gazed at me, I didn't think she would agree. For a long moment, she just stared.

"You're getting so involved with him," she finally said. "Are you sure you should?"

"I've never been happier with anyone, nor could I be. As soon as I can, I will tell the world and he and I won't have to sneak about. I can't wait for that day, but until then . . . Oh Trisha," I said, "I know it's unfair to ask you to lie, but you don't really have to lie. If I'm ever discovered, I will take all the blame. I'll say I did promise to go home with you and you thought I would, but I changed my mind at the last moment and there was nothing you could do about it."

"I'm not worried about myself," she said. "I'm worried about you."

"Don't be," I said. "I couldn't be happier or feel safer than I do when I'm with him."

"All right," she said, "I'll help you if you're positive this is what you want to do."

"Oh, I am. Thank you, Trisha, thank you," I cried and embraced her. She smiled, but her eyes were filled with concern.

I, of course, could fill my eyes with nothing but Michael. Everywhere I looked, I imagined him. He was walking through the school grounds; he was crossing a street; he was gazing back at me in my mirror. He lived behind my eyelids. I heard his voice, his whispers of love. When I closed my eyes and envisioned him, I felt his lips on mine.

I told Agnes I was going home with Trisha for Thanksgiving, being sure to do it when Trisha wasn't with me.

"Does your grandmother know?" Agnes asked suspiciously.

"I told my mother the last time she called," I lied. I hated all these lies, building one false story on another to create a foundation of deceit, but I told myself they were good falsehoods because they were making it possible for something wonderful and true to happen. The people I was deceiving were conniving behind my back all the time, and besides, my family wouldn't care if they found out the truth. I was lying only because I didn't want to make trouble for Michael.

And so early in the afternoon at the beginning of our school break, Trisha and I took a cab together that was supposedly taking us to the bus station. Everyone wished each other a happy holiday and we left. After we drove away from the apartment house, I gave the driver Michael's address. The moment I did, Trisha turned to me with surprise.

"I thought you told me he had an apartment on Park Avenue," she said.

"Did I say apartment? I meant his business was on Park Avenue."

Trisha was impressed with the apartment building. She leaned out of the cab to hug me after I had stepped out.

"Have a wonderful holiday," I said. "And thank you for making it possible for me to have one too."

"Call me if you change your mind and really want to come," she said.

We kissed each other's cheeks and then she left. I watched her taxi drive away. She waved to me from the rear window and then I went into Michael's apartment house to spend five glorious days with the man I loved.

9

SECRET LOVERS

Just before school had recessed for the Thanksgiving holidays, I had given Michael a list of groceries to buy for our Thanksgiving dinner. He had everything spread out over the kitchen table when I arrived.

"It's all here," he said, gesturing at the cans and boxes, the turkey and produce. "Just as you requested."

"Good. I'm going to make our pies tonight," I explained and took off my coat quickly and began to put on the apron he had hanging on the inside of the pantry door.

"You are? What kind?" he asked with an amused smile.

"Apple and pumpkin. I learned from an expert, Momma Longchamp, although we rarely had enough money to spend on desserts, even for the holidays." I began taking out the pots and pans and setting out the mixer.

"How poor you must have been with your first family," he remarked and sat in the kitchen watching me prepare and listening to my descriptions of what life had been like living with Daddy and Momma Longchamp.

"I remember having nothing more to eat than grits and peas. Daddy would get so depressed he would go to a tavern and drink up whatever extra money we had and then we'd find ourselves scrounging. After Fern was born, it became even worse. We had another mouth to feed and Momma couldn't do much work. I had to do the housework, care for the baby and keep up with my school work, while other girls my age were dreaming of boys and going to parties and dances."

"Well you're never going to suffer like that again," Michael said. He was moved to get up to kiss me and hold me and whisper promise after promise in my ear. "You're going to be a famous and very rich singer someday soon, so rich that you won't even be able to recall being that poor."

"Oh Michael," I said, "I don't have to make piles and piles of money. As long as I have you and you love me, I'll be as rich as I want."

He smiled, his eyes becoming soft, limpid pools of desire. His gaze made me tremble so, I had to look away.

"What's wrong, little diva? Don't you like looking at me?"

"I love looking at you, Michael. But when you gaze at me like that, it's as if you were undressing me with your eyes, taking me to bed with your eyes."

He laughed.

"Perhaps I am. Perhaps I should," he added and kissed me lovingly on the forehead. I saw he wasn't going to release me from his embrace.

"Michael, I've got to mix this batter," I cried, pointing to the bowl on the counter. "And I want to make a stuffing for the turkey and . . ."

"The food can wait," he declared. When that look came over him, there was no holding him back. It was infectious. I couldn't resist his kisses and soon I was kissing him back as hard as he was kissing me, and embracing him just as tenderly. Before I could protest, he scooped me into his arms and carried me out of the kitchen.

"Our dinner!" I cried.

"I told you—I get hungry after I make love," he said, laughing.

It seemed we were in bed most of the time for the first few days of the holiday, but I did manage to prepare a small turkey, stuffing, candied sweet potatoes, fresh peas, a homemade bread, cranberry sauce, and the two pies. Michael said it was the best Thanksgiving dinner he had ever eaten.

"I don't know many women who can cook like you can," he said. "All the women I know depend on maids and cooks and are helpless even when it comes to boiling water for tea."

It was the first time he had spoken about the other women he had known and I couldn't help recalling the beautiful red-haired lady he had been with at the museum recital. I asked Michael who she was.

"Oh, her." He shook his head. "She's the wife of a producer friend of mine. He's always asking me to do him a favor and take her places. She's the kind of a woman who needs more than one man, if you know what I mean," he said, winking.

But I didn't know what he meant. How could you need more than one man if that man was the man you loved with all your heart and soul? And if a man loved a woman, how could he want someone else to escort her places?

"Why wouldn't her husband be jealous of someone else showing her around?" I asked.

"Jealous? He was grateful," he said, laughing slyly. "Show business people can be like that," he said. "They think their relationships are just another performance. But don't worry, I'm not like that," he added quickly.

"You never found anyone you wanted to be with forever and ever?" I asked.

"Not before you. I never met anyone who was as innocent and pure. Your name fits you; you're as fresh as a new day." He leaned over to kiss me on the cheek.

I felt myself glow. I was never as happy as I was at that moment. It was the best Thanksgiving dinner I had ever had. Afterward, Michael made a fire in the fireplace and brought out one of his soft quilts. I lay with my head in his lap and we listened to beautiful music while the fire crackled and warmed us. Every kiss that night seemed sweeter than the one before. Michael stroked my hair and told me he wished all time would stop and we would be stuck right where we were forever and ever.

My heart was as full as my stomach. How could any woman love any man more than I loved Michael? I wondered.

We stripped off our clothes and made love in the glow of that fire, our kisses and embrace so passionate, I thought we were burning like the logs, consuming each other and yet fulfilling each other. We fell asleep in each other's arms, exhausted but never more content.

In the morning Michael told me he had an appointment with a producer downtown.

"And after my meeting, I'm going to bring home a small Christmas tree. It's traditional to begin decorating one during Thanksgiving, isn't it?" he said. "I've never bothered before, but now that I have you . . ."

"Oh Michael, I'd love that. It's been so long since I had a Christmas tree myself, or even cared about the holidays. When you don't have any family or a family you love and loves you, the holidays are just like any other day. Except you watch other people's happiness with an envious heart."

"No more pain and envy for you, my little diva," he said and kissed me softly on the lips before leaving for his meeting. While he was gone, I listened to music, watched some television and did a little reading. We had been given some assignments to complete over the holiday.

Late in the afternoon, Michael returned with a small, but beautifully shaped little tree, each branch full and very green. He had bought boxes and boxes of decorations. Both he and the tree were sprinkled with milk-white snowflakes.

"Guess what!" he cried as soon as he entered, one hand holding the tree while he clutched the boxes of decorations against his chest. "It's snowing. What a wonderful surprise and just in time to put us into the holiday spirit. Do you like the tree?"

"Oh, it's so darling," I cried.

"I spent a lot of time picking it out. I wanted something special for us. The salesman nearly went mad waiting on me. Nothing he had seemed good enough. Then I peered around a corner and saw this one just waiting for me to choose it. It practically cried out to me," he said, laughing.

He fit the tree in the stand and stood back. We decided it would look good just to the right of the fireplace.

"Looks perfect," he said and gazed at his watch. I had noticed that from the moment he had arrived, he had periodically checked the time.

"Is someone coming?" I asked.

"What? Oh no, no."

"You keep looking at your watch."

"Yes." He shook his head. "I've got to leave in a little while for a meeting. This producer I met with today went ahead and scheduled something without checking it out with me, but it's so important, I have to attend. There's a very, very good chance I'll star in a Broadway opening next season."

"Oh Michael, how wonderful."

"Yes, but these things take months and months of planning and endless meetings with investors and writers and production people. Everyone has an opinion. I hate preproduction, but it's a necessary evil. I'm sorry to have to leave you just when we've gotten started."

"Oh, that's all right, Michael. While you're away, I'll decorate the tree and make our dinner."

He looked troubled and shifted his eyes away quickly.

"Something wrong?" I asked.

"This meeting will probably run into dinner. I'm sorry, really I am," he said.

"Oh, then you won't be home until much, much later," I realized.

"Yes. Will you be all right?"

"I'll be fine. I'll eat all our leftovers. It will take me a while to decorate the tree anyway. Don't worry about me, really. I'll be fine."

"I'll try to call you later and let you know how late things will run," he said and then went in to change. He emerged wearing one of his beautiful wool sports jackets and slacks. When he put on his dark blue wool overcoat, I thought he never looked more handsome and told him.

"Well, you have to look good for these people. They expect it. That's one of the drawbacks to being a star: everyone wants you to look as though you had just walked onto a stage. You have to fit their image because you're continually in the spotlight. If a hair's out of place or you fail to smile, it could be a disaster. Next thing you know, they're spreading rumors about you and you don't get offered good parts.

"Are you sure you will be all right?" he asked again. "Maybe you should go to a movie? Let me give you some money for a taxi and a movie," he said and began to take out his wallet.

"Oh, no. I have plenty to do, even some homework."

He shook his head.

"Homework. Some of those teachers are such bores. Can you imagine giving homework over the holidays? All right. I'll talk to you later," he said and kissed me good-bye.

I had told him I would be all right, but the moment the door closed and I was all alone again, I looked around the empty apartment and felt like crying. How I wished we didn't have to be lovers in secret and he could have taken me with him. I would have been very interested in everything that happened, even though for him it had all become boring routine.

I turned to the little Christmas tree.

"Well," I said, "at least I have you. Now we'll get to know each other well."

I opened the boxes of decorations Michael had bought and began to dress the tree. The hours passed by ever so slowly just because I wanted them to fly by. I spent as much time as I could on the tree, fixing it and then changing it until everything looked balanced. After that, I ate my leftovers and listened to music and thought about Michael. I cleaned up and then tried to finish my homework, but I couldn't concentrate on my reading. Continually, I would gaze at the clock and become furious at those stubborn little hands just inching their way around. I tried to make a fire and distract myself by watching some television. It grew later and later and Michael didn't call. I dozed off a few times, but woke with a start, afraid I had failed to hear the phone ringing.

My poor attempt at a fire died. When I awoke from one of my short naps and checked the clock for the hundredth time, I was shocked to discover it was nearly twelve-thirty. Why hadn't Michael called? I wondered.

When I gazed out the window, I saw that it had snowed harder and the sidewalks wore a white blanket. The streets were wet and slushy. Horns blared as drivers cut and stopped around each other. People get into accidents in bad weather, I thought. Perhaps something had happened to Michael. How would I know? He didn't want anyone to know I was waiting at his apartment, so no one would call.

Despite my worry, it was hard to keep my eyes open, and after another half hour had passed, I drifted off again on the sofa and didn't awaken until I heard the door opening. I rubbed the sleep from my eyes and sat up. Michael turned to close the door behind him and fumbled with the handle and lock. I heard him go, "Shh."

"Michael?"

"Huh?" he said, spinning around. His hair was disheveled and his jacket looked quite rumpled. "Shh," he said, bringing his forefinger to his lips. "You don't wanna wake Dawn."

"Michael, I am Dawn," I said, smiling. I stood up. "What's wrong?"

"Huh?" he said again. He blinked and swayed.

"Michael, are you . . . drunk?" I asked. I had seen Daddy Longchamp enough times in this condition to know I didn't even have to ask.

"Naw," he said, waving his hand and nearly falling forward. "Not a bit. I just had . . ." He held up his right hand and squeezed his right forefinger and thumb together. "This much. Every ten minutes," he added and laughed again. His laughter carried him forward and he had to reach out to brace himself on the wall so he wouldn't fall on his face.

"Michael!" I cried and ran to him. He put his arm over my shoulder and leaned on me. How he smelled. It was as if he had taken a bath in whiskey. "Where were you? Why did you drink so much? How did you manage to get home?"

"Home?" he said. He gazed around. "Oh yes, home."

As I guided him toward the sofa, I noticed what looked like lipstick smudged on the side of his chin. There were also hairs on his jacket, red hairs!

"Michael, where were you? Who were you with?" I demanded. He didn't respond. He lowered himself to the sofa and fell back, gazing at me dumbly and blinking, obviously trying to bring me and everything around us into focus.

"Why is this room spinning around and around?" he muttered and closed his eyes. Then he slid down the back of the sofa until he was on his back, his eyes shut tight.

"Michael!" I shook him, but all he did was groan. "Oh, what's the use," I cried. I lifted his legs and took off his shoes. Then, with great effort and strain, holding him up as I did so, I peeled off his overcoat and sports jacket. He was too heavy for me to carry to the bedroom. Instead, I hung up his coat and jacket and got him a blanket. When I spread it over him, he moaned and turned on his side. I fixed the pillow under his head and then I sat at his feet, watching him breathe deeply and regularly.

My eyes drifted to our little Christmas tree. All decorated and lit up, it looked beautiful, warm, and very precious, but with Michael passed out on the couch, it looked as sad and as alone and disappointed as I was. Michael hadn't even noticed it. He had hardly even noticed me!

I rose slowly and turned the lights off on the tree. I took one more look at Michael. He was snoring. I put out the lights in the living room and then retreated to Michael's bedroom to fall asleep alone.

* * *

Michael was up before I was. I felt him sit on the bed and I fluttered my eyelids open just as he touched my face.

"Michael. What time is it?"

He was still wearing the clothes he had worn the night before. His shirt was open and his hair was wild, the strands going every which way. He yawned and shook his head.

"It's early. I'm sorry, Dawn," he said. "I'm sure I must have been some mess last night. I don't even remember falling asleep on the couch, or your getting me a blanket. I was what they call . . . blotto drunk."

I ground the sleep out of my eyes and sat up quickly.

"Where were you? What happened? Why did you get so drunk?"

"It was a celebration of sorts. I tried to leave them, but everyone insisted I go along. I was the life of the party, you see, the center of attraction. We had to wine and dine these investors, who paid for everything. The champagne flowed all night." He stretched and yawned again.

"But where were you?"

"Where was I? Let's see," he said, thinking as if it were a major question on a math exam or something. "Where was I? Well, first we were at this producer's office. Then we all went to dinner at Sardi's. After that, we started to hit nightclub row. I should recall one or two places, but they all seem to run together in my mind now."

He sighed and bowed his head into his cradling hands.

"Who was with you?"

"Who was with me?" He looked up, thought and then shrugged. "Some of the production people and the investors."

"Was that red-haired woman there too?" I asked.

"Red-haired woman? Oh, no, no," he said. "There was no red-haired woman. Well, I'd better get into the shower. I feel like last week's pot roast. I'm sorry," he repeated and leaned over to drop a quick kiss on my cheek. "Thank you for looking after me."

He rose like a cat, undulating and stretching. I lay back on my pillow and watched him undress and go to take a shower. Was he lying to me, I wondered, or were those red hairs on his jacket there from some previous time, maybe one of the times he had to escort the wife of his friend? I just couldn't believe he would lie to me. He loved me too much to hurt me.

I got up and went to the kitchen to put up our coffee and prepare some breakfast. When Michael appeared, he was bright and fresh, his hair neatly brushed. He wore a light blue, silk robe.

"Um, that smells good," he said, coming up behind me to embrace me. "I'm really sorry about last night," he repeated. "Everyone was so excited about the new show, it was hard not to celebrate." He kissed me on the back of the neck.

"Then it all went well?"

"Yes. You will soon hear and read about Michael Sutton opening on Broadway," he said proudly. I spun around in his arms.

"Oh Michael, how wonderful for you. You're right: that is very exciting. I only wish I could have been with you to celebrate last night."

"We'll celebrate tonight," he said. "We will take a cab to a small, out-of-the-way Italian restaurant I know in Brooklyn. No one will notice us there, but the food is great."

"But Michael, do you think we should? If someone should see us . . ."

"No one will. How sweet of you to be so concerned for me," he said. "Now, let me go look at the Christmas tree." He took my hand and we went into the living room. I turned on the tree lights. "Magnificent," Michael said. "On Christmas Eve you and I will roast chestnuts in the fireplace and drink egg nog and make love right beside the little tree. Our tree," he added, putting his arm around my shoulders and drawing me to him. "My little diva," he said again and kissed me gently on the lips.

"But for now," he said, snapping back, "I'm starving. Let's have breakfast."

The rest of the day went by quickly. Michael left to do some shopping. The telephone rang twice, but I didn't answer it. When I had first arrived, Michael had pointed out that if I did, someone would know I was at the apartment and that would lead to questions.

"And questions," he had said with raised eyebrows, "lead to answers we're not ready to give just yet."

When he returned in the afternoon, he had an armful of packages wrapped in holiday paper.

"What's a Christmas tree without gifts beneath it," he declared, setting them out.

"Who are those gifts for, Michael? Do you expect some of your family?"

"Family? No. These gifts are all for you," he said.

"All for me? Oh Michael, you shouldn't have bought so much!" I exclaimed, gazing at the enormous pile.

"Of course I should," he declared firmly. "Who else should I spend my money on, if not you. Certainly not my ungrateful family." He smiled impishly and reached into his jacket pocket to produce a small box wrapped in pink paper with a pink ribbon around it. "This," he said, "couldn't wait. It's a Thanksgiving present."

"People don't give each other presents on Thanksgiving, Michael," I cried, laughing.

"They don't?" He shrugged. "Well, I'll start a tradition and from now on, they will. For you," he said, extending his hand.

I took the small box and opened it carefully, my fingers trembling with excitement. There, in a bed of cotton, was a beautiful gold locket on a gold chain. The outside of the locket had tiny diamonds shaped in the form of a heart.

"Oh, Michael, it's beautiful."

"Open it," he coaxed.

I pressed the release and when the locket opened, I saw a bar of notes etched within. I played them quickly in my mind and smiled. It was the first phrase of one of his own love songs, "Forever, My Love."

"Oh Michael," I cried. Tears of happiness flooded my eyes. "It's the nicest gift anyone's ever given me. And it's so special."

I threw my arms around him and smothered his face in kisses.

"Whoa," he cried, holding me back. "We don't want to get ourselves all worked up right now. We've got to get ready to go to our quiet little dinner, remember?"

My heart was so full of happiness, I thought it was sure to burst. I had packed some things in my suitcase in anticipation of Michael and I having a night like this. Trisha had gone with me to buy an uplift bra. My deepened cleavage and my surging bosom made me look years older. I couldn't help the blush that settled at the entrance to the valley between my breasts, but I thought that made me look even more enticing in my black V-neck, three-quarter-sleeve dress. The tiny diamonds on my locket sparkled on my chest.

I brushed my hair until it was silky smooth and it lay obediently over my shoulders, shining softly. Then I put on a little rouge and lipstick and some eye liner. Satisfied that I looked more like the women Michael was used to having on his arm, I emerged from the bedroom to let him inspect me. He had just finished speaking to someone on the telephone and cradled the receiver. He turned and smiled with his dark eyes glimmering and his sensual lips opening in appreciation.

"You are beautiful," he said. "Very beautiful. I can't wait until I can introduce you to society. Everyone will be envious of my discovery, and," he added, stepping closer, "my love."

I beamed with pride. Michael helped me put on my coat and kissed me on the cheek.

"Our taxi is already here," he said and we left the apartment.

It was a long ride through the city. Michael wasn't exaggerating when he said he knew an out-of-the-way restaurant. The driver wound us around street after street until we finally arrived at a small Italian restaurant on the corner of a block. The restaurant was simply called Mom's. It was far from anything fancy—a small room with a very small bar and about a dozen tables, but to me it was the most romantic and wonderful restaurant I had ever been in.

Michael sat us at a corner table in the darkest section of the small room. He was right about our not attracting attention. No one seemed to notice us or care once we had entered and taken our seats. But everything we ordered and ate was homemade and delicious. Michael ordered the most expensive wine and we drank nearly two bottles of it. He knew so much about wines and foods because of his traveling. He described some of the famous restaurants he had been to all over the world.

The only thing I could tell him about was the food at Cutler's Cove Hotel. I described Nussbaum, the chef, and how special every dinner was at the hotel.

"Grandmother Cutler, with my mother sometimes accompanying her, greets the guests at the door and then visits them at their tables, making them all feel at home."

"She may be a tyrant," Michael said, "but it seems she knows what to do to make the hotel a success. She sounds like a very smart businesswoman. I wouldn't mind meeting her one day," he said.

"You would hate her. She would make you feel lower than an ant just because you are only an entertainer. She respects only pure bloods, wealthy pure bloods," I said, practically spitting the words.

I told Michael how she had tried to ruin my days at Bernhardt from the beginning by writing the letter of lies to Agnes.

"Soon you will be free of all that," he said, placing his hand over mine and squeezing my fingers lovingly. "And people like her won't be able to hurt you anymore."

"Oh Michael," I said, "I can't wait for that day."

"Well," he said, a sly twinkle in his eyes, "it may be sooner than you think."

"Michael," I cried, nearly jumping out of my seat, "what do you mean?"

"I shouldn't tell you this," he replied, a small, tight smile on his lips, "but there is a strong possibility I might be able to get you a spot in the new Broadway show."

"Michael!" I thought I would faint right then and there. I felt my heart begin to pound with excitement, making it so hard for me to breathe, I could feel my chest ache. Me, on Broadway? Already?

"It's nothing definite," he warned. "It's just a possibility. We've got to work a lot more on your singing. Being on stage in a musical is a lot different than stepping out to sing a tune or two at your local high school concert."

"Oh, I understand. Of course. But I'll work hard, very hard, Michael. I really will."

"I know you will," he said, patting my hand again. "It's in your blood. Didn't I tell you that from the start?"

After Michael paid the bill and we left the little restaurant, I didn't mind the long ride back to his apartment. I spent it in his arms, dreaming of the Broadway stage and of being with him from one glorious moment to another. Who would have thought that what Momma Longchamp had told me years and years ago would come true.

I knew now she had been trying to forget the tragic events that had led to my abduction. It was as if I had been born a lie. She couldn't live with that or her own sense of guilt either and in time, she got herself to believe the story she had created about my being born at the dawning of day with the birds singing.

"They put a song on your lips forever and ever," she told me. "Some day, people will hear you sing and they will know about the miracle that occurred when that beautiful songbird gave you its voice to celebrate your birth."

That day was drawing closer and faster than you could have imagined, Momma, I thought, and with love in my heart, my voice would be more beautiful than even I could have imagined.

The time that Michael and I had left together flew by more quickly than I wanted. When the morning of the final day came, I was reluctant to open my eyes to face it. Trisha and I had planned it all out. I was to take a cab to the bus station and meet her when she came off the bus from home. Then we would take a taxi back to the apartment house together so that Agnes would believe I had been with Trisha the entire vacation.

After I dressed and packed, I stood with my suitcase and gazed sadly around Michael's apartment. The rays of bright sunlight on a clear, crisp day came pouring through the windows, lighting up our little Christmas tree, making the glitter sparkle, the ferns almost kelly green. Even the holiday wrapping paper around the pile of gifts glittered in the pool of warm light.

"It's been wonderful," Michael told me at the door. "Every single moment. But don't think of it as an end," he chastised as my eyes filled with tears at our parting. "Think of it as just the beginning." He kissed me and pressed me to him. My throat was so choked up, I couldn't speak.

"Now get some rest, my little diva," he warned. "We have a great deal of work to do as soon as school resumes."

"I will. I love you, Michael," I whispered. His eyes twinkled with joy and we parted.

I was early at the station, so I sat on a bench and read a magazine until Trisha's bus arrived. She came bouncing down the steps of the bus, her long red scarf floating over her shoulders.

"Tell me everything," she cried after we hugged. "What did you do? Where did you go? I bet he took you to fancy restaurants and shows every day."

"No, we stayed in most of the time," I said and described how I had prepared Thanksgiving dinner. She looked very disappointed until I showed her my locket.

"It's beautiful," she said, eyeing it enviously. "And it's so nice of him to have had something musical put in it. What are those notes?"

"Oh," I said, realizing she might know Michael's song, "just notes. Nothing special."

We found a cab outside the station and continued talking about our holiday until we arrived at the apartment house. Trisha wanted me to know everything she had done so I wouldn't be caught in any contradictions.

"If Agnes asks," Trisha said, "we had ten people for Thanksgiving dinner and we had duck as well as turkey."

"It sounds like it was a wonderful dinner," I said. Now it was my turn to be envious, to be envious of a happy, loving family gathered around a dinner table on the holidays.

We were surprised to find Agnes standing in the corridor at the foot of the stairway when we entered. Obviously, she had been expecting us and had taken her position as soon as she heard us arrive, but one look at her face put a chill in my heart. She was dressed in black, her face pale, no lipstick, no rouge, nothing. Her hair was drawn back and tied in a bun. It was always difficult to tell whether Agnes was playing one of her roles or not. Right now, I thought she was playing a mourner.

"You lied to me," she snapped before I could say hello. I glanced quickly at Trisha and then at Agnes.

"Lied?"

"Your mother called for you two days ago. She didn't know a thing about your going to Trisha's. Did you go without asking your family for permission? I felt so foolish," Agnes added before I could respond. She twisted her white, silk handkerchief in her hands. "I'm in charge, yes, but I depended upon you, trusted you. When you told me you had permission, I believed you. I should have known better; I should have expected it," she spit.

"I expect a phone call from your grandmother any moment now," she said. She looked absolutely terrified of it.

"She won't call," I assured her. "My mother simply forgot," I declared.

"She must have been on some medication when we spoke last and she simply didn't recall. It happens often," I said and fixed my eyes firmly on Agnes, amazed at how easily the lies fell from my lips. I could see her considering the possibility.

"Oh dear," she said; she loved high tragedy. "I don't know what to think. You don't expect a problem then?"

"No." I shrugged. "It's happened before. Grandmother Cutler is used to it, too."

"Oh, how sad," Agnes moaned. "Your mother is such a pretty woman. I can't believe she's so ill."

"No one can," I said dryly, but Agnes missed my sarcasm.

"Did you two have a nice holiday then?" she asked, looking from me to Trisha.

"Yes, we did," Trisha said quickly.

"Mrs. Liddy has made something special for everyone's return. Oh dear," she said, wringing the handkerchief in her hands again. "I was so worried," she muttered and started away.

"She's getting worse," Trisha commented as we looked after her. "She got all dressed up in that old costume in preparation for some terrible scene. Every time a new thought or mood crosses her, she digs into her chest of old costumes and finds something to fit her temperament."

"I feel sorry for her, but she didn't have to become Grandmother Cutler's spy. I don't like lying, but I had no choice," I said.

Trisha nodded and we continued up the stairs to our room to put our things away. Of course, Trisha was fascinated to know what it had been like for me to have lived with a man in his apartment for so many days. She asked all sorts of questions and at least twice, I almost said something that would have given Michael away.

"My mother always says that nights are for fantasy and romance, but when you wake up in the morning and the man beside you is still snoring, reality comes crashing down and pops the bubble," Trisha said. "Did that happen to you?"

"Oh, no. Mornings were just as wonderful as the nights. I made us a big breakfast and we talked and talked with the same excitement. He has so much to say; he's been everywhere in the world."

"Why does he travel so much?" she asked quickly.

"Oh, it's his . . . his business."

"What is his business?"

"Something to do with importing," I said quickly.

"You're so lucky," she said. "You're talented and pretty and now you have a mature love affair."

"You're talented and pretty, too, Trisha, and I'm sure you will be in love very soon, too," I predicted. She thought about it and then shrugged with that happy little smile on her face.

"Erik Richards called me three times over the holidays."

"He did?"

"We're going to dinner this coming weekend. At the Plaza! I think he's going to ask me to go steady," she said.

"What are you going to do?"

Going steady sounded so childish to me now, but I didn't want to say anything that would make Trisha feel bad. Michael and I were talking about a life together, a life of performing and loving. Wearing your boyfriend's high school ring around your neck seemed something girls years and years younger than me would do. But Trisha wasn't younger than me.

"He is very good looking," she said. "I think I might just say yes," she concluded, her eyes sparkling with mischief. We laughed and hugged each other and went down to dinner.

Mrs. Liddy had prepared a dinner that rivaled any Thanksgiving spread. Agnes, who was now dressed in a very youthful white dress that had large puffed sleeves and an embroidered collar and hem, with a string of pearls around her neck that would choke a horse, made one of her short, dramatic speeches telling us how thankful she was we were all back safely from our holidays.

"And together again, a family united and ready to face anything the hard cruel world throws at us."

We all looked at each other. It was definitely a speech from one of the melodramas she had performed in during her younger days. Trisha was positive the dress was a costume from that very play.

But I didn't care. Nothing now, not Agnes's eccentricities, not Madame Steichen's temper, not even Grandmother Cutler's hateful actions could do anything to detract from my days of sunshine and happiness. I felt secure. I had been made invincible by the love between Michael and me. It was the fortress that would protect me from what Agnes called, "the slings and arrows of outrageous fortune," which, she always reminded us, was a quote from Shakespeare.

But there were "slings and arrows" I hadn't anticipated, falling on my bubble of joy and romantic bliss just the way Trisha's mother had described they might. The weight of reality was far too heavy for fantasy to bear.

It began the morning of the third day after our return from the Thanksgiving holiday. I woke up deathly sick and vomited for twenty minutes. Trisha was afraid I had caught the stomach flu and was about to inform Agnes and ask her to arrange for medical treatment when she asked me the question that dropped icicles down my spine and nailed my feet to the floor.

"You haven't missed a period, have you?" I didn't have to reply. She saw the answer in my face. "Oh Dawn, how long has it been?"

"Nearly six weeks," I cried out in dismay. "I just didn't think about it. I've been irregular most of my life."

"Which is more reason to worry and be careful," Trisha said. "Didn't your mother ever talk to you about these things?"

Which mother? I thought. Momma Longchamp always thought me too young to know about sex, and by the time I was old enough to know, she was too sick and worried about other things. I was sure my real mother would turn blue and go into a faint if I so much as brought up the subject. And she wasn't anyone to talk to anyway, I thought.

I shook my head, the tears beginning to trickle down my cheeks.

"Oh Trisha, I can't be pregnant. I just can't. Not now. I'm not," I said with determination. "It's just a stomach flu. You'll see." I nodded, forcing myself to believe it.

Trisha squeezed my hand and smiled.

"Maybe you're right; maybe it's just a little stomach flu," she said. "Let's not panic just yet."

I nodded and bit down on my emotions. I had little appetite at breakfast, but that could have been because of my nervousness as much as it was my earlier nausea. I walked about with the weight of worry on my shoulders all day. I didn't have vocal music so Michael didn't see me and I didn't want him to see me when I looked and felt this way.

I was very tired that night and went to sleep early. The next morning, I woke with the same spell of nausea and vomited again. I saw that Trisha was becoming increasingly worried and frightened for me, so I made it sound as if it hadn't been as bad as the day before.

"I think it is the flu," I told her. "And I'm getting better."

When Michael finally saw me in general music class, however, he said I looked a little peaked and tired, but I didn't say anything except I hadn't been sleeping well. Before he could ask why, there were other students around us, making it hard for us to talk.

Later in the afternoon, I went to the library and read about pregnancy so I knew what to look for when I went home. I took off my sweater and bra and examined my breasts in the mirror. I quickly realized that what I had thought was happening because I was maturing was happening for other reasons. My breasts were enlarged and my nipples, besides becoming larger, were darker in color. Tiny new blood vessels were visible just under my skin. Verification of the symptoms made my blood run cold. There was no denying what I saw and what it meant.

I bowed my head in defeat. Love had made me foolish and careless. Why didn't I think? Michael's love for me and my love for him had turned me into a woman very quickly. I had felt a woman's passion; I had kissed and had made love to him as a grown woman would, and I had captured his heart only the way a mature woman could. Why hadn't I realized that I could also suffer a woman's possible consequences when I threw myself into Michael's embrace with abandon?

"What are you going to do?" Trisha asked me after I returned to our bedroom and described all my symptoms and what it surely meant. "Maybe you should call your mother."

"My mother? I went to her when Grandmother Cutler was insisting I change my name to Eugenia, which was the name they supposedly first gave me."

"Eugenia?"

"It was the name of one of Grandmother Cutler's sisters, one who had died from small pox. When I complained to my mother, she almost went into a coma. The slightest tension drives her into a panic. She's useless. Of course," I added bitterly, "she just puts it on so that everyone will leave her alone and pity her."

"Well, you'll tell Allan, won't you? You would have thought a mature man would have been more careful and would have thought about this as much as you should have. After all, he has been married and everything."

I didn't say anything. I was afraid to tell Michael, afraid of what this would do to all our wonderful plans . . . my being on the Broadway stage, our being together forever and ever.

"Maybe he just didn't care," Trisha said, but her hard expression softened immediately. "I'm sorry if I sound harsh, Dawn," she added quickly.

"No, no," I said. "It's not that he doesn't care. He is just so much in love with me and love can blind you when it's that bright," I said. "You don't think; you lose yourself in the ecstasy. You heard the way some of those girls talk in the locker room, how they have trouble keeping their boyfriends from going too far, and those are just . . . just teenage romances."

"Well, you have no choice, you have to tell him," she said.

"Yes, yes, of course, I'll tell him. I'm just afraid he'll be quite upset."

"He has to share in the responsibility," Trisha snapped. "My mother always says, 'It takes two to tango.' "

"Yes," I said, fingering my locket nervously. "I know."

I didn't say it, but this was a dance I would have rather sat out.

10
BITTER FRUIT

I paused at the bottom of the staircase on our way to dinner.

"Trisha, tell Agnes I'll be right there," I said. She saw where I was heading: the sitting room where we had a telephone.

"You're going to call Allan now and tell him?" she asked, her eyes wide in anticipation.

"Yes. You were right. He has to know immediately." Trisha followed and lingered in the doorway. I knew she was dying to hear what I would say, but I couldn't let her listen in or she would know I was speaking to Michael.

"I'm sorry," I said. "I'm too nervous to have anyone around when I speak with him."

Disappointed, she left.

I lifted the receiver slowly. It wasn't until I began to dial Michael's number that I realized I could never tell him over the phone. I needed to see his face and have him hold me and tell me it would be all right, we would still find a way to do all the things we planned on doing. His phone rang and rang. I was about to cradle the receiver when he said hello. He sounded all out of breath.

"Michael, it's me," I said quickly.

"Dawn?"

"Are you all right? You sound like you're gasping."

"Oh no, no, I'm fine. I heard the phone ringing just as I was coming in and ran to pick up the receiver. Everything all right?"

"Michael," I said, "I . . . I've got to come over to see you tonight."

"Tonight? Tonight's not good, Dawn. I have another dinner meeting with the producers of the Broadway show and you know how those things can go on and on," he said, following it with a short trail of laughter.

"No, Michael. I must see you," I insisted. "When are you going to dinner?"

"In an hour or so. What is it? Why can't it wait? Can't you tell me at school?"

"I'm coming over right now," I said. "Please, wait for me," I begged.

"Dawn, what is it? Just tell me on the phone. There's no need . . ."

"There is a need. I must see you. I must, Michael. Please," I implored.

He was silent a moment.

"All right," he said. "Come over, but I do have to leave in an hour," he added. "These meetings are very important. A great many people are depending on me."

I wanted to say I'm depending on you, too, Michael, but I cradled the phone quickly and ran upstairs to get my overcoat instead. Then, without telling anyone anything, I rushed out of the house and ran up to the corner where there was more traffic and I had a better chance of hailing a taxi cab. It was bitter cold and a slight rain had begun, the drops like drops of ice pelting my face. Because of the weather and because it was rush hour, it took me nearly fifteen minutes to get a cab. Traffic was horrendous, so that even after I had managed to get a taxi to stop for me, we were at a crawl for blocks and blocks. I was terrified Michael would have to leave before I arrived.

"Isn't there any way to go any faster?" I cried to the driver. He behaved as if he didn't understand English. All he did was grunt. Finally, the traffic lightened up and we were able to make better time, but he dropped me off in front of Michael's apartment house nearly forty-five minutes after I had phoned.

The doorman had an elevator waiting for me. I thanked him and nearly pushed a hole in the button until the doors finally closed and I was on my way up to Michael's floor. I was panting, out of breath myself when he opened the door to greet me. My hair was soaked and messy, the strands stuck to my forehead and down my cheeks.

"What is it?" Michael asked, stepping back, obviously surprised by my appearance. "What could be so important to make you rush out in this weather?"

"Oh, Michael." I started to cry.

He went to embrace me, but then realized that my coat was wet and he would ruin his sports jacket.

"Take off that coat. You're drenched. Let me get you a towel," he said and hurried off to the bathroom. I took off my coat slowly and looked about what had been our rainbow room of dreams. The little Christmas tree was unlit and looked depressed and sad, even with the gifts wrapped in holiday paper beneath it. The walls of my heart quivered. I held the tears within and swallowed the cries that tried to emerge from my throbbing throat.

Michael came back with a towel and I wiped my head and my face. He looked at his watch.

"I'm going to be late as it is with this traffic and weather. All right," he added when he saw the way my lips and my chin were trembling. He guided me to the sofa. "Sit down, relax and tell me what the problem is. Whatever it is, we'll solve it together. Does it have something to do with that horrible grandmother?"

"No, Michael." I shook my head. "I wish that's all it was." I had to wet my lips which had gone dry. My legs betrayed me and began to shake. I couldn't hold back the tears any longer. I started to sob uncontrollably. Michael sat down beside me and took my hands into his. He kissed away some of my tears and put his arm around my shoulders.

"Here now, it will be all right. I promise. It can't be that bad; nothing is that bad. How can I help you? What's gone wrong?"

"Michael . . ." I swallowed. "I'm pregnant."

He didn't blink nor did he turn away, but a funny glazed look came into his eyes.

"Are you sure?" he asked. His tight smile widened and he looked like he would laugh. "Girls are always saying they think they're pregnant."

"Yes. I'm positive," I said firmly. I was surprised at his reaction. He didn't act upset or angry. He looked thoughtful and sat back to contemplate me.

"How do you know for sure?" he asked, folding his arms across his chest.

"It's been over six weeks since my period and I have some of the other symptoms."

"So you haven't gone to a doctor then?"

"No, but I'm sure. There's no sense pretending it isn't so. I've been sick a number of mornings now, and . . . and there are other changes in my body."

"I see. Well, we still have some time before you have to say anything. You certainly don't look pregnant. I bet you won't show it for a good two months more. By that time," he said, "my semester as visiting celebrity teacher will have been over. Does anyone else know?" he asked quickly.

"My roommate," I said.

"Oh." His face turned glum.

"But she doesn't know about you; she thinks the man I'm seeing is named Allan and he's a businessman."

"Very good," he said, brightening quickly. "Let's keep it that way."

"But Michael, what about afterward?" I asked.

"Afterward? Oh, afterward. I go directly to Miami from here. I have a short tour in Florida, but I don't have to be back in New York for rehearsals for the show until the summer. You'll have the baby down in Florida then," he said quickly.

"Down in Florida? You mean, I'll go with you?"

"Of course. You can't very well stay here once it's out." He smiled. "You don't think I would desert you, do you? Not after I have invested all this time and energy in making you a singing star."

"Oh Michael!" I threw my arms around him and he laughed.

"Now, now, take it easy. You're a pregnant woman, you know. You have to be careful how you toss yourself about." He kissed the tip of my nose. A tingle traveled through my fingers laced in his.

"But Michael," I cried, "a mother. I wanted to sing, to be with you on the stage as we dreamt I would be."

"And you will," he said. "What, you think a baby will hinder your career? Absolutely not. We can afford the best nanny in town. Only the best for my wife and child anyway," he added.

Just hearing him say "wife" made my heart glow and washed away all the sadness and tears. Those gray clouds that seemed to follow me everywhere I went were blown far off beyond the horizon.

"We'll take the baby with us everywhere. I have a number of entertainer friends who do the same thing," he assured me.

But I remembered the things Agnes had told me about marriage, a family and show business.

"Michael, isn't it so much harder to raise a family when you're in show business?"

"It's harder, but it's not impossible. Especially, if two people love each other as much as you and I do. So," he said, clapping his hands together and standing. "No more tears. Come on now." He held his hand out for me to take. "I'll have my taxi drop you off at your residence on my way to my meeting."

He helped me put my overcoat back on and put on his own.

"Now remember," he said after he kissed my cheek, "you must keep this quite secret until I'm finished at the Bernhardt School. There are some other teachers here who would just love driving me out on the furious waves of a scandal. It might even hurt my singing career."

"Oh Michael, don't worry. No one will know anything. I'd die before saying anything to anyone."

"But you already have . . . to your roommate," he reminded me.

"Yes, but Trisha won't say anything to anyone either. She's my best friend. I can trust her."

"I would still not tell her about me. Keep it as you have it. It's perfect.

You're quite ingenious, you know," he said and I beamed with pride as he put his arm around my shoulders and led me out.

By the time I returned to the residence, dinner had ended. It was Trisha's week to help so she was still clearing the table when I arrived. She was the only one left in the dining room.

"What happened to you?" she asked. She lowered her voice and looked toward Agnes's room. "Agnes is upset. After she went looking for you and you were nowhere to be found, she became very panicky. You forgot to sign out. Every time someone's not where he or she is supposed to be, she thinks they might have run off like Bones did. Where were you?"

"I went to his apartment and told him," I said.

"And?"

"He's not upset or angry. In fact, he's happy about it. Oh Trisha, we're going to get married."

"What? When?"

"In about two months."

"But what about school, your career?"

"It won't interfere. He's figuring it all out. He's so wonderful about it and he doesn't care about what kind of an expense it will be to hire a nanny while I continue with my career. He's always wanted a child," I continued, embellishing on my fabrication, a fabrication that had become a romantic dream to me. "He was sorry that he and his first wife never had any children.

"But I must keep it all a secret for a while longer, Trisha, so please don't tell a soul any of this. Will you promise?"

"Of course, I promise, but you can't hide it forever," she reminded me. She stared at me a moment and then shook her head, smiling. "Are you sure this is what you want?"

"Oh yes," I said. "More than you could ever know. I'll finally have a family, my own family, and even though we have a nanny to help, I'll never neglect my child or let him or her feel unloved."

"Then I'm happy for you," Trisha said, taking my hand.

"Thank you."

We hugged.

"But you had better go to Agnes's room and let her know you're back," Trisha said. "She's probably rifling through her chest of costumes right now, trying to find the appropriate one for a new tragedy."

I left her and went to Agnes's room. Just as I was about to knock on the door, however, I heard voices within. Someone else was in there with Agnes.

"It's always been like this for you," the other woman said. "You do something to drive them away. You might as well make up your mind—you will die a spinster and you have no one to blame but yourself."

"That's unfair," Agnes said. "I did nothing to drive him off. You drove him off; it was you and your jealous ways."

"Me?"

Who was in there? I wondered. What were they talking about? It wasn't about me. I turned to walk away when Mrs. Liddy stepped out of her room.

"Oh, m'dear, where have you been? Agnes was so worried. Come to tell her, have you?"

"I . . . yes, but, she's busy; she has company," I said.

"Company?" Mrs. Liddy raised her eyebrows. Then she smiled. "Oh, no. Just knock," she advised. "Go on."

I did as she said and Agnes opened the door. She wore a dark red peignoir and had her hair down. Her cheeks looked streaked by tears. When I looked past her, I saw there was no one else in the room. I looked back at Mrs. Liddy, who nodded slightly, her eyes closed. Then I realized: the other voice—it had been Agnes creating her own dialogue, rehearsing some scene from some play she had been in.

"Well, where have you been, young lady?" she said, folding her arms under her bosom and snapping her shoulders back. "You didn't sign out, nor did you tell anyone you were going anywhere.

"Well, where were you, Dawn? Why weren't you at dinner when you said you would be?" Her eyes took on a glassy stare, her pale hands trembling as they unfolded and fluttered up from her waist to her throat. "Only Mrs. Liddy prevented me from calling your grandmother."

"I'm sorry, Agnes. I was on my way to dinner when I remembered to call a friend who is in some terrible personal trouble. She was overwrought and I had to rush out to go to her before she did something terrible to herself," I emphasized, my eyes wide.

"Oh, dear," Agnes said, pressing her clasped hands to her breasts. I was correct in assuming the high drama would be something she could appreciate, but Mrs. Liddy looked very skeptical and tilted her head as she sucked in a corner of her mouth.

"I'm sorry," I repeated, turning back to Agnes quickly.

"Yes. Is everything all right now?"

"Oh yes, yes," I said, now thinking of myself. "Everything is . . . perfect."

And it was as far as I was concerned. Gradually, in the weeks that passed between Thanksgiving and the Christmas holiday, my morning sickness lessened and lessened until it came to an end entirely. In fact, I began to feel unusually well and found myself more energetic than ever.

When I gazed at myself in the mirror, I thought I'd never looked more radiant. My eyes sparkled with a brightness they had never before possessed. Other people noticed these changes in me, too; especially Madame Steichen.

"Now you are playing with a passion," she told me one afternoon. "Your fingers don't just roll over the notes; you have become one with the piano and the piano," she said, pulling her head back proudly to indicate she was responsible, "is playing you."

I was riding a soft, marshmallow cloud. I floated through the corridors. Young men who had given me only a passing glance or hello were now smiling widely and looking for excuses to stop me in the hallway for a chat. I had at least a half dozen invitations from a half dozen different boys to go on dates. Of course, I had to turn them all down. I was afraid they would all think me stuck up, so I took great pains to come up with reasonable excuses and be kind and friendly to them.

I wondered if Michael noticed these changes in me because he didn't mention them. Except for his occasionally asking how I felt, the subject of my pregnancy never came up. If anything, Michael acted more like my teacher and less like my lover since that cold, rainy day when I had gone to his apartment. His work on the plans for the Broadway show had kept him very busy every weekend since and one weekend, he had to go with the producers to Washington, D.C., to meet with some investors. I missed him and told him so. He promised that he would spend every available free moment with me as soon as he could, but it had been so long since he'd had any free time, I was beginning to worry.

"Is everything all right?" I asked him one afternoon as soon as Richard Taylor had left us.

"Oh yes, sure," he said quickly. "Why?"

"You seem so distant these days. I was just afraid you had thought things over and were sorry."

"Oh no, no. We have so little time now to accomplish what I had hoped we would, and I want to be sure you will be ready for bigger things. I'm sorry if I've been too hard on you in class," he said.

"You haven't been too hard on me. Besides, I like working hard on my music. Am I getting better?"

"Considerably better. We won't wait a day longer than necessary to have you audition after you've given birth. For now, though," he emphasized, "it's work, work, work, and for both of us. I'm off immediately to meet with the show preproduction staff right now. But please, don't think I'm neglecting you. Not a moment goes by when I don't think about you and how wonderful things will be for us."

"Oh Michael," I said, "it's the same for me." I was about to throw my arms around him when he reminded me we were still in school and anyone could walk into the music suite. We parted as we usually did with a quick kiss and then me leaving before he did.

I even enjoyed the cold days on my walks home. The colder it was, the more alive I felt as I strolled up the sidewalk, my little puffs of breath looking like puffs of smoke.

Trisha was true to her word: she hadn't uttered a syllable about my pregnancy to anyone, but she was fascinated with the physical changes occurring in me. Almost every night, she and I took out the tape to measure my waist. When it reached three inches over what it had been, I bought a girdle to keep my stomach in. In the meantime Trisha went to the public library and took out a book on pregnancy and we sat up nights reading it together and discussing the baby inside me—what stage of development it was in, what would happen next. Inevitably, we arrived at a discussion of names.

"If it's a boy, I think Andrew; it means strong and manly."

"And if it's a girl?" Trisha asked.

"That's easy, Sally, after Momma Longchamp," I said.

"I can't have babies until I'm at least forty," Trisha declared. "I can't risk anything interfering with my ability to dance. By forty, a dancer's career is on the downside anyway."

"You will have to marry a very understanding man then," I told her.

"If he's not understanding, he's not worth marrying," she replied. "Besides, it's not impossible. You found someone like that, didn't you?"

"Yes," I said. "I did."

She insisted I tell her more and more about Allan. I continued to fabricate, often forgetting one detail or another. Trisha, on the other hand, forgot nothing, and always reminded me of my contradictions. I knew she was growing more and more suspicious. A number of times I was tempted to tell her the truth. She was doing so well keeping my secrets as it was, why couldn't I trust her with the truth? I thought. But I was afraid, afraid of anything that might happen and ruin things for Michael and me; and I had, after all, promised Michael I wouldn't tell her.

Trisha and I were both amused by the next stage in my pregnancy: my dietary cravings. Some afternoons, I couldn't wait to get home to prepare myself a banana smeared with peanut butter. I would sneak into the kitchen whenever Mrs. Liddy was out doing an errand or off someplace else in the house, and get my strange snacks.

One afternoon, however, I opened the refrigerator and saw Mrs. Liddy had prepared jello for our dinner dessert. Suddenly, I was filled with a desire for jello on corn flakes. I filled a bowl as quickly as I could and scooped some jello on it. I couldn't wait to smuggle it up to my room and began eating immediately when Mrs. Liddy walked in on me.

"Oh, I'm sorry, Mrs. Liddy," I said quickly and tried to hide the bowl from her eyes. "I didn't mean to mess up your jello mold before dinner, but I just had this urge for some."

She continued to stare at me, now with very interested gimlet eyes. Her gaze moved from me to the counter where I had left the box of corn flakes and then back to me, scrutinizing.

"What are you eating . . . jello and cereal?"

I smiled weakly and shrugged, bringing the bowl out into the open, but I looked down. I had to be careful, I thought, and realize what my eyes might reveal.

"Yes, Mrs. Liddy."

"You're the one who's been dipping into the peanut butter jar every day, too, aren't you?" I nodded. "Don't you eat lunch at school, m'dear?"

"Sometimes. Sometimes, I'm just too busy, Mrs. Liddy."

She gave me that scrutinizing gaze again, her eyes full of questions.

"Are you feeling okay, m'dear?" she asked.

"Oh yes. I feel wonderful."

"Um," she said, nodding. I looked away quickly, gobbled down a few more spoonfuls of corn flakes and jello and then quickly retreated to my room, my heart pounding. Oh Michael, I thought, I can't hide the results of our passion and love much longer. I soon found out, he felt the same way.

I was upstairs in our room doing my math homework when I heard Trisha pounding the steps in her excited effort to get upstairs quickly. We had only two more days before the beginning of the Christmas holiday and all our teachers were piling on the work, especially the performing arts teachers who wanted their dancers and singers to reach certain plateaus before the long layoff that would occur during our holiday break. Trisha had three days of late dancing practice this final week of school, instead of her usual two days. I had been home almost two full hours before her.

She threw the door open and burst in as if the cold winds of winter were carrying her.

"What's wrong?" I asked quickly. I was in bed, my blanket pulled up over my protruding stomach. I took advantage of every opportunity I had not to wear the girdle.

"What's wrong? I thought I'd find you very upset. Don't tell me you don't know, or you didn't know," she said, closing the door behind her and approaching me. She dropped her armful of books on the bed.

"Know what? Trisha," I cried, smiling, "what are you talking about?"

"Michael Sutton," she declared and put her hands on her hips.

"Michael Sutton?" Oh no, I thought, had the school administration found out about us? Had those jealous teachers complained about him and gotten him fired? "What about Michael Sutton?" I closed my book slowly.

"He's leaving. He's gone!" she said, raising her hands.

"Gone? He was fired?"

"No. Why would he be fired? I can't believe you didn't hear about it before you came home today. The whole school's buzzing. It must have been posted after you left," she concluded.

"Posted? What was posted?"

"His notice informing his students." She sat down at my feet.

"Apparently," she began, "he's been offered the lead role in a major London production. It was something that couldn't wait. The scuttlebutt is that he had been having meetings about it for weeks and finally it came through. He has this letter posted on his music suite door, apologizing to the school and to his students, and explaining why he had to go with such little notice.

"Of course, the administration understands. This is, after all, a school for performing arts. That's show business," she said, raising her arms. "But his students are not very happy. You should see Ellie Parker. She claims he promised to get her a Broadway audition this year. I came rushing home because I knew you would be upset and in your condition . . ."

Somewhere in the back of my mind, I heard the roll of thunder. When I closed my eyes, I saw those ugly, bruised and angry dark clouds riding the wind and drawing a curtain of darkness over the light blue sky, dragging shadows over all that was green and bright below. My heart felt like a brick in my chest.

"Are you all right?" Trisha asked and leaned forward to take my hand. "Your fingers feel ice cold."

I nodded, my eyes still closed, my throat too tight for me to try to speak.

Don't panic, I told myself. Keep calm. This is all part of Michael's plan for us. Soon, he would call to let me know why he had had to do things so quickly without warning me. But he had said he was going to Florida, I thought, not London. Maybe he's just telling them London so they won't come after us. There has to be a logical reason for all of this, I told myself. Don't panic.

I opened my eyes and took a deep breath.

"Did anyone see him, speak to him?" I asked, wrestling down the note of hysteria that wanted to invade my voice.

"No. Richard Taylor says he's already gone."

"Gone?" I shook my head as if I didn't understand the word.

"Left the country," Trisha explained. "And boy is Richard Taylor angry. He says the man didn't give him an iota of warning, not a clue. He feels like a fool because he's the one left with all the explaining to do.

"Of course," she continued, "the school will assign someone new by the time we all come back from our Christmas holiday, but . . ."

She paused when she looked up and saw how I was shaking. I couldn't stop the trembling. I was almost a convulsion. Cold tears streaked down my cheeks. The ache in my chest grew so heavy I thought I would burst, and a burning had begun in my temples and spread across my forehead. I felt as if I had put on a crown of hot steel.

"Oh Dawn, I knew you'd be disappointed. You were doing so well under his tutorage, weren't you? And I'm sure he made you some promises about auditions, too. But you mustn't get yourself sick over this. I'm sure Allan would be so upset if he knew."

At first my tongue refused to form words, but as the silence stretched and became uncomfortably thick, I swallowed my tears and cried out.

"Nooooo!"

I buried my face in my hands and shook my head.

"Dawn."

I lowered my hands slowly and gazed into her sympathetic face.

"There is no Allan," I said in a hoarse whisper.

"What?" She started to smile. "What do you mean? Of course, there's an Allan. You can't tell me you're not pregnant."

"No, no," I said slowly, speaking like one who had been struck in the head and was in a daze, "there has never been an Allan. It was Michael," I said. "I'm carrying Michael's child."

"Michael? Michael Sutton?" Her mouth dropped open. "But . . ." Her eyes widened with shock. "But he's gone."

"No," I said slowly. I smiled. "It's all part of the plan, part of his plan for us. It wasn't supposed to happen until the end of the semester, but obviously he has had to move things up. I'll have to go to him," I said, swinging my legs off the bed and shoving my feet into my slippers. "He's expecting me, I'm sure."

Trisha simply stared as I went to my closet and chose one of my more loose-fitting wool dresses. I slipped it over my head quickly and sat down to brush out my hair.

"I wanted to tell you the truth, Trisha," I said, "but I had to promise Michael I wouldn't. He was worried about his job, you see. You understand, don't you?" I asked her. She nodded quickly, but she continued to look very confused. "There are so many jealous people around who would just love to destroy him because he's so talented.

"He's going to be in a Broadway show next year, you know," I said.

"And there is still a very good chance I'll be in it too. Don't look so glum, Trisha," I said, turning back to her. "I'm sure everything is fine."

She smiled even though her eyes were filled with tears.

"Really," I insisted. "It's going to be fine. I'll go to him now and he will tell me the specifics. We're spending the Christmas holidays together, you know. "I looked at myself in the mirror and continued to brush out my hair as I spoke, remembering. "He bought a darling little tree just for us, and you should see the pile of gifts he has bought me. All for me. He's spent so much money on me, it's obscene.

"Imagine," I said, turning back to her, "by New Year's Eve I will be Mrs. Michael Sutton. Doesn't that sound wonderful? You must let me know where you'll be celebrating so I can phone you and wish you a happy New Year from our apartment at exactly midnight. We'll be in each other's arms by the fireplace.

"So you see," I said, looking at myself in the mirror, "we have it all planned."

I got up to choose a pair of shoes.

"Why hasn't he called you yet?" Trisha asked me.

"He just expects me to come," I said. "What else could the reason be?"

"Should I come with you? Let me come with you," she said quickly.

"No, don't be silly. Besides, how would it look if I showed up with you at my side? I promised him I wasn't going to tell anyone about us until he said it was all right to do so, and here I appear with you. No, no, I'll be fine."

"It's starting to snow," she said. "There's another storm."

"I'm not going to walk all the way to his apartment, Trisha. You're acting like a nervous mother. I'll be fine, really."

I slipped on my overcoat.

"Tell Agnes . . . tell her . . ."

"What?" Trisha asked.

"Tell her I've eloped," I said and followed it with a thin little laugh much like hers.

"Dawn," Trisha said, standing.

"It's all right. When two people are in love the way we are, nothing else matters. You should hear the way we sing together. What am I saying? Before long, you will," I added and laughed again.

Then I rushed out the door and bounced down the stairs. Trisha called after me, but I didn't stop. I hurried out the front before anyone could see me. Trisha was right: the snow storm had begun. Flakes that looked nearly an inch thick were falling so heavily it was difficult to see five feet in front of me. I walked quickly up to the corner and waved and waved at every cab, not being able to see whether each had a passenger or not. Finally, one pulled up in front of me and I practically dove into the back seat. I gave the driver Michael's address and sat back thinking of the things I would say as soon as he opened that door and embraced me.

It would be just like a wonderful musical when the two leads finally overcome all the obstacles between them and meet on the stage to sing in each other's arms.

"I'm here, Michael," I whispered. "I've come, my love, to be with you forever and ever. No more secrets, no more hiding, no more clandestine rendezvous, no more quick, stolen kisses. Now we could walk hand in hand in public and all the world could see how much in love we are and how our talents make us something very special."

"Looks like we're in for it," the taxi driver said. "When the city gets four or five inches, all hell breaks loose and everything comes to a standstill. What a mess," he said.

Oh no, I thought as I gazed out the window. It's no mess. This snow looks beautiful. I'm happy it's snowing. Perhaps this means we'll have a white Christmas. I could hear the sound of bells and the Christmas carols. I could see Michael and I standing in the window looking down at the revelers, Michael's arm around me, both of us warmed by our eggnog drinks. Perhaps we had just made love.

"Merry Christmas, my love," he would say and kiss me.

"Merry Christmas, Michael."

"What's that?" the taxi driver asked.

"Nothing," I said, smiling. "I'm just dreaming out loud."

He looked at me in his rearview mirror and then shook his head. It's all right, I thought, why should I expect anyone else to understand how special and happy I felt.

In my excitement when we arrived, I nearly rushed away without paying the driver. After he called out, I returned and threw all my money at him, giving him nearly twice as much as the fare.

"Merry Christmas," I sang when he looked up in surprise. "Everyone should be as happy as I am."

He shrugged and drove off. When I entered the lobby, the doorman, who was more than familiar with me, gazed at me curiously as I made my way to the elevator. I smiled at him and stepped into the elevator as soon as the doors opened. The instant they opened again, I rushed out to Michael's door and pressed the buzzer. For a moment I thought he wasn't home. I heard no one inside and no one had come to the door. I pressed the buzzer again and then I heard footsteps.

My love, I thought.

The door opened, but Michael wasn't standing there. It was a much older man with curly gray hair and a round face. He had rosy cheeks and singing was even louder. The doorman opened the door for me and stood back.

"Do you hear him?" I asked. "Isn't it beautiful?"

"Huh? Hear who?"

He watched me step into the snowfall. The flakes struck my cheeks and eyes, but I welcomed the coolness which to me were as soft as Michael's kisses. He was just down the corner, singing. How romantic. I smiled and walked on, his voice drawing me, his promises of love growing stronger and stronger as I moved forward. But when I reached the corner, I found he was singing from another corner, again, just ahead of me.

Car horns blared as I walked on, ignoring everything but Michael.

"I'm coming, my love," I whispered, and then, I began to sing along, just as I had that first day. Soon I would be in his arms as I had been and he would kiss me again.

The snow was blinding, but I didn't need to see where I was going. Michael's voice kept me in the right direction. I could barely make out the traffic lights. Were they red or green? It didn't matter. Everyone in the world was watching us now, waiting and watching. The world was our audience. In moments there would be enormous applause, just the way I had always dreamt there would be.

I raised my voice and sang louder. He was only a few feet away now. I could see him standing there, his arms extended toward me.

"Oh Michael," I cried.

And then I heard the sound of a car horn. It seemed right on top of me. There was the squeal of brakes and something brushed across my right leg. It sent me spinning, but I felt as if I were rising, floating up into the snow storm, whirling around and around, going higher and higher.

Until all went black.

bushy eyebrows and wore a heavy woolen bathrobe with a towel aro his neck.

"Hello," he said. "I was almost in the shower."

I looked past him, but saw no one.

"I'm looking for Michael," I said.

"Michael? Oh, Michael Sutton?" I nodded, but he shook his he "Well, he's gone. By now he's somewhere over the Atlantic, I imagine. was supposed to see you today, Miss . . ."

"No," I said, "he can't be gone. All his things are here," I pointed o "The paintings, the furniture . . ."

"These aren't Michael's things, Miss. Michael was subletting my apa ment. I'm sure there is some confusion. I've got his forwarding address London if you want it, but . . ."

"No, he's got to be here," I insisted and walked by him. He didn't st me from entering. I ran through the apartment. *"Michael, Michael!"*

One look at the bedroom told me he was indeed gone. The things I kne were his were missing and different clothing was hanging in the close There was even a different bedspread. The gentleman who had let me i stood behind me, a look of annoyance on his face now.

"Listen, Miss, I told you, Michael Sutton is gone. Now do you want hi forwarding address or what?"

"He can't be gone," I repeated, but barely audible. I started out of th apartment and stopped to look at our little Christmas tree.

"Those are all presents for me," I said softly. The gentleman heard m and laughed.

"Really? Well, they're not very expensive gifts. All those boxes a empty. He put them there just for decorative purposes," the gentlema said. "I'm sorry. I see you're very disturbed, but . . ."

"No. He's waiting for me someplace else. That must be it. Maybe h called me. Oh, no," I said. "He's calling me and I'm not there."

"If he's calling you, it's from an airplane over the ocean," the gentlem said dryly. "Believe me, I know. I took him to the airport myself."

I stared at him a moment and then shook my head.

"No, he's waiting for me someplace else. That has to be it. Thank y thank you. Oh," I said, stopping in the doorway. "Have a Merry Chri mas."

"Thanks. You, too," he said and closed the door behind me as soon a stepped into the corridor.

I walked slowly to the elevator. It seemed to me I could hear Mich singing somewhere. He was singing that love song he had sung when had had our first private lesson. I began to hum along softly. I stepped i the elevator and went down to the lobby where the sound of Micha

11

NOWHERE TO TURN

I was falling through a great white tunnel, and as I fell, I spun around and around. Each time I turned, I saw another familiar face. There was Momma Longchamp looking so sad and tired; there was Daddy Longchamp with his eyes down looking ashamed; there was Jimmy holding back his tears in anger, and then there was baby Fern smiling and extending her arms toward me.

I dropped farther and farther down the tunnel and slipped past Grandmother Cutler who scowled. I saw Randolph looking distracted and busy, and I saw my mother, her face all pink, her head resting comfortably on a white silk pillow. Right below her was Clara Sue smiling gleefully at my helpless descent. Then Philip emerged, his eyes full of lust.

Finally, there was Michael, smiling at first, and then his smile evaporated and he became smaller and smaller and smaller as he fell below me, disappearing.

"Michael!" I cried. "Michael, don't leave me! Michael!"

I heard voices around me.

"Look at the monitor. Something's happening."

"She's coming out of it."

"Call Doctor Stevens."

"Dawn," I heard someone say. "Dawn, open your eyes. Come on, Dawn. Open your eyes."

My eyelids fluttered.

"Dawn."

Slowly, the whiteness around me began to take shape. I saw a milk-white wall and a large window, the tan curtain drawn closed. My eyes moved to what was nearer to me and I saw a metal pole holding an I.V. bottle. I followed the tube from it to my arm. When I turned my head, I saw a nurse looking down at me. She smiled. She had soft blue eyes and light brown hair and she looked like she was no older than twenty-five.

"Hi," she said. "How are you feeling?"

"Where am I?" I asked. "How did I get here?"

"You're in a hospital, Dawn. You were in an accident," she said calmly.

"An accident? I don't remember any accident," I said. I tried to move and did feel very stiff.

"Take it easy at first," she said. "The doctor will be here in a moment to tell you more." She brushed back my hair with the palm of her hand and fixed my pillow so I would be more comfortable.

"But what kind of an accident was I in?" I asked.

"You were hit by a car. Luckily, the car wasn't going too fast at the time, and you were just grazed really, but you were thrown back and knocked unconscious by the fall. You've been in a coma."

"A coma?" I looked around again. I could hear other nurses and doctors talking in the hallway just outside my door. "How long have I been here?"

"Today is the fourth day," she said.

"Four days!" I tried to sit up, but I got dizzy quickly and left my head on the pillow.

"Well, well, well," the doctor said, entering with another nurse, one who looked older and not as friendly. "Welcome back to the world," he said, coming to my side. "I'm Doctor Stevens."

"Hello," I said in a small voice.

"Hello, yourself," he replied. He looked like a man in his late fifties. He had dark brown hair, his temples a distinguished-looking gray. But his light brown eyes twinkled like the eye of a much younger man. He had a round face, even a bit pudgy. There was a dimple in his chin. He was stout with a neck like a wrestler and probably only about five feet eight or nine, but he touched me gently and smiled at me kindly.

"What happened to me?" I asked.

"I told her about the accident," the younger nurse said.

"That's what happened to you," the doctor said. "You were caught in a snow storm and were hit by a car just hard enough to spin you around and send you flying backwards. You must have struck your head on some hard-packed snow. The blow was sufficient to render you unconscious and you haven't been eager to regain consciousness since," he said, his eyes more inquisitive and curious now as he peered down at me. "All your vital signs are good and you have no fractures.

"However," he continued, his voice lower and even softer now as he brought his face closer to mine and took my hand into his, "I'm sure you are aware that you're pregnant."

The words brought tears to my eyes, for it reminded me quickly of Michael and his desertion of me. I swallowed back my tears and nodded.

"You were trying to hide it?" he asked. "That's why your family wasn't aware?"

"Yes," I said, barely audible. I expected a frown and a reprimand, but he simply closed and opened his eyes gently and smiled.

"The baby is a resilient one, for sure," he said. "Ordinarily, a mother would be in danger of losing her child as a result of such an accident, but everything is fine in that department."

A lump came to choke my throat and my eyes filled with tears.

"We'll start giving you some real food and get you off the I.V. In a day or so, you should be up and around. After that, our observation of you will be complete and you can go. I don't foresee any other complications," he added, smiling. "Any questions?"

"Does anyone know I'm here?" I asked quickly.

"Oh, yes. In fact," he said, "there's a young lady out in the lobby. She's been waiting hours and hours, coming back each day to see how you are. She's a very good friend and she's been very worried. Ready for a little company?" he asked.

"Oh yes, please. It must be Trisha," I said.

"Okay. We'll remove the I.V. and I'll have them bring you some soft foods and liquids. You'll be a little dizzy for a while until you regain your equilibrium and your strength, but that will pass. And your right thigh will be sore for a week or so more. That's where the car struck you. The main thing is that you eat whatever you are given to eat and don't try to do too much at one time. Okay?" he said, patting my hand.

"Yes. Thank you."

He nodded at the nurse and she began to remove the I.V. He made some notations on my chart at the foot of the bed. Then he smiled at me again and left with the older nurse. The young nurse turned a lever and raised the bed so I was in more of a sitting position. Even that little movement made me dizzy for a moment and I had to keep my eyes closed until it was over.

"I'll be right back with something for you to eat and drink," she said. "And I'll send your friend in."

"Thank you," I said. I took some deep breaths and tried to recall what had happened, but everything was a blur. I couldn't even remember going to Michael's apartment. All I was able to summon up were scattered images—an older man's face, Michael's bedroom looking different, and the little Christmas tree in the corner in the living room. Recalling it brought tears back to my eyes.

"Hi," Trisha said, stepping through the doorway. She had her dark blue wool jacket open and wore a white scarf. She had a small, gift-wrapped box in her left hand. Her hair was brushed back and tied in a ponytail. Her cheeks were still flushed from the cold weather, but she looked so fresh and bright, it was cheerful just looking at her within this white, bland hospital world.

"Hi," I replied and held out my hand. She took it quickly.

"How do you feel?" she asked.

"Tired, confused and a little sore. I get dizzy every time I lift my head from the pillow, but the doctor just told me that would soon go away as I eat and get stronger."

"I brought you some candy," she said, placing the box on the table beside my bed. "So you can get fat and ugly."

"Thank you." My smile faded when we stared at each other. "You know what happened to me?" I asked. She nodded and looked down, still holding my hand. "I went to his apartment, but he was gone; he deserted me," I said.

She looked up sharply.

"He's a horrible person to do this, horrible. I wish I had known it was Michael Sutton all the time. I would have warned you to stay away from him. Not that you would have listened to me, I guess," she added.

"Maybe he's just afraid of losing his career," I said.

"No. He's just selfish." She looked toward the doorway and then leaned closer to me. "Is the baby all right?"

"Yes." Using the doctor's words, I said, "Everything is fine in that department."

"What are you going to do about it now?" she asked quickly.

"I don't know. It's too late to do anything but have it. Anyway, I want it," I said firmly.

"You do?"

"I don't care what Michael is like now. I loved him and he must have loved me a little. The baby is a result of the good things, the nice things," I added, remembering. "The little Christmas tree is still there. We were going to have such a wonderful Christmas and New Year's together," I moaned.

"Don't," Trisha said sternly. "You will get yourself very sick and be in here longer."

I bit down on my lower lip and nodded. The nurse returned with a tray of juice and jello.

"Start with this," she said, placing the bed table over me and setting the tray on it. She fit the straw into the container of juice. My fingers trembled as I brought it to my lips.

"I'll help her," Trisha offered.

"Thank you," the nurse said, smiling, and left us. Trisha held the straw for me while I drank. It seemed like ages and ages since my mouth and throat had experienced any food, and not just three days or so. I never thought it would be so great an effort to sip juice.

"What's going on back at the house?" I asked after taking a breath. "Agnes must be fit to be tied."

"Oh, don't ask. When the police came and told her, she went racing through the apartment house, wringing her hands and telling everyone that she thought we were on a ship that was going down. Mrs. Liddy had her hands full calming her. All she kept chanting was, 'Nothing like this has ever happened before. It's not my fault.' Finally, she changed into one of her mourning outfits and paraded about like a bereaved person. It got on my nerves because it was as if you had died. Whenever she spoke about you, it was always in the past tense, telling us what a shame it was. You had so much talent and you were such a pretty girl, but you were too spoiled.

"Finally, I lost my temper and screamed at her. 'She's not dead, Agnes. Stop talking like that!' I cried. But it didn't do much good. She looked at me sadly and shook her head as if I were the one who was crazy and not her. All I could do was walk away. I came up here every free moment I had and waited for you to wake up."

"I know. They told me. Thank you for caring so much, Trisha," I said.

"You don't have to thank me for that, silly face. Look at you lying here like this. Just get yourself better and stronger and get out of here. I don't like hospitals. They're too full of sick people," she said and we laughed. It hurt to laugh. My stomach muscles were so sore, but I didn't mind.

"I'm sure she's called my family," I said. "You can see how much they care. No one's here."

Trisha nodded.

"I don't care anyway," I said.

"You better eat some jello now," Trisha advised and spoon-fed me.

Just being up and eating that small amount exhausted me. I could barely keep my eyes open to listen to Trisha's description of events at school. Finally, the nurse returned to take away the tray and advised her to leave.

"The next time you come, she will be much more alert," she promised. "She needs to rest now. That's all."

"I'll be back tomorrow," Trisha said. She squeezed my hand. "I'll tell Agnes how well you're doing and maybe she will change from a black dress to a blue one and put on some makeup."

I was too weak and tried to laugh. I barely smiled. Trisha kissed me on the cheek, but I didn't hear or see her leave. I was already in a deep sleep again.

When I awoke that evening, I was given hot cereal and tea. I tried to stay awake as long as I could and listened to the sounds coming from the hallway as the nurses and doctors went about their business seeing to other patients. But I dozed off and on.

The next morning I did feel stronger and a lot hungrier. I was given soft boiled eggs and toast. Doctor Stevens stopped by and took my pulse, listened to my heart and checked my eyes.

"You're coming along fast now," he said. "Maybe just a day or so more."

I ate a good lunch and even opened the box of candy Trisha had brought and ate two pieces. I gave some to the nurses, too. A nurse's aide brought me some magazines and I was able to read for nearly an hour. Late in the afternoon, Trisha returned with school news and a description of what was happening at the house.

"It's weird," she said. "I told Agnes how well you were doing, but she didn't seem to hear a word I said. She talks about you as if you were gone, as if you were one of her memories. At least she's wearing makeup and bright clothing and back to her dramatic self."

"I'm going to try to finish school," I said. "It's still very important to me."

She nodded and described Michael's replacement.

"He's tall and thin and wears these bifocals that keep slipping down the bridge of his nose. The girls tell me he's very mechanical. They're already walking around the school imitating him: 'A one and a two and a one and a two, and . . .'"

I started to laugh.

"Quite a change from the glamorous Michael Sutton, huh?" I said.

"Glamorous," she repeated, making it sound dirty. "I've got to shoot off," she said. "I have dance practice. Oh, I almost forgot," she said, reaching into her coat pocket to produce a letter. "This came for you yesterday and I got to it before Agnes did. She's been sending all your mail back."

"Why?"

Trisha shrugged.

"Who can explain why Agnes does anything. I thought you would want this one. It's from Jimmy."

"Jimmy!" I took it from her quickly. "Oh, thank you, Trisha."

"It's no big deal. Well, I hope the doctor releases you tomorrow, but if he doesn't, I'll stop by again in the afternoon." She kissed me on the cheek.

"Thank you, Trisha. Thank you for being my best friend in all the world," I said, tears flooding my eyelids.

"Don't worry," she replied. "I'll make you pay for it somehow. Maybe you will have to take my turn serving and cleaning up the dinner dishes for the rest of the term."

"Gladly," I said.

"See you," she cried and was gone. I sat there staring after her a moment. It was wonderful having a friend like Trisha during these horrible and trying times. But it was times like this when you found out who were your real friends. Out of all the good things that had happened to me in New York City, my work with Madame Steichen, my being chosen for Michael's class, the compliments I received from the other teachers, the shows and trips and all the excitement, nothing was more important than my friendship with Trisha. I realized that now and hoped and prayed we would always stay close.

I ground away my tears with my small fists and turned my attention to Jimmy's letter. How good it was to have it, I thought, even though I didn't deserve it. Not after the way I had betrayed him and his love. I would have to tell him soon now, I thought, and that would be one of the hardest things I had ever done.

I tore open the envelope gently and pulled out his letter. Then I sat back and began to read.

Dear Dawn,

Winter here has been very hard. We've had one blizzard after another, but the army doesn't pay much attention to weather. We have to go out and do what we're supposed to do no matter what.

You'll be happy to know I've been promoted to Private First Class. I'm part of a motor pool of mechanics who service tanks. Pretty impressive, huh?

Anyway, I couldn't help but notice how your letters continue to get shorter and far between. I suppose this means you've been very busy with your career, so I'm happy for you. I tell everyone I have a girlfriend who is studying to be a singing star.

I have one bit of news from the home front. Daddy's new wife is pregnant. I'm having a little trouble getting used to the idea of a new brother or sister, especially with Momma gone. It all seems so strange.

But he sounds happy about it. I think he's hoping for another daughter, one just like you.

I didn't tell him, but there can be only one you.

Love,

Jimmy

I put the letter down and closed my eyes. How my heart ached. Poor Jimmy, I thought, so far away and so trusting and loving. How would I begin to tell him what I had done and what had happened to me?

When the nurse came to look in on me again, I asked her for some paper and a pen to write a letter, but I never got to write it. Before I had a chance, I heard the sounds of sharp footsteps in the corridor outside my room, footsteps accompanied by the tap, tap, tap of a cane. I gazed curiously through my doorway and a few moments later, Grandmother Cutler appeared.

My heart seemed to flip over. For a moment she simply stood there, leaning on her cane and glaring in at me with her gray-stone eyes. She looked older, thinner. Her steel gray hair was still cut perfectly under her ears and just at the base of her neck with every strand in place. As always, she was elegantly dressed, not a crease showing. Under her mink stole, she wore a dark blue jacket and a white frilly collar blouse, with an ankle-length matching blue skirt and dark blue boots. Gold drop earrings dangled from each of her lobes, a small diamond glittering at the center of each earring. She wore a touch of red lipstick, just as she always did, but the brush of rouge on her cheeks looked brighter and larger than I remembered. I thought it was her way of trying to compensate for her more pasty and waxen complexion.

Her mouth didn't look as firm. The lower lip trembled either from anger or a bit of palsy. But the pride and arrogance that had put a rod of steel in her spine and hoisted her shoulders before was still there. Despite the onslaught of age, she looked just as formidable.

Being away from her this long, I had forgotten how much I despised her and how cold she could make my blood run whenever she turned those flintlike eyes on me. My heart pounded in anticipation. She began to shake her head slowly, her mouth curling into a smile of disgust and loathing. I wanted to sit up and scream that I loathed her twice as much as she loathed me, but I didn't move; I didn't utter a sound, afraid that I wouldn't be able to find a voice that didn't quiver.

"It doesn't surprise me one bit," she said, closing the door behind her and coming farther into my room, "to find you in such a place under such circumstances.

"Just a few weeks ago, I told your mother that you and she were cut of the same mold, that your own selfishness and lusts would take over and no matter where we sent you or what fine and expensive things we did for you, you would be the cause of some family embarrassment for us."

Her smile came bitter, wry.

"Agnes Morris has kept me quite informed as to your behavior. I knew it would only get worse and worse until something like this happened. And now it has," she concluded without disguising her satisfaction.

"I don't care what you think," I said quickly, but I had to shift my eyes from hers, for hers burned through me with more fire.

She flicked me a scathing glance and then laughed as she gazed about the hospital room.

"You've done your best to make that quite evident," she replied.

She lifted her cane and tapped the foot of the bed sharply.

"Look at me when I speak to you," she flared. I raised my head and tried to shout back at her, but the cruelty in her eyes stunned me so much, I was speechless.

A tiny smile came and went on her lips, lips that seemed to have forgotten how to smile.

"Don't worry, I didn't expect you to do anything wonderful here, despite the frequent reports we received concerning your supposed singing and musical talent. I knew how you were brought up and how you would turn out. I have been anticipating the eventuality of your causing more problems. I just didn't think it would happen as quickly as it has. In that respect you did surprise me."

I covered my face with my hands. I felt as if Fate had pulled me once again through a knothole and stretched me out, thin and flat. I trembled and had trouble bringing out my thoughts. It was as if I had lost my voice and everything would be trapped forever inside me, even my tears.

"There's no sense trying to hide your shame. Soon it will be sticking out prominently. Fortunately," she added, "you had the good luck to have had an accident."

"What?" I lowered my hands from my face. "How can you call being hit by a car, good luck?" I demanded. A small smile, tight and cold, met my question. No, it was not a smile, it was more of a sneer.

"The accident provides us with a proper excuse for removing you from the school," she replied, her sneer turning into a smile of victory. Whenever she looked at me now, it was at some particular part of me. She didn't see me as a whole person, but in sections that seemed to arouse her anger . . . and she would destroy whatever made her angry.

"Removing me from the school!"

"Of course." She gave me that tight, firm hateful look again, her eyes beady. "Did you think I would continue to sponsor you in this condition? Did you think I would tolerate you walking through the halls and attending classes with your stomach protruding? You're here as a Cutler. Everything you do, whether you care about it or not, reflects on the Cutler name. I have good friends on the board of trustees of this school. I have a reputation to protect."

She fixed her spiteful eyes on me, that detestable old woman, as if sensing all that I felt. I glared back defiantly, hoping that she could see how I abhorred the idea of even being thought related to her. Perhaps my eyes were only glass to reveal all the spinning wheels of revenge I harbored and vowed to let loose one day. If so, she ignored it. Nothing frightened her.

"Who is the child's father?" she demanded. I looked away. She tapped her cane sharply on the floor. "Who is he?" she repeated.

"What difference does it make now?" I asked her, my tears burning behind my eyelids, for I was trying with all my might to keep them from bursting forth. I didn't want her to have the satisfaction of seeing me cry.

She relaxed her shoulders and nodded.

"You're right. What difference does it make? You probably don't even know which one is the real father," she added.

"That's not true," I cried. "I'm not that kind of girl."

"No," she said, lifting her upper lip so that her pale white teeth were fully revealed in a scowl, "you're not that kind of girl. You're lying here in this hospital bed pregnant because you're a good girl, an asset to your family."

I covered my face again with my palms. She was quiet for a long moment. I was hoping she might just turn away and leave me alone, but she had come to take control of my life again. I was positive it gave her great pleasure to determine my future the same way she determined everyone else's in the family, even though she despised me and didn't want to consider me a member of the family.

"You can't return to the school," she began, "and you can't return to Agnes Morris's residence. I certainly don't want you back at the hotel. Can you imagine the embarrassment you would bring to us, parading about the building and grounds with your stomach out a mile?"

"What do you want?" I finally asked, lowering my hands in defeat.

"What I want I can't get, so I will settle for what must be. The story will be given out that you've been injured far worse than you actually were. You're being taken to a rehabilitation center. That's dramatic enough to satisfy the curious at your school.

"In reality, you will leave here tomorrow and be taken to live with my sisters, Emily and Charlotte Booth, until you give birth. After that we'll see," she said.

"Where do your sisters live?" I asked.

"Not that it should matter to you, they live in Virginia, about twenty miles east of Lynchburg in what was my father's home, an old plantation called The Meadows. My sisters have been told of your arrival and your condition. I have arranged for a car to take you to the airport. When you arrive in Lynchburg, there will be a driver waiting to take you to The Meadows."

"But what about my things back at Agnes's house?" I cried.

"She'll get your things together and see that they're shipped out. You can't imagine how anxious she is to get rid of any trace of you."

"No wonder, the way you poisoned her against me with your letter of lies," I spat out vehemently.

"Apparently, that letter of lies, as you put it, was quite prophetic," she replied proudly. "Anyway, your fling here has ended."

"But there are people I want to say good-bye to . . . Mrs. Liddy . . ."

"We're trying to salvage some dignity from this situation," she snapped. "I don't want you seen gallivanting about when you're supposed to be injured and off to a rehabilitation center."

"People will know it's not true!" I moaned.

"Decent people will not challenge the story I give out," she replied with icy assurance. "The school authorities have already been informed." she added, demonstrating how quickly and efficiently she could take control of my life.

But what was I to do? Where could I go? I was pregnant and essentially penniless. I certainly couldn't run to Daddy Longchamp, not now that he had a new wife and was expecting a new child.

"Your mother," she said, pronouncing "Mother" as if it were a profanity, "has been told about your accomplishments. Naturally, it has put her into one of her states of hysteria." She laughed. "She's even had her doctor, the tenth or eleventh, I can't keep track anymore, put one of those things into her arms," she said, pointing to the I.V. stand in the corner of my room. "She claims she can't eat, can't swallow. She has a nurse around the clock.

"And all because of you. So, I wouldn't bother trying to call her to ask her to help you. She can't help herself. But," Grandmother Cutler added, "there's really nothing new about that."

I saw the smile of satisfaction around her gray eyes.

"Why do you hate her so?" I asked. Somehow I thought it was more than only her love affair with an itinerant singer. Anyway, that was long over and my mother was still married to Grandmother Cutler's son and had given birth to two of her grandchildren.

"I hate anyone who is that weak and self-indulgent," she said slowly and with a sneer. "She has never been anything but a lead weight, despite her beauty.

"In fact, her beauty is a deception. My foolish son, just like any other man, couldn't see past it in time to save himself and still can't.

"I'm sure," she added, "someday you will find a doting fool to look after you just as Randolph looks after your mother, but until then you will do as I say.

"The doctor will release you after breakfast tomorow. I have already spoken with him. Be prepared to leave. All the arrangements are perfect and no one is to be made to wait on you. Do you understand?"

"I understand who you are," I said, finally fixing my eyes firmly on hers, "and how unhappy you must be and must have been most of your life."

Her eyes flared and she pulled herself up into her habitual queenly posture.

"How dare you . . . how dare you think you can feel sorry for anyone, especially for me."

"But I do," I said calmly, so calmly I even surprised myself. "I don't hate you as much as I pity you and hate the things that made you like you are."

"Save your pity for yourself," she snapped back. "You will need it," she added and spun on her heels so quickly, she almost lost her balance. Then she stalked out of my hospital room, her cane tapping like a tiny hammer over the tiles as she turned and disappeared down the corridor.

I fell back against my pillow, too weak and defeated now to bother with tears. What difference did it make anymore? I thought. Michael was gone; Jimmy was sure to hate me once he found out the truth; Daddy Longchamp had a new life and was even expecting a new child. All the people I loved and cared about were far away. Grandmother Cutler could do what she wanted with me, and I had no one to blame for it but myself.

Good-bye to dreams of singing and being a stage star. Good-bye to the magic of love and romance and believing that fairy tales sometimes come true. Good-bye to being carefree and young, hopeful and energetic.

I could see the clouds moving over the sun and dropping shadows like torrents of rain over the city. A gloomy darkness crept into my hospital room, chilling me. I pulled the blanket over myself and clung to the warmth within. Tomorrow, I would be whisked out of the city of my dreams. I would disappear as if I never existed. Poor Madame Steichen, I thought. How disappointed in me she must be. All her hard work and faith tossed aside.

When we had first met and spoke, Michael had told me that passion makes us desperate, but he never told me that it could leave us lonely and empty, too. He didn't want me to know the danger in letting myself love him.

Had it been the same for my mother? Is that what turned her into the weak person she was? Was Grandmother Cutler right in saying I was just like her? Would I become the same kind of person eventually?

Just thinking about these things exhausted me. I couldn't keep my eyes open and didn't want to, for it was only in sleep that I had any relief from the harsh reality that had fallen around me and trapped me. Now I was once again a prisoner of fate, and Grandmother Cutler was truly once again my warden.

Doctor Stevens appeared early in the morning to give me his final examination and declare me well enough to leave. He signed me out and the nurse arrived to help me dress and get ready after I had had my breakfast. I realized that by the time Trisha arrived, I would be gone, so I requested the use of a telephone. Agnes answered.

"Agnes," I cried, "it's me, Dawn."

"Dawn?" There was a silence.

"Yes. I'm phoning from the hospital."

"Dawn? I'm afraid you must have the wrong number," she said coldly. "I don't know anyone named Dawn."

"Agnes, please," I begged, "don't do this. I have to speak with Trisha."

"Trisha has gone to school," she replied, but I knew Trisha's class schedule. She couldn't have left yet.

"Agnes, please," I begged. "I'm leaving soon and I won't have any other chance to speak with Trisha. She will make a wasted trip to the hospital because I will be gone. Won't you tell her I'm on the phone. Please."

"Oh, dear," she said suddenly, her voice rising in pitch, "I do wish I could consider your production, but I've already committed myself to another."

"Agnes!"

"Perhaps you will consider changing your production dates." She laughed. "Other producers have done that to accommodate me."

I saw it was no use. She was either doing this because Trisha was nearby and she didn't want her to know she was speaking to me, or she had really gone off on one of her memories and was far gone.

"Agnes," I said through my tears, "won't you let me speak with Trisha."

"I'm sorry, but I'm very busy," she replied and hung up.

"Agnes!" I cried into a dead receiver. I cradled it and started to cry. How would Trisha know where I was or what had happened to me?

The nurse asked me what was wrong and I explained that I had a friend coming later in the day, but I would already be gone and I couldn't reach her now.

"Just leave her a note," she said, "and I'll see that she gets it."

"Oh, would you? Thank you."

I took out the piece of paper on which I had intended to write Jimmy a letter and began to write my good-bye note to Trisha.

Dear Trisha,

By the time you read this, I will be long gone. Grandmother Cutler has come and taken control of my life. I'm to live with her sisters in Virginia until the baby is born. This way I'll be out of sight and out of mind and the precious Cutler name will be protected. I don't even know the exact address. I don't really care anymore. I know you are the only person I will miss. I will write you every chance I get. Please say good-bye to Mrs. Liddy for me and to the twins, and even to crazy Donald.

And thanks, thanks from all my heart for being my one true friend in all the world.

Love,
Dawn

I folded it up and gave it to the nurse.

A short while later, a chauffeur appeared. He was just someone from a company Grandmother Cutler had hired in the city to take me to the airport. I could see that to him I was like a package to deliver. Since I had already been signed out and Grandmother Cutler had taken care of everything else, there was nothing to do but leave with him. The nurses bid me good-bye and wished me luck.

All I had on me was what I had worn the day of my accident. The chauffeur was surprised.

"No luggage?" he asked, lingering in the doorway.

"No, sir. Everything's being shipped or has been," I said.

"Fine," he said, obviously grateful that things had been made easier for him.

It was a luxurious limousine. I was surprised Grandmother Cutler had gone to the expense, but then I thought she was probably trying to impress everyone with how well she takes care of her own family. I sat in the back at a corner of the large, black leather seat and stared out the window as we drove out of the city and toward the airport. My memories of my arrival returned.

How full of hope and excitement I had been. Yes, I had been afraid, too, but when I had first set eyes on these tall buildings and had seen all the people rushing by, I thought I might just become a famous singer and live in a penthouse apartment. Now, with people scurrying up and down sidewalks to keep warm and the traffic moving at a slow pace through the slushy streets, the shine was certainly off. People looked troubled, frenzied, even bored to me. And the city looked brown and dirty.

Only the Christmas decorations in the store front windows gave me any feeling of warmth and happiness. It would have been wonderful, Michael and I strolling down Fifth Avenue, my hands in a fur muff. We would have heard the Christmas carols and seen the lighted displays and he would have hugged me to him. Later, we would have lain together at the foot of our little Christmas tree and made plans for our future.

As the limousine continued down the avenue, I saw a happy couple walking hand in hand just the way I had dreamt Michael and I would have. The young woman looked so happy and alive, her cheeks rosy, her eyes full of promise. Her young man was gesturing exuberantly and saying things that made her laugh. I could see the happy puffs of breath from both their mouths join in the air before them.

The limousine started to make a turn. I looked back at them as long as I could. Then the limousine sped up and they were left behind, just like all my dreams.

12

THE MEADOWS

Once I boarded the airplane, I fell asleep and woke up just before the stewardess announced we were going to land. The airport wasn't very busy when I arrived, so I didn't expect to have any problem finding my driver to take me to The Meadows, the home of Grandmother Cutler's sisters. But when I came through the gate and looked around, I saw no one holding up a sign with my name on it. In moments the people who had been there to greet arriving passengers left with everyone else who had gotten off the plane, and I was practically all alone in the lobby. I sat down and waited.

I wasn't sure what to do after the first hour ticked by. People scurried about rushing to other gates and departing planes, but no one appeared to be looking for me. I folded my arms under my bosom and sat back with my eyes closed. I was still very tired. Traveling so soon after my release from the hospital was exhausting, especially with all this waiting. I pulled my legs up under me and curled up on the chair and before I knew it, I had drifted off again. I dreamt I was in the back of Daddy Longchamp's car asleep, my head resting against Jimmy's shoulders. I felt comfortable and safe and was upset when I felt someone poke my shoulder sharply.

My eyes fluttered open and I gazed up at a tall, lean man with dirty brown hair, the strands going this way and that over his head and deeply creased forehead. He had a long, drooping nose and deep-set, dull brown eyes with a small web of wrinkles at each corner. He needed a shave badly. His rough, gray-brown stubble grew in ugly patches over his pale white face. Hair grew everywhere—on his neck around his Adam's apple and strands even poked out from the inside of his ears. I noticed how his lower lip hung open revealing teeth stained by chewing tobacco. There was a dry brown line from the corner of his mouth down his chin where some tobacco juice had drooled. He was dressed in faded blue overalls and wore a torn flannel shirt beneath. His boots were muddy and even smelly. I hated to think what he might have been stepping in before he arrived.

"You the girl?" he asked.

"Pardon me?"

"You the girl?" he repeated gruffly. It sounded like his throat was filled with sand.

"My name's Dawn," I replied. "Are you here to take me to The Meadows?"

"Come on," he said and turned abruptly. He started away before I rose, and I had to hurry to catch up.

"I've been waiting a long time," I said when I stepped beside him. He didn't look at me. He took long strides and glared ahead, his thumbs hooked in his overalls. I saw that his hands were covered with dirt and his fingernails were long and grimy.

"Got me butcherin' hogs all mornin' and then they expect me to drive all the way to the airport," he muttered.

"Do you know if my things arrived yet?" I asked as we turned toward the exit. "All my clothes were shipped from New York City," I added. I didn't think he was going to reply. He continued to walk and mutter and then reached for the door handle.

"Don't know," he finally said. I followed him out, practically running to keep up as he crossed the street and headed toward the parking lot. He didn't pay any attention to the traffic and cars had to stop short, the drivers shouting at us. But that didn't bother him. He kept his eyes forward, his head slightly lowered and continued his long, quick strides.

When we reached the parking lot, he turned abruptly and led me to a battered and rusted black pickup truck. Even before we reached it, I could smell it and the stench was enough to make my stomach gurgle and turn. I covered my mouth with my hand and looked away for a moment. He stopped after he opened his door, and looked back at me.

"Git in," he commanded. "I gotta git back and shovel out some cow manure and repair a flat tire on the tractor."

I held my breath and approached the truck. When I opened the door, I looked in at a torn seat, the springs showing everywhere. Where was I to sit? He got in and looked at me. Then he realized why I was hesitating and reached back behind the seat to produce a dingy and dirty looking brown blanket. He dropped it over the seat for me to sit on it. I got in slowly and lowered myself to the seat, making myself as comfortable as possible. Instantly, he started the engine. The truck sputtered and spit and then he ground it into reverse and backed us out of the parking spot.

I tried rolling the dirty window down so I could get some ventilation, but the handle just turned and turned without doing anything.

"That don't work no more," he said, not taking his eyes off the road. "Ain't got a chance to fix it. Not with the way that Emily's after me to do this and do that."

"How far do we have to go?" I asked, not relishing a long trip in this stuffy and smelly vehicle. It seemed to hit every bump in the road and announce it loudly. I was getting more and more nauseated every moment and had to swallow hard to keep whatever was in my stomach down.

"Close to fifty odd miles," he said. "Ain't no Sunday ride," he added. He shifted so the truck would go faster and we finally turned down a smooth highway.

"Who are you?" I finally asked since he never volunteered to tell me.

"Name's Luther."

"Have you been working at The Meadows long?" I asked. I thought if I kept talking, I could keep my mind off the horrible ride.

"Long as I could lift a bail of hay and heave it on a truck," he replied. "Never worked nowhere else." He finally turned to look at me. "You one of Lillian's kin, ain'tcha?"

"Yes," I said reluctantly.

"Ain't seen her for years and years. She don't never come back, but I heard she's a fancy rich lady now. She was always the smartest. Of course, it don't take much to be smarter than Charlotte. Hell, I got hound dogs know more than she does," he said and looked like he was smiling for the first time.

"What is The Meadows like?" I asked.

"Like most old plantations. It ain't what it was; that's for dang sure. But," he said, turning to me, "nothin' is—not the people, not the government, not the land, not the buildings, nothin'."

"What are my aunts like?" I asked.

He looked at me for the longest moment and then turned back to the road.

"You don't know?" he replied.

"No," I said.

"Well, it's best you find out for yourself. Yeah," he said, nodding, "it's best you do."

He was quiet most of the remaining time, muttering to himself about another driver or something he saw that annoyed him for reasons I didn't understand. I tried looking out at the scenery, but the window was so streaked, it made everything look gray and dismal, even though the sun was out most of the time. A little over a half an hour after we had left the airport, the sky grew more overcast and what had been cloudy and misty became murky, especially under the spreading magnolia trees. Fields and houses were draped in dim, purplish shadows everywhere.

Soon the nice, small farmhouses and tiny villages became few and far between. We passed long, dry, drab brown empty fields and when we did come to a house, it was usually sick looking with bleached clapboard siding and porches that leaned, their railings cracked or missing. I saw poor black children playing in front of many of these houses, the lawns covered with parts of automobiles or broken wooden chairs. The children stopped their make-believe and stared at us with empty eyes only vaguely curious.

Finally, I saw a road sign announcing our arrival in Upland Station. I recalled Grandmother Cutler telling me this was the closest town to the plantation. As we entered it, I realized it wasn't much—a general store which also served as the post office, a gas station, a small restaurant that looked like part of the gas station, a barber shop, and a large stone and wood house with a sign in front describing it as a mortuary. At the far end there was a railroad station that looked like it had been closed for ages. All the windows were boarded and there were NO TRESPASSING signs posted all over it. There were no sidewalks in Upland Station, and there was no one in the street, just a couple of hound dogs lying in the mud. It was one of the most depressing places I had ever seen and I had been in many rundown villages and towns when Daddy and Momma Longchamp took us from one place to another.

Luther turned as soon as we passed the old railroad station and started down a more narrow road that had only an occasional house here and there, all of them looking like poor farms on which people barely scratched out a living. The road began to look rougher and older, its macadam cracked and broken. The truck rocked from side to side as Luther tried to navigate it over the most solid pieces. He slowed down and turned right on what was nothing more than a dirt road with a mound of yellow grass running down its center. He drove slowly, but that didn't stop the truck from swaying so much it made me nauseous again.

"All this land still belongs to The Meadows," he said when we reached a broken wooden fence. I saw sections of it running far off to the right and far off to the left on both sides of the road. The fields were overgrown with bushes and dry grass, but it looked like acres and acres of it.

"They own all this?" I said, impressed. Luther grunted.

"Lotta good that does them now," he replied.

But how could it not do them good to own so much land? I wondered. They must be very, very rich people. I sat back, looking forward to setting my eyes on a wealthy southern plantation. I knew how some of these places could be, how some old southern families had held on to their wealth as well as their heritage. Perhaps it wouldn't be so bad here, I thought. After all I would rest, eat good food, and be in fresh, country air. It would be good for the baby.

Luther began to slow down even more. I leaned forward. Over the tops of the trees I could see the tips of the brick chimneys and the long, gabled roof of the plantation house. It looked enormous. At the entrance to the driveway were two stone pillars, each crowned with a ball of granite, but the driveway itself was nothing more than crushed rocks and dirt. As Luther turned into it, I gazed ahead and saw what was better described as a corpse, the remains of what must have once been a blossoming flower of the South, but what was now a phantom of itself.

I saw the dry and broken marble fountains, some leaning over precipitously. I saw the dead and scraggly hedges, the pockmarked flower beds with their gaping empty spaces, the chipped and battered stone walks, and the large, but ugly lawn only spotted here and there with patches of yellow grass. The shadows that had fallen with the twilight looked permanently glued on the immense two-story wood structure.

Over the great round columns of the full-facade porch ran thin leafless vines that looked more like rotting rope. Some of the multipane front windows had black shutters and decorative crowns; some had lost their shutters and looked naked. There was only the dim glow of light behind the lower ones.

Luther drove toward the right side of the house and I could see that behind the house was the barn and stables, all the buildings tottering and in need of paint. There was rusted and broken farm equipment everywhere and chickens ran freely over the driveway. Some even paraded arrogantly over the portico. I thought I saw a sow waddle just around the corner of the main house.

Luther stopped short.

"You might as well git out here," he said. "I gotta go on back to the barn."

I opened the door and slowly stepped out. When he pulled away, a cloud of dust rose from the driveway and nearly choked me. I fanned the air and when it cleared, I looked up at the tall plantation house. The windows in the gabled dormers were like mirrors reflecting the quickly blackening night sky overcast with brooding clouds. For the moment they looked like dark eyes peering down angrily at me. Above them, the peak of the roof seemed to touch the dark sky. I embraced myself. The wind that whistled past me was chilly and quickly turned my cheeks red.

I hurried up the shattered front steps to the enormous entrance. My boots clacked over the loose slats of the porch floor and blackbirds that had been hovering out of the wind just inside the columns rose in an ebony splash and flew into the night, complaining loudly of my intrusion.

I found the brass knocker on the tall panel door and let it tap on the metal plate behind it. A deep, hollow echo reverberated on the other side. I waited, but nothing happened, so I let the knocker rap again and again. Suddenly the door was jerked open, its rusted hinges rattling. At first I saw no one. There was barely any light on within the long entryway that led down a dark corridor to a circular stairway. Then, a tall, dark figure looking more like a silhouette stepped before me from the side, holding a kerosene lamp in her hands. Her appearance was so abrupt and silent, I felt like I had been greeted by a ghost in this dying house. I couldn't help but gasp and step back.

"Don't you have any patience?" she snapped. When she moved closer to me, I was able to see her face in the dim light of the lamp. It cast an amber glow over her long, ashen visage, turning her eyes into deep, dark sockets. Her mouth was a pencil-thin crooked line drawn across her narrow face. She had her long, thin gray hair knitted in a big knot behind her head.

"I'm sorry," I said. "I didn't think anyone had heard me."

"Step in so I can close the door," she commanded. I did so quickly. Then she held out the lamp and ran the light over me. "Humph," she said, confirming some expectation. When she brought the light closer to herself again, I was able to see more of her face.

There were resemblances to Grandmother Cutler, especially in the steel-gray eyes that gazed back at me with a similar iciness. Grandmother Cutler's face was just as thin now, the cheekbones just as prominent. Perhaps this woman was a little taller and had broader shoulders. She certainly stood as firmly with the same arrogant pride as she threw her shoulders back to gaze down at me.

"My name is Miss Emily," she said. "You are always to call me Miss Emily, is that clear?"

"Yes, ma'am," I said.

"Not ma'am, Miss Emily," she retorted.

"Yes, Miss Emily."

"You're too late for anything to eat," she said. "We eat dinner early and those who miss the dinner bell go without."

"I'm not very hungry anyway," I said. The ride in the smelly truck had taken care of any appetite.

"Good. Now march yourself up those stairs and I'll show you where you will stay." She started ahead of me, holding the kerosene lamp up to light our way. The entryway walls were bare except for a portrait of a dour-looking southern gentleman, his hair as white as milk. I had only a glimpse of him as the light washed away the shadows, but I thought I saw resemblances to Grandmother Cutler and Miss Emily, especially in the forehead and eyes. I imagined it was a portrait of their father or perhaps their grandfather. Lighter spaces along both sides of the walls indicated that there had once been other pictures displayed.

"Have my things arrived yet from New York, Miss Emily?" I asked.

"No," she said sharply without turning around. Her voice reverberated down the long, empty corridor and sounded like a chorus of "no's."

"No? But why not? What will I do? What I am wearing is all I have," I cried. She stopped to turn back.

"So?" she said. "What does it matter? You're not here to entertain yourself. You're here to give birth and then leave immediately after."

"But . . ."

"Don't worry, I have something for you to put on. You will have clean bedding and clean towels. If you keep them clean," she added.

"But maybe we should phone and find out what's happened to my things," I insisted.

"Phone? We don't have a phone," she said calmly.

"No phone?" So far away from anywhere in such a large house, with no phone? I thought. "But . . . how do you get important messages?"

"Anyone who wants us calls down at the general store in Upland and when Mr. Nelson has a free moment or is heading out in this direction, he brings us the message. We don't have any need to call anyone ourselves. There's no one left to call," she said dryly.

"But I have people who want to call me and . . ."

"Now listen to me," she said, stepping a few steps toward me. "This isn't supposed to be a holiday, young lady. You're here because you've disgraced yourself and my sister wants you here. Fortunately for you I've had experience as a midwife," she said and started toward the stairway again.

"Midwife? You mean I won't have a doctor?" I asked.

"Doctors cost money and are unnecessary when it comes to delivering a baby," she said. "Now would you please come along. I have many other things to do beside settle you in for the night."

I looked back at the doorway. With the kerosene lamp in her hands ahead of me, there was only a deep dark shadow to look at. I felt as if I had just entered a tunnel and the entryway had been shut up. I wanted to turn and run out, but where would I run to? We were miles and miles from anyplace and it was growing darker and darker by the minute.

Maybe in the daytime things would look better, I thought. I could probably get Luther to drive me to the general store when I wanted to call Trisha. And there was always the mail.

"You do get mail here, don't you?"

"We get mail," she said. "But not much."

"Well I'll be getting some," I replied.

"Humph," she said again and lifted the lamp so the light fell over the steps of the circular stairway.

"Isn't there electricity in this house?" I asked, walking behind her and embracing myself. There was a terrible chill . . . no fires burning, no scent of wood or coal, nothing but the musty odor of dampness.

"We use it sparingly," she said. "It's too expensive."

"Too expensive?" How curious, I thought, especially with all of Grandmother Cutler's enormous personal wealth. Why couldn't she send some money to these sisters to help them out? Where was the other sister? I wondered. I was about to ask when I heard a strange peal of laughter from above. It sounded more like a little girl than an elderly lady.

"Quiet, you fool," Miss Emily snapped. When the light reached the second-story landing, I saw a much shorter and much plumper little old lady leaning over the banister. Her gray hair was tied with yellow ribbons into two thick pigtails. That plus the faded pink shift with the yellow ribbon belt tied loosely about her waist made her look like an adult masquerading as a child. She clapped her hands together and then ran her palms quickly over her abundant bosom to smooth out her shift.

"Hello," she said when we reached the landing.

"Hello," I said and looked to Miss Emily for an introduction. She was reluctant to give it, but tightened her mouth in the corners and did so.

"This is my sister Charlotte," she said. "You can call her simply Charlotte. I told you to stay in your room, didn't I, Charlotte?" Miss Emily chastised.

"But I've come to meet our niece," Charlotte whined. As she drew closer, I saw she had a much softer face and bluer eyes. Although there were wrinkles along her forehead and some lines at the corners of her eyes, she looked considerably younger than Miss Emily and Grandmother Cutler. Her smile was far friendlier and simple, the smile of an excited schoolgirl.

I saw that the hem of her shift was torn and frayed and she was wearing what looked like a man's leather bedroom slippers with no stockings or socks. Her ankles were thick, even swollen, with little pink bumps around them.

"Well you've met her, now go on back and do your needlework," Miss Emily commanded.

"I do needlework," Charlotte said proudly. "I made all the nice towels and washcloths and Emily's got some hanging in frames in Daddy's office, don'tcha, Emily?"

"For God's sake, don't make a fool of yourself first chance you get, Charlotte. This isn't the time to talk about your needlework. Just go do it."

"I'll be happy to look at some of it later," I told her. Her eyes brightened and her smile widened. She clapped her hands together again.

"We'll have mint julep tea," she said excitedly.

"Not tonight," Miss Emily said, practically shouting now. "It's too late for that. I'm showing Eugenia her room so she can go to sleep. She's tired."

"Eugenia! My name's not Eugenia," I cried. "My name is Dawn."

"My sister told me your name was Eugenia. What difference does it make here anyway?" she snapped and started down right.

"It makes a big difference to me," I stated. All the while I had been at the hotel, Grandmother Cutler had tried to force me to accept the name Eugenia, the name of another one of her sisters, one who had died of smallpox. She had even gone so far as to cut off all food to me until I accepted the name, but I refused and she gave up when I discovered how she had arranged for my abduction.

Now that I was in trouble and desperate, she was going to have her way with me.

"Come along," Miss Emily ordered.

"Good night, Charlotte," I said. "I guess I will see you in the morning."

"I guess you will," she said and laughed again. She plucked up her skirt with her fingers and spun around. "I'm wearing Daddy's slippers," she cried.

"Charlotte!" Miss Emily screamed.

Charlotte dropped her skirt and gazed with frightened eyes in Miss Emily's direction. Then she spun around and hurried off in the opposite direction, that peal of childlike laughter trailing behind her.

"Come," Miss Emily repeated, glaring angrily in Charlotte's direction for a moment. Then she turned abruptly and we went down a long corridor to the right and turned a corner which took us down another corridor toward the rear of the building. The house was truly enormous. With its long, wide hallways dark, however, I couldn't appreciate any of the old artwork or the antique mirrors and tables. Above us hung unlit chandelier after chandelier, their crystal bulbs all looking more like pieces of ice in the dim light of the kerosene lamp. As we walked, I noticed that the doors to all the rooms, and there seemed to be an endless number, were all shut tight. I knew that some had been closed for a long time because there were cobwebs between the doors and the jambs.

Finally, Miss Emily stopped at an opened doorway and waited for me to approach.

"This is where you will stay," she said, holding the light so that I could gaze into the room.

It had to be one of the smaller ones, I thought. There was a narrow bed against the wall on the left. It had no headboard. It was just a mattress on a metal frame. Beside it was a bare night stand with a kerosene lamp. The floors of the room were wooden slats covered by a small, dark blue oval rug at the foot of the bed. The walls were dark gray. The remaining furniture was simple—a plain dresser with nothing on it and a small table with two chairs. There were no mirrors. I saw a closet on the right with two empty hangers dangling inside and there was another door down right.

"This is your bathroom," Miss Emily said, directing the light of the kerosene lamp at that door. "All right, go on in," she ordered.

I walked in slowly ahead of her. Even my little room away from the family at the Cutler's Cove Hotel was a palace compared to this, I thought. And then I realized what it was that made the room so depressing. There was no window. How could there be a room without a window?

"Why isn't there a window?" I asked. She didn't reply. Instead, she went to the dresser, put her lamp on top, and pulled open the top drawer. She reached in and drew out a plain gray gown made of cotton. It reminded me of a hospital gown. She tossed it on the bed.

"Put this on when we're finished," she said.

"Finished?"

"This is your light," she said, indicating the small lamp on the night stand. "The matches are here," she said, picking them up and then putting them down. "You have just so much kerosene a week so don't waste it."

"Isn't there any place nicer?" I asked. "There's no window here."

"It isn't for you to choose your room," she said sharply. "This isn't a hotel."

"But why was a room made without a window?" I pursued. She put her hands on her hips and glared at me.

"If you must know, this room was built long after the house had been completed. It was built especially for sick people, to keep them isolated from the others," she said. "Especially during the terrible smallpox epidemics and the epidemic of Spanish flu."

"But I'm not sick; I'm pregnant. Being pregnant isn't being sick," I protested, tears now burning under my eyelids.

"Pregnant like you are without a husband is the same as being sick," she replied. "There are all sorts of sicknesses, sicknesses of the soul as well as of the body. Disgrace can weaken and kill a person as quickly as any disease. Now take off your clothes so I can see how far along you are."

"What?" I stepped back.

"I told you; I have been a midwife. Everyone for miles and miles around here calls me instead of any doctor. I've delivered dozens of babies and all safely and well, except for those that were sick in the mother's stomach. Quickly," she snapped. "I have other things to do yet tonight."

"But it's so cold in here," I complained. "Where is the heat?"

"You have an extra blanket under the bed if you need it. Before I go to sleep," she added in a relenting voice, "I will bring you a hot water bottle. That's how we all sleep here and always have. We save the wood and coal for the stove in the kitchen. I've only got Luther now and I can't have him chopping wood all day to keep this house warm and coal costs money."

She lit the kerosene lamp on the night stand and turned expectantly toward me.

"I thought I would have a doctor," I said, "and be taken to a hospital at the right time. I was recently in an accident. I was hit by a car and I just got out of a hospital," I added, but she simply stared at me as if I hadn't said a word, stared and waited, her eyes fixed on me with the same cold, glassy glaze Grandmother Cutler had.

"I can't do what has to be done for you if I don't know what you need," she finally said.

"What do you want?" I asked.

"Take off your clothes and come stand here by me in the light," she ordered. She folded her arms under her small bosom and threw back her shoulders, her head high and arrogant again.

Slowly, reluctantly, I peeled off my coat and began to unbutton my blouse.

"I told you, I have many other things to do tonight," she snapped. "Can't you move any faster?"

"My fingers are cold," I said.

"Humph." She stepped forward and pulled my fingers away from my buttons roughly. Then she began to take off my clothing herself. She nearly skinned my arms when she unfastened my bra and drew the straps over my shoulders and down past my elbows. After she undid my skirt, she gave me a small push so I would step out of it. I stood before her in the pale glow of the kerosene lamps, my arms crossed over my naked breasts, shivering. All I wore were my panties and boots and socks.

Miss Emily circled me slowly, squeezing her narrow chin between her thumb and forefinger. As she drew closer, I saw the pockmarks in her cheeks and in her forehead. It looked like someone had taken sandpaper to her skin; it was that dry. Her eyebrows were thick and untrimmed and she had small dark hairs growing freely above her upper lip.

Suddenly, when she stood behind me, I felt her frosty, callous fingers on my sides. I started to move forward, but she pressed harder to hold me in place. I moaned in pain.

"Stand still," she commanded. She widened her hands so that they stretched around toward my belly button. Her cold, bony fingers felt more like wires. She continued to press and squeeze, which was starting to make me nauseous. I gathered she was measuring the size of my stomach. Then she pulled her hands away and came around in front of me.

Without speaking, she seized my wrists and pulled my arms from my bosom, holding them up as she gazed freely at my breasts. I saw her steel-gray eyes narrow as she leaned toward me to look closer. She nodded and released her hold on my wrists. Instinctively, my arms fluttered like broken bird wings and I brought my hands to my throat, pressing one on top of the other as I stared into Miss Emily's hard face.

This close her features looked chiseled from stone, the nose cut sharply, her thin lips sliced across a granite visage. A chilling shiver raced down my spine, making me want to run and hide.

"Take off those ridiculous underpants," she commanded. I knew she was referring to the lace trim.

"I'm cold," I complained.

"The longer you procrastinate, the longer it takes and the longer you remain naked."

Reluctantly, too tired and weak to offer any resistance, I did as she commanded. She told me to lie down on my back and then she brought the kerosene lamp to the foot of the bed so the light fell over my naked body. She took my ankles firmly in those strong hands and pulled my legs apart. I closed my eyes and prayed for the examination to end quickly.

"As I expected, it will be a hard birth," she declared. "The first birthing is always the hardest, but when you're young, it's even harder."

"You know why that is?" she asked, dropping my feet and stepping up to the side of the bed so she could gaze down at me. I shook my head. "It's because of Eve's sin in Paradise. Because of that all women have been cursed with the pain of labor. You will pay dearly for your fleeting moments of iniquitous pleasure."

She lifted the kerosene lamp high and held it above me. With her face so fully bathed in the light, it looked like it, too, was on fire. Her eyes blazed down. I had to shield my eyes.

"And when you conceive out of wedlock," she continued, "that pain and labor is even more horrendous."

"I don't care," I cried. "I'm not afraid."

She nodded and then those pencil-thin lips curled up at the corners as she slowly lowered the light.

"We'll see how brave you are when your time comes, Eugenia," she spat.

"Don't call me Eugenia. My name is Dawn."

She stopped smiling.

"Put on your gown and get to bed," she ordered. "We're wasting kerosene. I'll return with your hot water bottle."

She gathered my clothing quickly.

"What are you doing with my clothes? Those things are all I have right now."

"They have to be washed, purified. Don't worry, I'll keep them safely for you," she said, rolling everything into one ball within her embrace.

"But . . . I want my things. We've got to find out about my things," I demanded.

"Oh stop whining," she snapped, eyes blazing furiously. "You're just like all the other young girls today . . . I *want;* I *want!* Well look at what your I want has done for you," she spat. "Put on your gown," she repeated and turned and started out.

It was so cold, I had no choice but to quickly pull the ugly gown over my head. It smelled like mothballs and felt rough against my skin. I knelt down and looked under the bed for the blanket she had told me would be there. I dragged it out and shook it. Dust particles flew everywhere. Then I pulled back the cover sheet on the narrow bed. The bed sheet looked clean, but was cold and rough to the touch. I was shivering too much to care and quickly slipped into the bed and drew the blanket over me.

It seemed to take forever for Miss Emily to return. I was beginning to think she wouldn't when, finally, she appeared with a hot water bottle wrapped in a white towel. She thrust it at me and I took it gratefully and brought it to my trembling body. The warmth felt like a gentle pair of hands quickly wiping away the cold.

"It's so cold here," I said. "I'll only get sick."

"Of course you won't get sick. If anything, you will get stronger. Difficulties and hardships toughen us and allow us to battle the devil and his followers. Life was too soft and easy for you; that's why you got into trouble," she declared.

"My life was far from easy. You don't know anything about me," I cried, but I was weak and tired from the trip, the cold and the entire ordeal. My words had no fire. They sounded terribly pathetic, even to me.

"I know enough about you," she said. "If you behave and you are cooperative, we will succeed and you will have a second chance, but if you persist in being a spoiled young lady, you will make things harder for both of us and, eventually, impossible for you. Do I make myself quite clear?" She was waiting for my response. "Well?"

"Yes," I said, "but in the morning I want to go to the general store and call to find out where my things are. I need my things," I insisted. "Luther will drive me."

"Luther doesn't have time to spend on nonsense. He has his chores. It was hard enough for him to leave to get you. As it is he will have to work well into the night to make up for it. One final thing," she said, approaching the bed. I could only lie there all cramped up around the water bottle, borrowing from its warmth.

"I don't want you having much to do with Charlotte or encouraging her to say or do any of her silly things. You are not to pay attention to her," she warned. "Don't listen to any of the stupid things she says."

"What's wrong with her?" I asked.

"The same thing that will probably be wrong with your offspring," she replied.

"Why?"

"She, too, was born out of wedlock, the result of one of my father's sexual indiscretions. As a result she is an idiot," Miss Emily spat. "I keep her only because . . . she has no other place to go. Besides, it would be a disgrace to put her someplace because she still carries the Booth name.

"Anyway," she said, that sneer forming, "now you know what you have to look forward to," she added, and before I could respond, she bent over and blew out the kerosene lamp beside my bed. Then, she started away with her own, closed the door and left me in pitch darkness.

I began to sob.

Perhaps Miss Emily was right, I thought; perhaps I was a terrible sinner.

For surely, I was now as close as I could be to hell on earth.

13

UGLY REALITIES

"Get up, get up, get out of bed, you silly, silly sleepy head," I heard someone sing.

I unfolded myself slowly. I had been sleeping with my body as tight as a fist, the hot water bottle against my stomach. My muscles ached as I stretched out. Then I peered over the blanket toward the door. It was open, but there was no one there. Had I dreamt it?

Someone giggled.

"Who's there?" I asked, sitting up and embracing myself. Without the morning light through a window, the room was still quite dark, but there was some light coming through a window in the corridor.

"Who is it?" I demanded. When she giggled again, I recognized the childlike tones. "Charlotte?"

She stepped into the doorway. Her hair was still tied into two thick braids and she still wore the same faded pink shift with the yellow ribbon belt. I saw she continued to wear her father's old slippers, too.

"Emily sent me to fetch you. She says you should have been up and down to breakfast already," she added, forming as serious a face as she could. "Besides," she said, changing her expression quickly to a smile, "today is my birthday."

"Is it? That's very nice. Happy birthday," I said, yawning. I had had one of the worst nights of sleep ever. Every part of my body ached, from the back of my neck to my ankles. I was as stiff as a wet blouse frozen on a winter clothes line.

I swung my legs over the bed and found my boots. The insides were so cold it was like stepping into a puddle of ice water. I couldn't stop rubbing my arms: Charlotte stood there staring at me and smiling.

"How old are you, today?" I asked. Her smile evaporated quickly.

"Oh, that's not nice. You shouldn't ask a lady how old she is," she chastised, suddenly sounding remarkably like Miss Emily. "It's not good etiquette," she recited.

"I'm sorry."

"But we will have a cake and you can sing 'Happy Birthday' to me. We're going to have guests, too," she added. "All the neighbors and cousins and people from as far away as Hadleyville. Even Lynchburg!"

"That's very nice. I'm looking forward to it," I said. I lit the kerosene lamp so there would be some more light and carried it to the bathroom. "I'll be right out," I said.

The door didn't open easily. I had to tug and tug on it. Once I opened it and looked in, I thought it would have been better had I not been able to open it. The bathroom consisted of a small, rust-stained sink and a toilet with a cracked toilet seat. A lump of lard soap lay on the edge of the sink. There was a dark gray towel and a dark gray washcloth on a wooden rack above the sink, but there was no mirror, no tub, no shower. The floor had a yellowish linoleum on it, but it was peeled and cracked in the corners and around the toilet.

I closed the door behind me and went to the bathroom. Then I turned on the faucet marked hot, but nothing came out of it. Water only flowed from the faucet marked cold, and that water had a brown tint to it. I let it run, but it didn't clear up. Finally, having no choice, I wet the washcloth and washed my face using the horrible soap.

I realized I had no brush for my hair. I had had a comb in my purse, but Miss Emily had taken everything last night. I ran my fingers through my hair, which already felt dirty and scraggly and then emerged from the bathroom.

Charlotte was sitting on the bed, her hands folded in her lap. She smiled up at me. Her complexion was much softer than Miss Emily's, and there was even a bit of a rosy tint in her plump cheeks.

"You had better not waste your kerosene," she said, "or Emily will yell. She won't give you more," she warned.

"This is horrible," I cried. "I'm made to stay in a room without a window and there is no light except this small kerosene lamp and the kerosene is rationed."

Charlotte stared at my outburst, her eyes wide with surprise and confusion. Then she bit down on her lower lip and shook her head emphatically from side to side.

"Emily says there's a lot of waste going on. It's the devil's work when we don't cherish what we have and when we waste. Emily says waste not, want not. That's what Emily says," she concluded.

"Well, Emily's not right. I mean, Miss Emily," I corrected quickly.

Again, Charlotte stared at me. I could see from the look in her eyes that she either didn't understand my anger or didn't want to. Suddenly, her expression changed and she looked like a little girl about to whisper a secret. She leaned toward me, first looking toward the doorway to be sure no one was there.

"Did the baby keep you up all night?" she asked.

"The baby? What baby?"

"The baby," she said, smiling. "The baby was crying and I went to give him his milk, but when I got there, he was gone," she said, holding her hands out, palms up.

"Gone? Whose baby? I didn't hear any baby."

"We better get downstairs," she said quickly and stood up. "Emily's made oatmeal for us and if it gets cold, it's our fault."

She started for the door. I sighed and turned off the kerosene lamp. It would be a minor tragedy if I left it burning, I thought.

I followed Charlotte out. She walked with short, quick steps, shuffling her slippers over the floor, and kept her hands clasped to her body with her head down like a Geisha girl. Now that there was some light pouring through the windows here and there, I could see more of the house. When I had arrived in the dark, I hadn't realized just how run-down it was inside as well as outside. This wing, my wing, looked like it hadn't been used for years. Large cobwebs hung between the ceilings and the walls and through the chandeliers. The walls themselves looked caked with dust.

Here and there along the corridor were pieces of hall furniture: a dark oak chest, hardwood benches too uncomfortable looking to be sat upon, and upholstered chairs that looked like great dust collectors. Every dozen yards or so, there was an old painting, most depicting classic southern scenes: slaves picking cotton, a plantation owner sitting upon a great white steed and looking out over his acres and acres of crops, and pictures of young women holding parasols and talking to handsome young suitors on great, green lawns or in front of gazebos.

When we turned toward the stairway, the paintings on the walls were all portraits of ancestors—women with pinched faces dressed in dark clothes, their hair pinned back tightly, men unsmiling and stern, and an occasional portrait of a child who had obviously been forced to sit still and pose. At the end of this corridor, right before the stairway, stood a broken grandfather clock, missing its minute hand.

When we reached the stairs, I looked down the opposite corridor toward the west wing where Miss Emily and Charlotte lived in the great house. The hallways were cleaner and brighter and there were many more pictures. That side would get most of the sunlight, I thought. Why couldn't she find a place for me there?

Charlotte looked up from the stairs to be sure I was following and then continued quickly. I felt silly walking in my boots and wearing a gown that looked like a hospital gown, but what was I to do? Miss Emily had taken my clothes. I hurried along to catch up and turned at the foot of the stairs to follow Charlotte through a wide doorway.

The first room was a great dining room with a long, dark oak table and ten chairs. It had a light brown rug and a wall of windows which made it one of the brightest rooms I had seen. Above the table hung a large chandelier. There was a matching dark oak hutch in one corner and I could see dishes and ceramic figurines within. They still had some nice things here and there, I thought.

"Come along. Hurry," Charlotte said in the far doorway. I followed her into the kitchen.

It looked very little changed from what it must have been when the house had first been built. There was even a hand pump beside the sink instead of a faucet. There was a cast-iron stove for heat and cooking, a light oak table and six chairs in one corner and a counter beside the sink with cast-iron pots and pans dangling from hooks. The windows were covered with thin, white cotton curtains and the refrigerator was an old ice box.

Set on the table were three bowls of hot oatmeal and one piece of bread and an orange beside each. The place setting contained a single soup spoon and a napkin.

Miss Emily stepped out of the pantry, which was at the rear of the kitchen. Through the window in the doorway beside it, I could see some of the rear of the house: a bald field with an old wagon in the center and the corner of a barn.

"Well, it's about time," Miss Emily snapped. She wore a dark gray shift with a high white collar and black, high-top leather shoes. In the daylight, her face looked even more pasty and sallow. Her thin lips were so colorless they reminded me of long, thin dead worms. She had Grandmother Cutler's gray eyes, all right, but set in her narrow face, they looked sly, evil, conniving. The line of face hair above her upper lip was more pronounced in the light, and I saw she had a curly strand of gray hair here and there under her chin as well.

"Without a window, I didn't know it was morning," I replied.

She pulled her shoulders back as if I had slapped her.

"Um," she said, nodding. "I shall put a clock in your room so you won't use not knowing the time as an excuse to get out of your chores."

"Chores?"

"Of course, chores. Did you think this was going to be some sort of free ride? Did you think we were all born to be your servants?"

"I don't mind chores," I said. "I . . ."

"Sit down and eat before it's all too cold," she commanded.

Charlotte moved instantly to her seat and lowered her head. I sat down across from her and Miss Emily took her seat.

"I . . ."

"Quiet," she snapped. She clasped her hands and dropped her gaze to the table. "For this and all our other blessings, Dear Lord we thank you. Amen."

"Amen," Charlotte said and raised her eyes to me.

"Amen," I said.

"Eat," Miss Emily ordered. Charlotte began to scoop up her cereal, clutching her spoon awkwardly in her thick fingers. She looked like a little girl first learning how to eat by herself.

When I put my first spoonful of oatmeal in my mouth, I nearly gagged. It was not only bland; it was bitter. I had never tasted hot cereal so bad. Neither Charlotte nor Miss Emily seemed to notice or mind. I looked about hoping there was a jar of honey or a jar of sugar, but there was nothing.

"What's wrong?" Miss Emily asked quickly.

Having cooked and baked so often for my family when I lived with Daddy and Momma Longchamp, I knew seasoning and ingredients. It tasted as if she had added vinegar.

"Is there vinegar in this?" I asked.

"Yes," she said. "I put vinegar in everything I make."

"Why?" I asked, astounded.

"To remind us of the bitterness we must endure for the sins of our fathers," she replied. "It will do you good to remember."

"But . . ."

"This is all there is to eat," she said, smiling. "If you don't eat it, you will have nothing and you need your nourishment if you want to deliver a healthy child. God help it," she added, raising her gaze toward the ceiling.

I took a deep breath and closed my eyes, willing the cereal to taste better than it did. An old lady on her deathbed would have had more appetite.

"When can I get my things back?" I asked. "I don't have a hairbrush, but I have a comb in my purse."

"You won't have any reason to make yourself pretty here," she said, loud, cold and flat, her eyes challenging mine. Swallowing, I felt fear raise the hair on my neck.

"But why did you take my purse?" I asked softly.

"Everything has to be purified," she replied and ate her oatmeal as if it were the most delicious thing in the world.

"Purified? I don't understand."

She paused, closed her eyes to indicate that I was being very stupid and very annoying, and then turned to me.

"Evil is a disease; it clings to us and to everything associated with us. You brought it with you into this house and I have to make sure it doesn't stay. Now eat and stop asking so many questions."

I looked at Charlotte who sat there smiling dumbly.

"But Charlotte told me today was her birthday and you were having a party for her," I said. "I'll have to have my clothes back if I'm to meet anyone."

Miss Emily threw her head back and laughed the most hideous shrill laugh I had ever heard. Then she gazed at me, her eyes cold and narrow again.

"Didn't I tell you never to listen to anything she says? Every day is her stupid birthday," she added, glaring across the table at Charlotte. "She doesn't even remember the actual day anymore. She has no concept of time. Ask her what year it is or what month. Ask what today is. Tell her, Charlotte," she urged cruelly. "Is today a Monday or a Saturday? What is it?"

"It's not Sunday," she said. "Because we didn't have our service in the chapel," she added, smiling proudly at her accomplishment.

"See," Miss Emily said. "All she can tell you is it isn't Sunday."

I couldn't believe how harsh she was with her sister, but I swallowed my thoughts along with the rest of my terrible oatmeal. At least the bread tasted good and the orange was just an orange. She couldn't do anything to spoil that.

"Now that you have finished your breakfast," Miss Emily said with her elbows on the table, her hands clasped together, "I will tell you some of the rules.

"First, you are never, ever to go to the west wing of the house where Charlotte and I live. That section is off limits to you, do you understand?" She didn't give me a chance to reply.

"In fact, you are restricted to your room, the library, the dining room and the kitchen.

"Second, you are not to bother Luther. You are not to go out to the barns or the pens or the coops and pester him with stupid questions. He doesn't like it and it takes away from his work. Time is the most precious gift we have and it is not to be spent loosely.

"Third, from today on, after I put the clock in your room, you are to come down here at six, after you make your bed of course, and start the fire in the stove. Use only four pieces of wood. Luther keeps the wood in the pantry. After that, you set the table for our breakfast, a bowl for the cereal, one spoon, and a napkin, just as I have done today. On Sunday we each have an egg as well, so you will put out a small dish. I will show you where everything is and where everything goes after you wash it.

"Which brings me to four. Your first chore is to wash and dry all the dishes and polish the silverware every day. I want all the pots and pans scrubbed, even the ones we don't use because they gather dust.

"Five, after the breakfast dishes and silverware, and the pots and the pans are all washed, you will scrub the floor. There is a pail and a brush and soap in the pantry. Begin at the door and work your way to the pantry. Dump the dirty water off the steps in the back and then put back the pail where you found it. I like everything to be in its place.

"Six, every third day, you will take the linen I leave in a pile at the entrance to the west wing and, along with your own, wash it and hang it out to dry. Everything is to be washed by hand in the wash tub on the back porch and then put through the wringer. You will find the tub and the washboard on the porch. Once a week we do clothing and the pile will be in the same place. You will find you have a second gown in the top drawer of your dresser."

"But what about my own things?" I cried.

"I don't know about your own things. I know only about what is and this is what is and what must be done," she said quickly.

"Seven, you are to begin this afternoon with the cleaning of your wing. Since it is now being used because of you, you should be the one responsible for how it looks. I want the hallway floors scrubbed and the walls scrubbed. Use the same pail and brush that you used on the kitchen floor, but remember to put it back in its proper place," she repeated. "I want all the furnishings dusted, as well as all the paintings. Be extra careful when you touch the paintings; some of them go back a hundred years.

"Eight, on Saturdays we will do the windows on the first floor. Since that will take almost all day every Saturday, you will begin immediately after you clean the kitchen following breakfast.

"Dusting and washing furnishings and other things will take place almost every day in the afternoon. I will leave an apple on the table for you for your lunch.

"Do you understand all this?" she demanded.

I understood; I understood that she was turning me into a house slave. With the paltry and meager things I was being given to eat and to wear and with my horrible living conditions, I also understood I was doing far more than earn my keep.

"When will I have time for anything but work?" I asked innocently. Her eyes flared.

"There is nothing else for which time is meant," she declared. "Idle hands make mischief. Besides, the hard work is the best thing for you in your condition. It will make you stronger so when the time comes, you will be able to face your ordeal," she added, making it sound as if she were doing me a favor by turning me into a slave.

"Whenever you do have some idle time, you should fill it with sensible activities. Accordingly, I will permit you to go into our library and choose a volume or two to read. However, you should plan to utilize as much daylight as possible for this so you don't waste your kerosene. I don't want to see you sitting up all night reading some romantic novel and burning the oil," she warned.

"When can she see my needlework?" Charlotte interjected. For a moment Miss Emily glared at her, her thin lips so tight there was a patch of white at each corner.

"What did I tell you last night, Charlotte? Didn't I tell you Eugenia would be too busy to have you follow her around and babble nonsense all day? What did I tell you to do?"

Charlotte turned to me as if she thought I would give her the answer.

"You told me to wash my hair," she said.

"Oh Lord, give me strength," Miss Emily said. "That was last week, Charlotte. Last week." She spun around on me. "Do you see the burden I've been left to bear? My rich and fancy sister doesn't have any of this to contend with, does she? She has never once suggested Charlotte come visit her. Oh, no. Instead, she sends me you . . . another burden."

"I'm not your burden," I said defiantly. "Nor am I hers."

Miss Emily stared. Then she placed her hands flatly on the table and pushed herself into a standing position, rising slowly into her full height.

"I don't expect you to be grateful. Your sort rarely is, but I do expect you to fulfill your responsibilities while you are here under my roof and in my care. Is that understood?" she demanded. I looked away. "Is it?" she insisted.

"Yes," I said after taking a deep breath. "It's understood."

"Good. Begin your chores," she commanded. "Charlotte, get upstairs and clean your room."

"But it's my birthday," Charlotte protested.

"Then clean it so it will look nice for all your guests," Miss Emily said, a small, tight smile on her face. That seemed to please Charlotte. She rose and started out. At the doorway, she turned back to me.

"Thank you for the nice present," she said and left.

"Idiot," Miss Emily mumbled. Then she followed her out and left me with my work.

There wasn't even any hot water in the kitchen. Everything had to be washed in cold and it was very cold water, water from a deep well. My fingers grew so numb I had to shake them out periodically and rub them with a dish towel. Miss Emily had set out the polish for the silverware and had laid out the pieces on the counter. They were old and stained. Polishing them was something she obviously hadn't done often, but now that she had me to abuse, she decided to do so. It took me nearly an hour to get half of it looking decent.

Suddenly the back door was thrown open and Luther came in carrying an armful of fire wood. He barely acknowledged me with his eyes.

"Good morning," I said as he turned into the pantry, but he didn't reply. I heard him piling the wood and went to the door of the pantry. "Luther."

He paused and looked over his shoulder at me, his face almost a mirror of Miss Emily's—that same cold glint in his eyes.

"What do you want?" he asked.

"I was wondering if you were going to Upland Station any time today. I have to make a phone call. I have to see about my things."

He grunted and turned back to the wood without replying. I stood in the doorway waiting. Finally, he completed piling the wood neatly and stood up.

"I ain't goin' to no Upland Station today," he said gruffly.

"Will you be going tomorrow?" I pursued.

"Can't say. It ain't tomorrow," he replied and started out so quickly, I just knew if I didn't step back, he would walk right over me. I made up my mind that as soon as I got my clothes back, I would walk to Upland Station. Where were my clothes anyway? I wondered.

I completed the polishing of the silverware and washed and scrubbed the pots and pans. After everything was put in its place, I went into the pantry and got the pail, brush and soap. I had to get down on my hands and knees to scrub the floor, but this wasn't the first time I had done that. It was just that now, with my expanded stomach, it was harder to bend over and scrub. My lower back began to ache rather quickly and I had to continually sit up and rub it.

Washing the floor, just like polishing the silverware, was clearly something Miss Emily did not have done regularly. The floor was grimy and caked with dirt. I had to stop about midway and go out to empty the blackened pail of water. The moment I opened the door, the chill of the brisk December day came rushing over me making my teeth chatter, for the wintery wind had no trouble piercing the flimsy material of my hospitallike gown and I wore nothing underneath; nor had I any socks. I hurried down the rear of the small back porch to dump the dirty water over the side and that was when I saw it.

Down right, just behind the building, was a cauldron hanging over a robust fire built in a circle of rocks. The water in the cauldron bubbled, but I could clearly make out my clothing. I dropped the pail and rushed down the squeaky wooden steps. My clothing looked like it had been cooking ever since she had taken it from me the night before. I searched about desperately for something to use to pluck out my garments, but with the steam rising out of the large black pot and the fire burning briskly, there was no way for me to get close enough to rescue any of it.

"What are you doing back here?" Miss Emily demanded from the back door.

"What have you done to my things?" I screamed back. "You're ruining everything."

"I told you," she said, her arms crossed tightly over her stomach, "I'm purifying it. Now get back to your chores," she snapped.

"I want my things!" I cried.

"It's not for you to make demands on me," she snapped. "When and if they are purified, they will be returned. Now get back to work," she said and pivoted to go back into the house. I stared after her and then looked helplessly at my clothes. My purse wasn't even visible.

What a mean thing to do, I thought. I returned to the porch and got the pail of dirty water. Then I threw it over the fire. The dampened embers smoldered and hissed and sent steam everywhere. I stepped back and waited. The water continued to bubble. It would be a while before it cooled down, I thought, but as soon as it had, I would pluck out my things.

I went back to the kitchen floor and scrubbed the rest of it. I knew I had been working for hours in the kitchen because when I stepped out again, the sun was nearly directly above. I dumped the dirty water and turned to get my boiled things.

But the cauldron was gone! All that was left were the smoldering embers of the dying fire. I hurried down the steps and looked everywhere for signs of it, but all I saw was Luther coming around the far corner of the barn carrying a shovel over his shoulder as if he were a soldier carrying a rifle. I called to him, but he went into the barn and pulled the door closed firmly behind him.

Furious now, I went back inside and charged through the kitchen and the dining room, but I saw or heard no one.

"Miss Emily!" I called at the foot of the stairway. I listened. She didn't reply. I called again and then peered into the library which was just across the hall.

The drapes over the tall windows were open so I could see the shelves of books, the large desk and wooden file cabinets, a long table and chairs. There were paintings on the walls, one over the rear of the desk. It was a portrait of Emily, Charlotte, and Grandmother Cutler's father. I saw clear resemblances in the eyes and forehead. He stared down with the same arrogant air, his shoulders firm and his head high and slightly tilted in a condescending manner. He looked violently angry to me. I embraced myself and backed out of the doorway and right into the silently waiting Miss Emily. I jumped and cried out before I realized it was she.

"What are you doing? Why are you shouting? You should be starting on your wing of the house, not wandering about like this," she admonished.

"What did you do with my clothes?" I demanded. "That pot is gone."

"Do I have to keep repeating myself? I told you it was all being purified. Now, it has been taken to the second step."

"Second step? What does that mean?"

"It has been buried," she replied coolly.

"Buried!" So that was why Luther was carrying a shovel, I thought. "You buried my things? Where? Why? This is insane!"

"How dare you?" she snapped, her shoulders rising. Despite her slim torso, she looked formidable, as vicious as a buzzard. I had to step back. "You stand there critical of me," she said, lifting her long arm and pointing her witchlike crooked finger in my face. "You dare to reprimand and reproach me. You who stand in such disgrace with your stomach loudly announcing your sin. Don't you know that only he without sin can cast the first stone?"

"I'm not saying I'm pure and good," I cried through my emerging tears, "but that doesn't mean you have a right to torment me."

"Torment you?" She looked like she was going to break into laughter. "It is you who are tormenting me and the other members of the family. I have been willing to help you through this iniquitous time. I have opened my home to you and have assured my sister I will provide for your needs and you accuse me of tormenting you."

"You're not providing for my needs," I bawled. "I want my things back," I cried. I couldn't stop my sobbing.

"You don't know how ridiculous you look," she said. "All right," she added after a long pause. "After the earth has absorbed the taint of evil, I will see to it that Luther brings you those garments. "Now get back to work. You need to work, to build your resolve; your castle of righteousness must be fortified against any more incursions by the devil."

She started to turn away.

"But my other things . . . I've got to call to see what's happened to them. I don't even have a comb for my hair now," I said, holding up the knotted strands.

"There is no sense in calling," she replied with an alarming calmness in her voice.

"Why not?"

"Because I have instructed that those things are not to be sent here until after you have given birth and you will leave. It was enough I had to deal with what you brought on your back."

"But . . . . how could you lie to me? Everyone's lied to me," I added, realizing the truth.

"Everyone's lied to you?" She started to laugh. "What do you call what you've been doing? Now stop whining and do what has to be done. You must show some forbearance. Surely, you possess some grit. From what my sister has told me, the Cutlers all come from a strong stock."

"I don't have any Cutler stock," I muttered, but as soon as the words came out of my mouth, I knew I had made a terrible mistake. Her eyes widened.

"What? What did you say?" she demanded, stepping toward me again.

I felt myself begin to shiver. I had never seen a face so filled with both fire and ice. Her eyes flared, but her expression was so cold. Who knew what other horrors she would design for me if she knew the truth of my birth? I thought.

"Nothing," I said quickly.

She fixed her eyes on me, her gaze so intensely penetrating, I had to turn away. Each second ticked by with the boom of thunder. My heart pounded against my chest.

"Just finish your chores," she finally spit and pivoted again to march away. My thumping heart slowed, yet my skin felt clammy and the hair on my neck still bristled. I thought about turning around and running out. But penniless, with nothing but this ugly hospital gown on, where would I go? There wasn't anything to do but wait for an opportunity to leave, I thought. As soon as she did return my things, I would find a way to Upland Station and try to call Daddy Longchamp. Surely, he would find a way to help me.

Despondent and defeated, I returned to the kitchen to get the pail of water and soap and the brush and then climbed the stairs to begin work on the filthy and dusty wing of the great house.

As I dusted and cleaned the pieces of furniture near the stairway, I couldn't help but feel as though all the sullen looking ancestors with their harsh and severe expressions were gazing down at me hatefully. Miss Emily's portrait would easily take its rightful place along these walls, I thought. What an unhappy family, distrustful and afraid of the devil's presence in anyone and everything. It was easy now to understand why Grandmother Cutler was the way she was, I thought. In fact, one of the sour looking women looked just like her.

Every fifteen minutes or so, I had to carry the dirtied pail of water to my bathroom to empty it and fill it up again. It began to weigh heavier and heavier and the pain that had begun in a tiny spot on my lower back grew larger and larger like an expanding circle of fire. I had to rest more often and take deep breaths. The work was making my stomach feel like a heavy weight tied around my waist.

I was in the middle of wiping down one of the benches when I heard footsteps behind me and turned to see Charlotte holding an apple.

"You forgot to eat your lunch," she said, thrusting the apple toward me. I paused and sat back against the wall, exhausted.

"Thank you," I said, taking the apple. She stood there with a wide smile on her face, watching me bite into it.

"An apple a day keeps the doctor away, Emily always says," she sang.

"I'm sure no doctor would want to come here anyway," I mumbled. "Charlotte," I said, suddenly thinking of a possibility, "do you ever go to Upland Station?"

"Sometimes Emily takes me to the general store and buys me some sour balls," she replied.

"Then you don't go away from the house very much, do you?" I asked.

"I go to the gazebo when it's nice out and feed the birds. Do you want to feed the birds?"

"First day off," I said dryly, but she didn't understand. She smiled happily. I took another bite of my apple and started to stand, but the pain shot through my lower back so sharply and quickly, I couldn't breathe and had to sit back a moment.

"You got a baby in you," Charlotte said, "and it might have pointed ears."

"It doesn't have pointed ears," I snapped between gasps. "What a horrible thing to say. Did Emily tell you that it did?"

"Emily knows," Charlotte insisted, nodding. "She can see into your stomach with her fingers and she knows."

"That's silly, Charlotte. No one can see into anyone's stomach with her fingers. Don't believe it."

"She saw into mine," she said. "And saw the pointed ears."

"What?"

A door slammed down the west corridor and Miss Emily's click-clack footsteps reverberated through the house like one gunshot after another. The sound put a look of terror into Charlotte's face.

"Emily says I shouldn't bother you while you're working," she explained, backing up.

"Charlotte, wait . . ." I pulled myself up on the bench.

"I've got to finish a pattern," she said and turned to shuffle quickly away.

A few moments later, Miss Emily appeared. She glared down the hallway in my direction. Then she inspected some of the furniture and some of the portraits I had cleaned and dusted. Apparently, she was satisfied.

"I have put a clock in your room," she said. "Make sure you keep it wound up so it doesn't stop in the middle of the night and you don't know what time it is in the morning.

"Dinner will be at five promptly," she added. "I expect you to come to the table looking clean."

"But where do I wash? All I can get is cold water in my bathroom and there is no place to take a shower or a bath," I complained.

"We don't take showers," she said. "Once a week we take a bath in the pantry. Luther will bring in the tub and fill it with water he heats over the fire."

"Once a week? In the pantry? People don't live like this anymore," I protested. "They have hot and cold running water and they have nice-smelling soaps and they bathe far more often than once a week."

"Oh, I know how people live today," she said with that cold smile on her lips, "especially women with their fancy smelling perfumes and seductive clothing. Don't you know that the devil won Eve's trust by appealing to her vanity and that ever since that hateful day, our vanity has been the devil's doorway to our souls? Lipstick and makeup and pretty combs, lace dresses and jewelry . . . all devices to fan temptation and drive men to the promontory of lust. They fall," she chanted, "oh how they fall and they take us down with them, down into the fires of hell and damnation. You have been singed by the devil. I smell the odor of the black smoke. The faster you come to this realization yourself, the faster you will find redemption."

"That's not true," I cried. "I don't smell like something evil, and my baby won't have pointed ears!"

She stared down at me a moment and nodded.

"Pray to God that it doesn't," she said. "Pray that God won't take his vengeance on an innocent baby, but you have made Him angry and that anger is so great it rolls on and on through the heavens."

She took a deep breath and closed her eyes, her hands against her small bosom.

"Work," she said, "pray, and be obedient and, hopefully, you will find Him forgiving."

She turned and walked away. At the top of the stairway she paused and looked back.

"Don't forget, promptly at five and be as clean as you can," she added and descended, her head high, her back so straight she looked like a statue being slowly lowered.

I pressed my hands against my stomach and swallowed back the lumps in my throat. My baby was only something good, I told myself. No matter how Michael had deceived me, my baby was inside me and felt the power of my love. That power was something precious and heavenly and not the devil's work. Miss Emily never knew the power of love. At this moment I thought she was someone more to be pitied than to be despised. She lived in a cold, dark world peopled by demons and devils and saw evil and danger in every nook and cranny of her home and life. I imagined she rarely laughed, even rarely smiled.

She didn't know it, I thought, but the devil had already defeated her.

I washed my hands and arms and face the best I could. Without a mirror, I could only imagine how dirty and dingy my hair appeared, but Miss Emily didn't care about appearances. In fact the less attractive I was, the more she liked it. I had to replace the soiled gown with the second one in the drawer. Those two articles of clothing were all there was. She reminded me of that when I came down for dinner.

"Remember what I said about clothing—we wash it once a week, so if you dirty both your dresses, you will have to wear a filthy one until we wash."

"Why don't we wash clothing more than once a week?" I asked.

"We don't need to be extravagant about it. Take care of what you have and you need do it only once a week," she emphasized.

"But I don't have anything—just two ugly dresses," I replied.

"Simple things are not ugly things," she snapped. "Just because you are used to fancy clothing doesn't mean everything else is ugly."

"I'm not used to fancy clothing. But I need things that fit and I need my underwear and socks and . . ."

"I need, I need, I need. Are those the only words young people your age know these days?" she said. She uncovered the pot of potatoes and mixed vegetables. That, plus a glass of water and another piece of bread, was to be our meal. I had eaten better when I was living with Momma and Daddy Longchamp and we were scrounging to feed ourselves because Daddy had no work. But Miss Emily thought simple foods were good for the soul and things like chicken and eggs were to be eaten only on Sundays.

After saying grace, she didn't speak a word and Charlotte looked different, frightened. I imagined Miss Emily had castigated her harshly for the things she had said before and had probably forbidden her to speak. Every once in a while she lifted her eyes from her plate and glanced at me like a co-conspirator. It was curious, but I didn't find out what it was all about until dinner was finished and I had cleaned all the dishes, silverware and pots. I found her waiting for me in the shadows of the hallway just outside the dining room. Apparently she had been hiding there all that time, just waiting for me to appear.

She practically jumped out at me when I stepped through the doorway. I didn't think I would want to go to sleep so early, but I was so exhausted from my work and so full of aches and pains, even the dark, dingy room loomed promising. I had my hot water bottle wrapped in a dish towel under my arm.

"Charlotte!" I exclaimed, stepping back. "What is it?" I looked about, but Miss Emily was nowhere in sight.

"I gave you a present," she whispered. "It's on your bed," she added and then turned again and shuffled quickly away before I could reply.

I didn't know what to make of it. What could she have given me? Probably one of her needlework things, I thought. Or maybe she felt sorry for me and gave me one of her things to wear. I climbed the stairway slowly, each step an effort now, and walked down the dark corridor to my horrid room. I went to the kerosene lamp and lit it quickly. The light drove away the blanket of shadows and revealed something on my bed.

Slowly I picked it up and turned it about in my hand. It was a baby's toy rattle and from the looks of it, practically new. Miss Emily had ridiculed me when I had asked her about it being Charlotte's birthday and she had reminded me that Charlotte was not to be believed. So I didn't ask her why Charlotte had inquired if the baby had kept me awake or what Charlotte had meant by Miss Emily being able to see into her stomach and see a baby with pointed ears.

But why would she have a baby's rattle and one that looked just bought? Charlotte was certainly too old to have had a baby recently.

Miss Emily had forbidden me to go into their wing of the house, I thought, but maybe that was the only way I could eventually find out what all this meant.

For now, I was too tired and confused to care. I pulled back the blanket and crawled under it, placing the hot water bottle snugly against my stomach, thinking I was keeping my baby warm, too.

It didn't seem as cold tonight, and for that, I was grateful. One of the few things Miss Emily had said at dinner was the warm air meant a change in weather and probably a snowfall would come.

A snowfall, I thought. What was the date? I added the days I had been in the hospital to the last day I remembered and the two days I had already been here. The realization of what day and what night it was made me sit up in sorrow and horror.

It was Christmas Eve! And no one had even mentioned it or had even cared. I thought about Jimmy in Europe, probably celebrating and singing Christmas carols with his army buddies; I thought about Trisha home with her family in their warm house around their tree; I even thought about Daddy Longchamp with his new wife and the promise of his new child.

The tears streamed down my cheeks as Michael's loving promises returned. We had planned such a wonderful and romantic Christmas Eve together. We were to sit by a warm fire and unwrap our Christmas presents to each other, while beautiful holiday music played. Afterward, we would lie together in each other's arms and fall asleep with soft kisses on our lips.

I remembered the day he brought the beautiful little tree.

Was it still there and did it feel as completely deserted and alone as I did?

14
A LETTER TO TRISHA

Despite the difficulty and the tediousness of the work I had to do at The Meadows, I found I welcomed it, for it was only when I was scrubbing and dusting, washing and polishing that I could ignore the length of the day and the slow movement of time. It was truly like a prison sentence and Miss Emily didn't hesitate to treat me like a criminal. Incarcerated by my chores within the great house ruled by this horrible, sick ogre, every day ran into the next for me, each morning, afternoon and evening unchanged and unremarkable from the one preceding it. Like simple Charlotte, I began to lose my sense of time and couldn't remember whether it was a Monday or a Tuesday. Just like her, I used Sunday as my touching stone.

The Booth sisters didn't really attend a chapel for Sunday worship. I had hoped that would have provided a way for me to get to a phone or mail a letter, but Miss Emily said that the churches had become sanctuaries for the devil.

"People don't go there to pray and confess; they go there to socialize and be seen. Imagine, getting dressed up to say your prayers. As if the good Lord could be taken in by expensive clothing, the latest styles and rich jewelry. The way some churchgoing women paint their faces with makeup, too. Why it's sacrilegious is what it is. It's the devil in them and he's laughing all the way for he has successfully invaded the house of God.

"That's why we pray at home on Sundays," she concluded.

For the Booth sisters, the chapel was an anteroom off the library. Miss Emily had even had one long and very uncomfortable bench put in there, the back of it tilted forward so we had to lean because if you were too content and relaxed, you would forget the purpose for your being there.

The bench faced a large wooden cross. There was nothing else on any of the walls. She had long candles burning on a table before us and a kerosene lamp on each of the small tables around us. The moment the service ended, she would rush around to snuff out the candles in order to conserve the wax.

Naturally, I was required to attend the service which consisted of Miss Emily reading aloud from the Bible and then all of us reciting the Lord's Prayer together. Even Luther appeared, only he stood in the back by the door, his hands folded. Miss Emily's reading took more than an hour. Charlotte would get restless and fidget, but all Miss Emily had to do was stop and glare at her for a moment and she would freeze up and look remorseful. Then Miss Emily would throw a frosty look my way to be sure I understood. It was like someone tossing a pail of ice cubes at me; it stung that much and felt that cold.

Our reward for proper behavior was a special breakfast: eggs any way we wanted them, grits and butter, and blueberry muffins. The muffins were the only food in which Miss Emily permitted sugar and very little at that. To her sugar was the same as alcohol or drugs, something that could tempt us and make us vulnerable to evil. Self-denial made us strong and kept us properly fortified.

Another Sunday event was our baths. Just as Miss Emily had described, Luther carried in a large wooden tub and set it in the center of the pantry floor. We used the pantry because it was the closest to the rear door which led to the cauldron and the hot water. Luther started heating water right after the Sunday service and after breakfast brought in pail after pail of it. Cold water was added to the hot in just the right proportion to make it tepid.

Miss Emily was the first to bathe. Charlotte and I had to wait outside the pantry until she was finished. Then Luther was instructed to bring in another half dozen pails of hot water. Charlotte was next. What I found horrendous was that we had to bathe in the same water, Miss Emily being the only one who bathed in totally clean water. She claimed she was the cleanest of the three of us and therefore would leave the least amount of dirt behind.

By the time my turn arrived, Luther had to scoop out some water and replace it with another half dozen pails of hot. The first time I took a bath like this, Miss Emily burst in on me and dipped her fingers in the water to check the water temperature. She decided it wasn't hot enough and ordered Luther to bring in an additional pail or two of the hot.

"It's hot enough," I protested.

"Nonsense," she replied. "If the water isn't warm enough, you can't get the dirt that's deep down in your skin out," she insisted.

I had to sit naked in the tub while Luther entered with the water and dumped it around me. I covered my nudity the best I could, but I saw Luther's eyes travel with interest even though his face didn't show it.

I suspected that Luther had a nip or two of something from time to time, especially during the colder days in January and February. Sometimes, when I was finishing in the kitchen, he would come in carrying wood or bringing some hot water and I could smell the scent of whiskey. If Miss Emily smelled it, she didn't say. She wasn't afraid of Luther, for she didn't hesitate to snap at him or demand things from him in a sharp tone of voice, but she seemed to sense just how far she could push him.

Why Luther worked so hard for her and Charlotte was a mystery to me; I was sure he didn't get much more than his room and board. He slept somewhere downstairs in the rear of the house, another place that was off limits to me, but I couldn't help wondering about him and asked him questions every chance I got. That meant only when he and I were alone, for if Miss Emily was present, he wouldn't so much as glance at me.

"When did The Meadows get this run-down?" I asked him one morning after he had brought in the wood. I sensed that the plantation was his favorite subject and he would talk about it more willingly than he would talk about anything else.

"Not long after Mr. Booth died," he said. "There were some debts and most of the livestock and some equipment had to be sold off."

"What about Mrs. Booth?"

"She died years before him . . . a stomach ailment," he said.

"You work very hard, Luther. I'm sure you tried the best you could to keep it up," I said. I saw from the glint in his eyes that my words pleased him.

"I told her; I explained to her what had to be done to keep it looking nice, but appearances ain't important to her. Pretty things invite the devil is all she says. I wanted to buy some paint, but she says no to that. So it looks the way it does. I keep the machinery working as best I can and the house is still a sturdy structure."

"You're doing wonders with the little you have," I said. He grunted his appreciation.

One day I was bold enough to ask him why he remained working there.

"There's all kinds of ownership," he said. "Ownership that comes from a piece of legal paper and ownership that comes from years of workin' and livin' someplace. I'm as much part of The Meadows as anyone is," he added proudly.

"The truth is," he said with the closest thing to a smile on his face, "The Meadows owns me. I don't know nothin' else."

I wanted to get him to tell me more about Miss Emily and the family, but most of the time whenever I brought up anything remotely close to the subject, he would act as if he didn't hear anything I said. I didn't think he respected Miss Emily or even liked her much, but there was something about her that kept him obedient. Whenever I asked him to take me to Upland Station, he always had an excuse why he couldn't do it. Most of the time, he just went without saying anything.

By mid-January, I had concluded that Miss Emily must have forbidden him to take me along, so I waited until we were alone and I begged him to mail a letter to Trisha for me. He didn't say he would do it and he didn't say he wouldn't, but he wouldn't take it from my hands.

"I'll leave it on the counter here in the kitchen and next time you go, would you please take it along?" I asked. He watched where I put it, but he didn't respond. The next day the letter was gone. I waited for weeks for a reply from Trisha. I knew as soon as she received my letter she would write back, but whenever Luther did bring back mail none came for me.

One morning when Luther brought in the wood, I asked him about it.

"What letter?" he said.

"The one I left on the counter. You saw me leave it that day," I insisted.

"I saw it," he said, "but when I looked for it later, it wasn't there."

"It wasn't there?" He didn't add anything, but then he didn't have to. I knew where my letter had gone. It was with Miss Emily. A flame of anger traveled up my spine and whatever pride I had left came back in full dress parade. I spun on my heels and marched out to confront her.

Miss Emily spent most of her day reading the Bible, cooking our miserly meals, supervising Luther's work and keeping her account books to the penny. She worked on her bookkeeping in the office library at the big, dark oak desk with the enormous picture of her father's above her, his face in a frown as he looked down over her shoulder. I had the feeling she was haunted by him and believed that if she didn't do things the way he would have wanted her to, he would take some punitive action.

She sat there crouched over the bills making her calculations and small marks on paper. Her bony shoulders looked like iron framework with her head dangling in between. A grandfather clock ticked loudly in the corner. She had a single kerosene lamp burning because it was heavily overcast outside and there was little sunlight. The lamp cast a pool of yellow illumination over her face and hands. When she heard me enter, she raised her head and sat back so that her forehead and eyes were in dark shadows. The thin line of her mouth spread in a smirk. Her lips barely opened when she spoke.

"What do you want? Don't you see I'm busy?" she snapped.

"I just want to know why you took my letter to my friend Trisha," I said boldly.

"What letter?" she asked, her head unmoving. I thought I was facing a mannequin because she sat so stiffly. My eyes shifted for a moment to the eyes of her father in the portrait. He scowled down at me.

"The letter I left on the counter in the kitchen about a month ago. Luther was going to take it to mail for me," I replied, not backing away an inch. I thought she wasn't going to answer. Finally, she leaned forward, her eyes just entering the rim of light, which made them glow like the eyes of an alley cat.

"Anything left on the counter is garbage," she said, "and that's what a letter of yours to one of your city friends, who I am sure is just as wicked as you were, would be anyway."

For a moment my breath caught in my throat and seemed to stay. How could she admit what she had done so boldly? And what right had she to say such a terrible thing about Trisha, someone she had never met? Did Emily think she was the only good person on earth?

"How dare you say that? You don't know my friends. You had no right to throw away my letter," I cried.

"I didn't have any right?" she said, following it with her shrill laugh. "Of course, I did and do," she said sternly. "I have every right to keep any evil from entering this house. And I will not have Luther wasting his time on your correspondences," she insisted.

"But it was only one letter!"

"It takes only a word to bring the devil into your heart. Haven't you paid attention to any of the things I have been telling you? Now leave me. I have important work to do and you have your chores."

"You're treating me like a prisoner, a common criminal," I cried.

"That's because you are a common criminal," she said calmly. "You committed the most common crime of lust and now you are paying for it." She folded her hands and leaned farther forward on the desk so that her entire face was in the light now. "And why were you sent here for me to take care of you, eh? You have nowhere else to go; no one wants you. You're an embarrassment, a burden.

"My sister made that quite clear and also asked that you be treated as the sinner and the disgrace you are, not that she had to tell me," she said icily. And then she sat back so that her face was completely in shadows. "As long as you're living under my roof, eating my food, and depending on my care, you will do as I say," she roared in a voice that was so deep and loud, I thought it might very well have come from the face in the portrait above her. That terrifying thought took the wind from the sails of my rebellion. I felt my blood drain down into my feet; a stinging sensation began behind my ears and my strength grew small. I clasped my hands over my protruding stomach and backed out of the doorway. Immediately, she lowered her head and went back to her calculations, making sure that every single penny was spent wisely and accounted for.

I paused near the doorway of one of the sitting rooms. Even though I had been here for months, I had been restricted to a small part of the house and hadn't seen most of it, especially the forbidden west wing where Miss Emily and Charlotte had their rooms. But I knew that in this particular sitting room, there was an oval mirror. It was the only room downstairs that had a mirror. Miss Emily thought that mirrors encouraged vanity and vanity, after all, was what brought Eve's downfall and man's sin.

"It's not necessary to look at yourself," she had said when I asked for a mirror in my room. "Just keep yourself reasonably clean."

It had been so long since I had cared, but Miss Emily's treatment of me in the library had made me feel so diminished and horrible, I couldn't help but be curious about myself. Was this the way she saw me? What did I really look like? All this time had passed and I had been without a brush, without a comb, without skin creams or makeup. Having no place to go and not seeing anyone had kept me from thinking about it, but I so wanted to feel like a young lady again and not feel like some house drudge.

Slowly, anticipating in my heart what I feared was true, I entered the sitting room. The curtains were open, but the light was as dim as it was in the library. I found the kerosene lamp on a small table and lit it. Holding it before me, I approached the mirror. My silhouette appeared first and then I lifted the lamp and gazed upon myself.

My once beautiful hair was a dirty, tangled mop of split ends and mangled strains. Streaks of grime scarred my forehead and cheeks. My blue eyes looked dim and dull, as if all the light and life behind them was drained. I was pale, almost as pale and sickly looking as Miss Emily. My decrepit reflection turned my own stomach. It was as if I were gazing into the face of a stranger.

I couldn't recall when I had last put on lipstick or brushed my hair. I couldn't remember when I had last sprayed perfume on myself. And all my pretty clothes . . . my earrings and bracelets, even the locket Michael had given me . . . all of it was somewhere else. Perhaps Agnes Morris had sent it to the hotel and Grandmother Cutler had already disposed of most of it, just as she was disposing of me.

Look at me! I thought. Look at what Grandmother Cutler and Miss Emily have done to me. My face appeared bloated, even distorted. I stood there in this ugly shift which hung off my shoulders like a sack. I couldn't look at myself any longer and quickly turned off the kerosene lamp. I was grateful for the dark shadows that fell over my face immediately. As long as I was here, I wouldn't gaze into a mirror again, I vowed.

I rushed out of the sitting room and went up the stairs as quickly as I could, each high step an effort, for I was well into my fifth month and carrying heavy. Out of breath, I collapsed on my bed in the dark room and sobbed. I really was a prisoner here, I thought, a tormented prisoner.

"What's wrong?" I heard Charlotte ask and I stopped crying. I sat up and ground the tears out of my eyes. She was standing in my doorway with one of her needlework projects in her hands. She looked to her right down the corridor and then leaned in to speak in a conspiratorial stage whisper.

"Did Emily tell you your baby has pointed ears?" she asked.

"I don't care what Emily thinks," I said. "Least of all what she thinks about my baby." Charlotte stared at me a moment, the concept of defying Emily apparently too much for her, and then she smiled and approached me.

"Look at what I have made," she said proudly. I took a deep breath and leaned over to light my kerosene lamp. Then I looked at her work.

It was a very pretty piece done with pink and blue thread. She was filling in a picture of what clearly looked like a baby in a cradle swinging under a tree.

"Where did you get this pattern?" I asked.

"Pattern?" She turned the material toward her as if the answer were written on it.

"The picture? Did Miss Emily buy this for you someplace?"

"Oh no, I drew the picture," she said, smiling proudly. "I draw all my pictures."

"That's very, very good, Charlotte. You have a talent. You should show your work to more people," I said.

"More people? I just show it to Emily. She wants me to keep doing it so I don't get in her way." Charlotte began to recite, "She says idle hands . . ."

"I know; I know. Make mischief. Well, what about the mischief she makes?" I retorted. Charlotte's smile widened. I could see the whole idea of Miss Emily being evil was so farfetched to her she couldn't even imagine it. Her sister had her brainwashed. "Emily's not an angel, you know. Not everything she does and says is right and good. She's unnecessarily mean, especially to you," I continued. "She speaks to you like you were some sort of lower animal and she keeps you locked up here, just as she's keeping me."

"Oh, no," she said. "Emily's only trying to help me. I'm the devil's spawn and I've spawned the devil's child," she recited in a way that made me understand she had been forced to repeat it and repeat it until it was almost second nature for her to say it.

"That's a horrible lie. Wait, what do you mean, you've spawned the devil's child? What child?" I asked.

"I'm not supposed to talk about it," she said, backing up a step.

"She won't know," I coaxed. "I won't tell her. Can't we share a secret?"

She considered and then stepped toward me again.

"I made this for the baby," she confessed, holding up the needlework, "because sometimes, the baby comes back."

"Comes back? Comes back from where?"

"From hell," she said, "where it was sent to live because that's where it belongs."

"No one belongs in hell, Charlotte."

"The devil does," she replied quickly, nodding.

"Maybe just him . . . and Miss Emily," I mumbled. "Tell me about the baby," I asked, raising my head. "Was there a real baby?" She stared at me without replying. "Charlotte," I said, reaching under the bed to pull out the baby's rattle she had left for me one day. "Whose was this? Where did you get it?"

The wind made a loose shutter clack and the sound of it reverberated down the hall. Charlotte closed her eyes quickly and then stepped back, a shivering thought filling her eyes with terror.

"I have to return to my room," she said. "Emily will be angry if she knows I'm here bothering you."

"You're not bothering me. Don't go," I begged. The shutter clacked again. She turned quickly and walked out. "Charlotte!" I called, but she didn't return.

Charlotte was the only one here to talk to and Miss Emily had her terrified of doing so. I might as well be in some jail, I thought. I couldn't have a warden more cruel than Miss Emily and why? Because I had fallen in love too quickly and had been too trusting. My sin was believing in someone, I thought. Well, I would defy her; I would write my letter to Trisha and get it mailed even if I had to mail it myself.

I rose from my bed with new determination, hid the baby's rattle again and went back down to the kitchen where I sat and rewrote my letter to Trisha. Only this time, I told her all the ugly details. My tears splattered on the page as I wrote as quickly as I could.

Dear Trisha,

I've been trying to get in touch with you for months, but Grandmother Cutler's horrible sister Emily has kept me from doing so. There is no phone here so I cannot call and letters have to be taken miles to a place called Upland Station. Emily has also forbidden having my things sent here. She took my clothing the day I arrived and put it through some purification process that involved boiling and burying it and I haven't seen it or my purse since. I'm forced to wear an ugly sack gown and nothing else, not even underwear! At night I sleep with a hot water bottle to keep warm in a cold, dark, windowless room. I have a kerosene lamp for light, but I'm only given a small bit of kerosene that must last a whole week so I don't burn it as much as I'd like to for fear I'll be left in the dark for days and days.

All I do is work in the house, cleaning and polishing and dusting. I don't even have time to read, and if I did, I would be too exhausted anyway. I've grown bigger and bigger and my back has been bothering me more and more, but Miss Emily doesn't care. I think she enjoys seeing me in pain; she thinks the more I suffer, the more I will be remorseful.

I couldn't give you this exact address when I left New York because I didn't know it. I need you to do me a favor. I am enclosing Daddy Longchamp's address. He's the only person I can turn to now since Jimmy is still in Europe, I think, and anyway, has no idea where I am. Please contact Daddy Longchamp and tell him how desperate I am. I must get out of here. Miss Emily is a religious fanatic and her sister is mentally simple and helpless like me.

You don't know how much I miss you and our wonderful talks. I realize now more than ever how much of a friend you were to me and how much I love you. I miss the school, too, and most of all, I miss singing and music. There is no music in this house, except church music. According to Miss Emily, everything else is the devil's work. She sees him everywhere except where she should see him—in the mirror.

At this point I would even gladly choose to be living with Agnes again. No matter how weird she behaved at times, she was at least human.

Once again, I miss you.

Love,
Dawn

I stuck the letter into one of the envelopes I had found in the library one day. After I addressed it, I went back upstairs quietly and folded my one blanket as tightly as I could to conceal it under my dress. It would serve as my coat, since my coat was one of the articles of clothing boiled and buried. Then I started out, practically tiptoeing down the stairs. Miss Emily was still immersed in her work in the library. I saw the dim illumination from her kerosene lamp spilling out the doorway. Even so, I paused, waited to be sure she hadn't heard me, and then I walked rapidly to the front door. It squeaked terribly when I started to open it, so I opened it as slowly as I could, an inch at a time. As soon as there was a wide enough space, I slipped out and unfolded the blanket quickly and wrapped it around my body.

The late February air was still quite cold, especially with the sun buried behind the sea of soiled thick clouds spreading from one horizon to another. It was already late in the day as well. When I looked down the long driveway and off in the direction of the dirt road, I felt a deep pang of discouragement. The world looked so unfriendly. Trees were still bare; the grass and brush was still brown and yellow. I saw only black birds sitting as still as stuffed trophies on the bare branches and staring down at me with a distrusting air.

I had so far to go just to mail a letter, I thought. But I was determined to do it.

I clutched the blanket to my bosom and started away. Snow began to fall just as I reached the end of the long driveway. The flakes came down in tiny particles at first and gradually grew larger and larger. Parts of the roadway were soft and parts were so frozen hard and rocky my feet slipped and slid in the shoe boots I wore without socks. The cold air easily found openings in my blanket and rushed up and through my simple dress. I shuddered and tried walking faster and harder to keep warm.

If only someone would come along, I thought. I began to pray for it even though I knew this was a road built mainly to serve The Meadows. The sky grew darker and darker, but the snow flakes became whiter and larger. Caught up in a rough wind, the flakes were soon whirling about me, slapping me in the face and falling so hard and fast I had to walk with my eyes closed most of the time.

Unfamiliar with the road, I stumbled and fell over a large bump. I screamed and threw out my hands to break my fall. I landed on some gravel and skinned my palms badly. The impact shook me something terribly too and for a moment I thought I would be unable to get myself up. I felt a terrible pain shoot through my lower abdomen.

Oh, no, I thought, the baby. I struggled to my hands and knees and caught my breath. With the blanket open and mostly off, I was fully exposed to the wind and the snow. The icy flakes were falling down the back of my neck. I realized I had dropped my letter to Trisha, and had to search for it. After I found it, I stood up and took deep breaths as I clutched the blanket to my body. The pain in my abdomen subsided, but now my palms stung like there were needles jabbed in them.

I started to sob. I had only made things worse for myself, I thought. As I took renewed steps forward, I felt a pain in my lower back. It grew sharper and wider with every moment. I had to pause to catch my breath, but even then, the pain did not diminish. The pain began to spread around my sides toward my stomach. It felt like I was in the grip of fingers of steel, squeezing. I panicked and started to run. The snow was so heavy I could barely see in front of me anymore. I fell again, and again I scraped my hands. This time when I stood up, I spun around in confusion.

It had grown so dark so quickly, I thought. Was I heading in the right direction? Should I have turned left or right? My panic grew. I started in one direction and then stopped and started in another. Then, terrified that I was lost and would die in the cold, I broke into a trot, my stomach bouncing so hard, I had to keep my hands under it and consequently lost my blanket off my shoulders. But I didn't stop to retrieve it. I kept running and running and running. My foot got stuck in a soft part of the road and when I pulled up, it came right out of my shoe. It seemed as if the very earth were trying to swallow me up. I was so panicked I didn't even notice I was running with a bare right foot. I ran on and on until I was gasping for breath and had to stop. Then, clutching my stomach, the pain excruciating everywhere on my body, I fell to my knees and sobbed and sobbed.

Suddenly, I heard the sound of an engine and looked up. I screamed just as Luther's truck came to a stop directly in front of me, the bumper of the truck nearly touching my face. He got out and helped me to my feet, but I was mostly in a daze, my hands and feet numb with cold. He lifted me up and carried me around to put me into the truck. My head fell back against the window. My teeth were chattering so hard I thought they would break. He threw the old brown blanket over me and backed the truck down the road a few hundred yards and turned back into the driveway. Apparently, I hadn't gotten very far; I had been running in circles.

Luther drove up to the rear of the plantation house and carried me through the back door. Miss Emily, with Charlotte at her side, her face aghast, stood like a sentinel, her arms crossed under her small bosom.

"You little fool," she said. "You foolish little fool. Just lucky for you, Luther happened to gaze down the road and see you running about like a chicken with its head chopped off. You should have *yours* chopped off for this."

She nodded at Luther and he took me into the pantry and lowered me to the tub. Then he left and Miss Emily stepped up to pull off my wet and soiled dress. I couldn't stop shivering; my teeth continued to clatter. Luther brought in pail after pail of warm water. As the level built and more of my body was covered, I began to feel a deep fatigue in my lower limbs. No longer concerned about my nudity, I lay back and let Luther pour the warm water over my shoulders and breasts. Finally, Miss Emily declared it had been enough.

"Get out," she commanded and held up a towel. I rose slowly and, with Charlotte's help, stepped out of the tub. Miss Emily wrapped the towel around me quickly.

"You've lost a shoe, I see," she said. "You'll have to do without it and go barefoot now. I don't bear fools and sinners easily. March up to your room," she commanded.

My legs barely carried me along. The cold floor under my bare feet made it feel as if I were walking over a frozen pond. Charlotte held my arm as I started through the kitchen, but Miss Emily gave me no assistance. I struggled to climb the stairs, getting so dizzy at one point, I thought I would faint and roll down the steps. I reached out frantically and grabbed the banister.

"Just move on," Miss Emily said, her words like a whip striking my naked shoulders. I took a deep breath and continued. When I reached my horrid room, I remembered I no longer had a blanket. As soon as Miss Emily lit the kerosene lamp, she saw that immediately.

"You lost your blanket out there, didn't you. I should leave you without one just so you would learn your lesson," she said.

I didn't have the strength to talk back. I crawled under the sheet and pulled it up to my mouth, wishing I could pull it over my head and die.

"Go bring her another blanket," she ordered Charlotte and ranted and raved about my ingratitude and how much more difficult I was making an already horrible situation. I kept my eyes closed until Charlotte returned with the blanket and spread it over me.

"Thank you, Charlotte," I said in a voice barely strong enough to sound more than a whisper. She smiled.

"Leave her," Miss Emily said. When Charlotte left the room, she stepped up to me. "Where did you think you were going in this weather?" she demanded.

"I wanted to mail my letter," I said.

"Yes, your letter."

I looked up and saw she had opened the envelope and taken out the letter.

"You had no right to open the envelope and read that," I said.

"Again, you tell me what I have a right to do and not to? How dare you tell someone I should look into the mirror to see the devil? How dare you call me a religious fanatic and say I'm not human? How dare you call anyone else names anyway, you who bear the mark of sin? And who is this . . . this Daddy Longchamp? Is this the man who kidnapped you when you were a baby? Why would you want to contact such a person?" she asked when I didn't reply.

"Because unlike you and Grandmother Cutler, he's good," I said.

"Good? A man who steals babies is good? There's no question as to whether or not the devil is inside of you. The question is will you ever get him out?"

"The devil is in you, not me," I muttered. I couldn't keep my eyes open. "He's in you . . ." My voice trailed off.

Miss Emily droned on and on, spinning her talk about the devil and hell and my ingratitude into a blanket of venom and hate to throw over me. After a while I didn't hear words, just the droning and I fell into a deep sleep.

I awoke hours later in the darkness and for a moment, I didn't know where I was. But the aches in my arms and legs and shoulders helped refresh my memory. I groaned and turned in the bed. And then I heard the sound of a match and saw a single candle lit. The eerie amber light illuminated Miss Emily's face. She had been sitting in the dark near me waiting for me to stir awake. She leaned toward me. My heart began to pound as she brought her face closer and closer to mine.

"I have prayed over you," she said in a hoarse whisper. "And I have watched over you, but unless you repent of your ways, the devil won't release his grip on you. I want you to recite the Lord's Prayer now and every night, do you understand? Make the vessel of your body an unfriendly place for the devil to reside.

"Pray!" she commanded, her eyes two glowing embers.

"I'm tired," I said. "I'm so tired . . ."

"Pray," she repeated. "Drive the devil back into hell. Pray, pray, pray," she chanted.

"Our Father," I began, my lips trembling, "who art in Heaven . . ."

I couldn't remember the words and she claimed that it was the devil who was making me forget. She made me repeat it until I recited it perfectly and then she blew out the candle between us and slipped out through the darkness like one who was well acquainted with the night and the shadows and all the dark thoughts that haunt us in our most troubled moments.

I fell asleep again, not sure whether what had happened was a nightmare or not.

15

NEVER-ENDING NIGHTMARES

In the days and weeks that followed, I felt myself slowly but surely becoming more and more numb. I was deadened and dulled, moving about the plantation house like a robot, without feeling, uncaring, hardly seeing or hearing anything or anyone around me. It was as if the terrible cold that had engulfed me so viciously that afternoon when I had tried to walk to Upland Station still had a grip on me. I grew used to the house of darkness, the long shadows and the deep silences. I no longer glared defiantly at Miss Emily or challenged her authority and orders with questions. Whatever she told me to do, I did. Wherever she told me to go, I went.

One day she had me take out each and every volume in the library and dust the book jackets and the shelves. There were hundreds of books, some never touched for years and years, their pages so yellow and brittle they crumbled in my fingers if I pressed them too hard. I was there all afternoon and didn't even finish by the time the sun had begun to fall behind the trees outside the window. Miss Emily made me return after I had cleaned up the dinner dishes. I had to work by kerosene lamp and didn't finish until nearly midnight.

Exhausted, I pulled myself up the stairway and found myself grateful even for my decrepit room and bed. But I overslept the next morning, and when I didn't appear when I was supposed to, Miss Emily came up and poured a glass of ice cold water on my head. I screamed and jerked myself up abruptly out of a dead sleep. I felt something tear in my rib cage. The pain was excruciating, but Miss Emily wasn't interested.

"Sloth is one of the seven deadly sins," she declared as she hovered over me. "Rise early and be at your chores promptly and you will provide no sinful flesh for the devil to gnaw upon. Now dry yourself and come right down to the kitchen," she ordered.

Even at this outrage, I didn't moan. My flag of pride remained unfurled;

my dignity lay at my feet. I was tugged from chore to chore, room to room. I let myself be ridiculed and made an example whenever Miss Emily decided to preach to us at the dinner table. One Sunday, she made me the subject of the service in the make-shift chapel. I thought I was even beginning to see a look of pity for me in both Luther's and Charlotte's eyes.

But I felt helpless and lost. My mother never had inquired about me and I had been unable to contact Trisha or Jimmy or Daddy Longchamp. All that mattered now was putting in the time that remained and giving birth to a healthy and beautiful child, Michael's child.

Visions of the baby provided my only pleasant moments. Sometimes I would stop whatever I was doing and place both my palms over my stomach. I'd close my eyes and imagine the baby's little face. In my mind I saw a girl. She had my blond hair, but Michael's dark sapphire eyes. She had a robust little pink face and a happy disposition. I couldn't wait for the moment when I would hold her in my arms.

Despite the horrid circumstances and the tragic blows dealt me by the hand of fate, I foresaw only good things after the baby's birth. She would precipitate a change of luck. Somehow, I would make us a good life together and she would grow up to be beautiful and good. I could daydream for hours and hours about the two of us walking hand in hand in the sunshine on some beautiful beach.

Of course, I began to think about names. I had considered naming her after Momma Longchamp, but now I decided she should have an identity free of anyone else, an identity purely her own. Every chance I got, I thumbed through the dusty old volumes in the library, searching for unique names. One afternoon, Miss Emily caught me doing so.

"What are you looking for in those books?" she demanded, her eyes small and suspicious. "There are no erotic or provocative passages in my books."

"That's not what I'm trying to find," I said. "If you must know, I'm thinking about names for my baby."

She smirked.

"If it's a girl, call her Chastity or Virtue. She will have enough to overcome as it is. If it's a boy, name him after one of the disciples."

I didn't reply. There was no question I would reject any names she suggested. I liked the name Christie for a girl, but I was no longer sure what to call it, if it was a boy. As I mused over it, I realized Michael had never gone over names with me. I should have been more suspicious when he didn't have a proud father's interest from the start. I couldn't help wondering about him still. I was sure he was starring in some new spring production by now.

According to Luther, spring was late this year in the South and that played havoc with the planting. Days didn't finally warm up until the beginning of April, even though trees had formed buds and grass had begun to turn green. However, I didn't have much chance to appreciate the nicer weather, the birds and blossoming flowers anyway. Miss Emily's list of chores usually kept me busy all day. And despite the warmer days and nights, the great plantation house didn't seem to be any less cold to me. It was as if the sunlight pouring through the windows when the curtains were open lost strength the moment it entered this dark, brooding house.

By the time I entered the seventh month, I had grown quite large and I began to experience a shortness of breath during physical exertion. Miss Emily, although claiming constantly to be an experienced midwife, didn't reduce my chores. She continued to insist I get down on my hands and knees to scrub floors and move heavy furniture to dust and polish. If anything, she increased my load.

One morning, after I had finished washing the dishes, pots and pans and scrubbed the kitchen floor, she came in to inspect my work. I was so exhausted from the effort that I was still sitting on the floor, holding my stomach and taking deep breaths. She stood towering beside me, gazing down at me and what I had completed.

"Didn't you empty the pail now and then in order to use clean water?" she inquired.

"Yes, Miss Emily," I said. "I did as I usually do, using three pails full."

"Humph," she said, walking slowly over the kitchen floor. "This floor doesn't look as if it's been touched."

"It's a very old and worn floor, Miss Emily," I said.

"Don't try to blame your incompetence on the floor," she shot back. "From here," she said, making an invisible line with her toe, "to the end, it has to be redone."

"Redone? But why?"

"Because you used soiled water and simply ground in more dirt as you went along. How do you expect us to come in here to eat with a floor this filthy?" she said, her mouth twisted, her eyes filled with fire. How furious and ugly she could become, I thought.

"But I have furniture to polish and you told me to wash the windows in the library today and . . ."

"I don't care what else you have to do. What good is your doing anything if you're going to do it poorly. Redo this floor immediately," she insisted.

"Miss Emily," I pleaded, "I'm much further along in my pregnancy. It's getting harder and harder for me. Isn't it dangerous for me to work so hard now?"

"Of course not. It's just like someone like you to think so, someone spoiled and soft. The harder you work, the stronger you will be at the time of delivery," she said.

"But I'm tired. It's more difficult for me to sleep now and . . ."

"Wash this floor immediately!" she cried, pointing down. "Or when the time comes, I'll have Luther put you in the barn to give birth with the pigs."

"I should see a doctor," I mumbled, but kept my eyes down. I wanted to say more, but I was afraid she might just do what she promised and the only thing I would accomplish would be the death of the baby.

I struggled to my feet and went to fill a new pail of water. Then I put in the soap and returned to the spot she had indicated on the floor. She stood in the doorway watching me work.

"Press down harder," she commanded, "and make wider circles when you scrub. I thought you claimed to have worked as a chambermaid in my sister's hotel."

"I did, but we never had to do this!"

"That hotel must be filthy then. So much for what my sister knows. She was always the favorite, the apple of my father's eye and never did her share. She always managed to get me or poor, stupid Charlotte to do her work. She's still managing it," Miss Emily said. "You're here. Harder. Wider circles," she repeated and pivoted out the door.

I did the best I could and when I was finished, I found I couldn't get up quickly. My back was so stiff, I had to sit against the wall to catch my breath and wait for the ache to subside.

As time went by, the list of chores I usually completed by late afternoon now took me into the evening. When I was finished, I had to make my way alone through a dark house holding a candle. Gradually, the climb up the stairs became harder and harder and took longer and longer. I was terrified of passing out and falling down, for I was sure I would lose the baby.

One night toward the end of the seventh month, when I had completed my chores and pulled myself up the stairway to my closet of a room, Miss Emily marched through the door just as I entered. It was as if she had been waiting in the shadows in the corridor outside, for she was right behind me, practically breathing down my neck. She was carrying her kerosene lamp and something in a large paper bag.

"It's time to take stock," she said when I turned with surprise.

"What do you mean?" I cried. I was so tired I could barely keep my eyes open. I hoped she didn't mean doing some sort of inventory.

"We have to check you," she said.

"But why now?" I moaned. "I'm tired and it's time to sleep."

"What do you want me to do, adjust my schedule to fit your needs? Take off the dress," she ordered.

Reluctantly, I began to lift the garment over my head, but she was impatient and seized it in her hands and tugged it abruptly, nearly sending me to the floor. I embraced myself, covering my bloated bosom, and glared at her. She placed the palm of her right hand roughly over my abdomen, pressing so hard, I had to cry out.

"Just as I suspected: you're constipated," she declared.

"No, I'm not," I said, "I . . ."

"What do you mean, oh, no? Don't you think that after all these years and the dozens and dozens of babies I've delivered, I know when a pregnant woman is constipated and when that constipation is causing undo pressures on the womb and the fetus?"

"But . . . ." I shook my head. Was she right? I wondered. Was that why I had such trouble breathing?

"No buts. You want to do what's right for the baby, don't you?"

"Yes," I said. "Of course."

"Good." She reached into the paper bag and brought out a large bottle of castor oil and an enormous glass. She opened the bottle and filled the glass to the top. "Drink this," she said, thrusting it at me. I took it slowly.

"All of it?"

"Of course, all of it. I think I know how much you need. Drink it."

I brought the glass to my lips, closed my eyes, and swallowed and swallowed. The horrible tasting liquid bubbled as it settled in my stomach. To my surprise, she filled another glass.

"Again," she said, thrusting it back at me. She kept the glass in my face. "Drink it!" she snapped.

I took it slowly and emptied the glass as quickly as I could.

"All right. That will clean you out and take the pressure off your womb," she said. In the glow of the lamps, she almost smiled. Maybe now that my time was drawing closer and closer, she would behave more like the midwife she claimed she was, I thought. She put the nearly emptied bottle of castor oil back in the bag along with the glass. "You can put your dress back on," she said and marched out.

It was not long after she left that a cramp, sharp and dreadful, shot across my abdomen. The next time one came, it nearly doubled me over. Then the pains came quickly, one after another. I got out of bed as fast as I could and, without pausing to turn on the kerosene lamp, lunged for the bathroom door. I pulled on the knob firmly because the door was always stuck. Only this time, the knob came off in my hands and the thrust sent me reeling backwards. I couldn't stop myself from falling and sitting down hard. The impact caused me to have an immediate accident.

"Oh no!" I cried as my bowels rampaged. All I could do was lie there and wait for it to end. Then, slowly, as carefully as I could to keep myself from getting any dirtier, I slipped out of the soiled dress. I rolled it up quickly and returned to the bathroom door. I put my hand in the hole where the knob used to be and tugged until the door opened. Then I went in to wash myself. Yet the towel and cloth I used to clean myself wasn't enough. I groped about in the darkness and then went out back into the bedroom, deciding I would call for Miss Emily. But before I could open my mouth my stomach in reply began to rumble again. This time I made it to the bathroom. However, my bowels went wild and when it was finally over, I felt so limp and weak, I could barely stand. My abdomen ached. I had trouble catching my breath. My heart pounded so hard I thought it would split open my chest.

"Miss Emily!" I cried out, hoping she might hear me and come to help me. *"Miss Emily!"* I listened, but there was no response and no sound of footsteps in the corridor outside my room. She could never hear me shouting from here, I thought.

Terrified of what was happening, I pulled myself to my feet and desperately made my way back to my bed. The pains in my stomach spread to my back and became sharper and more intense. I realized I had to make another trip to the bathroom and quickly. I slipped off the bed and crawled on my hands and knees, just reaching the toilet in time, but the end of this ordeal left me as limp as a wet washcloth. I couldn't even crawl back to my bed. I collapsed on the floor, groaning, too weak to cry out. I realized I was in great danger of losing the baby, but I didn't have the strength to do much more.

Thankfully, the pain began to ease. I closed my eyes and held my stomach. In the morning Miss Emily found me still lying there. I had fallen asleep on the bathroom floor.

"This is disgusting!" she shouted. *"Look at this room. You're worse than one of my pigs!"*

"Miss Emily," I moaned, struggling to get up, "I couldn't get into the bathroom. You gave me too much castor oil," I cried, the tears streaming down my cheeks.

"How dare you accuse me of making an error, just because you're too stupid to take care of yourself."

"I'm not too stupid. I almost lost the baby." She started to smile. "You want me to lose the baby! That's why you did it and why you're making me work so hard."

"Why you ungrateful, spiteful . . . I would never do such a thing." Her eyes narrowed. "Do you think I would punish a baby for the sins of its parents? Get hold of yourself before I do put you in the barn. You're behaving no better than a barn animal anyway." She drew up her shoulders.

"I will send Charlotte up here with another towel and cloth and a fresh dress," she said. "I want you to clean yourself up and spend the morning cleaning this room. Then, and only then, can you come downstairs for something to eat. Do you understand? Disgusting," she added and marched out.

I remained where I was on the floor until Charlotte came with my things. Could I have been so confused as to leave them downstairs? I wondered. The last few days had been so hard, the work so difficult, my fatigue so deep, perhaps I had. But it seemed more likely to me that Miss Emily had done all this to me deliberately.

"Ugh," Charlotte said, squeezing her nose.

"I'm sorry, Charlotte. Thank you," I said, taking my things. "If I had a window in my room, I could open it," I added angrily. She stood outside the doorway looking in at me as I preceded to wash myself down. I felt like I had been dragged through a war. I was happy to get clean and I was even happy to put on the ugly sack dress because it was at least clean.

"The same thing happened to me," Charlotte admitted, shaking her head sadly as I went about cleaning up the room.

"The same thing?" I paused to look at her. "You mean you've been sick like this?"

"Yes, but Emily said it was because the baby had pointed ears and was a spawn of the devil."

I stared at her. What did all this mean—the baby rattle, the needlework for a baby, the references to her own pregnancy. Was it real or part of her imagination?

"Charlotte, when did you have this baby?" I asked.

"Charlotte!" we heard Miss Emily scream from down the hall. *"I told you to give her those things and leave her to clean up."*

Charlotte started to turn away and then hesitated and looked back in at me, an impish expression of defiance on her face.

"Yesterday," she said and ran off.

Yesterday? I thought. I nearly laughed myself. Charlotte really didn't have any concept of time. But did that necessarily mean that all she had told me was fantasy? And if she was pregnant out of wedlock, just like me, did Miss Emily do the same sort of things to her? Miss Emily wouldn't tell me. I knew that if I so much as had asked her about Charlotte being pregnant, Miss Emily would have chastised me for listening to her and encouraging her fantasies.

But I had to discover the truth, perhaps before it was too late for both me and my baby, I thought.

* * *

As I entered my eighth month of pregnancy, Miss Emily decided that I was too heavy. She decided to cut back on everything I was given to eat. Some days I was so ravishingly hungry, I gobbled anything in sight, even stale bread. I had to sneak food on the sly, for she left nothing out and easy for me to get. I would finish my meager meals and have to sit at the table and watch her and Charlotte continue to eat. I got to the point where I was eating whatever Charlotte left on her plate when she handed me the plate to wash.

Although my food was cut back, my work was not and I was carrying the baby much lower now. I couldn't bend down; I had to kneel to pick things up. One late April morning, Miss Emily decided that it was time to air things out. At first I didn't understand what that meant. Then I realized what she wanted to do.

First, she wanted me to take up every rug in the house and pound the dust out of it outside. Then, she wanted me to carry out every sofa and chair cushion and beat them the same way. When I started to protest, she ordered Charlotte to help and Charlotte was eager to do so. She was happy to be given any significant activity. Together, we began by rolling up the rug in the library. Charlotte did most of that, but carrying it out was a terrible strain. Even sharing the weight, it was too heavy for me to bear. I felt my stomach pulling and tearing. Off to the side, Miss Emily watched us like an eagle. We managed to get the rug out on the portico and draped it over the railing. Then we started to beat out the dust, months and months of it. The clouds of dirt nearly choked me.

"I had to get up early today," Charlotte told me when we paused for a rest. "The baby woke me."

"Charlotte, how can there be a baby if you told me the baby went to hell?" I asked.

"Sometimes, Emily lets him come back to visit. I never know until I hear him crying for his bottle," she said.

"Where is he today, Charlotte?" I pursued when I was sure Miss Emily wasn't listening to us.

"In the nursery. Where else?" she said and then she started to beat the rug, singing a child's tune as she did so.

"You better not go down to the woods today . . ."

I made up my mind. Tonight, I thought, when I was sure Miss Emily was asleep, I would do what I had been forbidden to do: I would go into the west wing and I would explore.

The airing out of things was the hardest work I had to do all month, but it at least permitted me to be outside and enjoy the warm spring day. I had almost forgotten how wonderful and happy the blue sky and soft milk-white clouds could make you feel. The breeze was gentle and delicately played with my loose strands of hair. I couldn't help but recall some of the happier spring days of my life, those unfortunately too rare but marvelous days when Jimmy and I were very young and didn't fully understand how hard and how terrible our lives really were. At least I didn't. I think Jimmy always knew and resented our poverty.

It had been so long since he had heard from me or I had heard from him. I was afraid he thought that I had forgotten him and no longer cared. One of the reasons I was anxious for the baby's birth and my leaving The Meadows was renewing my relationship with Jimmy, if I could. I was afraid that after he had learned all that I had done and all that had happened, he might very well not want to have anything more to do with me.

"Stop that daydreaming!" Miss Emily screamed from a window.

I returned to the sofa cushions and beat out the dust that had made its home in them so long.

Miss Emily was apparently satisfied with how much work we did accomplish, however, for after dinner she decided I could read or go to sleep as early as I wished. I did go into the library to peruse some family pictures I had discovered when I had done the thorough cleaning of the shelves. I turned the pages and gazed at the sepia photographs capturing Grandmother Cutler, Miss Emily, and Charlotte as children.

Grandmother Cutler was by far the prettiest of the three. Even as a child, Miss Emily had that pinched face and those cold, hard eyes. Charlotte was always on the plump side, but she always had that happy, innocent look of a child. There were even some pictures here and there in which Luther could be seen in the background. He was once a tall, strapping and even handsome man. In all of the pictures of Father and Mother Booth, Mother Booth was standing and Father Booth was sitting with Mother Booth behind him, her hand on his shoulder. Neither of them smiled—perhaps they thought that smiling would bring the devil. The pictures of the grounds were nice, however, and I understood that the plantation was once a bright and rich place. I couldn't help but wonder about the forces and events that had changed everything so dramatically and made this family so horrid.

Thinking about all these mysteries reminded me of my intention to explore the west wing. I went up to my room to get some rest and wait until it was much, much later when I would be certain Miss Emily would be asleep. I didn't anticipate how deep my own fatigue from the day's hard work went, however, and I practically passed out the moment my head hit the pillow. It was nearly morning when I woke up again, but it was still dark enough for me to begin my explorations.

I rose out of bed and lit the kerosene lamp, then I stepped out into the dark corridor and made my way toward the west wing, determined to discover if there was even the slightest shred of truth to Charlotte Booth's fantasies.

When I reached the stairway, I hesitated. It was almost as if there really was an invisible wall, a border that I would have to cross and the moment I did, I would risk bringing the full wrath of Miss Emily down upon me. The west wing corridor was pitch dark, and I had no idea where anything was, but I continued forward, hovering near the wall on the right as I did so.

Just like in my corridor, there were some decorative furnishings and many old paintings. There were two rather large portraits of Father and Mother Booth side by side, and as in all the other pictures, neither smiled, both looked angry and unhappy. These pictures hung on the wall directly across from the first door. I stopped and listened. Was this Miss Emily's or Charlotte's room? I turned the knob slowly and pressed against the door. At first, it didn't budge and then it got unstuck and I practically fell into the room.

I held up the lamp, afraid that I had blundered into Miss Emily's quarters, but it was immediately obvious to me that no one had lived in this room for years, so I turned up the lamp and gazed around. It was an enormous room with a great oak bed. It had pillars that went up as high as the ceiling and an enormous half moon headboard. The bed still had all its pillows and blankets, but the cobwebs on it were so thick it was clear no one had come in to clean it for ages.

There was a stone fireplace at least twenty feet long on the wall with large windows on either side. Long curtains were drawn tightly closed and looked weighed down with dust and grime. Above the fireplace was a portrait of a young Father Booth, I thought, or perhaps his father. He stood holding a rifle in one hand and a string of ducks in the other. It was one of the few pictures in the house where someone had something of a smile on his face.

There was a lot of dark, beautiful antique furniture in the room, and on the night table there was a copy of the Bible with a pair of reading glasses beside it.

The room smelled musty and stale and looked as if its inhabitants had simply been swallowed up one day, for the vanity table was still covered with brushes and combs and jars of skin creams. Some jars had been left opened, the contents dried and evaporated. Clothing still hung in the closets and there were pairs of shoes beside the bed, a man's pair on one side, a woman's on the other. I had the chilling feeling I had invaded the sanctuary of a pair of ghosts.

I backed out of the room I felt sure had once been Father and Mother

Booth's room and continued down the corridor. When I realized that the door to the next room on the right was open, I turned the kerosene lamp down again and approached as quietly as I could. There was some very dim light coming from this room. I hesitated and then peered around the door jamb and gazed within.

There, asleep on a long, narrow bed with a plain square head and foot board was Miss Emily. She looked laid out like a corpse, for she wore a shroudlike nightgown and the light of her small kerosene lamp made her face appear bone white. So she slept with a light on, I thought. How interesting that she permitted herself to be wasteful. Despite her iron face and steel cold eyes, she lived with fears that made her afraid of the darkness.

I moved across her open doorway quickly and hurried down the long corridor, for the next doorway was some distance away. That door, too, was open, and when I looked in, I found Charlotte asleep in her bed, her body folded into the fetal position, her fingers near her mouth. Her long pigtails had been unraveled and her hair lie about her head in a clump of gray that made her childlike face look strangely out of place.

Except for their parents' room kept like some museum chamber, what was here that would make Miss Emily want to forbid me from entering the west wing? I wondered. I lifted the lamp and directed the light ahead of me and saw that there was another room on Charlotte's side, the doorway much smaller than the others. I listened to be sure Miss Emily hadn't heard my footsteps and then I walked on. The door to this room was closed. I tried the knob, but the door didn't budge. Was it just like the first door, simply stuck? I pushed harder and it opened as if someone had been standing behind it and had suddenly decided not to resist. I practically flew into the room, carried in by my own efforts.

This time when I lifted the lamp to gaze about, I shuddered. It was a nursery. Charlotte hadn't been fantasizing about that. The walls were covered with her needlework in frames, all of it beautiful work, pictures of animals and the plantation, as well as simple scenes in nature—meadows, trees, flowers. There were dressers and closets in the room, but the centerpiece was a crib and it looked like there was a baby in it.

My heart began to pound as I drew closer and closer. There was a baby. All this time . . . but I never heard it cry and why keep it a secret? Whose baby could it be?

I stepped up to the crib and lifted the light slowly over it. Then I reached in and carefully drew the soft, pink blanket back from the baby's face and realized . . . *it was a doll!*

"How dare you come in here?" I heard Miss Emily scream and I nearly dropped my lamp. I spun around quickly to see her standing in the nursery

doorway. She was only in her nightgown, her hair loose around her shoulders, making her even more witchlike. She held her own lamp up so the light fell on me. *"How dare you come into this wing when I forbid it!"*

"I wanted to see why Charlotte kept telling me about her baby. I wanted . . ."

"You had no right," she roared, coming forward. "This is not your business," she hissed, only a few feet from me now. Her eyes were filled with hot anger, her neck strained, making her collarbone look like it would rip out of her skin. Death itself couldn't have appeared more horrid looking than she did with the light over her venomous face, her skin the same shade as her teeth and her eyes red. I could barely breathe, barely move. My throat closed up; my heart felt as if it had stopped and a cold chill rushed up from my feet and traveled with electric speed over my spine to the back of my head.

"I . . . didn't want to bother you by asking, but . . ."

"But you were curious," she said, nodding, "as curious as Eve about the Tree of Knowledge, even though she, like you, were forbidden to taste of it. Nothing's changed you all the time you have been here, not the work, not the Sundays in the chapel, not my lectures, nothing; you are what you are and what you will always be—sinful."

"I'm not," I protested calmly. "I only wanted . . ."

"To know where the devil has been before. I understand your interest," she said, nodding again. "Very well, feast your eyes upon it," she said, gesturing around her.

"I don't understand," I said.

"This room was where we kept the child until it died and went to hell."

"Died? What child? Whose child?"

"The devil's own," she said. "Charlotte gave birth to it, but it was the devil's own."

"Why do you say that?" I asked.

"Because no one but the devil himself could have made her pregnant. Suddenly one day she was pregnant, don't you see?" she said, her eyes maddeningly wide. "I knew it all the time and when the baby was born, I had only to take a look at it to confirm it."

"You told her it had pointed ears, didn't you?"

"It did," she said. "Thankfully, it didn't survive."

"What did you do?" I asked, my heart pitter-pattering so hard I could hardly speak loud enough for her to hear me.

"Nothing but say my prayers over it day and night," she replied, a far-off look in her eyes. She was silent a long moment and then remembered where she was.

"But my pathetic half-sister didn't understand, couldn't understand. And so . . . I let her keep this fantasy."

"This is cruel." I gazed into her terror-filled face. "You think my baby is evil, too, don't you? That's why you tried to cause a miscarriage by making me do such hard work and giving me too much castor oil and starving me. You're crazy," I said before I had a chance to prevent myself from uttering the words. She spun around on me.

"You would say that! Get out of here," she ordered. I started for the doorway. She walked toward me threateningly. *"Get out and back where you belong!"*

"I will and I don't belong here," I cried back. "I want to go away . . . anywhere else but here and you can't stop me."

As soon as I reached the doorway, I turned and started to run, the image of her hateful eyes lingering.

"Get thee behind me, satan!" she screamed. I ran faster, but I made the mistake of looking back when I reached the end of the west wing and I tripped. I screamed and spun around, slapping myself against the wall before falling to the floor. Miraculously, the lamp did not shatter, but the light went out leaving me in darkness. I groaned. This time, the pain in my stomach was accompanied by an intense tightening.

Oh, no, I thought. Oh, no . . . . I screamed in agony.

Slowly, Miss Emily came up the corridor, her light before her. I pressed my hands to my stomach.

"Help me," I cried out. "Something's happening . . ." I looked down between my legs and realized I was all wet. *"My water's broken!"* I screamed.

She lowered the lamp slowly and saw it was true.

"Get yourself up," she commanded. "Quickly." Charlotte, who had finally awakened, came up behind her.

"What's wrong with her, Emily?" she asked. "Why is she lying on the floor?"

"Help her to her feet," Miss Emily commanded and Charlotte stepped forward.

The walk back to my room was the most excruciatingly painful walk I could ever imagine. The pain grew worse as my stomach tightened and tightened. I fell on my back on the bed. Miss Emily came in calmly and put the lamp down on the table.

"Go wake Luther up," she told Charlotte, "and tell him to bring us a pail of hot water." She glared down at me, her face twisting into a smile of contempt. "She's gone and hurried things along." She turned to the amazed Charlotte who continued to gape. "Move," she commanded.

"Oh, God," I cried. "It hurts so much."

"The more sinful you are, the more it does," Miss Emily replied with great satisfaction.

She pulled up my dress and had me bend my knees. Then she put her palm on my abdomen. "You're contracting," she concluded. Then she smiled. "Now we shall see if you are strong enough to bear the burden of your guilt."

16

MY KNIGHT IN SHINING ARMOR

"Push!" Miss Emily screamed into my face. "You're not pushing. Push harder!"

"I am pushing," I cried. I took deep breaths and tried again and again. The pain was so excruciating I began to consider the possibility that Miss Emily had been right—my agony was more severe as part of some divine punishment for my actions. Momma Longchamp had never told me giving birth was this painful. I knew it was no Sunday picnic, but I felt as if someone with giant hands was squeezing my stomach. It seemed to become a knot of knives. I thought I would pass out before delivering and something terrible would happen. Finally, I felt the baby moving.

"Just as I thought," Miss Emily said, "the baby is coming feet first." She guided it out with her long, thin and bony hands.

Charlotte had returned with the pail of hot water and then Miss Emily had sent her for towels and a pair of scissors. I saw her standing by the door, her mouth agape, her eyes wide as she watched the miraculous event unfold.

"What are you doing with the scissors?" I cried when I saw Miss Emily reach back and take it from Charlotte's hands.

"I'm cutting the umbilical cord," she replied, annoyed at my asking.

"Why isn't the baby crying? Don't babies cry when they're first born?" I asked. My face was covered with sweat, some drops getting into my eyes and making me blink.

"Shut up and be patient," she snapped. "Don't forget, it's premature," she added.

"What is it? Is it a girl?"

She didn't reply, but I saw Charlotte nodding. A little girl, just as I had hoped. I closed my eyes and lay back, my head against the pillow as my breathing became more regular.

Suddenly, I heard the tiny cry as Miss Emily washed the baby and wrapped it in a towel.

"Let me see her," I cried.

Miss Emily placed her beside me. I was so tired, I could barely keep my eyes open, but when I gazed at that tiny pink face with a nose and mouth so small, I felt my pain and exhaustion recede, washed away for the moment by an overwhelming sense of elation. Her little fingers were curled and wrinkled like a little old lady's, and she had the smallest ears. She had a small patch of blond hair, my hair, just as I had hoped she would. Her eyes were shut tight. I couldn't wait to see if she had Michael's dark sapphire eyes.

"She's so perfect, so tiny," I said. "Is that a dimple in her cheek?"

"She's too small," Miss Emily muttered. She rolled up the other towels and dropped them in the pail. Then she gazed down at my baby and me. She shook her head and reached down to lift her from my arms.

"Where are you taking her?" I demanded. I was numb with fatigue, unable to resist.

"To the nursery. Where else? You sleep. Later, I will send Charlotte up with something nourishing for you to drink."

I thought she was holding the baby too roughly and I imagined even for a just-born infant, feeling those hard bony arms beneath and around her must be uncomfortable. She grunted and turned her head as if to deny what was happening to her.

"Why can't she stay with me?"

"You might very well roll over on her in your sleep," Miss Emily said, flicking me one of her scornful glances. Then she looked at the baby and shook her head again. "She's too small," she repeated and started away.

"But she is beautiful, isn't she? Isn't she?" I cried.

Miss Emily turned only her head and peered back at me over her sharp shoulder.

"She came into this world feet first," she replied.

"What does that mean?" I asked. She didn't answer. She continued out. *"What does that mean?"* I shouted, but all I heard were her footsteps moving farther and farther away. I wanted to get up and follow her out, but I was so exhausted that even the thought of it was too much. To lie helpless and too weak even to lift my hand or turn my head was an unnerving experience, so unnerving I closed my eyes and fell into a deep sleep.

I dreamt of my baby in my arms. She looked older already, her face fully formed and clearly combining my features and Michael's. Suddenly, she was lifted out of my arms just the way Miss Emily had just done so. My baby held out her arms toward me, but she kept moving away. The baby cried out and I cried for her. The cry in my dreams became a real cry waking me up.

I knew it was raining hard because I heard the torrents pounding the roof and the windows out in the corridor. Then I heard the rumble of thunder and the crack of lightning. It seemed as if the whole great house shook. Just the sounds made me feel cold and wet. I couldn't keep my eyes from closing again and fell asleep to the rhythm of the raindrops caught up in the gusts of wind and sweeping over the building in wave after wave.

When I woke again it was hours and hours later. I sensed someone at my side and turned to see Charlotte. She was holding a glass of what looked like milk, but had a brown tint and some tiny cereallike things floating in it.

"Emily says you should drink this now," she said.

"What is it?" I asked.

"It's a formula she made to help you regain your strength very quickly. It's something my grandmother drank after every one of her babies were born. Emily remembers what she told her to do to make it."

"Probably full of vinegar," I muttered and took it from her. But when I tasted it, it didn't taste bitter. It tasted like there was honey in it. From my life with Momma Longchamp, I knew that some of the old remedies, herbal concoctions and the like, were often better than so-called modern medicines. I emptied the glass in two gulps.

"Have you seen the baby?" I asked Charlotte. She nodded. "She's beautiful, isn't she?"

"Emily said she was too small," Charlotte replied.

"She'll get bigger. I'll nurse her and she'll be healthy and beautiful before long. I didn't want to give birth prematurely," I said, remembering it all now, "but Emily was so horrid to me. I thought she was going to attack me, so I ran and I fell. At least now it's all over and my baby and I will soon be out of here.

"Charlotte," I continued, reaching up to take her hand so she would come closer, "I saw the nursery and I know you were telling me the truth. You did have a baby, a real baby once."

"His ears were pointed," she recited quickly as if she had been hypnotized to repeat it every time there was a reference to her child.

"No, Charlotte. I'm sure they were not. Emily said you were just pregnant one day, but women don't just wake up and find themselves pregnant. There's always a father. Why didn't you ever tell her who the father was and make her stop saying those terrible things?"

She started to pull her hand from mine, but I held on.

"Don't go, Charlotte. Tell me. You're not as stupid as your sister says you are. You were ashamed, weren't you? So you kept it a secret. Why were you ashamed? Was he someone Miss Emily wouldn't have approved of? Did you think you loved him like I loved my Michael?"

Her eyes widened with interest, but I saw from the look in them that love wasn't involved.

"You can tell me, Charlotte. I won't tell Miss Emily. You know I won't. You and I are closer and friendlier. I want to help you and be your friend just as much as you've been mine. You let her think you didn't know how you were pregnant; you let her create that horrible fantasy with the devil, didn't you?"

She didn't reply; she looked down.

"You know how women get pregnant, don't you, Charlotte? You know what they must do with men, even though I'm sure no one's ever bothered to tell you. It's a subject I'm positive has always been forbidden in this house, especially as long as Miss Emily's ruled it. But you know, right?"

"The wiggles," she said quickly.

"The wiggles? I don't understand, Charlotte. What are the wiggles? How does that make you pregnant?"

"After he did the wiggles on me," she said, "the baby started to grow in my stomach."

"After he did the wiggles? Who, Charlotte? Who did the wiggles on you?"

"It was in the barn," she said. "He showed me how the pigs did the wiggles and then he did it."

"The barn? It wasn't Luther, was it? It was Luther," I concluded from the expression on her face. "And I believe Miss Emily knew that all the time. Of course," I realized. "And she's been punishing him for it all these years, weighing on his conscience. That's why he takes all her abuse and lives and works like a slave.

"Oh, Charlotte," I said, reaching out for her. "I'm sorry what happened to you was made into such a nightmare. But tell me, what happened to the baby?"

We heard Miss Emily's footsteps in the hall and Charlotte jerked her hand from mine quickly.

"I'll make you a nice needlework picture to hang in the nursery," she said quickly and took the empty glass. Then she started out just as Miss Emily turned into the doorway. Miss Emily seized her arm to stop her.

"Did she drink it all?" she demanded and Charlotte nodded and showed her the glass. "Good. Go rinse it in the sink," she ordered and then looked in at me.

"How is the baby?" I asked.

"The baby was too small," she said quickly. "I want you to sleep so you will be ready to leave in the morning. Arrangements are being made." She started to turn away.

"What do you mean?" I said, propping myself up on my elbows. "What do you mean the baby was too small?"

"When babies are born too small, they're not meant to be born," she replied nonchalantly and started away again.

"What's happened to her? *Where is she?"* I shouted. I swung my legs off the bed, but my head began spinning so much I had to drop myself back to the pillow and keep my eyes closed. I felt a warmth in my stomach and a gurgling. The warmth seemed to travel quickly up into my chest.

What was in that drink? I wondered. I shouldn't have drunk it after all. I shouldn't have . . .

I felt so groggy, so tired and weak. It took all my strength for me to get my legs back on the bed and I couldn't open my eyes. It was as if a heavy blanket, a blanket made of iron, had been pulled over me, holding me down. Soon I thought I was sinking deeper and deeper into the bed. I tried to fight it, but I couldn't lift my arms. In moments, I was in a sleep even deeper than the one before.

I slept on and off most of the day, but whenever I woke up and started to rise, my head began to pound. All that would relieve it was lying back and keeping my eyes closed, which eventually resulted in my drifting off again. I didn't know whether it was day or not, for the door to my room was kept closed, but some time much, much later, it was thrust open and Miss Emily returned.

I started to lift my head from the pillow. She approached quickly and put her hand behind it to help me into a more seated position. Then she brought a glass to my lips. It was filled with the same liquid Charlotte had brought. I started to gag on it, but she held the back of my neck firmly in her wiry, pincer-like fingers and kept the glass to my mouth.

"Drink this," she commanded when some of it began to run down the sides of my chin. "Drink or you will never get strong enough to leave."

I started to spit it back, and shake her hands from my neck, but her fingers clung to me like old rotten moss and she kept the glass between my lips, pouring, pouring, pouring. I couldn't keep from swallowing some of it. Finally, she released me and my head dropped back to the pillow.

"Where . . . is . . . my . . . baby?" I asked as she started away.

"I told you, she was too small," she said and shut the door behind her as she left, leaving me in pitch darkness.

I tried to fight off the sleep, to keep awake so I could get out of bed and go looking for my baby. I started to sing in hopes that would prevent me from drifting off, but I didn't have the breath to go on very long. My words grew softer and softer until I was only mouthing them and then only singing them in my dreams.

When I awoke again, I knew it was morning because the door of my room was open and I saw the light that came in through one of the windows in the hallway. Charlotte was there, this time carrying a plate of real food: a bowl of hot cereal, a piece of toast and an orange already peeled. She placed it on the side table and lit my kerosene lamp.

"Good morning," she sang. "Emily says you should eat a good breakfast and then get dressed so Luther can take you to the train station. You're going for a ride on a train!"

I started to sit up. I felt so weak and so tired. Sleep lay like a fog around me, making everything look blurry, misty, far away.

"Get dressed?" I asked. Charlotte nodded and then reached down on the floor to pick up the pile of clothes to show me. She put them on the bed.

"My *clothes!"* They were wrinkled and faded, but seeing them was like seeing an old friend. Even my missing boot, the one I had lost that cold afternoon, was there.

"Thank you, Charlotte," I said, taking the clothing from her. I started to pull off the sack dress. Charlotte helped me and then I put on my own things, relishing the feel of them on my skin. I found my purse at the bottom of everything and looked for my comb, but when I found it, I found it had been melted when Miss Emily had had all my things boiled. The comb's teeth were all stuck together. My hair would have to remain knotted and twisted awhile longer.

Despite my hatred for anything Miss Emily did or gave me, I couldn't help but eat some of the toast and all of the orange. I didn't touch her horrible cereal. Just the thought of it now made my stomach turn. But what I quickly ate gave me some renewed strength and energy and I was able to get to my feet even though I was still very wobbly.

"Where is your horrid sister?" I demanded.

"She's down in the library working, working, working on accounts," she replied. "I've got to go do my needlework because I have something nearly finished for you."

"Where is my baby?" I asked her.

"They took her," she said, shrugging. "Emily said she was too small so they took it."

"Took her? Who took her? Oh God, please tell me," I begged, seizing her at the shoulders. But I could see Charlotte simply didn't know much more.

"I have to go to work so I can finish your present," she said, turning and walking away.

I straightened up and attempted my first steps. I grew dizzy again and had to grab hold of the door jamb and wait until the whirling passed. Desperation gave me needed strength. I had to find out what she had done with my baby. I continued to walk slowly down the corridor, each step hard. It seemed it would take me hours just to reach the stairway.

But when I made the turn toward it, I heard the sound of someone's voice, a familiar voice, a voice that sent chills of hope up my spine and filled me with even more strength and determination. I heard my name being pronounced and then I heard Miss Emily's sharp, cold tones.

"She's gone," I heard her say. "She left early this morning."

I walked faster, pulling myself along the wall until I reached the top of the stairway and looked down just as Jimmy closed the big front door behind him on the way out.

"Jimmy!" I screamed with all my strength. *"Jimmy!"* The effort drained me. I felt my legs soften, and I crumbled to the floor, my face against the railing. I began to sob, even my crying a great effort, the sobs softer, harder to make.

Miss Emily turned to look up at me, a wry, evil smile on that pallid face.

"Jimmy," I said softly. Was it a dream? Did I really hear and see him?

I didn't have to wait for the answer, for the front door rattled open again and Jimmy came rushing back through it. He stopped in the entryway. It was him, handsome and tall in his army uniform, some colorful ribbons on his chest. I mustered all the strength I had and called to him. *"Jimmy!"*

He looked up and saw me. Then he rushed past Miss Emily, nearly knocking her aside, and lunged up the stairway, two steps at a time, until he was at my side, embracing me, holding me against his chest and covering my forehead with kisses.

"Oh Dawn, Dawn, what's happened to you? What have they done to you?" he asked, holding me out and gazing down into my face. I smiled, my eyelids fluttering as I fought to keep them open.

"Is it really you, Jimmy? Are you really here or am I dreaming?"

"I'm here," he said. "I came as soon as I was able to find you."

"How did you find me? I thought I was lost, buried in this madhouse forever and ever."

"I went to the school residence in New York City and spoke to your girlfriend Trisha. All my letters to you from Germany were being returned, simply marked 'No longer at this address.' Daddy hadn't heard from you either and said two of his letters had been returned the same way. I couldn't believe you would leave without telling me where you had gone, so as soon as I returned to the States, I went to your apartment building and asked to see your girlfriend."

He lowered his head.

"She told me what had happened to you," he said.

"Oh Jimmy, I . . ."

He put his finger on my lips.

"It's all right. Don't try to explain it all right now. My first concern was you and what was being done. Trisha told me about all the letters she had written to you. In a letter you had left her when you left the hospital, you told her you were going to someplace called Upland Station in Virginia and you mentioned the Booth sisters.

"She wrote to you, but you never wrote back and her letters were never returned, so she never knew if you had gotten them."

"Oh Jimmy," I moaned. "I never got to see them. That horrid woman kept them from me, just as she kept me from sending any letters or calling anyone. There's no phone in this house and it's miles and miles to one."

"Who is this woman? Why did she lie and tell me you had already left?" he asked, gazing down the stairway. But Miss Emily was gone.

"She's Grandmother Cutler's horrid sister, even more horrid than she is. I didn't think it was possible, but it is. There's another sister here, a simpleminded one named Charlotte, who she torments in a different way."

Jimmy shook his head and looked me over.

"What happened . . . I mean, I thought you were sent here because you were pregnant."

"I was. I've just given birth—that's why I'm so weak and tired, that and something Miss Emily has given me to drink so I would be no trouble until she was ready to get rid of me. I have no idea where they were sending me next."

"Well, where's the baby?" he asked.

"I don't know. She told me it was too small. I'm afraid of what she has done. Her sister told me some people came and took it. I hope and pray it wasn't an undertaker."

"An undertaker?"

"Oh Jimmy," I cried. "I gave birth nearly a month too soon. There were so many terrible things going on here. I was in the nursery and I saw this doll in the crib and then she came in behind me all in a rage, so I ran and I fell and . . ."

"Easy," Jimmy said, stroking my matted hair. "You will have plenty of time to tell me all of it. You're not making sense right now. You're too distraught."

"Distraught? Yes, yes." I touched my own face. "I must look so horrible to you. I haven't had a hair brush for months and these clothes . . ."

I tried to stand, but I got so dizzy, I fell back into Jimmy's arms.

"Whatever she gave me still hasn't worn off completely," I explained.

"Let me help you up and take you somewhere to lay down for a few minutes. Then, we'll get to the bottom of all this," he said with definite authority.

Gazing into his dark eyes, I saw how strong and mature he had become. Jimmy was a full-grown man now. His shoulders were broad, his face firm. I had always felt safer in his arms or with him near me, but now I truly believed he could take charge and do what had to be done.

He lifted me to my feet as if I weighed no more than a baby.

"Just take me right down here where she kept me, Jimmy. It's the closet bed. But as soon as I catch my breath, I want to find out what happened to the baby and . . ."

"We will," he said, guiding me along. "Easy. No one is going to hurt you ever again," he promised with assurance.

"Oh, Jimmy. Thank God you're here." I rested my head against his strong shoulder and started to sob.

"Don't cry. I'll take care of you now," he whispered and kissed my hair and my forehead.

When he set eyes on my excuse for a room, he gasped.

"It's like a closet," he said. "No windows, no fresh air. Just a little oil lamp for light! And it smells so stuffy and sour in here."

"I know, but I just need a short rest."

After he helped me lie down, he went into the bathroom to get a wet washcloth to wash down my face and place on my forehead. "I haven't seen hovels worse than this anywhere in Europe," he muttered as he wiped my cheeks. "Solitary confinement in a military prison must be a palace compared to this."

He put the cool cloth over my forehead, sat down beside me on the bed and held my hand.

"Jimmy," I said, squeezing his fingers tightly in mine. "Are you here, are you really, really here?"

"I'm here and I don't intend leaving you for long again," he promised. He leaned over and kissed me softly on the lips. I smiled. Now that I felt safe, I permitted my eyes to close and took a short and much-needed rest.

I didn't sleep long and Jimmy never left the room the entire time. When my eyes first fluttered open, I panicked because I didn't see him immediately and thought that what had happened had all been only a dream. But as soon as he saw I was awake, he was at my side again. He kissed me and embraced me.

"Feeling strong enough to walk out of here?" he asked.

"Yes, Jimmy, but not without knowing what happened to my baby," I said.

"Of course. I can't believe what they've done to you," he said, brushing back some loose strands of my hair. "I want to know every detail."

"I'll tell you all of it, Jimmy—the terrible chores she made me do, how I had to sleep in the cold, the meager meals, the prayer sessions—she's a religious fanatic who treated me as if I were the devil's child. And I'm sure Grandmother Cutler knew exactly what would happen to me when she sent me here. But I want to find my baby first."

He nodded, the lines of his mouth tightening and that all too familiar glint of anger coming into his dark eyes.

"Let's go," he said in a tone of command. "I don't want us to spend one moment longer than we have to in this hell hole of a place."

He helped me to my feet. I felt stronger and my head was a great deal clearer. We walked out of the room that had been my pathetic home for so many months. Oddly enough, I had grown used to every nook and cranny in it. It was like a deprived child itself, abused, forgotten and buried in the darkness and horror of The Meadows.

As soon as we descended the stairway, I knew where Miss Emily was. The light was on in the library.

"She's hoping we'll just leave," I said. "She wants to ignore us, ignore all that she has done."

Jimmy nodded, his eyes fixed firmly on the library doorway. I took his hand into mine and we walked quickly to it.

Miss Emily was in her usual place, seated behind the great desk under her father's portrait, only this time, she didn't seem as intimidating to me, nor did the portrait. I had Jimmy at my side and could borrow freely from his strength.

She sat back as soon as we entered and formed that crooked smile on her face, a face with pale skin so thin the bones of the skull within it could be clearly seen. It was like looking at the face of Death itself, but I didn't falter.

"Well," she said. "Actually, I'm glad someone has come for you. It saves me the expense of having Luther take you to the train station in Lynchburg, and besides, Luther has more important things to do with his time."

"Yes, you've made him into your convenient slave over the years, punished him and punished him and he's accepted it, but that's for you and Luther to live with. I won't leave here until I know what you did with my baby. Who came for her? Whom did you give her to? Why did you do that?" I added in a shrill tone and approached the desk.

"I told you," she replied coldly. "The baby was too small. You wouldn't have been able to take care of it anyway. My sister did the right thing," she added and looked as if she were going to go back to her work and dismiss us.

But I rushed up to the desk and slapped my hands over her precious papers.

"What do you mean, your sister did the right thing? What right thing?"

She glared up at me, unafraid, unmoved, her eyes filled with ice. She wasn't going to speak. But Jimmy came up by my side.

"You better tell us everything," he said. "You had no right to do anything with her baby and if we have to, we'll go to the police and bring them here."

"How dare . . ."

"Look," he said, putting his hands on the desk and leaning over toward her, his patience on a leash. "I don't want us to stay here a minute longer than we have to, but we'll stay here until hell freezes over if you don't cooperate."

My heart cheered to see someone finally speak to Miss Emily the way she should have been spoken to years and years ago.

"You can be brought up on kidnapping charges, you know. Now, what's been done with the baby? Talk!" he said, slapping the desk so hard and unexpectedly that Miss Emily jumped in her seat.

"I don't know who has the baby," she whined. "My sister made all the arrangements even before Eugenia," she said, spitting her words my way, "arrived. You will have to ask her."

"And that's exactly what we will do," Jimmy said. "If you are lying and you knew, we will be back with the police to charge you as an accessory to a crime."

"I don't lie," she said defiantly, her pencil-thin lips drawn so tightly I thought they would snap like rubber bands. Jimmy glared back at her a long moment and then straightened up.

"Let's get out of here, Dawn," he said.

"Yes, and good riddance," Miss Emily replied.

Something exploded inside me. All the pain and anger I had held in, all I had shut up in my heart came pouring out. Every harsh and cutting word she had said to me, all the bitter food she had forced me to eat, the darkness she had shut me up in, and the way she had made me feel lower than the lowest form of life was finally regurgitated like the sour things they were.

"Oh no, Miss Emily," I said slowly, walking around the desk toward her, "good riddance to you. Good riddance to your ugly, frustrated and hateful face. Good riddance to your religious hypocrisy, to your making everyone else feel evil and despicable while you are the most evil and despicable thing in this house. Good riddance to your miserly ways, except when it comes to yourself. Good riddance to your jealousy of everything soft and beautiful. Good riddance to your pretense of wanting everything clean while you yourself live in the muck of darkness of this coffin you call a home."

I stood right beside her and looked down at her.

"I have never in my life ever wanted to say good-bye to anything as much as I want to say good-bye to you. And do you know, Miss Emily, being here, living with you and seeing what you are has made me feel sorry for the devil, for when you die you are sure to go to hell and even Satan doesn't deserve something as horrid as you."

I pivoted on my heels and left her sitting there with her mouth open, her eyes frozen wide with shock, looking like a corpse. Jimmy took my hand and smiled.

"Momma would have sure loved to see and hear that," he said.

"I'm sure she did," I replied as we marched out of the dark library.

Just after we walked out the front door and down the steps of the portico toward Jimmy's car, I heard Charlotte call my name and turned to see her come running out of the house.

"Who's that?" Jimmy asked.

Charlotte had her hair in her long pigtails as usual and wore the same pink shift with the ribbon yellow belt she wore the day I had arrived. She had her father's slippers on and shuffled down the walk.

"It's Charlotte," I said. "It's all right. I want to say good-bye to her."

"Are you going for a ride?" Charlotte asked, her eyes on Jimmy.

"I'm leaving, Charlotte. I've got to go and find my baby," I told her.

"Oh, you have to go now," she said, looking from me to Jimmy.

"Yes."

"Well then, here," she said, thrusting her hands toward me. She gave me a piece of needlework. I opened it and gazed upon a picture of a young woman who looked remarkably like me, only her hair was long and pretty and she was in a beautiful light blue dress. In her arms she held a baby and gazed down at it lovingly.

"Oh Charlotte, it's beautiful. I can't believe you made it. You are very, very talented. You must have been working on it a long time," I said.

"Yesterday," she said and I laughed. Everything was yesterday. Maybe it was her way of erasing all the horrid days in between. Maybe she really was a lot smarter than Miss Emily thought.

"Well, thank you, Charlotte." I gazed back at the house. "Don't let her torment you or make you feel evil. You're better than she is, much better." I hugged her. "Good-bye, Charlotte."

"Good-bye. Oh, when you come back, could you bring some sour balls. I haven't had sour balls since . . ."

"Since yesterday," I said. "Yes, I will see that you get bags and bags of them."

She smiled and stood there watching us get into the car. As Jimmy pulled away and we bounced down the rutted driveway, I looked back at the brooding, dark plantation house with the shadows painted on it and saw Charlotte waving like a little girl. It brought tears to my eyes.

Jimmy turned out of the driveway and the mansion disappeared from sight, but it would never disappear from my mind. It had a place forever and ever in the closet of my most horrible memories. Being free of it, however, made me burst into tears. I sobbed so hard that Jimmy had to stop to put his arms around me and comfort me.

"I'm all right, Jimmy," I said. "I'm just so happy to be out of that place. Just drive and get us as far away from here as quickly as possible."

Ahead of us the sky looked blue. It was as if the darkest clouds always lived over The Meadows and its grounds, for as we moved farther and farther away, it became brighter and warmer looking. I had forgotten just how much I loved the sight of green and the smell of fresh grass. I felt like someone who had been released from prison, like someone who had been shut up from all that was beautiful and good in the world and was now able to feast her eyes on it all once again. It filled me with renewed hope and renewed determination. I felt myself growing stronger and stronger every passing moment.

"Jimmy, please take us to Cutler's Cove as quickly as you can. I want to see Grandmother Cutler and make her tell us where she sent my baby before too much time passes."

"Sure thing," he said.

"Do you know what she's done, Jimmy?" I asked, fully realizing it all myself. "She's done the same thing to my baby that she did to me. She's arranged for some other people to take her and bring her up as their own. She thinks she has the right to determine everyone's life."

Jimmy nodded.

"Well, we're going to stop it from happening this time," he said. "Don't worry about that."

"Jimmy, I don't deserve your help," I moaned. "I made promises to you when you came to see me in New York, and then I let it all go to my head, the excitement, the lights, the music, just as you were afraid I might. I told you it would never happen, could never happen, and hardly any time passed before it did. I tried to write you about it a few times, but I could never get myself to put it into words. Maybe deep inside myself I really didn't want it to be happening."

"Someone took advantage of you," Jimmy said with a wisdom that surprised me. "I've seen a lot of that sort of thing—young, impressionable girls are promised many wonderful things by older men who then take advantage of their hopes and dreams. Afterward, they're left crying and alone. Some of my army buddies were guilty of doing it," he added angrily. "I'd like to get my hands on the man who put you into this terrible spot." He turned to me. "Or do you still care for him?"

"No, Jimmy, I can't care for someone who would do the things he did."

Jimmy smiled.

"The main thing is we've got to put it all behind you now. We've got to right as many of the wrongs as we can and go on. You're still going to be a great singer someday. You'll see," he said, patting my hand.

"Right now, the most important thing to me is getting my baby back. The moment I looked at her tiny, precious face, I knew she was something good, someone to be cherished and loved. My mistakes brought her into this world and I want to make it as good a place for her as I can. You understand, don't you, Jimmy?"

"Of course, but first things first, and the first thing I want to do is get you to a store to buy you something nicer to wear. We'll get you some brushes and things and check into a motel so you can clean up and get some rest.

"I remember Grandmother Cutler, you know, and when we get to Cutler's Cove and confront her, I want you looking fresh and strong so she realizes she has a couple of tough cookies to deal with, okay?"

"Oh Jimmy, yes, yes." I hugged him and kissed his cheek.

"Hey, easy," he said. "You're kissing an expert marksman and a corporal," he said, brushing his stripes proudly. Then he turned and stuck out his chest so I could see his ribbons.

"A corporal! You got another promotion? I'm not surprised. I always knew you would succeed at whatever you did."

"Maybe I always knew you expected it," Jimmy said. "And that's what made me succeed."

I rested my head on Jimmy's shoulder as we drove on. How lucky I was to have him with me once again, I thought. Just a little while ago, I was convinced that I was the most unlucky girl in the world, cursed and lost forever and ever.

And now, like the rainbow after the rain, like the first rays of sunlight coming through a break in the clouds, Jimmy had come to me and where there was once only darkness and hate, there was now brightness and love. I was confident I would get my baby back.

My eyes were closed but I saw the sunshine everywhere.

17
AN UNEXPECTED TWIST OF FATE

Jimmy was anxious to buy me new clothes and new shoes and took me to a department store as soon as we drove into a town that had one. He was very proud of being able to do it, and I saw that if I began to protest that something was too expensive, he would immediately grow upset.

"I told you," he reminded me, "I'm going to take care of you from now on. In Germany, my buddies used to call me 'the little miser,' because I didn't go out and spend every penny I earned. I saved and saved, happy just thinking about the things I would be able to buy for you as soon as I had returned.

"Besides, I like the way you look in fancy new things," he commented.

"Jimmy, you can't fool me. I know how terrible I look. I'm pale and ugly and my hair is a mess."

"First things first," he said and finished buying my clothing. Afterward, he bought me brushes and combs and lipstick. When we completed our shopping, we drove for a few hours and then pulled into a motel.

I couldn't believe how good a hot water shower felt and how wonderful it was to scrub shampoo and conditioner into my hair. I was in the shower so long, Jimmy knocked on the door to ask if I had drowned.

When I had had enough, I wrapped a towel around myself and poked my head out the door. He was sprawled out on one of the double beds reading a newspaper. Seeing him relaxed like that brought back memories of him unfolded over our small sofa-bed reading comic books, his dark eyebrows lifting and turning in as he read something that annoyed or touched him. For a moment I felt I could close my eyes and turn back time, and all the terrible things that had happened since we were children would be only nightmares.

"Hey," he said, lowering the paper and gazing at me. "You all right?"

"Yes, Jimmy. I feel like a new person."

There was a small vanity table and mirror just outside the bathroom. I sat down and began drying my hair.

"Let me help," Jimmy said, jumping up. "You probably don't remember when I used to dry your hair when you were a pint-size kid," he joked.

"I remember, Jimmy," I said, smiling back at him. He took the towel and wiped my hair vigorously until it was fluffy dry. It felt so good, I closed my eyes and let him go on and on. Then he stopped and planted a kiss on top of my head.

"Maybe I'll become a hairdresser," he said.

"I'm sure you can become anything you want, Jimmy," I said with confidence, gazing at his face in the mirror. "What do you really want to do when you're officially discharged from the army?"

"I don't know." He shrugged. "I guess something mechanical or electrical. I like working with my hands."

He stood back and watched me brush out my hair with long even strokes. Of course, my bangs were long and uneven and I had to trim them down. Wearing my hair tied up most of the time I was at The Meadows, I hadn't realized how long it had grown.

"It feels so soft," Jimmy murmured, stepping up to run his hand over it. I caught his hand and brought it to my lips. For a long moment, I just closed my eyes and held it there.

"It's all right," he whispered. "Everything's going to be all right."

When I was finished with my hair, I lay down to rest. Our plan was to take short naps and then go have a wonderful dinner. It had been so long since I had anything to eat that really tasted good or had any seasoning in it. But neither of us realized just how tired we were. He had been traveling for days before finally succeeding in finding me. In fact, I was the first to awaken and realize we had slept into the night. I didn't have the heart to wake him, even though my stomach was growling because I was so hungry. I tiptoed out of bed and got dressed quietly. Then I sat in a chair, waiting for his eyes to open.

When his eyelids lifted, he blinked quickly and then he looked at me peculiarly for a moment before he shot up into a sitting position.

"What time is it?"

"Almost nine," I said.

"Why didn't you wake me up?" he asked, swinging his legs over the edge of the bed.

"I couldn't, Jimmy. You looked so content while you were sleeping."

"It's just like you to think about someone else while you probably sat there starving," he said. "When I first looked at you just now, I thought I was back in Europe having one of my dreams. I wanted to see you so much every day," he said while he put on his shoes, "I used to imagine you everywhere."

"Well, you don't have to imagine it anymore, Jimmy," I told him. He smiled and hurriedly got dressed so we could go to eat. We went to the restaurant connected to the motel because it was the closest and at this point, I knew that wherever I went to eat would seem like the most celebrated gourmet establishment.

After we sat down and we were given menus, I couldn't make up my mind. I simply enjoyed reading all the wonderful choices and seeing scrumptious things that had been forbidden and impossible to get for months and months. Jimmy teased me for taking so long. When I told him why, he suggested I put the menu down, close my eyes, and let my finger fall on a selection. I did it and chose the hot turkey dinner.

First, I had a delicious salad. I nearly ruined my appetite by eating three dinner rolls smothered in butter. I ordered a Coke and luxuriated in the sugary sweetness of it. Heavenly! Jimmy kept laughing and shaking his head. When the platter of turkey, cranberry sauce, sweet potatoes and broccoli was brought out, I began to cry. I couldn't help it.

"Hey, come on," Jimmy said, reaching across the table to take my hand. "You're going to spoil your appetite if you get yourself so upset."

"Nothing can spoil this appetite," I announced and attacked my food, savoring every morsel. Even though I was stuffed, I ordered a slice of chocolate cream pie. When we were finished, I could barely stand up.

"You put some of these truck drivers to shame," Jimmy declared.

It didn't take either of us long to fall asleep again once we crawled into bed, but when the sunlight came through the curtains, my eyes snapped open. Just the sight of it was a wonder to me. It had been so long since I had awakened to see golden morning rays lift the darkness. I thought it was truly one of the most beautiful sights on earth. How horrible it had been living like a mole in that depressingly dark old mansion.

My appetite for breakfast was no less than it had been for dinner. Just the aroma of bacon sent my stomach into ecstasy. I had eggs and sausage and little rolls, as well as cup after cup of coffee, something Miss Emily had considered as vile as whiskey.

Strengthened by the food and a good rest, wearing new clothes and having my hair washed and brushed, I did feel strong enough to face my horrible grandmother. Jimmy had been right in saying, "First things first." We drove on, now only hours away.

"You haven't asked me anything about my love affair with Michael Sutton, Jimmy," I said somewhat tentatively after he had talked and talked about his experiences in Europe.

"You don't have to tell me anything," he said somewhat tersely.

"I know, but I do. I want to," I stated in a rush. "He was my vocal teacher and he had told me he was going to make me into a Broadway star. Everything happened so quickly to me. Before I knew it, he was inviting me to his apartment and . . ."

"Dawn, please," Jimmy pleaded, his face grimacing in pain. "I don't want to hear it. It's over with now. You were hurt, I know. And I wish I really could get my hands on him. Maybe someday, I will, but you don't have to explain it to me. I told you, I understand how these things happen. I've seen it.

"The important thing is," he said, looking at me, his dark eyes narrowed with firmness, "it won't happen to you again."

I nodded, relieved that Jimmy had forgiven me.

"I love you, Jimmy. I really do. I didn't realize how much I did and I'm sorry."

"Just don't eat the way you did today," he joked. "I can't afford it."

It felt so good to laugh again, to be able to relax and feel comfortable with someone, especially someone who brought sunshine into your life. Oddly enough, as we traveled farther and farther away from The Meadows, I found myself hating Miss Emily less than I pitied her.

But I didn't have a smidgen of pity for Grandmother Cutler. She was such a vile, evil woman! In my mind no one could have been more of a villain. The same forces that had created Miss Emily had created her, only she had an added power—she could get most people to respect her and she had been able to achieve great things in the real world. There was no doubt that she was a formidable foe. My heart began to thump harder and harder as we drew closer and closer to Cutler's Cove and our inevitable confrontation. I hardly noticed how beautiful a late spring day it was with a deep blue sky and puffs of milk-white clouds. In my troubled mind, it seemed the world was gray and dark again and there would be no warm sunlight until I was reunited with my baby.

The first sight of the ocean sent a chill up my spine. A little while later I saw the familiar road sign announcing we were about to enter the seaside resort village of Cutler's Cove. Nothing looked any different to me. This early in the season, the long street with its small stores and restaurants looked quiet and quaint. There was little traffic and only a few people on the sidewalks here and there. It had a relaxed, lazy atmosphere about it, but to me it was like passing through the eye of a storm. The pretty shops, the boats and sailboats down at the dock, the rich green lawns and peaceful streets were all part of a deception, for the heart of Cutler's Cove pulsed with evil—Grandmother Cutler's evil.

"Almost there," Jimmy said and smiled his smile of encouragement.

"Don't worry," he added. "We're going to get to the bottom of it all and settle it once and for all."

I took a deep breath and nodded. We came to the coastline that curved inward and provided the guests of the Cutler's Cove Hotel with their own private beach, a beach of white sand that always looked combed clean. Even the waves that came up approached the shore softly, tenderly, as if the ocean were afraid of attracting the wrath of the powerful matron who ruled this kingdom by the sea. I could almost hear her voice and see her face when I read the sign declaring this beach was RESERVED FOR CUTLER COVE HOTEL GUESTS ONLY!

Jimmy turned up the long drive and the hotel itself loomed ahead of us, sitting on a little rise, the manicured grounds gently rolling down before it. The three-story wedgwood blue mansion with milk-white shutters and a large wraparound porch looked strangely quiet. The unlit Japanese lanterns swung softly in the breeze. Only some of the grounds personnel were visible off to the side, pruning some hedges and planting some flowers. I didn't, as I expected, see any guests sitting out on the porch, nor did I see any around the two small gazebos or sitting on the wooden and stone benches or strolling past the fountains and flower beds.

"It doesn't look open for business," Jimmy remarked.

It was mid-afternoon, so I knew people weren't at lunch or dinner.

"No, it doesn't," I said. I was nervous enough as it was. Seeing something unusual only added to it.

Jimmy pulled up in front and parked. For a moment, I just sat there staring out the window at the hotel's front entrance, recalling that morning when I left the hotel to go off to a performing arts school in New York City. I had been filled with fear and excitement the day I left, but I clearly recalled the expressions on the faces of Clara Sue and Philip, my mother and Randolph, and especially Grandmother Cutler. All those faces flashed before me now.

"Ready?" Jimmy asked.

"Yes," I said firmly and got out of the car. We walked up the steps quickly and entered the lobby of the hotel. The moment we did so, I knew something was definitely not right. Except for Mrs. Hill and an assistant behind the reception desk, there was no one in the lobby, not a single person.

"They must be closed," Jimmy remarked, looking around.

I started for the desk. Mrs. Hill looked up as soon as she realized someone had entered the lobby. I saw that her face was etched with worry. She shook her head softly as I approached the desk.

"Oh, you're back from school," she said.

Of course, I realized after she said "school," Grandmother Cutler would let everyone here believe I was still in New York.

"Where are all the guests?" I asked.

"Guests? Oh, you don't know," she said, the corners of her mouth dropping.

"Know what?"

"Your grandmother's had a bad stroke. She's at the hospital and we've closed the hotel for the week. Your father's been so distraught, he's been unable to do anything and your mother . . . well, your mother's very upset."

"A stroke? When did this happen?" I demanded too harshly. She nearly broke into tears. "I mean . . . I didn't know," I said softly.

"Just yesterday. We had only a small number of guests at the time, since we're not really in season yet. Your father gave everyone who was here a full refund and, of course, kept everyone on salary."

I looked at Jimmy. He shook his head, not sure what we should do next.

"Is my father here or at the hospital right now?" I asked.

"He's in his office. He hasn't come out all morning," she said. "He's taking it all very badly. It's good that you've come home," she added. "Perhaps you can be of some help.

"Poor Mrs. Cutler," she continued, dabbing her eyes with a tissue. "She simply collapsed at her desk in her office. Just like her to be stricken ill while right in the middle of work. Fortunately, your father was looking for her and found her. There was quite a commotion until the ambulance finally arrived and they took her to the hospital. But we're all praying," she added.

"Thank you," I said and indicated to Jimmy that he should follow me across the lobby to Randolph's office. When we got there, I knocked softly on the door, but we heard no response. I knocked again, much harder.

"Who is it? Who is it?" a frenzied voice cried. I opened the door and we stepped in.

Randolph was seated at his desk leaning over a pile of papers. He barely looked up. His hair was disheveled and looked like he had been running his fingers through it for hours and hours. His tie was loose and his shirt unbuttoned and he had a glazed look in his eyes. There wasn't even a note of recognition in his face.

"I'm sorry," he said. "I'm too busy now. Later, later . . ."

He turned his attention back to the papers, running a pen down one and then up another as if he were searching desperately for a single item.

"Randolph, it's me, Dawn," I said. He looked up quickly.

"Dawn? Oh . . . Dawn." He put his pen down and clasped his hands. "You don't know what's happened . . . my mother . . . she . . . my mother's never been sick," he said, following it with a mad, hysterical laugh. "She never goes to a doctor. I always say . . . Mother, you should get a regular checkup. You have so many friends who are doctors and they're always telling you to come in for a checkup. But she'd never listen to me. Doctors make me sick, she'd always say." He laughed again.

"Imagine saying that . . . doctors make me sick. But she's been like a rock . . . solid," he said, holding up his fist. "Never missed a day's work . . . not a day, even when my father was alive. I don't even remember her having a cold. I once asked my father and he said, 'Germs wouldn't dare enter her body. They wouldn't have the nerve.' "

He laughed hysterically again and then looked down at his papers.

"I'm falling behind . . . with everything . . . bills, orders . . . things she normally took care of, you see. I had to ask the guests to leave and cancel the few who were coming this week. I can't do everything right now . . . not until she's well enough to return."

"Randolph," I said when he paused long enough for me to interrupt, "do you know where I have been these last months? Do you know where Grandmother Cutler sent me?"

"Been? Oh yes, you've been in school . . . practicing your singing. How wonderful," he said.

I looked at Jimmy who stood there with his eyes wide, his mouth open in amazement.

"She never even told him," I muttered. I turned back to Randolph. "You didn't know I was at The Meadows?"

"The Meadows? No, I didn't know. At least, I think I didn't. But there's so much on my mind these days, I'm not sure about anything. You must forgive me. There's the hotel, of course, and of course, there's Laura Sue. She's taking all this very badly. A stream of doctors have gone up and down the stairs to her, but none have done anything to help her. And now . . . Mother's . . ." He shook his head. "Not a cold, not even a cold all this time."

"I must see her," I said. "I must see Grandmother Cutler right away."

"See her? Oh, she's not here, honey. She's in the hospital."

"I know that. Why aren't you there?" I asked.

"I . . . I'm very busy," he said. "Very busy. She understands." He laughed. "If anyone understands, she does. But you can go. Yes, go see her and tell her . . . tell her . . ." He looked at the papers on the desk. "The produce she ordered last week . . . it's gone up ten percent. Yes, my calculations say ten percent. What should I do?" He shrugged.

"Come on, Jimmy," I said. "He's useless."

"I'll spend time with you later," Randolph cried when we started for the door. "I'm just a little tied up right now."

"Thank you," I said and we left him mumbling over his papers.

"Maybe we should go see your mother first," Jimmy suggested.

"No, she would be worse. I'm sure she's milking this for everything it's worth," I added bluntly.

We went back to Mrs. Hill in the lobby and got directions to the hospital. Twenty minutes later we were walking down a corridor to the intensive care unit. A nurse met us at the door.

"I'm Mrs. Cutler's granddaughter," I explained. "I've been out of town and just heard what happened. I need to see her. How is she?"

"You know she's had a severe stroke," the nurse replied dryly.

"Yes."

"It's left her right side completely paralyzed and her speech is slurred. She can hardly make any sounds at all."

"Please, can I see her?" I begged.

"You're limited to five minutes, I'm afraid." She looked at Jimmy.

"This is my fiancé," I said. "She's never met him."

The nurse nodded and almost smiled. Then she stepped back to indicate what cubicle Grandmother Cutler was in. It was a room with glass walls. We could see her lying there with an I.V. in her arm and the screen of her heart monitor revealing the beating of her heart. I thanked the nurse and we walked to the cubicle.

Seeing her in the hospital bed with the white sheets pulled up to her neck, Grandmother Cutler looked far less formidable and terrifying. She looked her true size; in fact, she looked shrunken, diminutive, pale and old, a shadow of what she once was. Her steel-blue hair lay stiffly around her waxen face. She had her eyes shut tight. The only other part of her that was visible was her left arm in which the I.V. needle had been placed. Her hand was clenched, the long, crooked fingers twisted over each other. I saw the thin blue veins in her wrist and forearm beneath her parchment-like skin.

I might have been overcome with pity, even for her, if it weren't for a quick image of my baby wrapped in its blanket and in my arms. Grandmother Cutler's face and head didn't look much bigger than an infant's face and head right now and that resemblance quickly reminded me of my purpose and need. She knew where my baby had been taken. I had to find out.

I stepped up to the bed. Jimmy remained in the doorway.

"Grandmother Cutler," I said sharply. Her eyelids fluttered but didn't open. "Grandmother Cutler, it's me . . . Dawn. Open your eyes," I commanded.

The eyelids fluttered again. It was as if she were trying to resist opening them, but finally, they did so and she gazed up at me, her face expressionless, but the right corner of her mouth was twitching. Her eyes had not lost their icy glint.

"Where did you have my baby taken? You must tell me," I said. "Your sister was terrible to me. She tormented and punished me for months and months. I'll bet you knew she'd do that to me. She even tried to cause a miscarriage, but my baby was born healthy and beautiful. Nothing you did was able to prevent that. My Christie is beautiful and you had no right to give her away, to arrange for someone to take her from me. Where is she?" I demanded. "You must tell me!"

Her mouth began to twitch faster and her lips trembled.

"I know you're seriously ill, but this is the time to do something right and good." My voice softened. "I'm begging you, please . . . tell me."

Her mouth opened and closed without producing a sound, but I saw her tongue lift inside.

"You did this terrible thing once before, Grandmother Cutler. Please, don't do it again. Don't let my baby grow up believing one set of parents are her real parents when they're not. I need my baby with me. She needs me. She belongs with me. Only I can give her the love she deserves and help make her life good and happy. You *must* tell me where she is!"

She struggled harder to speak, her head now moving from side to side. Her heart monitor began to fluctuate and the beat became more rapid.

"Please," I begged. *"Please."*

She closed and opened her mouth again, this time producing sounds. I knelt closer to understand and brought my ear to her lips. It was mostly gurgling in her throat, but I began to make out some words.

She uttered them and then closed her eyes and turned away. The heart monitor began a high-pitched, monotonous ring.

"Why?" I cried. *"Why?"*

"What's going on here?" the nurse demanded, coming to the door of the cubicle. She rushed to the bed. She seized Grandmother Cutler's wrist and held it. Then she pressed a button and rushed to the door to stick her head out and call to another nurse who was standing at the desk. *"Code Blue,"* she cried.

"Step outside!" she ordered me and Jimmy.

"Maybe she'll wake up in a moment," I pleaded.

"No. You'll have to leave," the nurse insisted.

I gazed down at Grandmother Cutler. Her face looked like a shrunken prune. Frustrated, I turned away and walked out of the intensive care unit with Jimmy right behind me as the intensive care unit went into action.

"What happened?" he demanded as soon as we stepped into the corridor. "What did she say to you?"

"It was hard to understand," I said, sitting on the bench in the hall.

"What?" He sat down beside me.

"All she would say was 'You're my curse.' "

"You? Her curse?" He shook his head. "I don't understand."

"I don't either," I said and started to cry.

Jimmy put his arm around me and held me.

"She's going to die and take the information with her, Jimmy," I wailed, wiping at my tears. "She's that hateful and I don't know why. What are we going to do?"

A doctor came rushing down the hall and into the intensive care unit. Ten minutes later he emerged slowly, the intensive care nurse beside him. She saw us sitting on the bench and shook her head.

"I'm sorry," she said.

"Oh Jimmy," I cried and buried my face in my hands. My tears streamed uncontrollably down my cheeks and soon I couldn't see. The world before me was a watery blur. I wasn't crying for Grandmother Cutler—I *wouldn't* cry for her. I was crying for my baby who might very well now be lost to me forever.

Jimmy helped me to my feet and we walked out of the hospital, me moving like someone in a daze.

By the time we had arrived at the hotel again, everyone knew. Mrs. Hill and her assistant were sobbing softly behind the reception desk. Some grounds people were clustered in a group on the porch speaking softly and shaking their heads. I recognized some of the dining room staff off in a corner of the lobby and they recognized me and nodded. The hotel was already draped in a funeral air.

"I'd better go up to see my mother," I told Jimmy. "Maybe she knows what happened with my baby."

"Okay. I'll wait in the lobby," he said.

I started through the corridor which led to the old section of the hotel where the family lived. When I reached the living room, I heard sobbing and looked in to see Mrs. Boston, the black chambermaid who had been in charge of looking after the family's needs for years and years. She was seated on the couch and glanced up when I peered in.

"Oh, Dawn," she said, her eyes filled with tears. "You've returned from school too late. Have you heard the terrible news?"

"Yes," I said.

"What will become of all of us now?" she asked, shaking her head. "Poor Mr. Randolph. He's about as lost as a soul can be."

"How is my mother?" I asked.

"Your mother? Oh, I haven't been upstairs since Mr. Randolph came down. He went up to tell her not a half hour ago and then he came down, walking like a man who had been struck in the head dumb. He just looked at me and we both started to cry. Then he went off someplace and I sat in here."

"I'll go up to see her then," I said and climbed the stairs, stopping to gaze first in the direction of where my room had been, where I had been kept like some poor relative, away from the family, alone. Why was it, I wondered, that the people who worked here, people like Mrs. Hill and Mrs. Boston, as well as Nussbaum, the chef, held Grandmother Cutler in such high regard? Couldn't they see how bitter and cruel she really was? Being efficient and successful was one thing, but what about being a compassionate human being?

The outside door to my mother's suite was closed. I opened it slowly and entered the sitting room. It looked as untouched and unused as ever, the only change I noticed being that there was no music sheet opened on the spinet and the keyboard had been closed. The door to my mother's bedroom was partially open. I approached it slowly and knocked.

"Yes?" I heard her say. I pushed the door open farther and entered.

I had been expecting to find her lost in her king size bed as usual, her head sunk within two jumbo fluffy pillows. But instead, she was seated at her vanity table brushing out her long blond hair so that it rested softly over her shoulders and down her neck. It shone as brightly and richly as always. She turned her graceful neck and focused her innocent blue eyes on me. Never did she look so beautiful, I thought. Her complexion was plush peaches and cream and she looked positively radiant and happy.

She was dressed in one of her pink silk nightgowns, but as always, in bed or not, she wore a pair of diamond earrings and wore her heart-shaped locket between her breasts. Her eyes brightened with surprise and a small smile formed on her lips.

"Dawn," she cried. "I didn't know you were coming here today. I'm sure Randolph didn't know either, or he would have mentioned it."

"I thought you were very, very, very sick again, Mother," I commented dryly as I crossed over to her.

"Oh, I was, Dawn. Dreadfully sick this time. It was some . . . horrible new allergy, but thankfully, it's grown tired of tormenting me and has left my frail body," she said, sighing with relief and shaking out her luxurious blond tresses.

"You don't look very frail to me, Mother," I said sharply. Her eyes narrowed and her smile evaporated.

"You never did have any sympathy for me, Dawn. I suppose you never will, despite the terrible ordeals I have gone through," she complained.

"Ordeals *you* have gone through? What about me? Do you know where

I've been these past months, Mother? Do you? Did you once inquire after me to see if I were still alive or dead?" I demanded. *"Well?"*

"You made your own bed to lie in, Dawn," she admonished. "Don't start looking for other people to blame, especially me. I won't stand for it. Not now, not anymore," she said and pulled herself into a stiffer posture. "You haven't heard, I suppose, but Grandmother Cutler has unfortunately just passed away."

"I know, Mother. Jimmy and I have just come from the hospital. We were there when she died," I said.

"You were?" She looked astonished. "Jimmy, you say?" She wrinkled her nose in distaste. "You mean that boy . . ."

"Yes Mother, that boy. Thankfully, he arrived in time to rescue me from Grandmother Cutler's horrid sister Emily and that dreadful place."

"Emily," she said, smirking. "I met her only once. She never liked me and I certainly never liked her. She was a horrid woman," she agreed.

"Then how could you permit Grandmother Cutler to send me there?" I demanded, "especially, if you knew what Miss Emily was like?"

"Really, Dawn, we didn't have all that much choice," she said with exasperation, "considering how you behaved." She sat back and looked me over for the first time. "Apparently, your problem is over and you don't look all that terrible for it. It is good to see you've gotten your figure back."

"My *problem* is over? Mother, you don't know what torture I endured, how she treated me and worked me and tried to cause a miscarriage. She's a horrible, horrible person," I cried. My mother didn't even wince. She turned and looked at herself in the mirror again.

"Well, all that is behind you now, Dawn. It's over and done with. Grandmother Cutler is gone too, so you can return to the hotel and . . ."

"But Mother, you didn't even inquire about my baby. Don't you care?"

"What's there to care about, Dawn?" She turned and looked at me again. "Really, what do you want me to ask?"

"For starters, you could ask if my baby lived, if it were a boy or a girl, and most importantly, where it is! Unless," I added, hopefully, "you know."

"I don't know anything about any baby except that you were sent to The Meadows to have it secretly so it would bring no scandal to the Cutlers. I couldn't very well argue against that. You should have been more careful. Now, as I said, it's over . . ."

"It's not over, Mother! My baby is alive and I want to know where she is!"

"Stop that shouting. I *will not* tolerate anyone*ever* shouting at me again. Now that the queen is gone, I will be no one's whipping boy," she snapped back. Then, she smiled. "Be sensible, Dawn. You can be happy now, just like me. You will take your place in the family and . . ."

"Mother, do you know where my baby was taken after she was born? Did Grandmother Cutler tell you? If she did, please tell me," I begged, using a softer tone of voice.

"I never asked her any of those details, Dawn. You knew what she was like. She was in charge." She turned back to the mirror. "It wouldn't surprise me if she has already begun to order God Himself around in Heaven and He's had to toss her out." She laughed merrily. "What am I saying? That witch is probably burning in the pits of Hell, where she rightly belongs," she sniffed indignantly.

"But Mother, my baby . . ."

"Oh Dawn, why do you want to think about it? Your lover left you high and dry, didn't he? Why do you want his baby anyway? And just think what it would mean. How would you ever find anyone decent to marry? The choicest suitors, those who are rich and handsome, won't want to marry a young lady with a baby, especially someone else's baby."

"Is that why you gave me away so easily, Mother?"

"That was an entirely different situation, Dawn. Oh, please, don't start with that again and again and again. Be thankful for what you've got," she added, her eyes filling with anger and annoyance now. "Despite her methods, Grandmother Cutler made it possible for your indiscretion to be kept secret. No one has to know anything. It's over; you can start anew."

She turned to the mirror again and ran her finger over her eyebrows.

"I have so much to do before the funeral. I just hate funerals, dressing in black, looking glum and pale, afraid to smile or people will think it's blasphemous and disrespectful. Well, I won't look like a heartbroken mourner just to please the public. I won't. It makes wrinkles if you frown too much.

"Fortunately, I bought a very pretty black dress in New York when we saw you there. It's a little dressy, but I think it will do. I have to think about all the people who will come, people who will be at the hotel to console Randolph and pay their respects. I have to be the strong, perfect little wife and daughter-in-law and greet them all properly.

"I think you should go out and buy something appropriate to wear yourself, Dawn honey. Clara Sue and Philip are on the way home from school and the three of you should look very nice together."

"Didn't you hear anything I said, Mother? I had a baby; she was taken from me," I said softly.

She rose from her chair and started toward the bed.

"I want to rest now," she said. "I don't want to look tired and drawn. It doesn't do anyone any good for me to look that way. People expect me to look stunning and I can't let them down."

She pulled back the blanket and crawled under. Then she sighed and lowered her head to the pillows.

"Just think, Dawn. I'm the lady of the manor now. I'm the queen. Isn't that delicious?"

"In your mind you always were the queen, Mother," I said and turned away quickly, more disgusted with her than I had ever been.

Jimmy stood up quickly, the moment I returned to the lobby.

"Well?" he asked.

"She doesn't know anything and she doesn't even care. All she cares about now is looking like the new queen of Cutler's Cove. Oh Jimmy, what will we do?" I wailed, my tears fast returning.

"No sense in talking to Randolph anymore," he thought aloud. Then he turned to me and shrugged.

"I guess you and I will have to go into her office and search it for ourselves until we find a lead."

"Her office?" I looked in the direction. Here she was dead and gone and yet the thought of entering her office and touching her things without her permission seemed terrifying to me. She had been such a powerful person, especially in the hotel. Her presence seemed to still loom about us, her mark on everything and everyone.

"I don't know what else to do," Jimmy confessed.

"All right," I said, my heart pounding, "we'll do whatever has to be done to get back my baby."

I reached out and took hold of Jimmy's hand and then we started toward Grandmother Cutler's office.

18

STARTLING REVELATIONS

I hesitated when we arrived at Grandmother Cutler's office. The simple words, MRS. CUTLER, printed on it seemed to lift off the wood like a neon light before me. My hand froze on the doorknob. After a moment Jimmy put his hand on my shoulder.

"If your mother doesn't know anything and Randolph doesn't know anything, there isn't any other way," he emphasized. "It's not like we're in there stealing."

I nodded and turned the knob. When we entered, we didn't immediately notice Randolph sitting on the aqua-green settee. The curtains on the windows were drawn closed and only a small desk lamp was on low, casting illumination over a small area. Grandmother Cutler's lilac scent was as strong as ever. It was as if she had just been in here. For a moment my eyes played tricks on me and I even imagined her seated behind that big desk glaring at me as hatefully as she had the first day I had arrived.

Jimmy seized my shoulder again and when I turned to him, he nodded toward the settee and I saw Randolph sitting there simply staring ahead. Shadows deep and dark were in his eyes. Our entrance didn't phase him or surprise him. It was almost as if he had expected it.

"I can't get it into my mind," he said slowly, "that she's gone and won't be back." He shook his head. "Just the day before yesterday we talked about redoing the game room. She wanted new tables and chairs.

"She knew exactly when she had purchased the ones presently there, you know," he added, lifting his eyes to us. "One thing about my mother, she could remember the day she bought a packet of hairpins." He smiled and shook his head. "What a mind. There's not another businesswoman like her in the state."

He sighed deeply and turned to look at the desk again.

"It won't be the same; it will never be the same. I almost feel like giving it all up . . . just going off and waiting to die myself," he said.

"She wouldn't like that," I said. "She would be very disappointed in you, Randolph."

He turned back to me and nodded, a smile forming around his lips, but his eyes remaining sad.

"Yes, you're right, Dawn." He seemed to snap back into reality and the present. "How extraordinary it is that you've arrived just at this time," he said.

"It's not extraordinary, Randolph," I replied quickly and went to sit beside him. "You must have known about what happened to me in New York and how I was sent to live with Miss Emily at The Meadows. You must have," I insisted.

"Aunt Emily," he said, nodding. "I'd better get the news out to her right away. Not that I expect her to travel with Charlotte all that distance for the funeral," he added. "It's just she should know that her sister has passed away."

"Yes, it will break her heart," I said dryly, but he didn't hear my sarcasm.

"Randolph, you knew I was there, didn't you? You knew what had happened?" I pressed on. He turned to me and looked into my eyes.

"Yes," he finally admitted. "Mother told me. I'm sorry, Dawn. You spoiled things for yourself when you had an affair and got pregnant."

"I know, but I had my baby at The Meadows and Grandmother Cutler had someone come to take her as soon as she was born. I've got to get my baby back," I said firmly and seized his wrist. He shook his head, confused.

"Back?"

"From whomever Grandmother Cutler gave her to. She had no right to give my baby away. Please help us find out where my baby is. Please," I begged.

Suddenly, he looked terrified. He looked toward the chair and then back at me. It was as if he thought his mother could return from the dead to chastise him simply for talking to me.

"I don't know . . ."

"How would she go about it? Who would she call? What should I do?" I pleaded.

"There is so much to do now that she's gone, isn't there," he asked. "I suppose, the first thing is to call Mother's attorney, Mr. Updike. He handles all her affairs and has been the family attorney for as long as I can remember. He's not much younger than Mother," Randolph added.

"Mr. Updike?" I said. I looked at Jimmy, who widened his eyes hopefully.

"Yes," Randolph said, rising slowly. "I've got to phone him. He's also a close family friend."

"Will you ask him if he knows anything about my baby?" I cried as he moved around Grandmother Cutler's desk to get to the phone. I could see that he wouldn't dare sit in her chair.

Jimmy sat beside me on the sofa and we waited and listened as Randolph called the attorney. He began to choke up as soon as he told him what had happened. Then he just listened and nodded every few moments. I thought he was going to hang up without asking about my baby, so I jumped up.

"Can I speak to him, please," I pleaded. He looked at me a moment as if just remembering I was there and then handed me the receiver.

"Mr. Updike?" I said.

"Yes. Who might this be?" a deep, resonant voice inquired.

"My name is Dawn and . . ."

"Oh yes," he said, "I know who you are. In fact, I was about to tell Randolph to be sure that you are present at the reading of the wills."

"I doubt very much, Mr. Updike, that I will be included in any way in Grandmother Cutler's will. What I wanted to know is do you know anything about arrangements that were made for someone to take my baby."

There was a long pause.

"This wasn't something you had consented to?" he asked finally.

"Oh no, sir. Never."

"I see. And you are now telling me you want the child then?"

"Yes, sir."

"This is all unfortunate, very unfortunate," he muttered. "Very well. Give me some time. I will have information for you at the reading of the wills."

"I want my baby," I insisted.

"Yes, yes. I understand. Let me speak to Randolph, if he is still there, please," he said.

I handed the receiver back to Randolph and joined Jimmy.

"He knows about it?" Jimmy asked quickly.

"Yes," I said. "And he's promised to do something. We'll have to stay at the hotel for a few days until the reading of the will while he makes arrangements. And then, finally," I said sighing, "it will be all over.

"Come on," I said, taking Jimmy's hand, "let's pick out a room for ourselves."

"Do you think that's really all right to do? I mean . . ."

"Who's to say no?" I replied with a smile. I was so happy at the prospect of getting my baby back. "Besides, if my mother is the new queen, I'm one of the new princesses."

We went to the lobby and I had Mrs. Hill give us a key to one of the nicer suites. Then Jimmy went out and brought in his things. I didn't go up to tell my mother anything, but when Jimmy and I returned from dinner in Cutler's Cove, we found her dressed and in the lobby speaking to some of the staff. I was amazed at how strong and authoritative she sounded as she gave them instructions for the next few days. When she was finished, she approached us.

"So this is Jimmy," she said, extending her hand. "Last time you were here, we really hadn't had a chance to meet." She gave Jimmy a wide smile.

Meet? I thought. Why was she pretending Jimmy's last time here was like a pleasant visit? And I couldn't believe how charming and flirtatious she was. Had she no shame?

"Hello," Jimmy said, a bit confused. She held onto his hand as if she expected him to kiss the back of hers. Finally, she released his fingers, but she didn't take her attention from him.

"You've joined the army, I see. I just love a man in uniform. It's so gallant and romantic, even when he's only off to some revolting boot camp and not some foreign war. My, you have so many pretty ribbons," she cooed, running her fingers over them.

Blood rushed into Jimmy's face. Mother laughed and stroked her own hair gently. Then she turned to me.

"Clara Sue and Philip will be here late tonight," she said. "I'm arranging to have the funeral as soon as possible so they don't miss any more school than necessary. The year is almost over for both of them."

"How considerate of you, Mother," I said. She didn't change her expression. Her smile was beginning to look like a mask.

"You two don't have to go out for your meals, you know," she continued. "I've instructed the kitchen staff to continue working. The family will eat in the dining room as usual. Nussbaum is cooking for the hotel personnel, and I'm sure we'll reopen the hotel shortly after the funeral."

"How efficient," I said. "Grandmother Cutler would be very proud of you."

My mother blinked rapidly, but continued to beam, her eyes radiating with an excitement I had heretofore never seen. The flood of color into her face made her even more beautiful.

"As soon as the funeral is over and those offering their condolences have come and gone, I will instruct Mrs. Boston to move Grandmother Cutler's things out of her room so that you can move in there," she said.

"That won't be necessary, Mother. I have no intention of remaining here," I replied quickly.

"No intention to . . ." She looked at Jimmy. "Don't tell me you're planning something stupid, Dawn. Not now, not when you have all this new opportunity. Surely you have more brains than that!

"Just think what it will be like now—you can join me in supervising. In the evenings you and I will stand outside the dining room door greeting the guests. I'll buy you nice clothes and . . ."

"But Mother, considering your *fragile* health, do you think it's *wise* for you to take on so much added *responsibility?"* I asked, driving my words into her like needles. She did flinch, but she didn't lose her demeanor. Instead, she widened her smile and leaned over to kiss me on the cheek.

"How nice of you to be thinking of me, Dawn. Of course, I won't dive right into things. I'll go slowly, but that's more reason why I will need you beside me as my little assistant," she emphasized, still turning her shoulder and making her eyes wider for Jimmy's benefit. I saw how amazed he was.

"I'm afraid it's a bit too late for that, Mother," I said. "Once I have located the whereabouts of my baby, Jimmy and I will be leaving. You can try to stop me, of course, since I'm not quite eighteen, but I don't think you want that sort of scene right now and shortly I will be able to do what I want anyway."

Her smile finally evaporated.

"I was hoping you might have learned something from this past, terrible experience, Dawn, but obviously you haven't learned a thing, except how to continue to make your life and everyone's around you miserable. Mine especially. Why, oh why do I even bother to try?" she moaned theatrically.

"I'm afraid you're right," she continued with more spirit and anger than I would have thought possible for one so diminutive and delicate. "It is too late for you."

She turned toward Jimmy. "I have only pity for you, for the both of you," she added, her eyes burning with fury, and then sauntered off.

But the moment the captain of the bellhops crossed her path, her smile and charm returned.

Both Jimmy and I were exhausted from the day's traveling and the traumatic experience in the hospital. We went to bed early and had no trouble falling asleep. In the morning we showered, dressed and went down to the dining room for breakfast. We were the first of the family to sit down. I had forgotten that Clara Sue and Philip arrived the night before. They walked into the dining room together, with my mother and Randolph right behind them. As soon as Philip set eyes on me, he smiled, but Clara Sue twisted her mouth in disgust.

"Jimmy," Philip said, rushing over to the table to extend his hand. "How are you doing? You look great."

"I'm all right," Jimmy said. He shook Philip's hand quickly and sat down again.

"And Dawn," Philip said, gazing down at me. "You look as pretty as ever."

"Thank you, Philip," I said, quickly shifting my eyes from him because of the intense way he riveted his own on me.

Clara Sue eyed both of us without saying a word. She took her place at the table and immediately ordered one of the waiters to bring her some orange juice.

"Good morning," Mother sang. She appeared fresh and well rested, her hair looking as radiant as ever. I saw she had taken to wearing a little eye shadow as well as a slight touch of blusher. She was a very pretty woman. There was no denying that she had perfect, doll-like features: a face that never lost its childish innocence, but with blue eyes that could tempt and tease a man to the point of pain. She wore a blue silk dress with a provocative neckline and tapered sleeves.

Randolph, on the other hand, looked as though he hadn't yet gone to sleep. His eyelids drooped; he was pale and his shoulders were bent. He wore the same clothing he had worn the day before, only it looked wrinkled. Perhaps he had fallen asleep in them, I thought. It wouldn't surprise me to learn he had never left Grandmother Cutler's office.

"I'm glad to see you two rose early," she said as she sat down. Randolph looked confused for a moment until Mother tapped the back of his seat and he sat down. She ordered juice and coffee and eggs for herself. Randolph wanted only coffee.

"Well," she continued, "we have a great deal to do today. Randolph and I will be going to the funeral parlor to make the final arrangements. We thought it would be a nice touch if after the church ceremony, the funeral procession came up to the hotel so Grandmother Cutler could pass by the front entrance one last time and the hotel staff could bid her their final good-bye.

"Don't you all think that would be a nice touch?" she asked, practically singing.

Philip agreed. Clara Sue gulped down her juice and continued to glare my way. Finally, she mustered enough courage to assail me.

"We heard you visited Grandmother in the hospital moments before she died," she commented.

"What of it?" I replied.

"You must have done something to aggravate her to death. You were always aggravating her," she accused.

"Oh Clara Sue," Mother pleaded. "Please don't make a scene at breakfast. My nerves can't take it."

"Grandmother Cutler didn't need me to aggravate her," I said, "she had you," I added, taking the wind from the sail of her attack.

Philip laughed loudly and Clara Sue's face turned crimson.

"I didn't have to be sent off to have a bastard," she sneered. "Whose was it? His?" She pointed at Jimmy. "Or don't you know who the father was?"

"Please," Mother said, "stop this right now. We're a family in mourning," she reminded.

Philip dropped his eyes to the table, but kept his silly smirk. Clara Sue embraced herself and turned away in a sulk. I looked at Randolph, but he seemed distracted, lost in his own world and unable to hear anything. Under the table Jimmy found my hand and squeezed it.

Mother took over the conversation after that, describing all the arrangements for the funeral in great detail, down to the flowers she had chosen to be placed around the coffin, the cards she had had printed to be given out, and the food she had ordered Nussbaum to prepare for afterward.

"Naturally, we have to make this the most impressive funeral Cutler's Cove has ever seen," she declared. "People would expect it."

With a joy and a pleasure she had trouble disguising, Mother had taken complete control of Cutler's Cove. Randolph sat by nodding in silent agreement with everything she said and did. It was almost as if he were a puppet and Mother had her hand behind him, manipulating him.

She went at her own preparations with relish, acting as though she were preparing for a gala celebration. The day of the funeral she descended the stairway like a queen about to greet her subjects. Never did she look more radiantly beautiful. Her black dress had a string of tiny diamondlike stones along the V-neck collar, which I thought showed more cleavage than proper for a memorial service. It was a short-sleeved dress with a firm waist and pleated skirt. She wore her most ostentatious diamond necklace and matching earrings. She had had Randolph get her one of Grandmother Cutler's beautiful silk shawls to wear over her shoulders.

Randolph and Philip both wore black suits and ties. Clara Sue had a black dress that she had to have let out at the waist and bosom. I overheard some of the staff talking about how she had abused the seamstress when the poor woman came to do the fitting.

Mother insisted I go to the boutique in Cutler's Cove and charge something to her account. I had Jimmy take me and I bought a simple black dress.

Jimmy and I followed Mother, Randolph and Philip to the church in Jimmy's car. It was as if Grandmother Cutler had ordered the proper weather for a funeral, too. The sky was completely overcast and gray, and a cool wind blew in from the sea. Even the ocean looked dismal and depressed, the white caps barely rising and the tide barely making its way up the shore.

Mother had been correct in predicting the importance and size of Grandmother Cutler's funeral. The church was overflowing with the residents of the community. Every lawyer, doctor and politician was there, as well as every businessman, many of whom prized the hotel as one of their chief clients.

All eyes were on us, especially, I thought, on Mother, as we took our places up front. The coffin was before us. Mother had decided it should be kept closed. The minister made a long sermon, talking about the special obligation more fortunate people had to their communities. He cited Grandmother Cutler as an important community leader who had used her skills and business sense to help build the community and thus help those who weren't born as fortunate as she was. He concluded by saying she had lived up to the assignment God had given her.

Only Randolph showed any sincere emotion, his eyes filling with tears, his head bowed. Mother maintained her perfect smile, turning and nodding at this important person and that from time to time. Whenever she thought it necessary, she dabbed her eyes with the corner of her white silk handkerchief and lowered her head. She knew how to turn her emotions on and off like a faucet. Clara Sue looked bored, as usual, and Philip kept glancing at me, an impish glint in his eyes and a flirtatious smile on his lips.

Afterward, we proceeded the way Mother had described. The funeral procession followed the hearse up to the hotel where we all got out to listen to the minister say a few more words from the front steps of the hotel. The staff was gathered all around, everyone looking glum. I caught sight of Sissy in the background with her mother. She had come even though Grandmother Cutler had ruthlessly fired her. When she saw me, she smiled.

We went on to the cemetery. The first thing I noticed when we drove in and walked to the Cutler section was that the tombstone Grandmother Cutler had put up with what was supposed to be my name was gone. Now it seemed more like some nightmare I had had.

The minister read some psalms over the grave and then we were all asked to bow our heads while he offered the final prayer. I prayed that Grandmother Cutler, wherever she was, would finally realize the cruelty and harshness of her ways. I prayed she would repent and beg God to forgive her.

Again, as if Grandmother Cutler commanded the weather, the skies began to clear and the sun dropped its rays around us. The ocean looked blue and alive again, and the terns that sounded a mournful cry in the morning now chatted gaily as they swooped down on the beaches searching for some plunder.

Randolph was so confused with grief, he had to be led back to the car. Mother thanked the minister for his nice service and invited him to the hotel to join in what was supposed to be the mournful gathering.

She had arranged for everything to be set up in the lobby. I thought all that was missing was live music. The staff were on duty just the way they would have been for any hotel affair. Waiters walked around with hors d'oeuvres and glasses of whiskey and wine. Tables of food were arranged at the far end. At mother's behest, Nussbaum had prepared all sorts of salads and meats, including Swedish meatballs, small frankfurters, and sliced turkeys. There were jello molds with fruit and a separate table just for desserts.

Just about everyone who had been at the church arrived. The small murmur of conversation that had begun when we first returned from the cemetery exploded into a loud roar of voices. Randolph tried standing beside my mother, Clara Sue and Philip at the front entrance to greet people, but he had to sit down after a while. He was given a glass of whiskey and sat there, still looking quite dazed and confused. Once in a while, he would focus his faraway eyes on me and smile.

Before long, I heard my mother's peal of laughter and saw her escorting the men she obviously considered the most important around the room to the various tables of food and drink. I saw her everywhere, and everywhere she was, she looked like a fashion plate, vibrant and beautiful and always surrounded by clusters of male admirers.

Late in the afternoon, the mourners began to leave, most stopping by to shake Randolph's limp hand. Older people, especially the older women, tried to give him real comfort and some hugged him. It was only then that he looked like he knew what was happening and what had happened.

Finally, when just a half dozen or so people remained behind, a tall, stout gray-haired man with a robust slightly tanned face and dark brown eyes approached Jimmy and me. His forehead had deep furrows and there were webs of wrinkles at the corners of his eyes, but despite his apparent age, he stood firm and had an air of authority about him that told me he must be Mr. Updike even before he had introduced himself.

"I have contacted the people who thought they were adopting your baby," he said when he pulled us aside. "I have their address here," he indicated, handing me an envelope, "and they expect you to come by in a day or so. Naturally, they're very upset because we were all given to understand this was something you wanted to do."

"I was never even asked, and I would never have agreed," I replied. He nodded and then shook his head.

"It's a bad business, bad business. I'm conducting the reading of the wills in about a half hour in Mrs. Cutler's office," he added. "Be there."

"What would Grandmother Cutler leave you?" Jimmy asked as soon as Mr. Updike walked away.

"A pail and a mop," I replied. I really could think of nothing else.

Mr. Updike sat behind Grandmother Cutler's desk with the papers and documents spread before him. Randolph, my mother and Clara Sue sat on the settee. Philip sat in a chair to the right of them and Jimmy and I took the chairs on the left. Even with all the lights on and the sunlight streaming through the windows, the office looked dreary, drab and gloomy.

But I couldn't get over how brilliant my mother looked. Supervising the funeral and its aftermath had brought a healthy flush into her face. She sparkled, her eyes dancing with a youthful glint. Clara Sue, who had been pouting all day, glared with hatred every time she looked my way. Our cheerful mother looked more like her sister.

"Since everyone who is required to be present is present," Mr. Updike began, "I shall commence with the formal reading of the wills and disposition of the estates of William and Lillian Cutler, both deceased," he said in a somber tone of voice. My mother was the first to realize something odd.

"Did you say William and Lillian, John?" she asked.

"Yes, Laura Sue. There is some unfinished business as concerns the instructions William left."

"Well, why wasn't it done before this?" she pursued.

"Please be patient, Laura Sue," he replied. "The answer is here," he added, tapping a document. My mother's smile wilted and I thought she looked rather uneasy suddenly, but Randolph didn't seem to notice or care. He sat there coolly, his legs crossed, his eyes focused on some memory rather than on Mr. Updike.

"I shall begin then," Mr. Updike said, "with a letter of instructions left by William B. Cutler, deceased." He fixed his glasses firmly on the bridge of his nose and held up the document to read.

" 'Dear John or whom it may concern,

" 'This letter is to serve as my final will and testament and is to be read only immediately after the event of my wife Lillian's death. I have left these instructions specifically to ensure that my wife suffer no embarrassment during her lifetime.' "

Suddenly, my mother rose, her hand on her bosom. Mr. Updike looked up from the documents.

"I . . . I'm not feeling well. I've got to lay down!" she exclaimed and bolted from the office. Randolph started to rise.

"You had better remain here, Randolph," Mr. Updike said firmly.

"But . . . Laura Sue . . ."

"She'll be all right," Mr. Updike said and made a gesture with his hand to indicate we must forget her for the moment and return to the business at hand. Randolph sat back slowly, looking frightened as well as dazed. Mr. Updike continued to read.

" 'I realize I have no real way to make amends for my actions, but I feel I must not permit my sins to echo on and on punishing the innocent. Accordingly, I hereby confess to having fathered the second child of my son's wife. I make no excuses for this other than to say I succumbed to the same animal lusts and desires men have succumbed to since Adam and Eve. I blame no one, but myself.

" 'Accordingly, I hereby instruct that on the event of the death of my wife Lillian and on the eighteenth birthday of my son's second child, who is in truth my son's half-sister, sixty percent of my holdings in the Cutler's Cove Hotel be deeded to the second child and the remaining forty percent, heretofore deeded to my wife Lillian, be distributed as she sees fit in her last will and testament.' "

Mr. Updike looked up. For a moment it was as though a streak of lightning had passed through the room and we were all waiting for the clap of thunder. Everyone, including me, wore the same expression of disbelief and shock. Randolph shook his head slowly. Philip's Adam's apple bobbed as if he had just swallowed a live frog. Clara Sue finally broke the silence by bursting into tears.

"I don't believe it!" she screamed. *"I don't! I don't!"* she repeated, pounding her own leg. *"This can't be happening!"*

"This has all been properly notarized and witnessed. Actually, I witnessed it myself years ago," Mr. Updike said calmly. "There is no question about its authenticity."

"Daddy," she cried, shaking Randolph's shoulder. "Tell him it isn't so; tell him it's a lie."

Randolph lowered his head in defeat. Clara Sue glared at me and then turned back to Mr. Updike.

"But why should she get so much?" she demanded. "She's a bastard."

"It's the way your grandfather wanted it," Mr. Updike replied. "And," he reminded everyone, "it was his to do with as he wanted."

"But she's a . . . *a freak!"* Clara Sue screamed. "That's what you are, a freak!"

"No, she's not," Philip said with a smile of amusement as he turned to me. "She's your half-sister and your aunt."

"That's freaky. I don't believe it; it's all a lie," Clara Sue insisted. She got up and turned on me just as she reached the door. "I hate you," she spit back at me. "I won't let you get away with this! I won't let you get away with taking what is rightfully mine. Mark my words. One day you're going to pay." Then she ran from the room.

"What about my grandmother's will?" Philip asked Mr. Updike.

"I'll read it in a moment. She leaves various things to various people, but her share in the hotel goes to your father."

Randolph continued to sit with his head bowed. Had he known all along? I wondered. Was that what made him the way he was? There was no question in my mind now that Grandmother Cutler always knew. Now I understood why she called me her curse on her deathbed and why she hated me so. Despite my hardened heart, a small part of myself even felt sorry for her.

But I didn't feel sorry for my mother. I stood up.

"Mr. Updike," I said, "since the rest of this doesn't concern me . . ."

"Yes, of course. You may go now. I will be in touch with you concerning documents to sign."

"Thank you," I said and turned to go. I hesitated a moment and crossed to Randolph, who lifted his head and looked up at me with eyes flooded with tears. I touched his shoulder and smiled at him.

"I wish," he said through his tears, "that you really were my daughter."

I kissed him on the cheek and then Jimmy and I walked out of the office.

"Well," Jimmy said, shaking his head. "From a girl with barely enough to eat to the owner of a major resort."

"I'd give it all up in a second for a normal life, Jimmy."

He nodded.

"Let's go get Christie," he said.

"You go to the car, Jimmy. I'll be right out," I said. "I want to speak to my mother first."

I hurried across the lobby, through the family's section of the hotel and up the stairs. The doors to my mother's bedroom were shut, but I didn't knock. I opened them abruptly and marched in to find her spread on her stomach on her bed. She had been sobbing into one of her big, fluffy pillows.

"Why didn't you ever tell me the truth, Mother?" I demanded.

"I'm so embarrassed," she cried. "Why did he have to do that? Why did he have to write that horrible letter and let the whole world know?"

"Because he couldn't die with it on his conscience, Mother. You know what a conscience is, don't you? It's what haunts you and haunts you when you lie and deceive people you are supposed to love. It's what haunts you when you are so selfish you don't care who you hurt, even if the people you hurt are your own flesh and blood," I lectured.

She slapped the palms of her hands over her ears.

"Oh stop it, stop it!" she cried. "I don't want to hear this. Stop it!"

"Stop what? The truth. You simply can't take the truth, ever. Can you, Mother?

"So this was really why you permitted Grandmother Cutler to arrange for my kidnapping? She knew that Grandfather Cutler was my father, didn't she? *Didn't she?*" I demanded.

"Yes," my mother confessed. *"Yes! Yes! Yes!"*

"And this was why she hated me so much when I was returned and why she couldn't stand the sight of me," I continued, extracting each piece of truth out of her like a dentist pulling teeth.

"Yes," she moaned. "That woman despised me because of what William had done. She wanted to hurt me . . . to have her revenge."

"And so you let her give me away, Mother. And you let her torment me when I returned. Because I reminded her of your liaison with Grandfather Cutler. You let her do it, Mother. You permitted her to get away with it. Not once did you try to help me."

"I tried," she said, turning toward me. Her face was red and streaked with tears. "I did what I could."

"You did nothing, Mother. You let her humiliate me. You let her put up that tombstone symbolizing my death. You let her make a slave of me. You let her send me to her horrible sister to be tortured. You let it all happen and why? *Why?*" I screamed, burning with frustration from the unanswered questions smothering me and because for my entire life I had been a pawn in a game I hadn't orchestrated.

"Because you were afraid," I said, answering my own question. "You were always afraid she would reveal the truth and the truth must have been that you seduced him."

"No!"

"No? I'm not blind. I see the way you flirt, even with Jimmy. It's in your nature to be like this. I'm sure that story about my real father being some traveling entertainer, a story both you and Grandmother Cutler led me to believe, wasn't all fantasy, was it? You probably did have a line of lovers, didn't you? *Didn't you?*" I demanded.

"Stop it!" she screamed, her hands over her ears again.

"I don't pity you anymore, Mother. I despise you for what you've done. You've hurt so many people, Mother, that if you had a conscience, it would tear you apart," I said.

"Oh Dawn," she replied wiping her face with the backs of her small hands. "You're right to be so angry," she said in that softer, childish tone of voice she could easily manage. "I don't blame you for feeling the way you do. I really don't. I should have done more to help you, but I was afraid of her. She was such a tyrant. I am sorry. Really, I am.

"But," she said, smiling, "amends have been made. You're about to become a very rich young lady and there's this hotel to run. Randolph will be useless to you. He's always been useless. But we can be friends again. We can work on our mother-daughter relationship. Maybe even become friends. I'd like that, Dawn, wouldn't you? I've always loved you, Dawn. Honestly I have. You must believe me. I'll help you and together we will make the hotel into something and . . ."

"Right now, Mother, all I care about is getting back my baby. And don't think that money makes it all right again. As for this hotel . . . I couldn't care less if it burnt to the ground," I flared and stormed from her room.

"You will feel differently, Dawn," she cried. "After you calm down, you will feel differently. And then you will need me. You *will* need me . . ."

I slammed the outer chamber door behind me, stifling her cries, and hurriedly descended the stairs. As soon as I stepped out of the hotel, I stopped to catch my breath. Then I looked up at the now-deep-blue sky with the previous layers of clouds far off toward the horizon.

God couldn't have wanted all this to happen, I thought. He didn't write the scripts for the puny little players down here. We wrote them ourselves—with our lusts and our greed and our selfish ways. These rich and powerful people feasted on each other like cannibals and if someone got hurt in the process, well, too bad.

Then afterward, like my mother up in her luxurious suite, they tried to make it seem like nothing significant had occurred. Well, it was terrible, and they should be made to suffer even more than they had, I thought.

"Hey," Jimmy called from the car. "Come on, Dawn." He came forward to take my hand. "Say good-bye to the past, and hello to the future. We're wasting time. Christie is waiting for you."

"Yes," I said, smiling. "She is, isn't she?"

It was just like Jimmy to say the right words to make me feel alive and free, free enough to forget thoughts of revenge and think only of blue skies and warm breezes, days of happiness filled with music, music I wanted so much to make.

I took his hand and let him lead me away from the hotel. In moments we were driving off toward a rainbow and all the promises it pledged.